KISSING MR WRONG

Sarah Duncan

WINDSOR
PARAGON

First published 2009
by Headline Review
This Large Print edition published 2010
by BBC Audiobooks Ltd
by arrangement with
Headline Publishing Group

Hardcover ISBN: 978 1 408 46082 5
Softcover   ISBN: 978 1 408 46083 2

British Library Cataloguing in Publication Data available

Printed and bound in Great Britain by
CPI Antony Rowe, Chippenham and Eastbourne

*For Nancy Kinnison, with thanks
for her friendship and support*

Acknowledgements

For the first time I've used a background that I wasn't already familiar with so I'm very grateful to Nick de Larrinaga of the War Studies Department at King's, London, for all his advice and suggestions, and especially for being my guide to the Imperial War Museum. If I've got any of it wrong, it's undoubtedly my fault, not his. In France, Martine Warlop of Maison Warlop was a knowledgeable and gracious hostess.

Several of the people who gave me information about the life of an illustrator wanted to remain anonymous, but thanks to Isabel Freeman for letting me use her picture book texts and Steve Lavis for telling me what Cockadoodledo was in nineteen different languages.

My thanks, as ever, to Nancy Kinnison and Rachel Bentham, Linnet van Tinteren and Sue Swingler for their feedback on the draft manuscript. Thanks also to my agent, Lavinia Trevor, and my editors at Headline, Marion Donaldson and Leah Woodburn. Working with you all was a real pleasure.

Finally, thanks to my family and friends, especially Steve who did all the driving in France.

Chapter 1

'The trouble with men is . . . oh, where do I start?' Lu said, balancing the box of wine glasses on the edge of the table as she cleared a space free of paper napkins and five plastic trays of supermarket smoked salmon party nibbles before pushing the box on to the table properly with her left hip.

'Knowing you, you've probably got a list,' Briony said, puffing as she dumped a case of sparkling wine next to the glasses.

'Not a list exactly,' Lu lied, busy taking wine glasses out of the box and lining them up neatly along the table. For a second she toyed with the idea of staggering the glasses slightly so they took up the least space, but decided against it on the grounds that the lines would look untidy when some of the glasses were removed. 'You wouldn't have thought it would be difficult to meet a nice, normal man without major hang-ups, but it seems impossible. They all have masses of baggage—if it isn't their ex-girlfriends, it's their mothers—or they're controlling or workaholics or alcoholics or—'

'Sexaholics?' Briony began arranging the bottles, but was then distracted by one of the paintings hanging on the gallery walls. She adjusted its position.

'At least there would be fringe benefits,' Lu said, laughing. 'It needs to go a bit up on the left.'

'Like this?' Lu gave her a thumbs-up. 'So, no date for tonight?'

Lu shook her head in response. 'Maybe I'll meet

1

Mr Right tonight,' she said lightly and began ripping the packaging off the plastic trays ready to lay the smoked salmon parcels out on plates. 'Maybe even now he's ploughing through his afternoon's work, thinking about going to this fabulous private view and meeting the woman of his dreams.'

Briony was still squinting at the painting to see if it was level. 'What sort of work does Mr Right do?'

'Something serious. A lawyer maybe, or a doctor. Or someone in business.' Lu licked her fingers, contemplating. 'A banker perhaps.'

Briony snorted. 'You mean, someone like no one you've ever gone out with before.' She left the painting and peered out of the gallery's front window.

'Exactly,' Lu said, delighted that her friend understood. 'I realised the other day that that's where I've been going wrong. Everybody I've been out with before has been a creative of some sort— artists, writers—'

'Bricklayers?' Briony turned, and raised her eyebrows at Lu.

'Phil was a mistake,' Lu conceded. 'But you know, bricklaying can be quite creative, in its own way.'

Briony laughed. 'I expect bankers and lawyers say the same thing.'

'I shall find out, and report back.' Lu paused from arranging salmon parcels in neat concentric circles. 'I fancy a man in a suit who talks to me about stuff I can't understand, who works regular hours doing something unbelievably important—'

'Well paid?'

Lu waved a salmon parcel in the air. 'Goes without saying. Certainly enough so I can give up flat-fee illustration and do nothing but the best creative work on the most beautiful picture books.'

'And let me guess—he's also devoted, caring, sensitive, understanding, intelligent, listens to you, cherishes you . . .'

'Of course.'

'An amazing lover?'

'Naturally.'

'Incredibly good-looking?'

Lu put her hands on her hips in mock outrage. 'Are you calling me shallow?' She pouted, then laid both hands on her heart. 'Of course he's devastatingly good-looking and unbelievably attractive, but that isn't why I love him. I love him because he's Mr Right.'

'Ahhh, it's love, it's so romantic,' Briony said, coming back and joining Lu. 'And you haven't even met him.'

'I will, just give me time,' Lu said, glancing at her watch. 'Speaking of which, we ought to get a move on or we'll never finish putting out this stuff before people start turning up.'

'I hope they do turn up. It's always a worry, the first exhibition in January. Everybody's exhausted from Christmas, and the weather's always dreadful.' Briony pulled a bottle from the case and started peeling off the gold foil cap. 'Fancy one to get us in the mood?'

Lu grinned at her. 'Oh, go on. It's not every day you celebrate ten years in business.' She got two glasses ready while Briony popped the cork.

'To Briony Vickers and the Bath Originals Art Gallery,' Lu said, raising her glass. 'Ten years on, and still in business—thereby proving miracles do happen.'

'Tell me about it,' Briony said, taking a hefty swig from her glass. 'The miracle will be if I'm here in another ten years.'

'Don't worry, everybody will come, bad weather or not. And no talk about recession,' Lu said firmly, topping up Briony's glass. 'Tonight we're celebrating your achievement. And it is an achievement,' she added, hugging Briony's shoulders. 'I think you're amazing to have done all this.'

'It does seem incredible,' Briony agreed.

There was silence for a second as they both looked about the gallery. They had met at art school, although they'd been on different courses, Lu doing illustration and Briony fine art. After graduation Briony had tried making a living as an artist for a couple of years until a windfall inheritance gave her the money to invest in a run-down gallery near the centre of Bath. Lu thought how much the gallery had moved on from those first days, from the haphazard exhibitions of friends from college shown on peeling walls, to the sleek (replastered) off-white walls hung with paintings bearing serious price tags.

The exhibition for the tenth anniversary was a mixed show of work by all the artists Briony represented. As Lu looked round, she could recognise paintings by several friends from art college days, but they were now outnumbered by other more well-known artists, even a couple of Royal Academicians and one of the rare artists to have become a sir. 'You're becoming part of the establishment,' she said, almost in surprise. 'You're growing up.'

'We are grown up,' Briony said, raising her glass to Lu. 'We're in our thirties.'

'Just,' Lu said, sipping her champagne. She looked across at Briony, at her sleek hair pulled into a chignon like Betty Boop grown up, the beautifully cut dress that exposed her slim arms but otherwise covered her in origami folds. It would have been made by some famous designer, Lu guessed, hardly conscious of fingering her own skirt, a cheap one she'd picked up from the market and customised with appliqué roses. The champagne felt cold against her lips, the glass clammy in her hand. 'You won't get too grown up, will you?' she said.

'Course not,' Briony said, giving Lu's shoulders a squeeze. 'Look at me, drinking champagne in the afternoon when I've got a big private view in a couple of hours. That's hardly grown-up behaviour, is it?'

Lu laughed, and they went back to setting out the food and wine ready for the party, but she noticed that Briony hardly touched her drink, and her glass stayed at the same level throughout the evening, and what could be more grown up and sensible than that? Her friend was slipping away from her, and she hadn't noticed until that evening.

She looked around the now full gallery, crammed with people talking and laughing and drinking. Briony needn't have worried about the January weather: people were out in force, and some were even looking at the paintings. Lu could recognise about a third of them, some old friends, some acquaintances, but this evening they seemed

5

different, they seemed . . . She scanned the crowd, looking for faces she knew. There was Saffron, another illustrator from college, now married to some rich farmer and living outside Bath with two kids and a studio in a converted barn; Stephen, who'd given up art and gone into his uncle's advertising firm, with an expense-account stomach to prove it; Abby, who'd ended up with a chain of fashion shops, a souped-up sports car and a Caribbean suntan in January.

As Lu looked at her contemporaries, she realised it wasn't just Briony who was slipping away; it was all of them. They were settled, with partners and houses and sports cars and children and careers that were expanding. Even the struggling artists weren't struggling any more; if they'd stayed in the business this long, they'd either become successful or were teaching regular hours or had a supportive partner.

I was supposed to be one of the best, Lu thought. The one who was going to go far and do great things and change the face of illustration. Instead, she lived alone in a one-bed apartment doing hand-to-mouth flat-fee commissions for the lower end of the illustration market that hardly covered the bills let alone any extras. She now knew what the hare felt like when he'd been lapped by the tortoise. But at least the hare had known he was entered in the race. Lu hadn't realised there was a race until now, but everyone else seemed to be heading for the winners' enclosure while she was still meandering around the perimeter fence.

An arm snaked around her waist. 'Lunabella, where have you been hiding?' Lu turned to see

Jerry, Briony's partner. 'Briony keeps saying she's seen you, but it's never when I'm around.'

'I've been busy working,' Lu said, moving fractionally away from him. She knew Briony had in the past fretted about Jerry's wandering eye, but recently that seemed to have calmed down. Still, she wasn't going to give her any reason for suspicion, however unfriendly it might appear to Jerry.

'What is it now? Kittens in coats? Or talking vegetables?' Jerry laughed, flashing a lot of over-whitened teeth. 'Seriously, Lu, when are you going to get some proper painting done?'

'I expect about the same time as you do,' Lu answered sweetly. Jerry painted big, splashy, untidy nudes in sweet-shop colours, which sold well to men with Porsches and brittle-faced blonde girlfriends. He worked to a formula that was so effective it could probably be used to remove built-up limescale as well, and was easily the most successful financially, if not critically, of the class of '96.

'Miaow,' he said, mimicking a cat's paw.

No more than you, Lu was going to say, but was stopped from descending into bickering by the man Jerry had been talking to.

'Have you got any work in this exhibition?' He was a big man, the sort you could imagine on a rugby field or playing mine host at the bar.

'No, I'm an illustrator, I don't do this sort of thing. Jerry's just being stupid,' she answered, still annoyed.

'I'm Nick,' he said, smiling and holding out his hand, and she suddenly realised that for all his bulk the man wasn't unattractive, a bit like Gerard

7

Depardieu, though no hint of a French accent. 'How do you know this reprobate?'

'Lu,' she said, taking his. Her hand felt small in his palm. 'I was at art school with Briony, but not on the same course—I did illustration.'

'Kittens in coats?' Nick looked at her quizzically, a twinkle in his eyes. No, not unattractive at all.

'Afraid so. Not all the time, of course,' Lu added quickly. 'I mean, I do other things. Other animals. Fairies. Whatever.' She inwardly winced. Why had she said 'whatever'? That was what bored teenagers said.

'Which explains why Lu lives in a dinky little one-bed flat and not in a palace,' Jerry butted in like a hyperactive three year old, and Lu felt herself shrivel up inside. 'You ought to go where the money is. Wizards and witches! I know, be the new J.K. Rowling!'

'Shut up, Jerry,' Lu said with a smile she didn't feel. Honestly, she didn't know how Briony put up with him. She was about to ask Nick how he knew Jerry when a woman pushed past her.

'Jerry! What an exciting exhibition! Briony must be so pleased,' she said, large diamond brooch twinkling on an expansive dark navy bosom, as if she'd come dressed as the sky at night. A man trailed in her wake, looking so like a pillar of the community in his charcoal grey pin-striped suit and regimental tie that it was a surprise he wasn't topped with a bit of architrave.

Jerry quickly introduced them as Briony's neighbours, Clive and Fenella, then turned to Lu. 'And Lu writes children's books.'

Clive's jowls wobbled. 'Like Harry Potter?'

8

'No, not at all like Harry Potter,' Lu said, thinking perhaps she ought to get a T-shirt printed with 'I am not J.K. Rowling' on it. 'I'm an illustrator really, although I have written a couple of picture books.' It was at least five years ago since she'd written and illustrated her last picture book, she realised. Five years since she'd felt proud of what she was doing.

'I've always fancied writing a couple of kiddies' stories. They're not very long so they wouldn't take much time,' Fenella said airily, wafting coral-tipped fingers like parrot claws in Lu's direction. Lu could have stamped on her toes. Just because picture books were short, people always thought they were easy to write. If anything, they were much, much harder *because* they were so short. 'Clive's written a novel,' Fenella continued, picking a scrap of imaginary lint off his shoulder as if just finishing dusting a museum exhibit.

'I think we'll leave these writers together,' Jerry said, turning to Nick. Lu telepathically flashed an SOS towards Jerry, begging him not to leave her with Clive and Fenella, but intuition didn't seem to be his strong point. Instead he put a hand on Nick's shoulder. 'Come on, mate. Time to show me what your wife's been up to. I hear she's gone abstract.'

And with a quick wink at Lu that told her he knew exactly what he was leaving her to, he steered Nick away. Typical Jerry. And typical—you meet an attractive man, and he turns out to be married. Ah well.

'My grandchildren love my little stories,' the woman continued blithely. 'Tell you what, I'll give you some of my ideas and you could illustrate

9

them. We could split the royalties.'

Lu counted to three, then ten. 'I'm quite busy with my own work at the moment.'

'Have you ever thought about writing a proper book?' Clive said. Lu could imagine him stepping into Prince Philip's shoes quite easily.

'In what way do you mean, a proper book?' But Lu knew what he meant.

'Well, for adults of course.' Clive didn't actually put his thumbs in braces and stick his chest out, but it was a near thing. 'Like mine.'

It couldn't have been more of a leading statement if he'd taken it three times round the paddock. Despite herself, Lu felt compelled to ask the question. 'What's it about?'

'It's a thriller about this group of old friends who've all been at university together and are going on a boating trip in the Norfolk Broads. It's about what happens next.'

'And what does happen next?' Lu asked, secretly hoping they all drowned.

His eyes bulged. 'That's about it so far. I've only done the first couple of chapters, no point in wasting time if it's not a best-seller. I'll do the rest when a publisher wants it. I've tried sending it out, but it's a closed shop, everyone knows that. They don't like to think that there are people outside London who have ideas that pop their little bubble. Either that, or it's nothing but nepotism. Some of them don't even have the courtesy to write back. And they don't read it all, you can tell.'

'I think that's dreadful,' Fenella said, diamonds quivering. 'I mean, it's their job, isn't it?'

'Not really,' Lu said, not wanting to get into a discussion about the state of publishing. She took a long slurp of champagne, surreptitiously looking around for an excuse to slip away, but inspiration was lacking. She was going to have to accept she was stuck in the publishing conversation from hell. 'What books do you like reading?'

'Oh, I don't have time for fiction,' Clive said, rocking back on his heels. Lu wondered if she should rethink her fantasies about men in suits. 'I'm far too busy. Besides, I don't really see the point of it.'

Lu thought about asking him why he was trying to write a novel if he didn't see the point of fiction, but she felt she didn't have that much life to spare. 'What about you?' she asked his wife.

'She likes all that slushy romantic stuff,' Clive said with a superior smile.

'I certainly don't,' Fenella said, bristling so much at his statement it could only be true. 'Occasionally I might read something a bit lighter, but I really only like Literature.'

Clive looked Lu up and down as if he didn't approve of what he saw. 'So how did you get published?' The emphasis was on the word *you*, as if he didn't believe her. Did he realise he was being rude?

'My grandfather was a Flopsy Bunny,' Lu said brightly. 'Us Bunnies have been in the business for generations. Of course, it was my great-great-grandfather Old Mr Rabbit who founded the business, along with his nephew Peter. It was a terribly paternalistic company—my great-aunt Cottontail was cut right out of the will. Luckily for me, they're a bit more enlightened nowadays.'

'Sorry to butt in,' and there was Briony, her arm slipping round Lu's shoulders and gently steering

11

her away from a confused-looking Clive. 'I've promised to introduce Lu to a friend so I'm going to drag her away.'

'I have never wanted to see someone more,' Lu said with feeling once they were a safe distance from the neighbours.

'Did I really hear you tell them you were a Flopsy Bunny?' Lu nodded. 'Oh Lu, grow up,' Briony said, laughing.

'Do I have to?' Lu asked. She wasn't sure she wanted to, if it meant becoming like Mr and Mrs Clive.

Briony lowered her voice. 'Listen, I've come across the most gorgeous man for you. Absolutely perfect. Ticks every box. If I wasn't with Jerry . . .' She took Lu's arm.

'So long as he doesn't want to write a novel, he'll do,' Lu said, following Briony to a corner near one of Jerry's paintings.

'This is Marcus, who plays squash with Jerry, and this is Lu, who I told you about, and I must leave you to it and go and sell some paintings,' Briony said, disappearing.

Lu looked at him. Oh. Oh, oh, oh.

At first sight Marcus ticked a lot of boxes, being tall, dark and yes, handsome. All her romantic clichés had arrived rolled up in one, she thought as she looked up into his chocolate-brown eyes. Her heart was thumping. Could she hear violins in the distance?

'Briony said you play squash with Jerry—I hope you pulverise him.' Amazingly her voice sounded quite normal.

'I grind him to dust,' he said. God, even his voice was wonderful, slow and sexy. And he looked athletic too, with long legs and not much spare flesh on him. It must be all that squash-playing. He was lightly tanned with a golden glow, or maybe it was emanating from him like rays of sunshine. 'Do you play?'

'No, it's far too energetic for me.' Oops, she didn't want to give him the impression she was a couch potato. 'I go to the gym, do Pilates, things like that.'

'I've heard of Pilates.'

'It's very good for your back and your pelvic floor. I mean, I do it for my back,' Lu babbled quickly, hoping he wouldn't think she needed to do work on her pelvic floor. 'I spend most of my day hunched up on a stool over a drawing board so I need to stretch my spine out or I'll end up doubled over.' She pulled herself up straight, settling each vertebra on top of the other as she'd been taught.

'Does the drawing board mean you're an architect?'

Damn, she should have been an architect. It would have been possible: she liked houses and could do technical drawing. The physics would have been a bit of a problem, but . . . 'No, not an architect. An illustrator. And you?'

'I'm an engineer by training, but nowadays I mainly push paper around for a multinational company.' He sounded offhand, but he was obviously high up within the company, judging by the quality of his clothes. An engineer . . . Not wearing a suit right now, but she bet he did most of the time; his trousers had that dry-clean-only look and the creases on his shirt were so sharp it was either brand new or professionally laundered. Which was good, because she didn't like the idea

13

of ironing a man's shirts, not even for the man of her dreams. She glanced at his shoes. Not quite right, being too shiny and smart, as if he was trying a bit too hard, but you couldn't have everything, you had to compromise on something. She checked his hands. No sign of a ring, apart from a gold signet ring on his little finger, but that meant nothing. Not every man wore a wedding ring.

'A multinational sounds as if you travel a lot.'

'Sometimes. I've spent time in Hong Kong, Germany and the US.' He was saying normal things with his mouth but his eyes were saying something else, something warm and intense; he could have used them as a microwave the way he was melting her from the inside out.

'Moving around must be difficult for your family.' Did that sound too much like she was fishing for information? Oh well, couldn't be helped.

'If I had a family it might be, but I'm not married.'

Hallelujah. It wasn't just violins playing, but trumpets too.

'And you?' he added.

Double hallelujah. He wouldn't ask if he wasn't interested. 'I'm not married either,' Lu said, as the full angelic choir joined in and cherubs blew horns and the roof opened up and radiant sunshine filled the gallery.

*   *   *

Lu rang the doorbell three times in quick succession, then waited. She could hear Scottie yapping and could picture him scuttling backwards

14

and forwards along the hall as her grandmother approached. She quickly checked the garden. Everything looked neat and as it should be; even the crazy-paving path leading to the front door was less of a random arrangement of oddly shaped leftovers than a carefully ordered plan. One day she would arrive to discover the leaves hadn't been swept away, the deadheading hadn't been done, and the brass letter box hadn't been buffed up and polished, but that day hadn't yet come, thank heavens.

A few minutes later she heard a muffled voice. 'Lu, is that you?'

'Yes. Were you expecting anyone else? Burglars? Your lover?' She said it casually, to amuse herself, knowing Delia would be too busy concentrating on undoing the deadlock and the safety chain to answer, but the word 'lover' seemed to reverberate around the front garden. Would Marcus be her lover? Marcus the Wonderful, the Perfect, who'd asked for her phone number. He'd ring, they'd go out, they'd fall in love, everything would be perfect . . . Lu shook her head. She was mad to think like this; he probably wouldn't even ring her.

The door opened a chink, then widened, and her grandmother peered out. 'It is you.'

'If I was an enterprising burglar I'd have said yes,' Lu said, stepping in and embracing her grandmother. Her cheek was as soft as ever, but her shoulders were frail under the sensible navy cardigan layered over a jumper and shirt, and probably a thermal vest underneath. Delia felt the cold.

'You can't be too careful nowadays,' Delia said.

15

'You could have been anyone. You read about them in the paper, preying on pensioners, coming in for a glass of water and stealing your handbag. It's not safe to go out. Stabbings, muggings, it's dreadful what they do.'

'I think you should stop reading the paper,' Lu said, bending down to pat Scottie. 'You'd be much happier.'

'I want to know what's going on,' Delia said, leading the way to the sitting room. Lu followed, her eyes anxiously scanning her grandmother's back for signs of infirmity. The thought of Delia not being there made her catch her breath with worry. She had always been there when Lu needed her, a refuge from the chaos that followed her mother around. It was a mystery how Delia had managed to have a daughter like Susan, or Pixie as she preferred to be called, the name she had given herself at some point in the sixties—to Delia's horror. It suited her free spirit better, Pixie had once explained to Lu. However, Pixie had displayed similar horror when at secondary school age, Lu refused to answer to Lunabella. Lu might equate to toilets, but it was better than being a loony, especially when you had a loony mum to cope with. Besides, Delia had always called her Lu.

The sitting room was so old-fashioned it could have been used as the set for Miss Marple's house. It was incredibly tidy and well dusted, the opposite of the jumble that Pixie had created in the string of homes they'd lived in while Lu was growing up. Lu suspected that Delia dusted each china ornament jostling for position on the mantelpiece, each photograph frame, even each dried flower head every day. When anyone said to Lu that she was very tidy, in that slightly disapproving way that suggested that she was too tidy, Lu always replied, 'You should see my grandmother's house. I'm not nearly as bad as she is.'

Lu loved Delia's tidiness; it was always a relief not to have to worry about what you might sit on on the sofa, what you might step in when you crossed a room, what might be lurking under the bed when you tried to find your school shoes in the morning. Even now when she came to her grandmother's house she could feel a layer of tension dissolve.

'You sit yourself down there and I'll bring the tea,' Delia said. She'd never been a currant-bun sort of grandmother, soft and squidgy, but her outline had become more indistinct as the years progressed, blurring as if she were fading out of the picture.

'I'll get it,' Lu said quickly. She went back into the hall and into the kitchen, where, as she'd expected, she found a tray laid with tea cups and a pot, all on an immaculately ironed white linen cloth. As she waited for the kettle to come to the boil, she touched the lace edge of the cloth, knowing that it had been hand-crocheted by Delia many years ago. There were little ziggurats of yellow cross-stitching in each corner, the stitches as neat as any machine. Forgotten arts, she thought. Little girls no longer learned to make those immaculate tiny stitches; instead they played computer games along with their brothers.

But they were girlie enough to read Princess Butterfly, she thought, seeing a pad of Princess Butterfly paper perched by the phone. Princess Butterfly had been a series of books Lu had illustrated a few years ago. She touched the illustration lightly, thinking how typical it was of Delia to be supportive and have something Lu had illustrated about the house, even though Princess Butterfly was aimed at four year olds rather than ninety-two year olds. Her lovely, caring grandma.

Don't forget to ask Lu, was written on the top sheet.

Lu poured the boiling water on to the tea bags, thinking that it was a good thing she was there to do things for her grandmother. Little things—changing the times of the central heating when the clocks went back, opening jars that Delia's arthritic fingers could no longer manage, hanging yet another picture on the crowded walls. Mind you, you had to watch Delia—given half a chance she'd be up a ladder trying to change a light bulb or clearing out the guttering. She wanted her independence, of course, but seemed sometimes incapable of seeing that if she fell and hurt herself, she could kiss that independence goodbye.

'Ask Lu what?' Lu said, coming back into the sitting room with the tea things.

Delia looked up. 'What was that?'

'On your pad, by the phone. It says, don't forget to ask Lu.' She had expected Delia to ask her to retrieve a box from the attic or explain the meaning of the council tax bill, but instead her grandmother patted the sofa. 'I've something to show you, and something I want you to do for me.'

'Of course,' Lu said, putting the tea things on to the coffee table in front of the sofa and sitting down. 'Tell me what it is you want me to do.'

Delia reached behind her and brought out a cardboard shoebox, which she placed on her

18

knees, her hands resting on the lid as if Lu might snatch it from her. She suddenly looked up. 'Now I don't want you to go telling your mother.'

It was so unexpected, Lu almost dropped her tea cup. 'Mum? Why ever not?'

'I'll tell her later, when we know what's what, but I don't want her to know yet. She'll want to do it all with those cards of hers, or go dowsing, and I can't abide all that nonsense.' Delia reached over for Lu's hand. 'It'll be our secret.'

'I won't say anything if you don't want me to,' Lu said. 'I hardly ever get a word in edgeways with Mum anyway.'

'You're a good girl,' Delia said, patting Lu's hand. 'Now, I've been watching that programme where they look up their family history and find out about their ancestors. I expect you've seen it.'

'I know the one you mean. It's with celebrities, and they trace back through the generations and find out about their long-lost relatives, where they came from, that sort of thing. Oh—do you want me to trace our family tree?' Lu frowned. 'I thought you'd got that all written out in the big bible you got from your mother.'

'No, not the family tree.' Delia reached into the box and took out a photograph in an ornate mahogany frame. She stroked it gently, then handed it to Lu.

'I want you to find him,' Delia said.

Lu took the photograph. The picture was faded round the edges, but the eyes of the young man in uniform were clear as he looked steadily towards the camera. The vaguely painted backcloth landscape and pot plant on a stand gave it an Edwardian feel. Who was he? She looked at Delia,

19

trying to read her face. A former boyfriend? Except they didn't call them boyfriends in those days. A sweetheart, maybe. But Gran's courting days must have been in the thirties and forties, and this chap looked older. First World War, perhaps? He'd have to be at least a hundred, if not more.

Lu cleared her throat. 'Um, Gran, I don't like to say this, but won't he be dead by now?'

Delia clicked her tongue. 'I know that, but you can track down dead people, can't you? I want you to find him on the Internet. You're always saying it's wonderful and can find anything. Well, I want you to find him.'

Lu looked at the photograph again. 'You know, it's funny, but the person he reminds me of is Mum.' Maybe it was the way their heads were tilted, or the shape of the eyes. There was something about Delia's stillness that sharpened her senses. 'Who is he?'

'His name is Jack Havergal,' Delia said. She cleared her throat. 'I think he's my father.'

Chapter 2

Lu couldn't have been more surprised if Scottie had suddenly announced he was the winner of *The X Factor*. She looked around the room, thinking that she'd see the tables rocking and the ornaments quivering in the wake of the earthquake, but everything was still. Even Scottie, instead of launching into a pop ballad, was flat out on the old rag rug in front of the gas fire.

'Your father?' Lu blinked. 'But your father was

20

Percy.'

'I grew up believing that.' Delia lay back on the sofa cushions. 'He was a lovely man, my dad, he wouldn't have hurt a fly, so I'm sure it was all my mother's idea. She had some funny notions in her head, she did. Ever so proper. Looking back, I reckon she didn't like the idea I was . . .' Delia sighed. 'Well, there's no nice way to say it. I'm illegitimate, that's all there is to it.'

'What?' Lu couldn't believe what she was hearing, and Scottie, disturbed by her virtual shriek, sat up and barked. 'So Maud and this man . . .?' Lu looked at the photograph in amazement and some awe—she'd seen photographs of her great-grandmother looking completely impenetrable, like the elderly Queen Victoria.

'Certainly not. Whatever gave you that idea? Scottie, hush now,' Delia soothed, as the dog danced and yapped at them. 'Really, Lu, you should know better.'

Lu wasn't sure if she should know better than to disturb Scottie by raising her voice, or to suspect Great-grandmother Maud of an illicit liaison. Probably both, knowing Delia, who, while generally loving, had a nice sideline in universal disapproval, especially when it looked as if Lu was picking up bad habits from Pixie.

Scottie soothed and back on the rag rug, ears cocked for any further excitement, Delia continued. 'When I say I was illegitimate, I mean I was born illegitimate. My real parents were Jack Havergal—this photograph is a portrait of him—and Anne Morgan. When I was four years old, Percy and Maud adopted me.'

'So do you remember your real parents?' Lu

21

said, sitting forwards. 'And how long have you known? Have you only just discovered this? Oh Gran, it must have been an awful shock—are you all right?'

'Yes, yes, dear, don't fret and fuss me. I've known for years that I was adopted, ever since I was married. My parents—and I still think of them as that—decided it was right I should know when I got married, and that my future husband should know. Though what I'd have done if it'd put your grandfather off I don't know.' Delia looked quite cross.

'But it didn't put him off,' Lu said, glancing across to the photograph of her grandfather in pride of place on the mantelpiece.

'Certainly not. Your grandad was the salt of the earth, he was. Said it made no odds, he wanted to marry me wherever I'd come from.'

'That's so romantic,' Lu said, wondering if Marcus would ever say anything like that to her. She could just see him now, going down on one knee and looking up at her with his brown eyes— they were brown, weren't they? Yes, brown eyes, dark brown hair. She dragged her imagination away from this delightful vision. 'So if you were only adopted when you were four, you must remember your real parents.' She hesitated, suddenly wondering if poor Delia had started life in an orphanage or even the workhouse. She wasn't sure if they still had workhouses in the early twentieth century or if they'd gone by then.

'It's a strange thing,' Delia said, 'but I can't remember anyone else other than my mother when I was small. And I'm sure I can remember things from when I was two or three, but they're

22

always at my parents' house. Nothing from anywhere else. I did ask my mother, but she didn't want to talk about it—I think if she'd had her way, nothing would have been said in the first place. It was my dad who thought I should know. I think she didn't want to be reminded that I hadn't started life in a respectable way. She was always very strict when I was growing up, very keen that I should stay nice until I married. Still, that's all water under the bridge now.'

'So why do you think this man's your real father?' Lu examined the photograph again, looking for similarities between his face and her own. 'And what about your real mother?'

Delia took a deep breath. 'When my mother died, I found all sorts of papers. Rubbish, a lot of it, but there were the adoption papers, so that's how I knew my real parents' names.' She patted the cardboard box. 'There were also letters from Percy to my mother, and from a man—Jack Havergal—to Percy. They're all dated to the time of the Great War, so I think my father and this Jack met then. Now, my dad had this photograph and he told me that the man in the photograph, Jack Havergal, had saved his life, so that's how I know this is Jack.'

'What about your real mother?' Lu said softly. 'Didn't your parents tell you anything about her?'

Delia shook her head. 'I know this sounds strange to your generation, you're always busy talking about everything, but my parents didn't say much, and I didn't like to ask. I could see my mother found it upsetting and, well, people didn't talk about things like that in those days. We let sleeping dogs carry on sleeping.' Delia looked

23

affectionately at the snoring Scottie, little paws twitching as he terrorised dream rabbits. 'Apart from the name, I know nothing about my birth mother. When we married, your grandad and I, we did a bit of looking, but it wasn't like now, there wasn't this Internet and we couldn't find anything. We had to give up.'

'Isn't there an agency that keeps all the records?'

'There is now, but not back in them days. People adopted children just by private arrangement, they didn't make a fuss out of it. Girls had babies out of wedlock, and thought it better to pretend it hadn't happened. It's easier now—you can get in touch if you want, but not then. People didn't think children would want to know.'

Lu nodded. 'But you would. I can see you'd want to know. So what can I do?'

'I've seen it on the telly,' Delia said. 'They look it all up on the web thing, the one you're always saying I should do. But my love, I can't do it.' She turned her palms towards Lu, the gnarled and arthritic fingers bent together. 'I tried, down at the library, the lady was ever so nice, but I can't do the typing and I can't move that mouse, my hands just won't do it. I'm ninety-two and I'm an old dog. I can't be learning new tricks.'

Lu grimaced, thinking of how she'd tried to encourage her grandmother to become a Silver Surfer. Stupid of her not to realise that Delia would have difficulties with her arthritic hands. 'I'm sure it's not as easy as it looks on the telly, but I'll do what I can.' She looked up as something else struck her. 'Why do you want to know now?'

Delia looked shifty. 'It's on the telly.'

'Gran . . .' Lu looked sternly at her grandmother. 'Why now?'

*   *   *

'It turns out it's her teeth,' Lu said, sipping her mojito. 'She's got to have her wisdom teeth out, and she's terrified of having a general anaesthetic. Of course, she's ninety-two, so it is more dangerous but, just imagine, she's never had one before.' The bar was busy; they had to sit close to hear what the other was saying, but Lu didn't mind. The closer the better as far as she was concerned.

Marcus nodded. 'I've not had many. My appendix, and I broke my arm playing polo and it set badly so I had to have it broken and reset under a general, but that's about it.'

Lu tucked away the knowledge that he'd played polo. Of course he had; he had probably been to Argentina and played chukkas on the pampas. 'Anyway, I've got to find out about my real great-grandparents. It looks so easy when you see it on television: you go to the right site, and there's all the information, and Bob's your uncle—or Jack's your great-grandfather.'

'So there isn't the information?' Marcus ate a salted almond, licking his lips to get the salt off. For a second Lu wondered what he'd do if she leaned forward and kissed the salt away. She quickly started talking instead.

'No, just the opposite. There's too much. I've tried typing things into Google and you just get millions of sites coming back at you.' Family

25

history was a booming industry, if the entries on Google were anything to go by. Books and societies and people wanting information on long-lost relatives all jostled across her screen. Defeated by the deluge, Lu had thought she'd try a bit of First World War research, and discovered that there were millions of people out there with sites to visit and books to buy. She had only the haziest ideas about the war in the first place, which didn't help. It had coagulated into her mind as four years of fighting in trenches, with a few poets scooting around talking about foreign fields, and posters of Kitchener saying Your Country Needs You.

She gave the mojito a cautious sip. The barman had stuffed it full of ice and mint and she didn't want to risk making a horrible dreggy sucking noise with her straw. 'I'm sure once I get started it'll be easier, but it's hard to know where to begin. A lot of the sites you have to pay to subscribe to, and I don't know if it's worth it. I don't suppose you've done any family history research?' She looked up at Marcus hopefully, but he shook his head.

'Afraid not. My family history is, as far as I know, fairly straightforward. I think there are a couple of distant cousins who've done some research and they've sent my parents copies of the family tree. I'm not going to be any use to you.'

Don't say that, Lu thought, lowering her eyes in case he could read her thoughts. I can think of lots of uses for you. 'What about the First World War—do you know anything about that?'

But again Marcus shook his head. Still, it would be quite unreasonable to expect him to be an expert in precisely everything she wanted to know, when he was really absolutely perfect in every other way.

'Science all the way for me, that or making things.' Marcus spread out his hands as if ready to make something. He had very practical hands, Lu thought, tanned and strong, with neat fingernails. She hated men who had long fingernails, but his were just right.

'Do you make things now, for your company?' She knew engineering had a wide application, but in her head it meant building bridges, bridges spanning vast gushing rivers, a bit like in the film *The Bridge on the River Kwai*.

'I could do, if I had to.' He explained that his company manufactured precision technical equipment using lasers.

'Like the baddie in *Goldfinger*?' Lu put on a fake German accent. ' "I don't expect you to talk, Mr Bond. I expect you to die." '

Marcus laughed. 'Right sort of kit, but on a slightly smaller scale. Most of our equipment would fit into the palm of your hand.' He explained how his company's laser equipment was used for machinery all over the world, for pattern-cutting and engine-tooling and surgical equipment and . . .

Fascinating, Lu thought, gazing into his eyes as he talked. He was so knowledgeable, so articulate, so passionate. So . . . perfect. Not that she could understand much of what he was saying; phrases like electrode deposition, vacuum bonding, the Czochralski method, athermal birefringent filters flew around her head like exotic humming birds. She took a long sip of her mojito and made an equally long slurping sound.

'I'm sorry,' Marcus said. 'I must be boring you.'

'Not at all,' Lu said honestly, putting down her glass in case of further oral embarrassment. 'I don't think you could.'

Marcus gave her a sideways look, as if he wasn't a hundred per cent sure she wasn't joking. 'Anyway, it's your turn. Tell me about what you do. You said at the exhibition that you're an illustrator. What are you working on at the moment?'

'Vegetables. To be precise, some peas in a pod called . . .' she gave a little drum roll on the bartop with her forefingers, 'the Sugarsnaps!'

Marcus looked uncertain. 'Is that what you like illustrating?'

'It's got its charms,' Lu said. 'It's quite interesting working out how to draw them, given that peas are round, and identical, and don't come with any foliage you can use for legs or arms. Bit like doing a crossword puzzle or sudoku. And they're having lots of adventures with other vegetables, which is fun to draw. But really, it's not a question of what I like doing, I'm a freelance illustrator; I take the work I'm offered, and if that's vegetables, then I draw vegetables.' It wasn't what she'd trained for, she felt like saying, it wasn't what she had dreamed of. But that would have been way too heavy for a first date. 'At least it's not animals dressed up and doing human things. Or fairies. A couple of years ago I did a series on a princess fairy, and I have to say, I'm fairied out for the moment. Anyway, I think the bottom's dropped out of the fairy market,' she added.

'That sounds vaguely obscene.' Marcus sipped

his drink with a raised eyebrow, suave as James Bond—no embarrassing slurping noises for him.

'You should hear some of the conversations us illustrators have. I had one the other day about pigs—how do you draw the rear view of a pig complete with tail but without showing its bottom, if you're not going anthropomorphic and allowing trousers.' What was she doing talking about pigs' bottoms to Marcus? It wasn't exactly a come-hither line. At least she hoped it wasn't. 'People have no idea of the complexities of the job.'

'So you don't do anything like Jerry?'

'No, it's a quite different discipline.' Lu felt in safer waters. 'Though I like to think that if I decided to be an artist, I'd find it easier than Jerry would find it being an illustrator.'

Marcus smiled at that. 'Perhaps I should ask him what he thinks.'

'Noooo, it would be embarrassing,' Lu said, wincing. She wondered whether she should order another round of drinks, which might prompt Marcus into suggesting they went out for dinner. The barman was busy down the other end of the bar, which was filling up even more. It was getting harder to hear what Marcus was saying. She decided against another drink here. 'Did you have a chance to look round the exhibition? It was very crowded, I'm amazed anyone could see any of the art. Pity, because there was some really good work there.'

'I bought something, actually.' Marcus swirled the ice round in his glass nonchalantly.

'Really?' Lu leaned forward, although if she got much nearer she'd be sitting on his lap. 'What?'

'I should really make you guess, but . . . I bought

29

one of Jerry's.'

'Right.' Lu had to admit it sent him down a bit in her estimation. At least he bought art, which was more than most. 'Was it the one with the . . .' She stopped, embarrassed.

'Nipples that look like lumps of bubblegum? Yeah.'

'That was what I was going to say.' Lu knew exactly which one it was. You could hardly miss it: the paint was heavily applied in great vibrant blobs. It wouldn't have been her choice. She looked up at him, suddenly less certain. 'Do you buy much art?'

'When I can. I can't paint or draw to save my life, so I'm in awe of those who can.' Marcus gave her a teasing sideways glance. 'Perhaps I should buy something of yours.'

Lu smiled back at him, uncertainties evaporated, her skin tingling with anticipation. 'I don't sell my illustrations.'

Marcus leaned towards her. She could smell his aftershave, fresh and lemony. 'You might make an exception.' His voice was enticing.

Lu shook her head. 'Never,' she said, her eyes on his.

'A challenge for me, then. I like a challenge.' To her surprise, instead of following up with something wonderfully seductive and flirty, he withdrew slightly, fiddling with his cufflinks. 'Pity I won't be able to take it up in the near future.'

'Oh?'

'I'm going away next week. To Minneapolis.'

'On business?'

'Yes—I wouldn't be there for any other reason. It's not exactly Barbados.'

30

She should have known Marcus went to Barbados on holiday, Lu thought. First class, most likely. He could probably waterski. He drank from the minibar and never smuggled the rolls from breakfast up to his room for lunch. 'So how long are you in Minneapolis for?'

Marcus gave a rueful smile. 'For ever, perhaps.'

So it turned out the gods weren't smiling on her after all.

*   *   *

'There's good news, and bad news,' Lu said as she plonked herself down the next day in the seat opposite Briony at the café around the corner from the gallery. Briony ate there so often she nicknamed it her second office. Her first office was a damp cubbyhole down in the basement under the gallery. Lu thought she probably did more work in her car than either of her offices.

Briony looked up from the stack of papers she'd been making notes from and pushed them to one side. 'Oooh, let's have the good news first.'

'Marcus rang.' Lu quickly ordered a cappuccino and a piece of carrot cake from the waitress. No point in being on a diet now.

'And?'

'And we went out for a drink, and he's absolutely wonderful, just what I was looking for. He's really interesting, got a great job, knows lots of stuff, has the most gorgeous eyes.' Lu sighed and rested her chin on the heel of her hand. 'In fact he's perfect in every way.'

'I knew he would be.' Briony squealed with delight. 'I'll have to pump Jerry for information—I

31

wonder when he's next playing squash with him.'

Squash meant quick reactions, Lu thought. Lovely legs. Adrenalin . . . testosterone . . . Mind you, that would also have been true for Jerry, and she didn't fancy him one little bit. 'Jerry will never play squash with Marcus again. That's the bad news.' Lu sat back in her chair. 'He's going to Minneapolis.'

Briony frowned. 'Where's that?'

'Minnesota.' She could sense that Briony was about to ask where *that* was, and got in first. 'North USA, to the left of the Great Lakes. The starting point of the Mississippi, land of ten thousand lakes. Home once of the Chippewa and Dakota Indians, now home to Marcus.'

Briony looked doubtful. 'Might be a nice place to visit . . .'

'I'm not sure it's my sort of place—I Googled it, and the first site that came up was one for rogue taxidermists. They stuff roadkill.' She supposed that at least it was a form of recycling and a bit whacky, but then there was whacky in a good way, and whacky in a bad way. 'Anyway, it's hardly likely that we're going to see each other again. You wouldn't just happen to be passing by, or be able to pop out for a quick drink.'

'There's always email.'

'Come on, it's not as if we'd got together and then he's going. We've only just met. You can't build a passionate, earth-shattering relationship on the basis of a couple of glasses of mojitos and a bunch of emails.' The waitress placed Lu's coffee and cake in front of her and she murmured a thank you before picking up the fork and spearing a corner of carrot cake.

'No, but you could keep things going until he gets back. How long is he going for?'

'That's the point. He might never come back. He's got a wonderful opportunity to go out there and build his own division blah blah blah. It's just too depressing. I meet someone who has real potential, and they're going away practically the next day. I really thought he could be Mr Right, just the timing's wrong.'

'Mr Right at the wrong time is Mr Wrong.' Briony sipped her espresso, dark as her hair and clothes. The only colour on her was her scarlet lipstick.

Lu slumped in her seat. Nothing was going well; every direction she tried came to a dead end. No wonder she needed carrot cake. 'I am so fed up with this. All I want is a nice normal relationship with a nice normal man, one who doesn't have vast quantities of baggage. You'd have thought it wouldn't be too much to ask.'

'But they've all got baggage. Everyone has, even you.'

'Not me. I've no ties, own place, own car, own career—not that that's brilliant at the moment, but at least it exists—no dodgy exes lurking round the corner, nothing.'

'No dodgy exes? You've got more exes than I've had hot dinners.'

'I haven't.'

'Come off it. You're always falling for men, and they're all wonderful at first and then they turn out to be wrong in some way. What about Bill? Or Alec? Or what was that one called? The one you dumped because he was too needy? Dan, that was it.'

'He *was* needy,' Lu protested, realising she'd eaten a huge slab of carrot cake in record time.

'He was normal. Maybe a bit OTT, but most women would have loved it. Blimey, if Jerry did half that stuff—no, correction, ten per cent—I'd be thrilled.'

'It was nice,' Lu said, thinking back to the regular supply of flowers, the attentive phone calls, the cute texts. 'But it got too much. Anyway, how is Jerry? Did he sell well? I know Marcus bought one of his.'

'The gallery did pretty well. I was a bit nervous, what with the state of the financial markets, but I think people have decided to invest in art. After all, if you're only getting pennies in interest, you might as well take a punt on something you can enjoy on the wall. All of Jerry's work went; I was worried that his market would have dried up, but it seemed to be fine.'

'Trust Jerry.'

Briony laughed. 'I know it's not to your taste, but it is a lot of people's.'

'And the man himself? He seemed on good form at the party.'

'Oh, Jerry's always on good form. Life's one big party to him.' There was a bitter edge to Briony's voice.

'Is everything all right?'

Briony twiddled her pen in her fingers. 'Same old stuff: I complain because he's peering down girls' cleavages; he says he's just having fun and enjoying himself; I feel like a miserable old prune. I know he doesn't mean anything by it, but it's just so obvious. And he's always got some model in his studio without her clothes on. He just says nudes

34

sell, and I know they do, I just wish he'd do something like landscapes.'

'But you're not really suspicious, are you?'

'No. Yes.' Briony doodled a scribble on the cover of her notebook. 'I know a lot of it is just in my head, but then you think, no smoke without fire.'

'To be fair, he's always been a bit like that.'

'I know, but you'd have thought he'd have changed by now, settled down. I want us to sell our flats and buy somewhere together, but he says it's a bad time to sell and we should wait. I know it's a bad time to sell, but also I don't see why we have to put our lives on hold. So we have a row and he stomps off, and then we make up and it's as if none of it's happened. I just don't feel we're going anywhere, apart from in circles.' Briony looked at her hands, silver rings on most fingers. 'Sometimes I think I might be better breaking up and moving on, finding someone who does want to settle down with me.'

Lu didn't know what to say. On the one hand, Jerry was not her favourite person; on the other, Briony had been through this cycle so many times before. The next time she saw her, Jerry might have suddenly become Mr Wonderful again. 'It's tricky . . .' she started to say.

'I know, if you were me, you'd have dumped Jerry years ago. But most of the time it's so good together. It's only that last ten per cent, and it's not even that. We all have to make compromises somewhere along the line.'

Lu didn't say anything. She didn't intend to compromise, not ever. When she met Mr Right, that would be it. She didn't want to waste her time

35

on Mr Wrongs. Oh Marcus, why do you have to go to Minneapolis?

Lu's phone rang. She checked it, then let it fall back in her bag.

'Not answering?'

Lu shook her head. 'My agent. It'll either be to tick me off for being behind with my deadline or to offer me more work that I don't want to do.'

'How very glam to be offered work you don't want to do.'

'Hardly.' Lu slurped her cappuccino, not caring if she made noises or got a foam moustache. 'I don't know, I had such high ideals when I left college about what I was going to do. It was only going to be top-end picture books.'

'And that's what you did.'

'So how come I'm here, doing flat-fee work about vegetables? Sometimes I feel like a machine. They give me the brief, they wind me up, I churn the work out by a set time to a set fee. Half the time they give me the brief late, so I end up delivering the work late, but that's somehow my fault, so they're pissed off and my agent gives me an ear-bashing about being reliable and professional.'

'You sound pissed off too.'

Lu spooned the last dregs of cappuccino out. 'I don't know. Sometimes I can remember how I used to feel about illustration, how it was the most important thing in the world to me, but to be honest, that seems a long time ago. The creativity has gone out of it; it feels like the books are designed by committees.'

'You could go back to individual top-end picture books rather than this flat-fee series work. You did that once.'

'Somehow I seem to have slipped out of that market and I can't get back into it. My agent doesn't appear to be able to get me the commissions.'

'What about writing your own again?' Briony checked her watch, and started to gather her papers up.

'But that would mean turning work down—paying work. I'd have to develop a book with no guarantee it would get published, and the illustration market is tricky at the moment.' Lu rummaged in her bag for her purse. 'It's a Catch 22: I need money to live off so I can't afford to turn work down, but because I'm fully booked with flat-fee work I'm not free to even have a crack at the sort of jobs I'd like to do. When I started this series, I thought it was really cute, but now I could murder the person who wrote them.'

'I always thought cute was king in the illustration business.'

'It is, it is.' Lu put down the money to pay her bill, thinking she was going to have to give up having coffee and cake with Briony quite so often at this rate. 'I know it sells, but I wish I could do something a bit more meaty.'

'Like what? Farmyard animals?'

Briony looked so pleased with her joke that Lu laughed as she stood up. 'I didn't mean to come and dump all this on you.'

'No problem.' Briony got up too. 'It makes a change from artists whingeing about the gallery's commission.'

Lu looked around the café, the walls hung with art for sale. Many of them had red dots beside them. 'You were better than any of the stuff here. Don't you miss it?'

'Never.' Briony looked at the art. 'And while it's nice of you to say so, I don't think I was that good to start out with. Plus I never had the drive that some people had, regardless of talent. I mean, look at someone like Jerry. He works hard at his painting, yes, but he also has one eye on the market all the time and he networks furiously. I can think of other people in our year—Maria, for instance—who were really, really talented, but they didn't have any of the other skills you need to make a career of it. Actually, someone at the party told me she'd got four kids under five.'

Lu pulled on her coat and wrapped her scarf twice round her neck. 'Yuck. As far as I'm concerned, my biological clock can tick until it's blue in the face and I still won't want them.'

'Not even with Mr Right?' Briony slipped on her coat, a square kimono sort of affair in what looked like blanket material. It radiated I Own An Art Gallery.

Lu shook her head, thinking that her own coat radiated I'm Seriously Broke. 'Not even with him. Speaking of children, I know what I wanted to ask you—do you know anything about tracing your family history?'

Briony shook her head. 'Nothing. I've always known who my lot were. Why?'

'You know my gran? She's got to have her wisdom teeth out and, while it's a pretty routine op, because of her age and everything, she's really worried about it. I think she thinks she's going to die.' Lu shivered involuntarily at the thought and Briony wrinkled her nose sympathetically.

'Anyway, she's asked me to do a bit of research into our family history and, in particular, this photograph she's got of a First World War soldier. And I haven't a clue where to start.'

'Can't you look it up online?'

'In theory, yes, but it's really hard to know where to start. There must be about twenty zillion sites on the First World War—which one do you go for? It's the sort of thing that if you know what you're looking for it's really easy, but if you don't know anything about it, you're lost.'

Briony looked thoughtful. 'Actually, I might be able to help, or at least I know someone who could. Nick Jones. He was at the party. Not obviously attractive but quite sexy. Looks a bit like Gerard Depardieu.'

Lu nodded. 'I know who you mean, I think. I met him briefly with Jerry.' She had a hazy picture of the man, before he was eclipsed by the wonders of Marcus.

'He's something to do with war, ex-soldiers, I'm not sure what exactly. I don't think he's a historian, but he seems a really nice guy, so I'm sure he'll help if he can. Look, I've got his number somewhere here . . .' Briony put all her papers back down on the café table and started to flick through the numbers on her mobile.

'Brilliant. Anything is better than floundering around the Internet for hours. How do you know him?'

'His wife is one of my artists—does abstract landscapes, sells well. I had thought there was some problem with them because I hadn't seen him about for ages—not that Morwenna said anything because she's very private, keeps it all

39

professional—but I assume it's all fine; anyway, they seemed very amicable at the private view. Look, here's the number—do you want me to call him now?'

Lu blinked. 'Um, yes, why not?'

Briony rang the number and after a bit someone answered. They exchanged pleasantries about the exhibition, then Briony said, 'I'm after a favour for a friend. Lu Edwards—I think you met her briefly at the party. Long brown hair, a bit hippyish.' Lu frowned at Briony. A bit hippyish? Just because she didn't wear black all the time like Briony.

'Yes, that's right, an illustrator.' Briony nodded at Lu and did a thumbs-up. Lu was cheered by this proof that she was memorable, even if hippyish. 'She needs some help tracking down a First World War soldier, and I thought of you. She's right here—shall I pass you over?' Briony handed the phone to Lu.

'Hi. Um. Sorry to bother you.'

'That's fine. Briony says you need some help tracking down a soldier?'

Lu explained the situation, and how she was finding it difficult.

'It's not too bad when you know your way around the sites.' He spoke slowly, his voice reassuring. 'I'm quite happy to help get you started.'

'Thank you so much, that'd be great.' They arranged to meet at a local pub the next evening, then Lu hung up and handed the phone back to Briony. 'He was nice.'

'He seems to be. Attractive too,' Briony said as they walked to the exit, Lu's face suddenly feeling brittle as the cold air hit it after the warmth of the café.

'Not my type. Too broad. Too married. Anyway, I'm after him for his knowledge, not his body.' Outside on the pavement, Lu gave Briony a hug. 'Thanks for helping, and cheer up. You're always having ups and downs with Jerry; perhaps you're just having another down right now.'

Briony hugged Lu back. 'Expect you're right. Good luck with Nick.'

*　　　*　　　*

Lu got to the pub the following day earlier than she'd expected. Inside it was dark but welcoming. They'd taken a tired pub, badly modernised in the seventies, and ripped out the old interior, revealing the original features such as the fireplace and oak floors. They'd made a snug area in the darkest corner, with over-scaled flock wallpaper in purple and black. It should have looked wrong, but here it worked, although it did make the corner very dark. Lu looked around hoping to see Nick, but she couldn't spot him. She felt a frisson of fear, a bit like on a first date—what if she didn't recognise him at all? Perhaps the pub was filled with men who looked like Gerard Depardieu but dark-haired. On the other hand, looking around, perhaps not.

She got herself a drink from the bar and chose a table, settling down with her back to the wall so she could see the main entrance without it looking as if she was staring anxiously. She got out her notepad, more to give herself something to do, then she noticed the couple two tables down. The man had the most enormous nose. It was huge.

Humongous. Quickly she sketched the outline as best she could. He was staring morosely at his plate, as if he'd asked for steak and been served salad—rabbit food, he probably called it, she thought as she started cross-hatching round his cheeks. And his eyebrows—like prawns stuck on to his brow ridges. There, off they went like firecrackers, shooting sparks from his eyes, his hair like wire wool, tight as a terrier's, and then down and round to the ears, mottled red like old meat on the butcher's counter, and then—

'Lu. Hello.'

Lu looked up, reluctantly focusing on the shape in front of her. Oh, yes, Nick. She gave herself a mental shake. Yes—Nick. 'I'm sorry,' she said, closing her sketchpad. 'I was miles away.'

Nick raised his eyebrows—no prawns there. 'Remind me never to ask you to draw me.'

'What? Oh no, this is nothing, I always carry it with me.' Lu slipped the pad into her bag. 'Thanks so much for meeting me.'

'No problem.' He sat down next to her. 'You said on the phone you needed to track down a First World War soldier.'

'Gosh, yes, but let me get you a drink first.'

Lu went to the bar and ordered a pint of bitter. Nick was and wasn't what she'd expected. Her memory of him had been hazy, a big guy, not as tall as Marcus but broad, his demeanour relaxed and pleasant. He was still all these things, but shaggy might have been a better description, although he wasn't unkempt in any way. Maybe his hair was a bit too long and needed a decent cut, maybe his shirt looked as if it was about to become untucked. For a second she saw him as a little boy, the sort with scabby knees and socks concertina'd round the ankles and a Swiss Army penknife in his pocket, the sort that was always busy doing something, the sort that was fun to draw.

She paid for his pint then carried it back carefully. Nick took a long drink, as if he needed it.

'Hard day?'

He nodded. 'I've not been doing this job for long, so I'm still on the learning curve.'

'I don't know what it is you do—Briony just said it was something to do with war.'

'Not exactly. I work for a charity that helps former members of the armed forces, whether it's helping them to adjust to civilian life, or deal with disabilities or pensions or any other issues.'

'So not the First World War then.'

'Not directly, but I know my way around.' Nick sipped his pint again. 'I was brought in to run a project linked with the centenary of the First World War in five years' time, so although my background's in marketing and fund-raising rather than military history, I'm starting to learn about it. Now. What did you want to know?'

'My grandmother's given me a photograph of a soldier; I'm guessing he's in First World War uniform. She thinks he might be her father and she wants me to find him, but I don't know where to start.' Lu had scanned the photograph into her computer and printed off a copy, not wanting to lug the heavy photograph frame around with her. She handed the copy to Nick.

'Do you know his name? His regiment?'

'I've got his name, but I don't know anything else. He looks terribly young,' she added.

'Some of them signed up at fifteen, fourteen even,' Nick said, shaking his head. 'Poor lads, they had no idea what they were letting themselves in for. Though it has to be said, most of them were a lot older. The Army paid well, much more than most ordinary men could earn.' He bent his head to look at the photograph more closely. 'It's a bit blurry, but with a magnifying glass we'd be able to work out his rank and regiment from the buttons and insignia, and then it will be a lot easier. Do you know if he was a regular soldier or just enlisted?'

Lu shook her head. 'I don't know.'

'And did he die in the war?'

'I know nothing at all about him beyond his name and the fact that my grandmother believes he's her father. Which would make him my great-grandfather.' Lu peered at the photograph in Nick's hands, hoping to feel some connection. But he remained just a man in uniform. 'Would it make a difference if he had died?'

'It's much easier to look up soldiers who died while serving in the Army.' He leaned forward. 'The Internet makes it so easy.'

'That's what everyone keeps telling me, but it isn't!'

Nick laughed. 'No, really, it is.'

If you know where to look, Lu thought as Nick pulled out his iPhone and flipped it open. He pressed the keypad a couple of times, waited for Internet access, then tapped in a site. 'Right. What was his name?'

'Jack Havergal,' Lu said, peering over his arm at the screen, trying to see what he was doing. In the dimly lit pub interior, the screen glowed in his hand.

'Good, that sounds like an unusual name. That'll make it more straightforward if he's there and . . .' Nick typed in the name, pressed enter. 'Yes, there he is. Private Jack Havergal, Somerset Light Infantry, died first of July 1916. Thiepval Memorial.' He showed the screen to Lu.

'Is that it? You've just found him.' She stared at him in disbelief. 'How did you do it?'

'Like I said, the Internet makes it easy.' His eyes twinkled at her. 'If he'd been Jack Smith, we'd have been searching for ever.'

Lu thought of all the time she'd spent getting frustrated sitting in front of her computer. 'I can't believe you just did it. You're a genius.' She shuffled nearer to him, peering over his shoulder at his iPhone, trying to see the details of Jack Havergal, her great-grandfather. She was surprised at how excited she felt. Somehow the man in the photograph had just become real. 'What else can you tell me? Where was he born? What did he do?' She looked up at Nick expectantly, but he shook his head.

'This site just deals with soldiers who died. I know you can search the births, deaths and marriage registers online, but I'm not sure of the sites; you'd have to do a bit more research for that. Then you can send off for his birth certificate, marriage certificate, whatever you need, and that should tell you some more. That's all family history and it's not my field. What I can tell you is that he was probably a volunteer in the infantry and died at the Somme on the most beautiful summer morning.' His voice had an edge to it and Lu looked at him with surprise.

'How do you know that?'

'The date. First day of the Battle of the Somme.'

Lu knew the Somme was one of the major battles of the First World War, but she'd thought the war was all about mud and rain, not beautiful summer days. 'Sorry,' she said. 'I didn't do history at school.'

'Do you want a potted history?' Lu nodded, with a shamefaced smile. Nick took a deep breath. 'Right. The war started in 1914, and at the beginning there was a lot of direct fighting, actual battles, but neither side could establish victory. So there was a stalemate. By 1916 the enemy had been stuck in their trenches for a year, and it was becoming clear that something extra was going to be needed to get them out. So the British and French came up with a plan. They decided to focus all their attention on a section of the Western Front and throw everything at it. If they could break through the enemy defences, there was a good chance that the whole line would collapse and the war would be won.'

Something stirred at the back of Lu's brain. 'Is that the Big Push?'

Nick nodded. 'They shelled the Western Front for five days in the area around the River Somme, then on the first of July they sent wave after wave of soldiers over the top into no-man's-land to attack the enemy trenches. That first day . . .'

'Was it bad?'

'It was the worst single day of the whole war. Sixty thousand casualties, of whom a third died. I'd guess your man was one of them, in which case he probably died fairly early in the morning.'

Sixty thousand. Lu couldn't begin to imagine

46

that many. That was like nearly the whole population of Bath being gathered together and wounded or killed on one single day. Impossible to imagine. 'How do you know it was in the morning?'

'That's when they went over the top.' Nick examined his hands, fingers spread out. 'Did you notice on the entry that it gave his cemetery as Thiepval? That's where the Lutyens memorial is. On it are carved the names of seventy-two thousand soldiers who have no known grave. They could only bury men who they could retrieve from the trenches or from no-man's-land, and they could only do that if the fighting had stopped. So at the Somme, they were only able to start burying the dead in early 1917, six months after the worst day. There's not much left of a man by that point.'

Lu couldn't take it in. Yes, she'd known that lots of men had died, but the numbers seemed so vast, so impersonal. But now she had a stake in it: the man who was her great-grandfather. She touched his face. It was so young-looking, the steady eyes, the serious expression. 'How can I find out more about what he did in the war? Or where he was from and what he did. I want to know everything about him.'

Nick shifted in his seat as if coming back from somewhere far away. 'The war I can help with. You now know his regiment, the Somerset Light Infantry, so you can order his war record and find out where the regiment went, what they were involved with and so on. It's not really my area, but I'm sure I can help you—I can certainly put you in touch with people who are experts.'

'You sound pretty expert to me.'

Nick shook his head, and Lu thought he'd got a very appealing smile. 'Not at all. Since I started this job, I've been reading up on it. There's a lot of interesting material out there; you can see why it becomes a bit of an obsession.'

'What exactly are you doing? You said you'd got a project.'

'We want to raise awareness, so hopefully we're going to plant a line of poppies along the line of the Western Front as it was on the first of July. Four hundred and fifty miles or thereabouts. It's a mad idea.'

'Was it yours?'

' 'Fraid so.'

Four hundred and fifty miles of scarlet poppies. Lu could see them now, bobbing in the breeze. Perhaps you'd be able to see them from outer space, like the Great Wall of China, a ribbon of scarlet like a scar across the earth. 'Wow. It'll be like a great landscape installation; it'll make Richard Long and Andy Goldsworthy look tiny in comparison.' She looked at Nick with fresh eyes. He must have an incredible imagination to come up with such an original idea. The scarlet line of poppies would really bring home the scale of the war. 'Was the front really four hundred and fifty miles long?'

'From the sea coast of northern France right down to the border in Alsace.'

'I'd no idea it was so long. Four hundred and fifty miles.' And made out of poppies. That would be something unforgettable. 'That's going to be amazing.'

'If it happens,' Nick said cheerfully. 'There's so much politics behind the scenes. That whole area

48

of France was devastated, villages destroyed, the countryside turned into a wasteland. A lot of people in France would rather forget, and move on. And perhaps they're right.'

'But you don't think so.'

Nick looked at his hands again. 'So many men died,' he said simply. 'They need remembering, both for themselves and for the future. Perhaps if more politicians remembered, they wouldn't be so quick to go to war.'

'I hope you succeed.'

'Thanks. I hope you find your soldier.'

It seemed time to go. Lu stood up and held out her hand. 'Thank you so much for all your help.'

'No problem.' He stood too, shaking her hand. 'Let me know how you get on. I'd be interested.'

'Okay. I'll do that. Good luck with your poppy project. It sounds fascinating.'

'Thanks.' He let her hand go. 'Would you like me to do a bit of research on your soldier? Making no promises, but I'm sure I could find out some more about him.'

Lu smiled broadly. 'That would be great.' It wasn't so much that she wanted someone to do all the work, but she could see that finding out about one soldier among so many would be like searching for the proverbial needle—let alone finding Anne Morgan, her great-grandmother. It would be much easier if there were someone else looking alongside her, someone who had specialist knowledge. 'You've been so helpful I don't like to ask, but do you know how you'd go about tracking down a woman who lived around that time? I've got hardly any information on her, just a name.'

Nick dug around in his pockets. 'I can suggest a

couple of websites to look at . . .' Lu handed him a piece of paper from her notepad and a pen. He wrinkled his brow as if thinking, then wrote down a couple of web addresses and handed the paper back. 'There's quite a lot of detective work involved in these searches.'

'Just call me Sherlock,' Lu said.

Nick gave her a considered look. 'Perhaps I will.' To her surprise, he bent and kissed her cheek. 'Good to meet you again. I was rather annoyed with Jerry for whisking me away, to be honest.'

'Really?' Lu frowned. 'He took you off to look at your wife's work, I think.' She emphasised the word 'wife' slightly. She didn't want him getting any ideas.

'My ex-wife.'

Ex-wife? Perhaps she did want him getting ideas. 'Briony didn't say . . .'

'She probably doesn't know. Morwenna doesn't like to mix professional and personal, and we tried to keep our dirty linen as private as possible. Neither of us wanted to slag the other off in public.' He looked across the pub as if in embarrassment at talking about something personal, then turned back to Lu. 'Nor in private, to be honest. We're still friends, as much as it's possible to be in the circumstances.'

Lu didn't know what to say. She could see the hurt in his eyes. 'I'm sorry. I'm always blundering in.'

'Not your fault. I should have said something to Jerry, but it didn't seem the right place or time. Besides, he was busy being the successful artist and trying to get me to buy one of his paintings.'

Lu liked the slightly caustic edge to his voice. 'And did you?'

'Heavens, no. I can't afford his stuff,' Nick said, before lowering his voice. 'Actually, I don't like his work very much. It's a bit flashy for my taste. But don't tell him I said that.'

'I won't.' She leaned closer to him. 'I don't like his work much either.'

'A secret we share.'

They smiled and said goodbye, and Lu watched Nick as he left the pub. At the door he turned and raised his hand, a fleeting gesture of farewell. Lu raised her hand too. What a nice man he was. She hoped she would meet him again.

Chapter 3

Looking things up on the Internet proved to be the ideal displacement activity from work. Lu started with the sites Nick had suggested and gradually began to penetrate the maze of websites on family history and the First World War. It was lucky that Jack had an unusual surname; it was fairly easy to find references to him and his family. Because she discovered that he did have a family. Using a births, deaths and marriages site, she tracked down his place of birth in a small Somerset town in 1890—he was in his mid-twenties when he enlisted—and then, using the birth certificate, was able to find his father, George. Once there, she could go backwards in time to his father's marriage, in the same small town, to Jack's mother, Mary. Her surname had been, most

51

inconveniently, Smith, so that meant a dead end— or rather, too many ends to explore. Next she tried to find out if Jack had any brothers and sisters. Guessing that any other children would be registered in the same area, she tried different dates for the surname Havergal either side of Jack's birth. Bingo—Harold in 1887, Arthur in 1885, Louise in 1891. And there were other children with the Havergal surname but with different parents. Cousins? Lu began to see how this could be addictive.

When she went to the library to check out the local area phone directory, there were hundreds of Smiths living there, too many to begin to check. However, there were also a few Havergals, few enough for her to deduce that they might be related to Jack in some way, descendants of brothers or cousins. She was tempted to phone them up and introduce herself as a potential long-lost relative and see if she could work out where they fitted into the family tree, but she resisted the temptation as being premature. She needed to find out more, and there was Delia to consider as well. Lu recognised that she herself was excited about it because she was at several removes from it, but Delia might not want to be 'discovered' as an illegitimate cousin.

Lu reported back to Delia. 'If you like, we could drive down and visit. It's not that far, it'd probably only take an hour to get there. I expect there are lots of Havergals in the graveyard. And I haven't even started on the census returns. I might be able to get an address for George and Mary, and imagine—the house might even still be standing.'

Delia didn't touch the sheets and sheets of

paper that Lu had printed out from the Internet and spread over the coffee table. 'That's all very interesting,' Delia said faintly. Scottie came over and nuzzled her leg and she reached down to stroke his wiry head. 'It's a lot to take in.'

Lu kicked herself for dumping everything she'd discovered on Delia all at once. 'I'm sorry, I didn't think—I rather got carried away.' She pressed her lips together, not sure what to do. She'd expected her grandmother to be thrilled and delighted by her research, but instead she was looking shrunken, her face small and closed, her skin pale. 'Shall I make you a cup of tea?' Lu asked gently. Delia nodded, so Lu took herself off to the kitchen.

Why am I so stupid? she berated herself as she made tea. This is Delia's father I'm babbling on about. It's not a detective puzzle; it's about people, real living people and their feelings. Jack is Delia's father—how would you like it if someone suddenly blurted out lots about . . . Lu stopped herself, gripping the sides of the sink. She never thought about her own father. Never. And she wasn't going to start now. As far as she was concerned, he was nothing, and that was that.

She took a deep breath. Nothing. Quick, quick, think about nice things, think about . . . Marcus. No, he was no good, he was probably on a plane right now, en route to Minneapolis and out of her life for ever. Think about . . . Nick. Now he was nice. And so helpful, he'd made the search for Jack into a pleasure. She smiled, thinking of how frightened she'd been about the scale of the information out there. What a silly thing to be frightened of. What was that saying—the journey of a thousand paces starts with the first step? Something like that. Nick had shown her how to take that first step, and afterwards it had been much easier. She sighed, thinking how useful it was that Briony should have known him. Sometimes life just slotted into place in a most pleasing manner.

Tea made, she returned to the sitting room and was pleased to see that Delia had lost some of the pinched whiteness about her face. She set the tea things down gently, turned the handle of Delia's mug towards her, picked up her own mug and a ginger biscuit and settled down next to her grandmother, waiting for her to speak. The grandfather clock ticked loudly in the background.

After a little while, Delia leaned forward and took her mug. 'Thank you for doing all this work. It must have taken you a long time.'

'It was no problem,' Lu murmured, dunking her biscuit. 'A really nice man showed me how to look up stuff about the war, and various sites. I wouldn't have got this far without his help.'

'That was kind of him.' Delia nodded, as if thinking. Lu waited, guessing that what was to come was, for her, the most important thing.

'Did you . . . did you find my mother?'

Lu felt her insides contract in anxiety. She'd been so carried away with her success in tracing Jack, she'd almost forgotten about Delia's mother. She put down her mug and took Delia's hand. 'I couldn't, I'm afraid. I tried inputting her name into Jack's town, and then the local area, but I couldn't find anyone who fitted the bill, unless she was either eight when she had you, or in her fifties. And if you don't know the specific area and you're just searching the records for someone with that name . . .' Lu shrugged, desperately wishing she was able to tell Delia something else. 'Well, there are thousands of Anne Morgans around. If you don't have an unusual surname, you need other information—even having someone's middle names makes it easier to find a match.'

Delia patted Lu's hand. 'Don't you fret, you've done wonders for me. Fancy being able to find out so much! It's amazing.' She smiled brightly at Lu as if nothing was amiss. 'Amazing.'

Lu felt like crying. 'I wish I could have found out more for you,' she blurted out. 'I'll go back and have another look, I will, and I will find something.'

'Don't you worry. It's my fault, when all's said and done. I should have asked more questions when my parents told me I was adopted. But I was getting married and setting up home, and then the war came—the Second World War, that is—and then Susan arrived . . .' Delia waved arthritic fingers, and Lu caught echoes of Pixie's flamboyance. 'I'm more than happy with what you've found. It's been as good as on the telly.' But without the tearful family reunions, Lu thought.

Her phone began to ring. She picked it up from her bag, checked who it was and put it back without answering.

'Who was that? Aren't you going to answer?' Delia's eyes were as sharp as Miss Marple's on the trail of a murderer.

'It's only my agent, Yolanda. She's been trying to get hold of me for ages, but I don't want to speak to her right now.' Lu poured herself another mug of tea. 'She'll only be cross with me for not having done some work, or want me to sign up for something I don't want to do.'

'Lunabella Edwards, that's downright rude. I'm surprised at you.'

Lu shifted in her seat, squirming under the weight of Delia's disapproval. 'Oh Gran, you don't understand.'

'I understand rudeness. This lady's been trying to get hold of you for some time, you say? Then you're wasting her time by not answering her calls. That's not right.'

'I suppose so,' Lu said, thinking of all the calls she'd avoided. She was going to have to speak to Yolanda at some point. 'I just don't want to speak to her now.'

Delia eased herself off the sofa, puffing slightly. 'I'm going to take Scottie for a little walk in the garden,' she said firmly. 'He needs some air, and you can be on your own in here while you make your phone call.'

'But Gran . . .' Lu said, knowing she sounded like a sulky teenager. Delia looked at her, that special grandmotherly look that didn't take any nonsense, young lady. The sulky teenager in Lu submitted and she dutifully took out her mobile phone. Delia nodded approval and went out, Scottie trotting at her heels.

*   *   *

Yolanda was in full flow at the other end of the phone. Lu only half listened, letting the torrent of words wash over her, even though she knew her agent fully expected her to pay attention. You should have done this, you should have done that,

56

and what about the other? And then she was surprised that Lu didn't want to return her calls. That was the trouble with illustration agents, they seemed to think they employed the illustrator rather than the other way around.

Yolanda finally ran out of steam—Lu doubted she'd noticed that the conversation had been decidedly one-sided. 'Anyway, let's move on,' she said briskly, as if it was Lu who'd been holding things up. 'They want you to sign up for four new Sugarsnap books, two now, and then two later on.'

Lu bit her lip. 'But that means for the next year I'd be committed to the Sugarsnaps.' A whole year of her life with peas. Was there enough green paint in the world? 'I'm not sure . . .' she let her voice trail off. 'I was thinking of doing something different when I've finished this book.'

'Different?' Yolanda's voice sharpened. You'd have thought the golden goose had just announced that instead of laying eggs, it wanted to drive a motorbike across South America on the trail of Che Guevara. 'What sort of different?'

'I was thinking of writing my own stories again.'

'Fine. Can you show me the texts?'

'No, I haven't had time to get anything down,' Lu had to admit. She'd got lots of ideas flowing around, but they never graduated into something more concrete, because she always had to leave them to draw yet another picture of peas in a pod. She traced a circle on the floor with the toe of her shoe. 'Don't you sometimes think this is a ridiculous job for an adult to be doing? Painting vegetables?'

'No more than painting anything else, like fairies or field mice.' Yolanda sounded baffled.

57

'You chose to be an illustrator, that's how the job is.'

'I know. Just . . . I sort of feel I've exhausted vegetables.' It was so hard to explain without knocking her own work. This feeling that she had lost her way. At some imperceptible stage she had shifted from being a creative artist to being part of a production line, where sales figures and targets were more important than any creativity. 'Perhaps I just need a bit of a break.'

'Lu. The Sugarsnap series is a good job. Take it. I have lots of illustrators on my books who'd jump at the chance to do it. Illustrators who want to work.'

'I want to work, I just don't want to work on peas.' Put it like that, and it didn't sound unreasonable. 'I want to illustrate work that has merit. It's been five years since I've done a top-end picture book.'

'I can't make publishers give you top-end jobs. The offer on the table is for the Sugarsnap series, and can I point out that there isn't that much work out there at the moment. If you turn this down, I can't guarantee getting you any more for a while.'

It was like blackmail. Do this, or else. Lu looked around Delia's neat sitting room, photographs of a younger Lu lined up along the mantelpiece. Lu winning the cup at the local show for her painting of a tern; a shot of Lu and Pixie out sketching together; Lu graduating top of the class from art school having just won the illustration prize. I can't carry on like this, she thought. But I need the money. 'I'll say yes to the first two books, and when I've done them, I'll decide about the second pair.'

'Okay.' And with that, Yolanda disengaged without saying goodbye.

Lu dropped her head into her hands. What should she do? She really didn't want to do another Sugarsnap book. Bugger Yolanda. Bugger bugger bugger. And bugger the Sugarsnaps.

*   *   *

Delia hadn't really understood why Lu was so angry with herself for agreeing to do another two books. As far as she was concerned, work was work. Lu was an illustrator, so when an illustration job was offered, she should take it. Lu tried to explain that the Sugarsnap jobs weren't that well paid, so they just kept her afloat, but they also took up her energy and time, which meant she couldn't develop her own creative work, which might lead to better-paid jobs. She searched around for something Delia might understand. 'It's like when you gave up your job to train as a teacher,' she said. 'You didn't know it would lead to anything, but you couldn't do the training and carry on working in the shop.'

Delia still looked puzzled. 'I had a grant for my teaching,' she said. 'And your grandfather was working.'

'Well, I can't get a grant, and I'm not married. I have to do it on my own.' A vision of life as a lady who lunched wafted in front of her. She could have married Marcus and been an ex-pat in Minneapolis and shot moose, or whatever it was they hunted around the lakes. 'Never mind, it wasn't a good analogy. Just, I wish now I hadn't said I'd do the work.'

59

Delia stroked her hair, and Lu hugged her. She wished she could stay like that for ever, safe and with nothing to worry about because Delia was looking after her. Delia's back felt fragile, her collarbone sharp against Lu's cheek. Lu pulled away gently. Delia was the one who needed looking after.

'Now, don't think I won't be so busy with illustrating the new books that I can't carry on looking for Jack and Anne.' She held Delia's hand. 'I will find out what happened. I promise you.'

*   *   *

After a short discussion about how Lu was too busy, despite being adamant that she would never be too busy to give Delia her time, Delia finally handed over the shoebox full of papers. Lu felt a bit guilty—had she bullied Delia into letting her carry on looking? Perhaps deep down Delia didn't want to know. After all, she hadn't looked for her parents until now. But then, as Lu carried the precious box home, she rationalised that it wasn't just Delia who was finding out about her background, it was also Lu herself. Jack and Anne were her ancestors too.

She shuffled through the letters. The writing was faded, the paper brittle. Some of them were little more than notes. There was also a faded maroon notebook that had doubled up as a diary for Percy. Lu diligently read everything, and felt she was not much wiser at the end of it. The trouble was, she didn't get the references to locations and regiments, to battles fought and fields sat in. She liked the names—Sausage Alley,

Mash Wood—but as to their whereabouts in France, she had no idea. Percy was also an annoying diarist from the researcher's point of view, being (understandably, Lu supposed) more interested in the quality and quantity of the food and the successful procurement of a bed to sleep in than anything useful about his friendship with Jack. However, she suspected that someone with more background knowledge might be able to tease out some clues, someone with more access to military personnel might be able to decipher Percy's cryptic abbreviations, someone with previous experience of dealing with war history might be able to work out what, exactly, had been going on. Well, that was what she told herself as she dialled Nick's number.

*   *   *

Lu had bought her flat five years before. It had stretched her financially, but at the time work was looking good and she could see that property prices in Bath were steaming ahead. If she didn't buy now, she'd felt, she'd miss out completely. It was small, a one-bed flat carved from the ground floor of a Georgian house in a crescent. Bath was famous for its Georgian crescents, but hers wasn't a famous one up on the hills of Lansdown or Widcombe with stunning views across the city centre. It was in an area that had been badly affected by first bombing during the Second World War and then what was called the Sack of Bath, the 1960s onslaught of architects and the council with progressive views about architecture and utility. The area was a curious mix of square modern blocks interspersed with Georgian buildings, mainly divided up into flats.

Lu's flat consisted of a living room with a lovely view out over a green towards the river, and her bedroom looking out over the back, with a minute kitchen, bathroom and hallway squeezed into the space between them. The big plus was that she had a section of the garden, which had been paved with large grey flagstones. She'd added gunmetal-grey planters filled with pyramid box trees. In the autumn she planted white tulip bulbs for spring, overplanted with miniature white cyclamen for the winter months; in summer she bought masses of cheap white busy Lizzies. Briony thought it was monotonous, but Lu argued that whenever she looked out of her bedroom window she saw a calming mix of green and white that needed hardly any maintenance.

She'd toyed with continuing the white theme throughout the flat, but couldn't resist displaying her finds: vibrant paintings, sculptures, bright rugs and tapestries, a collection of decorative vases and jugs, and bits and pieces she'd picked up from trips abroad, like an intricately woven bag in shades of blue and green like the sea that came from backpacking round Thailand, and a gloriously embroidered scarlet kimono from a flea market in Paris displayed as a work of art. The walls were still white, but colour filled the rooms, not least from her drawing board and desk in the front room where she worked.

'I put the letters and the diary out on the table,' Lu said to Nick, indicating with a hesitant gesture. It had been a bit cheeky to ask him round after work to look at the letters; she knew he was busy. 'Would you like a cup of tea? Or a glass of wine?'

'Oh, definitely alcohol,' Nick said, making a beeline not for the table but for her drawing desk, and the character sketches she'd pinned up against the wall behind it.

'Don't look at those, they're not very good.' She pulled a sheet of paper over her day's work so he couldn't see.

'They're clever. I like this one.' He pointed to a cross-looking turnip. 'And that one's funny.' He was peering more closely at one that showed a turnip reading a paper, *News of the Wurzels*.

'Those are just sketches,' Lu said, feeling edgy. She wanted him to like them; on the other hand, she didn't usually show her work to anyone at this stage.

'How does it work? You do sketches, and then paint from them?'

'I do sketches, then rough out the drawings in pencil, then paint them up. The blue lines show where the edges are going to be when the pages are cut to size.'

'It's a lot more complicated than I'd realised. When you look at a picture book you don't see the work that goes into it, you just enjoy the story and the pictures.' He touched her drawing board. 'I expect it's like watching Wimbledon: the best tennis players make it look so effortless, you think that a couple of games at the public courts and you'll be able to play like that too. You're obviously very good.'

'No, no, just ordinary,' Lu said, torn between embarrassment and pleasure. 'Red wine okay for you?'

'Please.' Nick moved away from the desk and followed her to the doorway of the kitchen—it was too small for more than one person at a time. He lounged against the door frame and examined her noticeboard.

She poured out two glasses of wine. 'Are you always this nosy?'

'Always.' Nick smiled, completely unabashed. 'Do you buy much art? You've got a lot of invites to private views.'

'I can't afford to buy, but I know a lot of artists,' Lu said, handing him a glass.

'Drat, Sherlock Nick misses the obvious solution.' Nick took the glass from her. 'Too busy looking for the egg stains on your tie.'

'But I'm not wearing a tie.' Lu held her hands up in mock alarm.

'I knew there was a fatal flaw in my theory.' Nick winked at her. 'Cheers.'

'Cheers.' Lu didn't know quite what to make of him. Nick was nosy, noisy, perhaps a bit pushy, and yet she liked him. There was something good about him, an openness, a feeling that he'd not let you down. It made him attractive, even though compared to Marcus he wasn't conventionally good-looking at all.

They went back to the sitting room, glasses in hand. Nick showed alarming signs of veering back to examine Lu's drawing board. 'How's your project doing?' Lu asked, hoping to deflect him from her work again.

'It's early days.' Nick turned to her, his back against her desk. 'I need to get a political heavyweight or two on board. If only I knew President Sarkozy. You don't happen to . . . no, me

64

neither. I need to enlist a few useful people to the cause.'

'Like who?' Lu doubted she'd know anyone useful, but she'd like to help if she could.

'Farmers, a couple of local mayors, tourist board officials, politicians, rich people—anybody will do.'

'Why do you need rich people?'

'Have you ever been to northern France?' Lu shook her head. 'It's a bit like Norfolk, or Lincolnshire. Huge fields, intensively farmed, highly mechanised. The farmers will want compensation for planting weeds across their fields, and fair enough.'

'Don't the poppies grow naturally?'

'On the verges and other rough ground, but the fields are sprayed with weedkiller. According to my agricultural adviser, it's not going to be as easy as scattering a couple of packets of seeds about. Still, the whole point of problems is to overcome them.' Nick sounded positively cheerful about the prospect. 'Right, let's have a look at these letters.'

He hummed to himself as he began to read. Lu had sorted the letters into date order, as far as she could. Percy had been a keen correspondent, writing frequently to Maud. He mentioned his pal Jack in quite a few of the letters. Jack was, Lu was relieved to know, the best of fellows, according to Percy. There were also some official letters, including one that looked like a cross between a birth certificate and a ship's log, except that the entries were all in cryptic acronyms and abbreviations. She watched Nick's face as he read. It was expressive, eyebrows raising, lips making little twitches as if he was thinking of saying something. But he didn't, not until he came to the official birth certificate cum ship's log one. 'This is a discharge note. It shows he was sent back to the UK from the front. They were called Blighty wounds; in other words, bad enough to be sent back home to Blighty, but not so bad you died from them. People shot themselves in the foot hoping to get sent home, but it was a difficult one to gauge—most injuries were treated in field hospitals; it was only the most serious that went home.'

'I can remember Gran telling me Percy had lost his leg in the war.'

'There you are. Lucky, or unlucky, depending on your point of view. It says he was discharged to a hospital in Kent on the nineteenth of August 1916.' Lu peered at the paper. As far as she could see it didn't say anything of the sort, beyond the date. Nick tapped the paper with his finger. 'I wonder if this is the answer. It's just the dates have been worrying me.'

'Dates? What's wrong with them?'

'We know that Jack died in July 1916 on the Western Front, and you said your grandmother was born in December 1916.' Lu looked at him, not sure where he was going with this. 'So, think about it. Her parents must have had—how can I put this—access to each other nine months beforehand; in other words, some time in March or April.'

'Do you mean Jack wasn't her father after all? Or maybe her mother was French?' Lu mentally tried to say Anne Morgan with a French accent, but it didn't work particularly well.

'It's not impossible for her to have been conceived in France. There were some women around, mostly those few remaining French people who hadn't evacuated their land or those involved in running the bars. But then your grandmother would have been born in France, not in England.'

'It definitely says England on the birth certificate.'

'And it's in the middle of a war. People couldn't just go travelling to another country on a whim; it was hard enough going to the next town. If she was born in England, then I can't believe that her mother was French. Everything points against it.'

'Then who could she be? Were there any British women out there? Oh . . .' Lu stared at the discharge note. 'You mentioned field hospitals. Were there nurses out there?'

Nick nodded. 'Not that many female nurses— most were men—but there were some. What if Jack had been injured, but not badly enough to be sent home? Or he could have had a minor illness—there wasn't penicillin in those days, people died of flu.'

'Wasn't there a flu epidemic at the end of the war?'

Nick nodded. 'Spanish flu—they reckon more people died from that than in the whole war. Anyway, what about, Jack has an injury, gets sent to a field hospital where he meets Anne, she becomes pregnant, returns home to England where she has her baby.'

'Brilliant! Can we prove it?'

'We can ask for a copy of Jack's medical record, and there are lists of nurses who served out there. Not sure if they're online or not.'

'I can find out,' Lu said, grabbing a piece of paper and starting to make a list of what she was going to chase up. The whole energy behind the search had shifted now she had a target to aim for. 'If there were so few nurses out there in the first place, it won't matter that Anne Morgan is a common name. It would be an amazing coincidence if there was more than one. And even if there were a couple it wouldn't matter so much, I'd be able to trace them all and see if anyone matched. Then I'll have to work out how Percy and Maud came to adopt Delia. It's a shame Percy's diary doesn't have anything useful like: "Today I adopted a baby. Stew for supper."' She frowned. 'It's a bit odd, because according to the certificate she wasn't adopted until 1920, but she can't remember living anywhere else, or with anyone else apart from Maud and Percy.'

'She's ninety-two . . .'

'She's still got all her marbles. Besides, older people usually remember their childhoods well; it's what happened yesterday that defeats them.'

Nick made a non-committal noise at that, and went back to the letters. 'What are you going to do with these?'

'I hadn't thought—read them through, then return them to my grandmother, I suppose.'

'I meant long term. Have you thought of loaning them to the Imperial War Museum in London?'

'They're not mine to loan, they're my grandmother's, and I don't know how she'd feel about that.' It was the sort of thing that was hard to predict, even from someone you thought you knew well. Delia might be horrified at giving up her father's letters; she might be proud they were going into a national museum. Proof, Lu thought, that we never really know people as well as we think we do. 'But surely the museum wouldn't be interested. The letters aren't very detailed or even that interesting, to be honest, if you're not searching for a long-lost relative.'

'I think the museum would be interested. It's got the largest collection of documents about the war, including an archive of personal experiences such as letters and diaries. You ought to visit if you want to know more about the First World War; it's a fascinating place. My boys love it.'

His boys. So he had children. The feeling of high energy evaporated suddenly. 'How old are they?' she asked, the polite automatic question.

'Seven and ten.'

'Do they live with you?'

'Half the time. I veer between being a hands-on, full-time dad, and then go back to being a bachelor. It can be a bit confusing at times. What about you? Any children?'

Lu peeped under the table. 'Not when I last looked.'

Nick shook his head. 'You don't know what you're missing,' he said.

Au contraire, Lu thought. I know exactly what I'm missing. Sleepless nights, sticky fingers and mess, snotty noses and nappies for starters. Instead she said, 'It's never been on the cards. Not so far, anyway.' Oh heck, that might sound as if she was fishing for a bloke to father her babies. 'I mean, I haven't been in a relationship where it's been a possibility.'

'Or you've got some hidden flaw that means you haven't been snapped up yet.'

'You mean like the dense layer of body hair I have to shave off every morning?'

'Something like that.' Nick shook his head. 'Seriously?'

'I haven't met Mr Right yet.' Lu smiled. 'What about you? What are your hidden flaws?'

'Hardly hidden, tragically. I'd have thought they were pretty obvious. I am, according to my ex-wife, completely impossible.'

'And are you?'

'Probably. I suspect all women think all men are completely impossible. I'm no exception.' He swirled the wine around the glass. 'To be honest, we grew apart, we wanted different things in life. It seemed better to make the split while we were still friends and liked each other rather than hang on for ever and risk ending up hating each other.'

'It sounds very civilised.'

'I don't know about that. Practical, maybe. What's your story?'

'According to Briony, I'm a perfectionist. I think I have high standards. Take your pick.' Lu tucked her hair behind her ears. 'Truth is, I'm a hopeless romantic. I believe true love will turn up and announce itself with trumpets and cymbals, and that it'll last for ever and ever, day after day of blissful togetherness.' She looked at the floor. 'Stupid, I know.'

'Not stupid, just—well, it might be real life, but not as I know it.' Nick drained his wine. 'So, what now?'

'What do you mean?' Lu said, feeling herself go slightly pink. Was he propositioning her? Surely not.

'What do you want me to do with Jack? See if I can find out any more?'

'Oh, yes, sorry.' Now that was stupid of her,

70

jumping to the wrong conclusion. Just because they were talking about relationships didn't mean he was going to ask her out. 'Um, no, I think I can manage, certainly for the time being. I've got my to-do list.'

The doorbell rang, conveniently breaking the conversation. She murmured excuses to Nick and went to answer it, expecting it to be Jehovah's Witnesses. But instead . . .

'Sweet pea! You must answer your phone.'

'Mum!'

'Don't call me Mum,' Pixie said, pushing past Lu and into the flat before stopping suddenly. 'Hello,' she said, her voice alight with speculation, just as if she'd been Leslie Phillips in one of those black-and-white films from the fifties. As Leslie Phillips she might have rested a navy-blazered arm on the edge of her open-top sports car and twirled her moustache; instead, as Pixie, she leaned on the door jamb and twiddled the long string of papier-mâché beads that hung from her neck. As she was dressed in a leopardskin-print tunic, it was a miracle she hadn't decided to purr seductively. At least the tunic was reasonably long over her black leggings, and her trainers appeared almost normal, once you'd got over the fact that they were made of bubblegum-pink patent leather and had two-inch-thick rubber soles. Mothers might not wear twinsets in the twenty-first century, or demand that bags and shoes coordinated, but, Lu thought, she must have got the only mother in the world who had gone in for matching shoes and hair. Certainly Nick seemed transfixed by Pixie's hair colour, as bright pink as the nipples on Jerry's nudes.

Lu cleared her throat. 'Mum, this is Nick Jones.

71

He came over to help me with some research.'

'Research? No need to explain yourself, darling, you're well over the age of consent,' Pixie said archly, looking between Lu and Nick in a way that made Lu shrivel up and die inside.

Nick stopped being a living statue and put out his hand. 'Hello, Mrs Edwards.'

'Ms. And it's Pixie, just Pixie,' her mother announced. 'I can't be bothered with all those patronymics, they make my skin itch. So what's this research? You never told me; I'd have come and helped. Is it more about vegetables? I wish you'd move to herbs. I've so much information it's coming out of my ears.' Pixie's hands darted for the letters. 'What are all these?'

'Gran asked me to look something up for her.' Lu started to tidy the letters back into the shoebox. 'Why are you here, Mum?'

'Now you're doing it just to annoy me. What sort of research are you doing?' Pixie picked up the diary, and closed her eyes as if about to go into a trance. 'I'm picking up . . . vibrations,' she murmured.

'The central heating's just come on,' Lu said, taking the diary from Pixie, putting it in the shoebox and shutting the lid. 'We've finished here.' She looked towards Nick pleadingly.

'I must go,' Nick said, putting his glass down.

'Don't leave on my account,' Pixie said, eyes sparkling between the heavy fringes of false eyelashes. 'What are you all drinking?'

'We've finished,' Lu said firmly.

'Nice to meet you, er, Pixie.' Nick gave a sheepish grin as Lu swept up his briefcase and ushered him to the door.

'And you.' Pixie waved with both hands, rings sparkling on her fingers and thumbs.

Lu followed Nick out of the front door, keeping one hand on the latch. 'Thank you so much for coming over,' she whispered. 'I'm sorry about my mother, but . . .'

'Never mind. Everybody's got embarrassing relatives,' he said easily. Lu was pretty certain not many people had mothers like Pixie, but it was nice of him to say so. He carried on, 'I was going to say, I'm going to the Imperial War Museum next Wednesday for a meeting. If you liked, you could come up, and I'd have a go at showing you round.'

'I'd love to.' A day out in London. Going to the museum with Nick. It had huge appeal. 'I ought to work. I've got a lot on,' she said reluctantly, thinking of all those peas waiting to be coloured up.

Nick was about to say something when Pixie's voice floated through. 'I'm still here, you know.'

Nick grinned, then bent and kissed Lu's cheek. 'My meeting should be over by two, so we could spend the afternoon researching the museum.' Was it her imagination, or had he put a slight stress on the word researching? 'Give me a ring if you want to come.'

'I will.' Lu suddenly felt shy. 'Thanks for coming over.'

He gave her a nod, and then went. She watched him go down the street.

About halfway down, he turned and caught her looking at him. She smiled, and gave a little wave. He waved back, then continued jauntily on his way.

'He's nice,' Pixie said, lounging against the door jamb.

'Very,' Lu said, tidying the rest of the letters up.

'No, don't put them away. Tell me what you're up to.'

'Nothing.'

Pixie made a tsk noise. 'I'm not prying into your love life, sweet pea. In fact, I'm delighted there's evidence there is a love life. You ought to be out there having fun, not working all the time.'

'I am out having lots of fun, Mum, just I don't tell you about it. Because it's none of your business actually.'

'Other people's daughters share with them . . .' Pixie looked at Lu with huge hurt eyes, like a very small kitten about to be drowned.

'Other people's mothers . . .' Lu took a deep breath. What was the point of going into this? Pixie was Pixie, and as far as Lu could tell, she wasn't like any other mother on the planet. Sometimes, when Lu had been small, she'd fantasised that Pixie wasn't her real mother. Her real mother was someone who worked regular hours and lived with a regular husband in a normal house. Someone more like Delia, in fact. 'I don't share with you because you then go and share with everyone else.'

Pixie pressed a hand to her chest as if Lu had just stabbed her. 'Me? Me? I'd never, never tell someone else's secrets.'

'What about the time my periods started and you threw a party to celebrate?'

Pixie beamed and clapped her hands together. 'But that was lovely, you were becoming a woman. These milestones should be marked—would be marked in a matriarchal society that celebrated female wisdom and knowledge. Instead we're stuck in this patriarchal, monotheistic, oligarchical—'

'Do you know what any of those words mean?'

Pixie drew herself up to her full height, which, given the platforms, was not inconsiderable. 'Lunabella! You shouldn't interrupt your mother.'

Lu folded her arms across her chest. 'Go on. What does oligarchical mean?'

Pixie narrowed her eyes. 'Your aura is very small and mean,' she said. 'It's a little purple fug around your head.'

Lu laughed. 'Don't worry, Mum. I don't know what it means either. The point is, I was a teenager. I was embarrassed—it was private. It was my choice if I wanted to share, and I didn't. And certainly not with all your friends.'

Pixie looked contrite. 'I did say I was sorry.'

'I know.' But saying sorry after the event didn't count for much when practically every day there was a betrayal of Lu's confidence. Lu had learned to keep her private information to herself.

'So . . . tell me about Nick,' Pixie said brightly. 'He's lovely. Lovely aura.' About ten years earlier, Pixie had been on a Wise Woman retreat and discovered that she could not only see auras, but paint them too. Since then she'd made her living from portraits with a difference. They were usually highly coloured, Pixie having discovered early on that not many people were happy at being portrayed with a black or muddy-brown aura.

75

Happy colours for happy people, Pixie said, happily. She was certainly more settled since she'd begun painting.

'Nick's just a friend. Really,' Lu added as Pixie raised her eyebrows suggestively. 'It is possible for men and women to be friends.'

'After they've had sex,' Pixie said. 'Then you can be friends. Not before. Unless they're gay, of course, but I'm sure that Nick isn't gay, his aura is definitely straight, so you don't need to worry about that.'

'I don't—he's been married, and has children,' Lu said, then kicked herself for getting involved in discussing Nick with Pixie.

'Sweet pea, that means nothing, as you know.' Pixie sucked in her breath. 'A divorced man with children. Still, probably means he's house-trained. And he's definitely interested in you. I can tell.'

Lu knew she shouldn't but she couldn't help herself. 'Is he?'

Pixie looked knowing. 'I thought he was just a friend, mmm?'

'He is, he is. Heavens, he's got children and I'm so not into that.' Quick, stop it, before you get in too deep. That was the trouble with Pixie: she was able to winkle information out of you that you really didn't want to tell, a skill that came in handy when she'd made her living from reading Tarot cards. 'This is irrelevant. He's helping me with some research I'm doing.'

'Have it your own way. So, what is this fascinating research that attractive man has been helping you with?' Pixie examined the table, then darted to pick up the photograph. 'Isn't this Delia's? And these letters—they're Grandad's,

76

from the war. Has she asked you to research our family history? Why didn't she ask me?'

'She knows how busy you are, what with the painting,' Lu said, hoping Delia wouldn't mind Pixie knowing. 'And she knows I like doing research on the computer, whereas you don't have an Internet connection.'

'I have other connections,' Pixie said mystically. She held the photograph carefully with just the tips of her long fingers. Lu thought that although her mother didn't look particularly old, her hands were where she couldn't disguise her age. Pixie inhaled deeply and closed her eyes. Lu waited politely. You could never be sure how long these things would take, but as a teenager she'd become aware that Pixie usually took as long as she thought her audience would bear.

Pixie opened her eyes. 'He's dead,' she pronounced. 'He was a soldier.'

Well, durr. But Lu felt a twinge of disappointment that her mother's psychic abilities hadn't produced anything more useful, even though she didn't believe in them.

'He's very nice. Sexy.'

'Really?' Lu looked at the photograph, wondering how Pixie could tell. He had managed to father a child despite being stuck out in the trenches, which pointed to a healthy sex drive, so maybe she was right.

'He's got a lovely aura, all golden.'

'That's the sepia.'

'No, sweet pea, keep up. That man. Nick. Lovely. And he's very good in bed.'

Lu looked up at that. 'How do you know?'

'See? You are interested.'

'No I'm not. But how do you know?'

'It's the hands. You can tell from a man's hands.' Pixie had a faraway look in her eyes. 'The eyes tell you about intellect, the hands about physicality.'

'So what did his eyes tell you?'

'Darling, I hardly noticed, I was so busy looking at his hands.'

Lu felt this conversation had gone far enough. 'Anyway, what are you doing here?'

'Visiting you. Aren't I allowed to do that? Can't your mother impinge a little on your nicely ordered world?' She looked around at Lu's tidy sitting room with a mournful sigh. 'How I managed to have a daughter like you, I don't know. So sensible, so organised, so tidy.'

Lu laughed. 'Most people think those are good qualities to have.'

'But dull, dull, dull.' Pixie shook her head sadly. 'Of course, your father was a very dull man.'

Lu picked up Nick's wine glass and took it through to the kitchen. She washed it up carefully, soaping the rim of the glass repeatedly, trying to regain her equilibrium. Had Malcolm been dull? She could remember bedtime stories, snuggling up to him as he turned the pages, trying to make out the words. It was Malcolm that Lu could remember putting her to bed and insisting on a routine. That was dull, she supposed, and after he had gone, there was no more routine. Pixie had no time for books. On the rare occasions she told Lu a story, it was straight from her vivid imagination, featuring a heroine who bore a striking resemblance to Pixie herself. But most of the time she hadn't bothered. Lu had learned to put herself to bed.

Pixie sidled up behind her and put her arms around her. 'I didn't mean to call you dull. You're really very creative.'

'It's okay.' Lu rinsed the glass and put it to drain, not giving in to the hug.

Pixie squeezed tighter. 'I know I'm a bad mother. But I was trying to do my best. And I was so young when I had you, practically a child.'

Lu deliberately kept her voice neutral. She imagined her aura as some sort of beige. 'Twenty-four's hardly a child.'

Pixie released her, as Lu had known she would. 'No, no, no, it was much earlier than that, you must have got your dates wrong. Maths was never your strong point.'

Lu raised an eyebrow at her. No point in saying that Pixie was fifty-six; her mother simply refused to acknowledge she'd gone past fifty. If she carried on, in less than twenty years she'd be younger than Lu. But, Lu thought, she'd always been younger. Lu had had to be the grown-up half the time, putting her mother to bed on more than one occasion. When Malcolm had left home, Pixie had skittered off course, like a little sailing boat in a gusty breeze with no hand on the tiller.

As if Pixie could read Lu's thoughts—something she had been known to claim to do—she felt around in her capacious fringed and beaded bag. 'I wanted to see you, but I also wanted to give you this.' She held out a letter. Lu could see it was addressed to her, in neat round handwriting. The handwriting of a dull man.

'No.' Lu turned away and went to the window.

'You don't know who it's from.' Lu didn't reply. 'Won't you even look?' Pixie's voice was coaxing,

79

as if enticing a small animal out of a corner.

Lu stared at the brick wall of the yard. Don't think about him, make your mind a blank, close it down.

'He's your father.'

Lu shook her head. 'No he isn't. Fathers don't disappear. He chose to go, he chose to leave us.' He chose to leave me, she winced inwardly. 'We managed just fine On Our Own.' It had been Pixie's battle cry when Lu had been young. We can manage On Our Own.

'It's not good for you to harbour grudges. It damages your soul. Your aura's gone all murky purple again.' Pixie took Lu's hands into hers and peered anxiously at her daughter through her fringe. 'I may be the world's worst mother, but I do care for you, and I think you'd be happier if you made it up with your father.'

'I'm perfectly happy now.'

Pixie hesitated. 'That's not what your aura's saying.'

'I don't believe in auras.'

'I shall ignore that,' Pixie said with dignity. 'Sweet pea, what harm would it do to at least read his letter? See what he's got to say? It'll probably be terribly boring, I admit, because I doubt he's improved with age, but . . . it makes me feel guilty that you're not in contact. I feel it's my fault,' she added, suddenly looking vulnerable and childlike, legs like sticks in her clompy trainers.

'How could it possibly be your fault? He left you for someone else.'

'Yes, but . . . it's never black and white, breaking up. Sometimes things get blurred. I really think you ought to be in touch, even if it's only once.'

Pixie must have picked up from Lu's aura that the answer was going to be negative, because a crafty look came over her face. 'Perhaps he's got terminal cancer. Just imagine how guilty you'd feel if he died and you'd never made it up. You'd never have the chance again.'

Despite herself, Lu had to laugh at Pixie's tragic tone. 'Mum, you should have been an actress in Victorian melodramas. You're wasted in this century. Look, I appreciate that you think it would be a good thing for us to have contact, but honestly, I don't, even if he were dying. I've sorted it out in my head and moved on. I know you think it's best to talk about everything, but I don't. I'm like Gran, I keep it to myself. Maybe if he'd stayed in touch when I was growing up it would have been different, but he didn't, and it's too late now. He means nothing to me.'

'Sweet pea, we both know that's not true.'

There was silence. Maybe it was the silence, so unusual for Pixie, but something triggered inside Lu, something sharp and painful. She squeezed her eyes shut. Think of nice things, think of work, think of Jack and all the research she was going to do. Think of Nick, think of the list: wouldn't it be wonderful if she could tell Delia that her mother had been a nurse on the front line. She could picture herself phoning Nick and telling him she'd traced Anne. The sharp tightness inside her eased. She opened her eyes.

'Fancy a glass of wine?' she said, uncorking the bottle. 'You can tell me all about your latest portraits.'

Pixie accepted a glass and started chatting about her latest sitters; one man's aura had been so enormous, darling, that she'd needed to support the canvas on the wall, instead of using her easel as usual. They walked through to the sitting room, glasses in hand, but Lu hung back. She darted back to the kitchen and swept the envelope from the worktop where Pixie had left it and into the bin. There. Gone.

She gave a deep sigh as she went back to join Pixie, who was so busy being outraged by this man's enormous ego that she'd not noticed Lu's momentary disappearance. Lu sipped her wine and smiled at her erratic mother. Whatever her eccentricities, she was the only parent she'd got.

Chapter 4

'I can see your knickers!'

'What?' Lu said, aghast.

'I can see your knickers!' the boy repeated loudly, tugging at her hand.

'You can't,' Lu responded, automatically checking that the waistband of her jeans was covered by her jumper.

'I can,' the boy said, his eyes fixed on her crotch. 'They're red!'

Lu relaxed, relieved that she'd put on a pair of sky-blue ones that morning.

'Don't say that, Barry,' one of the teachers droned. 'You'll upset our guest.'

'It's fine,' Lu said quickly as she continued to set up her material for the workshop. School visits and workshops were part and parcel of being an illustrator, and she usually enjoyed them, but today the room was already echoing with high-pitched voices bouncing off the ceiling, reverberating round her skull. She needed a couple of paracetamol. She checked her bag. Nothing. Memo to self: always remember the paracetamol when doing school visits, especially when it's been snowing and the children haven't been able to play outside as much as they would normally do.

But after the inauspicious start, the day actually went quite well. The children were reasonably well behaved, and seemed to enjoy the stories, and the illustrations that went with them, and afterwards they came with their parents and bought the books. Now they'd gone, and Lu was left to load her stuff back into the bags, counting the books. Quite a few sold, she thought with satisfaction. It was always interesting which ones they chose. Of course it was girls mainly, they were her audience. Let's face it, princess fairies and cute vegetable families weren't aimed at boys. They wanted farting and burping and snot and gore. Boys might not actually be made of puppy-dog tails and slugs and snails, but sometimes Lu found the old rhyme not hard to believe. Especially as she herself was made of sugar and spice and all things nice. She put the illustrations back into their folder carefully, thinking of how many hours' labour they represented.

The two teachers who'd been with her during the day came up, and Lu thanked them for inviting her. 'You've sold quite a few, then,' the droning one said.

'It's been good. I hope they like them.'

'Perhaps you'd like to draw something for the

school magazine. Nothing much, just perhaps a nice picture of the school.'

Lu counted to three, then answered, 'I don't think I have time before I go.'

'Oh,' the teacher replied, her expression one of disdainful surprise. 'I wouldn't have thought it would take you long to knock something out.'

Lu couldn't think of anything polite to say, so instead she smiled, grimly thinking that they wouldn't ask Dostoevsky to knock something out.

'A little sketch would do,' the other teacher said cheerfully. Perhaps years of dealing with children had rendered her immune to the nuances of frost that Lu hoped she was giving out. 'We could use it as a card to raise funds for our charity. We're supporting Children in Need this year. It's a jolly good cause.'

'I'm afraid not,' Lu said. She toyed with the idea of explaining that she was a freelance, and therefore giving out sketches was like giving out chunks of her income. Yes, she wanted to help good causes, but were the teachers donating chunks of their salary? She thought not. 'I'm in a terrific hurry.'

She quickly packed the rest of her things and left the school building. Perhaps if I did something else they would have more respect, she thought, stacking the bags in the boot of her car. Like breed chickens. Or cats. Or chinchillas. She paused. In her mind she could see a little girl called Caroline, surrounded by cats, chickens and chinchillas. She lived in a cottage along with her cousins, but what she wanted more than anything else was . . . was . . . was . . . Lu tried for a few seconds to think of something beginning with C that a little girl could long for, but all she could come up with was Christmas. She got out her notebook and jotted the idea down. It could make a series—the Alphabets—each book starting with a different letter. She looked at what she'd written. On the other hand, maybe not.

*   *   *

Back home that evening, Lu bent her head over her drawing board, trying to catch up on the time she'd lost by doing the school visit. She had sent off the roughs for the latest book, they'd been approved by the publisher and now she had to trace them down on to the paper that she'd paint on to. She stared at the pages. The pages stared blankly back. This was the most mechanical part of being an illustrator, the copying from the roughs to the finished paper ready to paint. Most of the creativity went into the rough sketches, then the paintings gave a chance to play with colour, balancing it in each section and as a whole, working with depth and texture. But now the mechanical part had to be done.

She picked up her pencil, placed the tracing paper over the rough and began to outline the design. One of the advantages of working on a computer was that this section could be done instantly. And yet . . . She had experimented with using the computer to produce artwork, but the drawing had lacked the charm and simplicity of her hand-drawn work. Perhaps it didn't matter to others, but it did to her. Watercolour had a freshness that couldn't be matched by computer-

85

generated images. She'd gone back to the old-fashioned way, the techniques she'd learned initially as a child in primary school, she thought. Then it was greaseproof paper, and what was being copied was a map of Great Britain, or the world, or some such, the carbon lines laid roughly on to the pages of her exercise book, waiting to be filled in. She'd always got marks for her neat colouring. Different counties, different countries.

Her mind flicked back to the little boy at the workshop shouting 'I can see your knickers!' She smiled at the memory. He'd been so certain, so sure, it had made her doubt herself. On a sheet of scrap paper she sketched a child, a little boy with glasses, pointing. His expression was one of utter glee. She drew a speech bubble coming from his mouth: *I can see your knickers!*

She could remember being told that if you had to see someone scary, like the head teacher, you had to imagine them sitting on the loo, and that would stop them being scary. But she'd never really been able to imagine her teacher, Miss Sawyer, doing anything as human as sitting on the loo. It was as if she was immune to all bodily functions. But her knickers . . .

Lu quickly drew an outline of Miss Sawyer, her helmet hair, her glasses that swooped, her sharp nose, her black, black outline. But magically Miss Sawyer's bulky skirt had vanished and in its place was a pair of bloomers of doughty proportions. *I can see your knickers!* If only she'd been able to conjure up Miss Sawyer's knickers, perhaps Lu wouldn't have found her so terrifying. Perhaps that was what that little boy was doing—puncturing the school visitor's self-importance. Thank heavens they hadn't been red, because for a split second she had believed him.

What had the droning teacher said? Don't say that, Barry, you'll upset our guest. Lu quickly drew another, friendlier teacher, cosy and cuddly where Miss Sawyer had been spiky. 'Don't say that, Barry,' the new teacher said from a face like a currant bun. Lu shook her head and went back to tracing down the images.

More peas, more vegetables. What had Yolanda said? They're so eco-friendly. She felt like a production line, generating idea after idea. I feel stretched, her imagination complained, stretched and thin, forced to go one way when I want to expand. Perhaps soon she'd burst and something new and exciting would come out, like a butterfly.

Abruptly she stood up. This wasn't getting her anywhere. Soon she'd start making mistakes. She went to the kitchen and put the kettle on, not because she wanted a cup of tea but because it gave her something to do while she tried to get over this feeling of restlessness.

She picked up Jack's photograph, the frame heavy and too ornate for the portrait within. She'd started to transcribe the letters from Percy in case it would make it easier to spot clues. Percy did describe things he and Jack had done, but it wasn't that exciting. She couldn't imagine the Imperial War Museum being interested in his account of soldiering, which was mainly limited to drills and marching. Perhaps that was the most interesting thing about them: what they omitted. Overall, the impression was not of downtrodden soldiers, depressed and sad, but of lads out on a lark, jolly japes and a good show all round. It almost sounded as if they were enjoying the war.

Lu touched the face in the photograph frame. Jack's face was a good one, with strong features and clear eyes. He did look like Pixie, in a strange way. My irrepressible, lunatic mother, she thought with a smile and a shake of her head. Always looking forward, never looking back. She'd be useless as a researcher.

Ping! Like a Pavlovian reaction at the mere mention of research, her mind winged off to memories of Nick looking at the diaries. Pixie had said he was interested in her, but then Pixie saw romance everywhere, falling extravagantly in love with new men throughout Lu's childhood and rushing off to live on a commune, in a gypsy caravan, once for three weeks in Middlesbrough, Lu's sole sojourn in the north. Pixie's intuition on matters romantic was not to be relied on. Actually, Pixie's intuition on almost anything was pretty unreliable. Lu touched her cheek where Nick had kissed her on parting. On the other hand, perhaps this time her mother was right. Not that Lu was interested back; after all, Nick was divorced, with children, and that was far too much baggage for her to handle, and he wasn't her type, but still . . . It was always nice to know someone was interested. And he'd asked her out. Not that a trip to the Imperial War Museum was exactly a date, but it was an invitation. And since Marcus had buggered off to Minneapolis, there wasn't anyone else on the scene. A little bit of flirting wouldn't do any harm, she thought as she flipped her phone open.

*   *   *

The train pulled into Paddington on time, and Lu got out feeling that strange momentary dislocation that she always did on arriving in London. It was so much bigger, busier, noisier than Bath. People bustled back and forwards, or stared at the screens as if awaiting the imminent announcement of the destruction of the universe. Two policemen strolled along, the younger one looking alert, as if expecting a terrorist event any second, the older looking bored, as if whatever happened, he'd seen it all before. A luggage trolley rattled past, beeping furiously at a group of tourists marooned on the concourse, all standing facing different directions, their mouths hanging open.

What was she doing here? She should really be at home finishing off the Sugarsnap book. Jack Havergal was such an insignificant cog in the war machine, extinguished so early, there wouldn't be anything for her to find out at the museum. It wasn't as if there was going to be a special display on him, in the way there would be on General Haig, for example, or any of the other military leaders. But she would see Nick, and he would show her round. Lu checked her watch. She'd got several hours before she was meeting him.

Despite not being in a hurry, her pace quickened as she went out of the station and caught a bus to Trafalgar Square, preferring it to the tube. She liked travelling through London, seeing the streets change from the multi-ethnic Edgware Road to the brash shop fronts of Oxford Street, the more upmarket Regent Street to the classical townscape of Trafalgar Square.

She took out her sketchbook and drew vignettes of life spotted through the slow-moving bus window: two girls clutching cardboard coffee cups and giggling as the wind flirted with their skirts; a tourist looking at a map as if it was written in Sanskrit; a huddle of office workers in dark suits and thin shirts, shoulders hunched against the cold, drawing on cigarettes with hollowed cheeks; a woman strutting on Regent Street with glossy shopping bags in both hands, her downturned mouth sour as a month-old lemon.

'You're good,' a voice said next to her, and she turned to see an elderly man. 'Draw me!' So she quickly sketched in his face—grizzled cheeks and rheumy eyes, but still with a twinkle—and tore the sheet out as she stood up to go.

'Thanks, love,' and she left him admiring himself as she hopped off the bus at Trafalgar Square. She'd intended to walk down the Strand to the Courtauld, to see the Cézannes, but on impulse she decided to go to the National Gallery instead. Inside, she found herself drawn to the early Renaissance galleries, smooth-faced Madonnas with golden halos, surrounded by saints and angels, gleaming like jewels in ornate gilded frames. After an hour she grabbed a sandwich from the coffee shop and headed south on the tube to Lambeth.

There were signs directing her to the museum when she emerged from the station at the other end. She followed them along a busy road, then went left. Iron railings along one side enclosed a park, and inside she could see a large white building, like an enormous church. The front of the museum was a vast portico with steps leading up, and in front of that was a huge cannon. Lu hadn't realised cannons could be quite so big; the barrel of this one must have been forty feet long at least and pointed directly at the grandly gated entrance. Not exactly the friendliest of welcomes, she thought, as she made her way round the cannon and up the steps.

Inside, the similarity with a church continued, in that it was a huge open space, but a church with tanks and armoured vehicles on the floor and biplanes and Spitfires overhead. Children in school uniform clasping clipboards darted between the exhibits, the boys avidly noting down details of the tanks, the girls more occupied with their own whispering games. The museum seemed much brighter and busier than she'd imagined, as if war was a cheerful cartoon and everybody got up after being shot down or run over by a tank. She wandered around the vehicles, checking her watch. Nick was late. Perhaps he wasn't coming.

She spotted him before he saw her and her spirits lifted. He was shaking hands with another man, full of smiles and good humour as they parted. They were both wearing suits, although Nick's looked distinctly lopsided compared to the other man's military precision. Goodbyes said, he hurried off towards the front hall where they'd agreed to meet, briefcase swinging like a schoolboy.

'Good meeting?' she said, intercepting him.

Nick turned, a huge grin on his face. 'Lu, I'm sorry, the meeting ran on.' She turned her face up towards him, and he kissed her cheek in greeting, quite naturally, his hand lightly touching her shoulder, warm and friendly.

'No problem. I had a look at the tanks. I'm now an expert.' She realised she was grinning back at him. Strange to be so pleased to see him. Perhaps Pixie was right: he did have a good aura that others subconsciously picked up on.

'Right, what would you like to do first?' His hand was on the small of her back as they walked through the hall to the back of the museum, though where they were going she didn't know.

'I was hoping you were going to show me.' She was still smiling, she realised. 'I don't really know much about the First World War, beyond lots of men dying in trenches.'

'The exhibits we want are mainly downstairs.' Nick paused at the top of the stairs and looked directly at her. 'It's good to see you.'

'Good to see you too,' Lu said, feeling warm all over at his open pleasure in seeing her. They walked down the stairs at the back of the great hall, the air tingling between them. Downstairs was divided up into a maze of exhibition cases. They wandered through the different sections about various aspects of the war, Lu staring diligently at the exhibits, finding it hard to make sense of what she saw. Yes, there were mannequins dressed in uniforms, and yes, the artefacts were the real thing, but she had no sense of the reality of the events. It had all become history, something far away, to be studied and discussed. Not about real men like Percy and Jack, one losing a leg, the other his life out there in France nearly a hundred years ago. In one photograph an officer was wearing an early steel helmet that had only been patented in 1915, more than a year after the start of war. The other officers were all wearing sheepskin fleeces over their uniforms, as if going to a fancy dress party as Neanderthals rather than heading off for war.

Nick was staring intently into a display case of close-combat weapons: knuckledusters with knives sticking out, trench clubs, brutal weapons designed specifically for use up close and horribly personal. Lu wandered off to a corner where a small display case showed examples of lucky escapes: bullet holes through diaries and bibles, a buckled hip flask that had taken the impact. Next to it, a screen was set into a wall. The display explained that you could look up any soldier who had died during the war. Enter details, it instructed. She typed in Jack Havergal, and in seconds, his details came up as they had done for Nick in the pub. Amazing. Percy drew a blank, of course, having been only wounded rather than killed. Then she randomly tried John Smith. Plenty of those had died. She stared at the screen. All those young men, all those lives, squandered so carelessly.

'Are you up for the Trench Experience?' Nick said, stirring her out of her melancholy.

Lu looked up to where he was pointing. It was an innocuous-looking doorway. 'Sure,' she shrugged.

They entered a dimly lit passageway. It was mocked up as a trench, surprise surprise, with painted fibreglass walls. A small cubbyhole contained a rather shabby-looking mannequin of a soldier, apparently searching for a radio signal. A voice-over started, triggered by their entry, as if he were speaking. There was something slightly disturbing about it, so Lu moved along the trench, peering through periscopes to get a view of no-

93

man's-land at the top. It was decorated with trench signs: Suicide Corner, Petticoat Lane, Tattenham Corner with a racehorse galloping across the top. The ceiling was painted dull grey-blue like the sky, and while it looked nothing like the sky, there was an eerie quality to it. She found it hard to judge how far away it was, as if distance was immaterial here in this claustrophobic space. More mannequins of soldiers lurked. They were obviously models, but she began to feel they were watching her, as if they knew quite how flip she'd been previously. Her mouth tasted sour, as if fertile French soil lingered among the coffee she'd drunk earlier. Nick was nowhere to be seen.

What must it have been like, waiting here to be fired on, or to haul your gun up to the edge and shoot across the lines? So many men died. Would friendships have formed easily, under the stress of imminent death, or would they have been ephemeral, a linking of comradeship to be dissolved by death? It would have been hard to make connections with the man standing beside you when you knew that he, or you, might be blown to bits tomorrow. We are so lucky, she thought. So lucky that no one asks this of us.

Suddenly the trench was overwhelming, as if the air had been sucked out of it by the staring dummies. Lu looked around for Nick, wanting reassurance that somewhere there was life, but he had gone. She moved forwards down the trench, round the command posts. Her heart was pounding, her face felt hot and a noise in her ears sang like wind along electricity lines, penetrating into her skull. She couldn't look the soldiers in the eye. The passageway narrowed, and she had to squeeze past them, frightened to touch.

Then one moved, and unable to help herself, Lu gave a little scream.

'Are you okay?' Nick said, his arm around her. 'You're very pale.'

'I just want to get out,' Lu said, reaching blindly in front of her. Her fingers touched Nick's coat, feeling the warm, rough texture under her fingers, and her heart slowed to something more manageable.

'Hey, it's all right. Let's get you out of here.'

With Nick's arm around her, they went out of the trench and into the brightly lit corridor.

'I'm sorry,' Lu said, shaking her head. 'I don't know what happened.'

'Are you claustrophobic?'

'Not usually. I thought . . . I felt . . .' But she couldn't say what she'd felt, that sense of being there, as if the next man's hand she touched would have been Jack's. But looking down, the hand she was holding was Nick's.

'You need a cup of tea,' Nick said.

She let him lead her back up the stairs, still holding his hand, and to the tea room on the ground floor. He let go of her hand to pick up a tray.

'What would you like? Tea? Coffee? The cakes are excellent here.'

'Just a tea, please.'

He looked down at her, his face concerned. 'You look pale still. You ought to have something to eat. It's compulsory.'

'Carrot cake, then.' Nick was an attractive man, Lu thought as he ordered for them both, although not her sort. She liked lean men, and Nick was

95

veering to teddy bear. But there was no denying he had charm; she could see the girl behind the counter responding to it, getting slightly pinker when he smiled at her. Charm. What was it that made one person charming and another not? She'd once been out with a man who looked perfect, who had the good looks of a young Sean Connery, but who completely lacked charm to the point of sexlessness.

But it wasn't just about sexual attraction. Everyone responded to Nick: the girl behind the counter, and now the cashier, who had originally looked bored to tears but who brightened up as Nick paid. Pixie would say it was his aura. It wasn't that he pushed his way forward or was noisily the life and soul of the party; life just seemed on a larger, more colourful scale when he was around. He took up more room than other people, she decided as they settled down at one of the tables, feeling like a pale little waif beside him. Yes, he was physically large, broad-chested and frankly a little overweight, but he seemed to occupy more space. She'd seen that same effect with teenage boys lounging around dominating rooms by virtue of their presence. It must be some male energy, she thought idly, taking a sip of tea. I wonder what he's like in bed. She choked on her drink. What?

'Okay?' Nick asked, leaning forward, his blue eyes intent.

'Fine, thanks,' she spluttered. 'Some went down the wrong way.'

'Shall I thump you on the back? I'll get some napkins.'

'No, no, I'm fine,' she managed, as Nick bounded off.

The trouble with being single and looking for someone was that you couldn't help speculating what men would be like in bed. Years ago, when she'd been at college, one guy had had the reputation of being a major-league womaniser. He went through the college choosing the most beautiful of the students to sleep with in a series of one-night stands. Honestly, you almost felt it was an insult not to be targeted by him, one of her girlfriends had confessed. 'Not that I'd succumb,' she'd added. 'Nor me,' said Lu, wondering what it would be like to have sex with someone so experienced, so devastatingly attractive. Surely he, if anyone, would know exactly what to do in bed. She'd watched him out of the corner of her eye at parties, half hoping that one day he'd try to seduce her. And then he did. She'd literally bumped into him outside the college cafeteria, he helped pick up the books he'd just knocked out of her hands and that was that. His seduction technique was simple: unwavering attention and flattery combined with sudden bouts of ignoring her. She found herself in bed with him. And there she discovered the secret of all those one-night stands: he was useless in bed. No self-respecting woman would ever want to go through the experience more than once, but similarly, no self-respecting woman would ever want to reveal that she had become yet another notch on the bedpost.

Nick flopped down next to her with a fistful of napkins. 'How are you feeling? You're looking better.'

'I'm fine, thanks. Don't worry about me.'

'I was worried, you were horribly pale,' Nick said. 'You're such a little thing, I thought I'd overdone it.'

'I'm not that fragile,' Lu said. 'I'm as tough as old boots really.'

'So, appearances are deceptive.' He took a mouthful of chocolate brownie.

'Why—do you think we can tell people's characters from the way they look?' Lu asked, taking a forkful of carrot cake.

'Yes,' Nick said with a heavy emphasis that surprised her.

'Goodness, it sounds as if that's something you feel strongly about.'

'Not really. I just wanted to appear decisive.' He looked sideways at her. 'Let me guess your character from your appearance.' He looked her up and down. 'I think you're precise and fastidious. A bit prissy, even.'

'Why do you think that?' Lu said, bridling at being thought prissy.

'Your hair,' Nick said. 'It's so straight you must spend hours every morning with hair straighteners doing whatever it is you do with them. And you look neat. I can't imagine you with your shirt hanging out and wearing sloppy old tracksuit bottoms. And your hands . . .'

He picked up one of Lu's hands and held it in his. It looked small against his palm. 'Delicate, precise.' He turned her hand over. 'Your nails are short, and unvarnished, so that says practical to me. Creative, maybe?'

'That's cheating.' Lu laughed, tugging her hand away from him, but he didn't let go. 'You know I'm an illustrator.'

'No, Gypsy Nick sees everything, knows everything.' He turned her hand over and peered at her palm, running a finger lightly along her life line. As he did so, a ripple of excitement, cool and electric, followed in his wake. 'A long and happy life,' he announced.

'That sounds good,' Lu said, taking his hand in hers. 'My turn.' Pixie had never gone in for palmistry, preferring the Tarot for predictions. Nick's hand was broad, the palm at least an inch wider than hers, and she'd never thought her hands were particularly small for a woman. She could imagine him working with his hands, making things. Something outside, she thought, like dry-stone walls, or hewing wood. Nothing fiddly, something large-scale. His thumb was huge, she realised, at least twice the size of her own. What had Pixie said about hands? She bent forward so Nick wouldn't see her blush. 'You've got big hands.'

'You know what they say,' Nick said. 'Big hands, big heart.'

Lu looked up at him. 'Is that what they say? I always thought it was something else,' she murmured.

'Oh really?' Nick said innocently, but his blue eyes challenged her. 'And what might that be?'

'Nothing,' she said, ducking out of the challenge by bending her head back over his hand. 'Oh look, you're going to have a very short life if you continue with this conversation.'

'Why's that? We're only talking about old wives' tales and sayings.'

'Well this old wife thinks you've got a very short life line.'

'That's because I'm so young,' Nick said. Lu looked up at him, puzzled by the comment. 'Think about it. Your extremities carry on growing throughout your life, which is why old people have such enormous ears. So your life line carries on growing too. The older you are, the longer your life line. If you did a study of old people, you'd find out their life lines were long and could conclude that a long life line predicted a long life. But it doesn't, it's just physiology.'

'So you don't believe in palmistry. What about things like the Tarot? Horoscopes?'

Nick shook his head. 'Nope, nothing psychic. It can all be explained by science. But then I would say that, being a Leo,' he added.

'You've just lost my mother as your number one fan. She believes in all that stuff,' Lu said as what looked like an entire Boy Scout group squeezed and jostled on to the table next to theirs.

'I didn't know she was a fan of mine.' Nick raised his eyebrows. 'What about you?'

'Sometimes I think there's something in it, but as you say, there's nearly always a logical explanation, even though Pixie doesn't agree with me.' The voices of the Boy Scouts bounced off the high ceilings so she had to lean forward to hear Nick's reply.

'I meant, were you a fan?'

'Of course I'm a fan,' Lu said lightly. 'You've just bought me tea and carrot cake.'

'Doesn't take much, then.' Their shoulders were nearly touching.

'Oh no, I'm easy.' Oh God, she couldn't believe she'd just said that. She could feel her cheeks going scarlet. She ate the last bit of carrot cake and downed the last dregs of her tea. 'Let's go round the rest of the museum.'

They went up to the top floor, where there was a display of personal items from soldiers and their families back home. Letters and sketches, photographs, official messages, postcards. The walls were hung with posters from the time asking for volunteers and for everyone to do their duty, or with paintings from the battlefields, some showing serene landscapes marred by the soldiers trudging off to the Front. One etching caught her eye, and she studied it more closely.

She'd heard of Otto Dix before—at art school she'd studied his work as a member of the German Expressionist school—but she hadn't realised that he'd been a soldier in the war. It was almost abstract, a landscape in grey and black, pitted like the moon. Shell holes, the display card said. Another showed a horse, rearing and bucking to escape, but there was nowhere to go, crammed into the blackness of the etching. This caught the horror of the war far more effectively than the carefully arranged display cases in the basement. Next to the Dix etchings was an aerial photograph of the Ypres battlefield in October 1917 with the terse information that during the Third Battle of Ypres an average of 3,200,000 shells were fired a week.

An announcement came that the museum was closing in ten minutes. Lu checked her watch. 'It can't be nearly six,' she said in disbelief. 'We haven't finished here.'

Nick looked equally surprised. 'Time flies.'

They moved into the next room, one they hadn't been into before. On the back wall a black and white film was playing, the images wobbly, the people moving jerkily and slightly fast. The back drop was a barren landscape, like the one in the Otto Dix etching, and in the foreground a soldier grinned for the camera, cigarette half to mouth, as if caught off guard. Lu immediately thought of Percy's letters, the sense that war was something to be endured with a cheery 'mustn't grumble'.

'Is this real footage?' she asked Nick.

'Yes. It's of the Battle of the Somme. They sold twenty million tickets to see it after it was released in August 1916. It caused a great stir: most soldiers kept the horror of war out of their letters home—it was felt to be unpatriotic—so people hadn't realised the scale of the shelling.'

'You know a lot about it.' In answer, Nick pointed at a card next to the screen. Silently they watched a cavalry regiment passing, the horses tossing their heads, sunlight shining off polished brass. A sudden cut to a trench, men waiting to advance. Some were joking, but others stared at the camera with mad, frightened eyes.

The museum guard walked by. 'The museum is now closing. Could you please make your way to the exit.' Reluctantly Lu headed for the stairs, wishing she had more time to spend there. War as a subject had limited appeal to her, but the way it had been presented, especially up here on the top floor, the use of individual accounts, had brought it home to her in a way that any amount of exhibits of trenching tools and spent grenades could never do.

'Have you enjoyed it?' Nick asked as they got to the ground floor and moved through the main hall.

'Enjoyed is the wrong word,' Lu said. 'It's been interesting. To be honest, it's made me realise how little I knew about it. How little I still know. It's

102

too big to take in. I feel I ought to be saying thank you to these people, but they're all dead and gone. It's impossible.' The only thing she could do was try to remember them. For the first time she understood the desire to have one's memoirs privately printed. It was a means of putting those memories down, honouring them for all time. Perhaps she could make something of Percy's letters and diaries . . . but she couldn't see how. They were so mundane.

'Perhaps we need to make sure nothing like the First World War will ever happen again.' Nick was subdued, as if the energy she found so attractive had dissipated in the grim reality of war.

'But it won't, will it?' Lu said, dismayed by his seriousness. 'I mean, they won't send men to their deaths in their thousands again. Not like that.'

'Technology has moved on, but they still need the men in the field.'

'Scary thought.'

'Especially when you have two sons.' He pushed the door open for her to leave the building.

It was dark outside, and raining, but there were patches of a lighter blue amongst the indigo, as if a sunset was struggling to break through.

'I think this'll pass over if we hang on for five minutes,' Nick said, peering out through the columns of the front portico. Beyond the gates of the museum the black shapes of rush-hour traffic streamed past, red tail lights blurred by the rain, headlight reflections shining on the wet tarmac.

Lu huddled into her coat, the chill dampness of the air sharp against her face. She knew she was standing very close to Nick, much closer than required, given that they were the only people on the portico, the uniformed guard having retreated into the warmth of the foyer. It was very bright inside, and looking through the glass doors she could see the outline of a plane suspended. In front of the museum was the gun from a boat, so big that if they'd managed to dismantle it and get it inside the hall, it would have filled that vast space. It stood in front of her, the barrel stretching out towards the traffic, ready to blast and destroy the traffic lights at the junction of Lambeth Road.

'Are you cold? We can always wait inside for the rain to stop—look, I think it's starting to ease off now. Or we can get a taxi,' Nick said.

'I'm fine,' Lu said, shaking her head. But she edged a little closer towards him, being drawn by his warmth. He put his arm around her, and quite naturally she turned towards him. His hair was black in the darkness, his face white in the sodium flare of the street lights, but his hand was warm as he touched the side of her face, tilting her head towards his, and his mouth was warmer still as it pressed against hers. She closed her eyes and lost herself in the sweetness of his kiss, her arms reaching out for him, holding him close to her, and then the kiss ended and she opened her eyes to see Nick smiling at her, and knew his smile was mirrored by her own. Their hands were drawn to each other, fingers interlaced, and the world was a different place, no longer wet and dank, but shining with possibilities and laughter and joy.

'The rain's stopped,' Nick said, his eyes bright.

Lu inhaled, feeling she was breathing in pure happiness. 'So it has.' She couldn't stop smiling.

'What shall we do now?'

She peeked up at him. 'Kiss me again?'

'Are you always this bossy?' he murmured as he gathered her into his arms.

'Always,' she replied, her mouth against his, and then they didn't say anything more for a while.

Arm in arm they walked back to the tube station, feet splashing on the glistening pavements. They could have walked all night for all Lu cared, walked the entire A to Z of London, like a taxi driver learning the Knowledge, except the only knowledge she wanted was Nick. They found a pub and nestled into a corner, watching the staff write that evening's menu on the board. And so they decided to eat there, talking all the while about the museum and Nick's project and Lu's work and where they'd gone for holidays when children and what their favourite television programmes were, and every inconsequential piece of information seemed vitally important and a revelation and a miracle.

At Paddington they bought an evening paper and had a brief argument over whether to buy fruit pastilles or wine gums before getting both, even though Lu wasn't that hungry.

'Penny sweets!' Nick said with a sigh as they made their way back to the concourse. 'Blackjacks and fruit salads. And sherbet spaceships. And those prawns made out of foamy stuff that should have been really disgusting but were incredibly addictive.'

'Probably with a million E additives,' Lu said, staring up at the departures board. 'I liked sherbet fountains.'

'But you could never get the sherbet to suck up the liquorice tube,' Nick said, putting his arm around her shoulder. 'It ended up getting

105

everywhere except your mouth.'

'Speak for yourself.' Lu could see Nick as a schoolboy covered in sherbet, a look of disgust on his face, pretty much the same as the one he had now. She leaned her body into his as if the more places it touched the better the chance of being absorbed into him, becoming one. 'I managed okay.'

'You must have better suck than me,' Nick said. Their eyes met, his sparking with mischief, and they both laughed far more than the double entendre merited. The departures board clicked round and displayed their train. 'Platform five,' Nick said, and kissed her. Everything shone and sparkled, became an adventure. Going through the ticket barrier, the whoosh as the ticket shot through the machine, made her laugh as the barrier released and let her through, knowing that Nick was behind her. The whoosh of his ticket, and then he was with her, his hand in hers as they found the right platform, checked the departure board again, just because that meant stopping, and stopping meant kissing.

Then the train, and finding two seats together, enclosed in their own world, talking about, oh, anything, everything; it was all interesting, fascinating, everything Nick said was incredibly funny, and she sparkled back, trying to keep quiet as the two of them giggled like children at the back of the bus on a school trip.

She'd been intending to walk home from the station, but Nick had his car, so he naturally offered to drive her home. Should she invite him in for coffee? She glanced across at him as he swung the car round a corner. Funny, she would

106

have invited him in if they hadn't kissed, if they'd been just friends, but now . . . it was such a loaded question. He stopped the car outside Lu's flat but left the engine running, and she liked him all the more for not making assumptions.

'Thank you for inviting me today,' she said, suddenly shy.

He touched her cheek. 'It was delightful.'

Did he expect to be invited in? She undid her seat belt, playing for time. Did she want to invite him in? Oh yes, but she didn't want to rush things. She hesitated.

Nick leaned over and kissed her. 'I'll call you tomorrow,' he said.

'Come in for coffee.' There, she'd said it.

In response, Nick switched the engine off. The silence was startling. They got out, and Lu was suddenly pitched into a state of nerves, not able to remember how tidy she'd left the flat.

But it was okay, she thought, swiftly gathering a few things into a bundle as she went through to the kitchen. She made coffee and they drank it, all the while talking and touching and kissing. Finally he pulled away from her. 'I must go,' he said. 'Work tomorrow, and I've got to get the house ready for the boys.'

But he didn't leave for another twenty minutes, and then ten minutes on the doorstep kissing and hugging as if he was going for ever.

'Thank you for a wonderful day,' Lu said as he finally got into his car. She stood on the pavement and waved him goodbye all the way to the end of the street.

Chapter 5

'I've not got much news,' Lu said to Delia, and then felt her cheeks flush as she suddenly remembered Nick's hands on her hips, pulling her to him. She fiddled with one of Delia's china ornaments on the table to hide her face as her insides squeezed into a knot of delight, a hot wave of desire flickering over her. Nick. She'd see him again soon; perhaps he'd phone this evening and she'd speak to him.

Delia's voice overlapped her memory of Nick. 'It's nice to see you, and looking so well too.' Her eyes scanned Lu's face, and for a moment Lu wondered if there was a neon sign above her head: *I've met someone, someone wonderful.* Not that she would say anything, of course; it was far too early to tell anyone, let alone Delia. Besides, what if Nick didn't get in touch with her? She'd look pathetic, getting excited over a man who didn't call afterwards. But she knew he would be in touch. Nothing in the way they had been together indicated that he would do anything else. It was inevitable.

'I went up to the Imperial War Museum yesterday,' she said. Was it really only yesterday? So much had happened, it felt like a whole new world, as if she'd been living in black and white before and now everything was Technicolor. She could remember Nick's mouth on hers, that first kiss, how everything seemed to fizz with excitement, the need to stand close to him.

'That's in Lambeth, isn't it?' Delia said, sitting

108

down at the table. Scottie settled by her feet with a loud sigh. Delia had put a tablecloth out, one of the ones embroidered by her mother. Lu ran the tip of her index finger over the edge of one of the flowers, the nerve ends tingling, remembering tracing the line of Nick's cheek, him kissing her palm.

'Sorry?' She realised that she hadn't caught what Delia was saying, and sat up straight, ready to concentrate.

Delia smiled. 'It doesn't matter. Tell me about your visit.'

What to tell? She couldn't remember anything about it except Nick, Nick, Nick. 'I went with Nick—he's the man who's been helping me . . .' And kissing me, and . . . She couldn't stop herself from grinning like a dolphin. Stop it, she had to be serious. 'Nick had a meeting so he offered to show me around.' Nick, Nick, Nick. She wanted to say his name all the time.

'We think there's a possibility that Anne was a nurse and she met Jack when he was injured. I've sent off for copies of the documents, but they haven't come in the post yet.'

'A nurse? That's interesting.' Delia's face was tired, and Lu noticed for the first time that there was a cross-hatching of wrinkles across her cheeks. That was new.

'Are you okay?' Her phone gave a beep. A text—from Nick? She went to her bag, her hands shaking slightly as she flipped the phone open. Read text? Yes, she thought, pressing the button. Oh yes.

Thanks for a wonderful day. Missing you already. When can I see you again? Nick.

Lu read the message three times, the bit about missing her five times over. He was missing her. She snapped the phone shut, laughter bubbling up. He was missing her. He wanted to see her.

'That looks like an important message.' Delia's eyebrows were arched. 'Now, would it be your agent?'

Lu grinned at Delia; she couldn't help it. Everything was wonderful. 'I've met someone,' she said.

'Someone special?'

She cradled the phone in her palm as if it were a connection with Nick, then slid it back into her bag. 'I think he may be,' she said, and the mere voicing of the idea sent delicious shivers all over her body. 'But it's early days.' She let the phone go. She'd reply later, when she'd had a chance to think about what to say. Anticipation was half the fun.

Delia put her cup down as if about to speak, but she said nothing, just stared into her cup as if she could read the leaves, a feat that would have been difficult given that she used tea bags. Lu shivered again, but this time the hairs on her arms were cold.

'Gran—is everything all right?' Her beloved gran couldn't be ill, it wasn't allowed. Delia was always there, was always herself, maybe a little frailer than when Lu was a child, but essentially unchanging.

Delia looked miserable. 'They've written to me. My operation is going to be in June.'

'Gran, it'll be fine, I promise you. People have anaesthetics all the time nowadays; there's really nothing to worry about. The last time I had one, I

110

was awake before I'd realised I'd gone to sleep.' She smiled reassuringly at Delia. 'You get an injection, go to sleep, and then when they wake you up, da-dah! No more problems with your teeth.'

'Ay, but what if you don't wake up? It'll be like Death Row, the lethal injection. I'm ninety-two, you know, no good to anyone. I've had my time. They'll want to put me down, save me being a drain on resources.' She sighed. 'It's probably for the best.'

'A drain on resources? Now you're just being silly.' Lu held Delia's hands, half exasperated, half concerned, wholly wanting to say the magic words that would stop Delia being this pathetic, hunched little old woman that she seemed to have become. 'You're going to get that telegram from the Queen, remember? I'll be very cross with you if you don't.'

Delia smiled grudgingly. 'I think the Queen will have to do without me.'

'Now stop it this minute,' Lu said, wagging a finger at her. 'Besides, what about Scottie? You don't want to make him an orphan, do you?'

Delia leaned down and pulled one of Scottie's ears. 'There's another thing. What's to become of Scottie when I'm inside?'

'It's not prison, Gran, it's hospital. And it's only for a few days. I'll look after him, it's not a problem,' Lu said, thinking she really ought to check the small print on her lease, because she vaguely remembered a clause saying no dogs allowed. Still, Scottie was a very small dog, and who would know, especially if she kept him plied with so many biscuits he'd be too stuffed to bark.

'I don't like to ask you, because I know how

busy you are, and you've gone to quite enough trouble trying to track down Jack and Anne.'

'I'm going to bully you now,' Lu said firmly. 'You're not to worry about your operation and I'm going to look after Scottie. Is that understood?' Delia looked as if she was about to protest, but Lu wagged her finger again. 'Is it?'

Delia capitulated with a sigh like the air going out of a balloon. 'I've been worrying about what to do ever since I heard. I don't think he could cope with kennels, not at his age.'

'He'll be fine,' Lu said, patting Delia's hand. 'And so will you, darling Gran.'

* * *

Lu parked by the green as Nick had told her to. She was longing to see him, to see where he lived, and yet she sat in the car, anticipation like a golden glow around her. Or maybe that was just the low-angled evening sunlight hitting the windscreen. Whatever: in a few minutes she was going to see him. She got out of the car, blood fizzing round her system. It had been like that throughout the fifteen-minute drive out of Bath to the village where he lived, a drive that she couldn't remember; it was a miracle she hadn't crashed. Now here she was in the perfect picturesque village, the hamstone cottages arranged around the green glowing gently in the sunlight. Each cottage, though small, was perfectly formed, each with a thatched porch over the front door, a wooden gate leading on to the front path lined with lavender or box or a patchwork of flowers.

112

A man got out of his car further up and a woman passing with a small Cairn straining at its lead waved a cheery greeting to him. Two women up beyond the green rode tall horses, chestnut haunches swinging gently, tails swishing. White ducks waddled across the green before launching forth into the pond. Love in a cottage had always been one of Lu's daydreams. But then so had a Scottish castle, and what about the French modernist pad? She shook them away; they were all just dreams. Except perhaps this cottage— Nick's cottage—would be reality.

She locked her car, walked through the gate with Rose Cottage painted on it in peeling paint, up the flagstone path. In summer, lavender bushes would billow over the edge, but the remnants of last year's stalks were still unpruned. The cottage was small, smaller than she'd imagined, one of a terrace of workman's cottages, just one window wide, one downstairs, one up, and a dormer window in the stone-tiled roof. Achingly pretty, but small. Ahead was a porch smothered with the starry pink flowers of Clematis montana, and a white door with a knocker shaped like a dolphin.

Deep breath. You're going to see him. Be calm. She knocked on the door.

Nick opened it, and for a moment she just stood there, drinking him in, cottages and castles forgotten as they stared at each other in wonder. Wordlessly he stood back to let her in.

Lu stepped over the threshold and reached up for Nick. Even though she was dying with curiosity to see his house, seeing him was better. They kissed, Lu inhaling his warm, lemony smell, rubbing her cheek against his like a cat. It was

113

good to be held by him. She could have stayed like that all day, all evening, all night, just wrapped in his arms.

'Hello,' she said, remembering the last time they'd met, and she knew from his answering smile and the way his eyes lit up that he too was remembering. All nervousness had dissolved; she was living for this moment, here and now.

Finally Nick pulled away. 'Right. Conducted-tour time. This is the hall.'

Lu looked around. Yup, this was the hall. The cottage was lopsided, with beams overhead and a flagstone floor. A clutter of cricket bats and tennis racquets filled a tall wicker basket in the corner beside a line of wellies in three sizes, big, medium and little, just like the three bears. Anoraks and coats and scarves smothered a line of hooks, and for a second she wondered exactly how many people lived in this small cottage. A bookcase stuffed with books filled one wall, books lying on top of others so the whole was a jumble of spines that Lu itched to straighten.

An oil painting hung over an oak chest of drawers. At first glance she thought it was an abstract, blues, greens and whites swirling together, but then she realised it was the sea, that point where the waves lapped the shore, the water foaming over sand, deeper blues further out into deeper water. Nothing else beyond a line of brown, rocks or sand, at the bottom. 'I like this,' Lu said, peering more closely, appreciating the artist's skill. Most seascapes were of dramatic curving waves frozen in paint, but this water looked real, alive, ever moving even when calm. There was energy and power here, but understated.

Nick smiled briefly. 'Come through into the kitchen,' he said, ducking slightly under the doorway. Lu took one last look at the painting, then followed him. More beams and flagstones, a traditional scrubbed pine table circled by units that had definitely seen better days. It was the sort of room that would never look tidy even if you removed all the clutter, but—oh my, there was enough clutter to sink the *Titanic*. Still, look on the bright side, it was certainly homely.

Nick passed her a glass of white wine so cold that condensation had formed on the glass. 'It's good to see you.'

'And you.' They clinked glasses, eyes locked together. Nick hesitated, put down his wine glass, then leaned forward and kissed her properly.

'You've made me spill my wine,' she murmured, coming up for air.

'Should I stop?'

'No.'

After a million years of bliss, the guided tour continued. The sitting room next: more books, a sagging sofa squarely placed in front of an enormous television on a stand squashed full of cables and black boxes and DVD cases. Several remote controls perched along the top edge, along with some games-player consoles. Lu could imagine Nick and his boys lined up along the sofa, all playing computer games, thumbs and fingers frantically working the handsets. Not that she knew what the boys looked like, and scanning the room, there weren't any photographs of them either. She imagined them as miniature versions of their father, although for all she knew they took after their mother. No photographs of her either,

115

fortunately.

She followed Nick up the stairs. The first room contained two bunk beds with startling primary-coloured duvets of superheroes. The skirting boards were hidden by a layer of castles, forts, guns, shoeboxes—stuffed, she guessed, with warlike toys rather than Jimmy Choos. Dark posters of fantasy fortresses and dragons backlit against stormy skies made the small room even darker, despite the whitewashed walls. More bright primary colours on the curtains, this time supercars rather than superheroes, all gleaming fenders and scarlet bodywork and Ferrari prancing horses. Not a smidgeon of pink anywhere. The bathroom was at the back, towels shoved over the radiator any old how. Then, behind a panelled door, another flight of stairs twisting into the roof.

Nick's room was equally masculine, although quite different in style from the boys' room, being positively monastic in atmosphere. It was dominated by two pieces of furniture: an antique linen press of dark oak that Lu guessed might be eighteenth century, and a large double bed.

'This is my room,' Nick said, rather unnecessarily. He gave a little shrug as if not certain of himself, his hand on the brass knob of the bedstead.

There was a pause as they both stared at the double bed.

This time, Lu put her glass of wine down first.

*   *   *

'So where's my supper?' Lu said, running her hand lightly over Nick's chest. He had just the right

116

amount of hair: not so much that it was like a rug, nor too little so he looked like a boy. It was just right. She kissed the slight dip in his sternum, nuzzling her nose into his chest, feeling his heart beat steadily.

Nick stroked her hair. 'In the oven,' he said, his eyes shut. 'Hopefully it hasn't completely evaporated.'

Lu made a tsk noise. 'I don't know, what sort of host are you? I come here for supper, and where is it?'

'Are you hungry?'

Lu rolled over on to her side and smiled up at him. 'Not right now.'

'Good thing too. I can't move. You've exhausted me.' His eyes were still closed and she wondered if he was the sort of man who liked to be completely still and quiet afterwards. So many things to discover when you started a new relationship, so many preferences, big and small, to be unearthed. This might be the best it was going to get, or the start of something that would take her into a new dimension. Maybe he was the love of her life, or maybe this would be the last time she saw him. It was difficult to predict. Lu stared at his face, relaxed in apparent sleep. Perhaps she would be looking at this face for the next forty years. But if he was The One, how would she know? It would be so much easier if people came with a forecast: you're not going to see him again after tonight; he's the love of your life; he's about to be posted to Minneapolis. She frowned as the thought of Marcus flitted inappropriately across her brain. Mr Perfect, and yet here she was lying next to Nick.

She snuggled herself up to him, gaining

reassurance from the touch of his skin. 'Are you asleep?'

'No,' he murmured, then sighed deeply and opened his eyes, blinking a few times. 'Sorry,' he said. 'Almost dropped off there.' He kissed the top of her head and hugged her to him. She fitted perfectly into his arms, she thought, as if she'd been made for them.

*   *   *

'This looks delicious,' Lu said, watching Nick ladle out stew from a well-used casserole dish. Judging by the density of the sauce, another few minutes lolling in bed and it would have evaporated. She inhaled the meaty aroma as she took the plate from him. 'What is it?'

'Beef stroganoff,' Nick answered. 'My signature dish. Every man should have one surefire, failsafe dish he can produce, and beef stroganoff is mine.'

'Do you do it every time you first cook for someone?' Lu asked, slightly archly, and Nick nodded.

' 'Fraid so. Mind you, the first time I made it, it was a complete disaster. I could follow the recipe all right, but the soured cream floored me. I'd never heard of soured cream. In the end I got a carton of ordinary cream and put it outside in the sun for a couple of hours.'

Lu grimaced. 'That would certainly make it sour. Was it disgusting?'

Nick shrugged and shook his head, his face amused at his long-gone self. 'It was so long ago I don't remember.'

'And did you get the girl?' Lu said, fascinated by

118

this vision of Nick as an inept young man, busy trying to impress someone.

'Which girl?'

'The one you were trying to impress.'

Nick paused, then nodded, his expression serious. 'Eat up,' he said abruptly. 'Don't let it go cold. I promise I've used the right stuff this time.'

Lu ate a mouthful of beef, aware that the atmosphere had shifted from something light and frivolous to something more serious. 'Mmm, it's lovely,' she said. And it was, not a hint of sun-soured cream at all, just smooth and rich and flavoursome. She swallowed. 'Was the girl you were impressing that time your wife?'

Nick put his fork down. 'Yes. Yes it was.'

His wife, who Briony said painted abstract landscapes. Lu remembered the seascape in the hall. One of hers? 'Morwenna's an unusual name.'

'It's Cornish.'

It could have been Cornwall in the painting. 'Is that where she's from?'

Nick sighed. 'Yes. Look, do we have to talk about her?'

'No, of course not,' Lu said, longing to talk about her. 'I was just curious, that's all.'

'There's nothing to be curious about,' Nick said.

If you really believe that, you don't know anything about women, Lu thought. You're my lover; of course I want to know about the woman you were married to. My lover . . . She slid her hand across to him under the table and squeezed his thigh. You're lovely, she thought happily. My lovely lover.

They began to discuss art, and Lu found him surprisingly knowledgeable, which she put down to the fact that he'd lived with an artist for years. Not that she was going to ask. Instead she talked about the illustrators who had inspired her, artists like Maxfield Parrish and Arthur Rackham, Brian Froud and Alan Lee. 'Not many people know that Lee inspired the whole look of the *Lord of the Rings* films,' she said earnestly. 'He did all the preliminary drawings, right down to things like the design of Gandalf's staff. He really ought to have got an Oscar.'

'And what about you?' Nick asked, holding out his hand for her now empty plate. 'Any Oscars in the offing?'

'I don't do Oscar-winning stuff, though I wish I did,' Lu blurted out. 'Not Oscar-winning, but something more important than just drawing peas. I want to do something . . . bigger.' She felt breathless merely voicing such a thing. 'Something less trivial, less ephemeral. I know that there are lots of people who do horrid jobs they hate, who would think me mad to be complaining about what I do—and I'm not complaining, not really, because I do love it,' she added. 'But compared to being a doctor, for example, you've got to admit that drawing vegetables is a pretty frivolous sort of occupation.'

'If you take that as your standard, then most occupations are fairly trivial,' Nick said, dumping their plates in the sink. 'I expect that's why we complain about administrators so much: we don't think their jobs are essential. But then not many people's jobs are that essential taken by themselves. It's how they connect with the rest that matters. Small children need to learn to read, so someone needs to write and illustrate books that

120

appeal to them. That's all. You're a cog. What you do isn't essential to the day-to-day functioning of the machine, but the machine as a whole needs you to be there, creating. Just as I suppose it needs someone to be doing the filing.' He squinted at the serving spoon. 'Hmm, not so sure about that one. Still, same principle.'

'It's nice of you to say it, but illustration is not in the same league of usefulness as being a doctor.'

'No, but the doctor needed to learn to read, didn't he?'

'I'd not thought of it like that.' Lu turned the idea over in her head. 'No, it's no good, I'm not buying that argument. Drawing peas is a daft way for an adult to make a living. But you're incredibly good at spin.'

Nick gave a little bow. 'It's what I do.' He served pudding, great scoops of vanilla ice cream with blueberries and raspberries scattered over the top. 'Antioxidants and vitamins to go with the calories.'

Lu smiled as she took the bowl from him. 'Have you always done marketing?'

'I read history at uni, but since then it's been marketing. I started with one of the megacorps, working on bubble bath and shampoo ads, so when we got married I think Morwenna hoped I was going to keep her in the style she was looking forward to getting used to. Then one day I realised I couldn't think of another synonym for "shiny", and switched to working for charities and not-for-profit organisations, even though they pay peanuts.' He tossed his hair back and simpered. 'Because I thought they were worth it.'

Lu laughed at his supermodel impersonation, but she had clocked the reference to Morwenna.

'Was your move into the charity sector why your marriage broke up?'

'It didn't help—but no, no. That would make Morwenna a complete bitch.' Nick contemplated a blueberry. 'You're a freelance, you know what it's like. It helps if one of you has a decent regular income.' Lu blushed, thinking back to her list of requirements for Mr Right. Nick shrugged. 'Our timing was bad. Morwenna was two months' pregnant with Ben when I had my conversion from rampant capitalism. Then we had Tom . . . They say all marriages break up for one of two reasons, money or sex. We were a bit of both.'

'It can't have been the sex,' Lu drawled, thinking back a few hours.

Nick smiled. 'Thanks for the endorsement. It helps not having two small children around. Kinda cramps one's style. Not that I wouldn't be without them, but life changes the day they're born.'

'Were you there for both births?' Nick nodded. 'And was it the most amazing thing you'd ever seen?' That was what everyone said, wasn't it? It was the moment that changed my life, I felt instant love. She couldn't imagine feeling instant love for anything, beyond a painting maybe.

'It was very intense, certainly, the first time, with Ben. As a man you feel so helpless: there's nothing you can do and your wife is going through all this pain and drama, and you're the cause of it all. I was terrified, to be honest. The second time round it was much easier.'

'I always think it must feel like you're carrying some alien around with you and then it bursts out,' Lu said.

Nick laughed. 'Not having been pregnant

122

myself, I can't say, but I don't think Morwenna felt like that.'

No, she was probably good at being a mother, as women were supposed to. 'I don't want to have children,' Lu said.

'Not ever?'

'Nope.' Lu thought about saying she didn't like them, but given that Nick had two, that seemed tactless. 'I don't feel at all motherly,' she said. 'I decided when I was thirteen that I wasn't going to have children and I haven't felt any biological urges to change that.'

'No ticking clock?'

'Not even a tock.'

'Why did you decide not to have children at thirteen?'

'Lots of reasons. My mother, mostly.'

'The fabulous Pixie.' Nick smiled, as if remembering. Lu winced inwardly. Why the leopardskin tunic, why the pink hair? 'I thought she was great. Different, sure, but you said she was my fan, so what could possibly be wrong with her?'

Lu groaned. 'You've seen her—she's not exactly your usual mum, for starters. She wasn't a bad mother, I suppose. I mean, she didn't beat me or anything like that—I'm not about to write a misery memoir called *Mummy Stop Hitting Me*, but she wasn't like a mother should be.'

'No tidy-bedroom patrol? No cake-baking?'

'Only if they had hash in them.' Nick's eyebrows shot up. 'Yup, she was the original hippy chick. It's funny, because my grandmother is so ordinary, and my mum—who's an only child—should have been such a good little girl, with sensible shoes and pigtails, but instead she ran off with a rock band

123

when she was sixteen and that was that.'

'I can see she's still in touch with her inner hippy chick.'

'And how,' Lu said. 'In fact, half the time I feel older than her. More responsible, certainly. Sometimes I think we're like Saffy and Edwina in *Absolutely Fabulous*.'

'Are you an only child? I sort of imagine a massive brood.'

'Think again. Pixie would agree with you that children cramp your style, so I'm an only. What about you?'

'I've got a younger sister, Judith. My parents are the opposite of Pixie, I'm sad to say, because I think she'd have been the coolest mum in the world, but that might be because they are very conventional and managed to organise a boy and a girl, two years apart. Judy and I were really close as children, but she married a Canadian and now lives near Montreal. We email and chat on Skype. I was thinking of taking the boys out there in the summer.'

Now was her chance to ask. Lu hoped she appeared casual when she said, 'How does it work with the boys—do they live with Morwenna or you?'

'Two weekday nights a week here, and every other weekend. As Ben's got older it's got more complicated—football practice and things like that. We play it by ear. In the holidays it depends what Morwenna is planning, and what I can manage workwise.' He shrugged. 'It sorts itself out.'

'It sounds civilised.' Lu was wondering if she could live with the boys being around every other weekend. It wouldn't be too bad, she thought, picturing two little Mabel Lucie Attwell cherubs in pale blue pyjamas and shiny hair and huge innocent blue eyes as they stared adoringly at her while she handed them their warm milk before bedtime.

'We tried to be civilised, for the boys' sake,' Nick was saying, dragging her away from the image of herself as not a mummy substitute, more a glamorous older sister. 'We were very careful not to have the sort of divorce that means you can never speak about each other without spitting. I have to admit I sometimes thought I'd be left with ridges in my tongue from holding it between my teeth.'

'I didn't notice,' Lu murmured. 'Seriously, I admire you for that. So many people when they split up seem to go in for mud-slinging, when a few years ago that person could do no wrong.'

'People change, fall out of love, want different things.' Nick looked up. 'What are you doing on the other side of the table? Why don't you come and admire me on this side.'

So she did.

Chapter 6

The next two months were bathed in a golden glow. The terrible weather in February improved over March and April and the days became warmer. Lu met Nick several evenings a week after work, usually ending up at her flat, and they spent every other weekend either there doing city activities like visiting art galleries, or at Nick's, taking long walks and going to country pubs and cuddling up together in front of the fire in the evenings.

Together they managed to trace Jack's military history; Nick's guess had been right in that Jack had been wounded. It had been a Blighty wound—a bit of shrapnel had gone through his arm—and he'd been in England at the right time to father a child. But there was no record of an Anne Morgan as a nurse, whether as part of the Army or Navy, or as a Voluntary Aid Detachment with the Red Cross, so Anne and Jack hadn't met as nurse and patient. How then? Lu went back to Delia's original birth certificate. Anne's residence was given as the same town as she'd given birth in, but Lu couldn't find her listed there for either births or deaths. The only connection was that Percy and Maud had lived in the same area before and during the war when Percy had been a gamekeeper on a big estate. Was there a possibility that Percy and Maud had known Anne? There appeared to be no way of knowing, no matter how many hours Lu spent poring over the records on the evenings and weekend that Nick was absent with his boys.

'Of course it leaves me with a weekend completely clear to go shopping, like today, or settle down and get some extra work done. For the first time in my life I'm ahead of myself,' Lu explained to Briony as they walked down Milsom Street in the May sunshine. 'But it feels odd. He has this whole other life that I know nothing about.'

'Not nothing, surely. He must talk about them.' Briony stopped to look in the Jaeger window.

'Too much, at times.' Lu surveyed the window display with a disinterested eye, not having a Jaeger lifestyle. 'He knows everything about my life, and it's weird I don't know the same about his. He says the boys are the most important things to him, and I haven't met them.' She didn't add that she felt a twinge of jealousy whenever Nick said it, because she wanted to be the most important thing in his life.

'It's early days.' Briony presumably felt she didn't have a Jaeger lifestyle either, because she moved on down the street. 'He's being a responsible father. He can't introduce them to every girl he goes out with; that wouldn't be fair.'

'To the girl? Or the boys?'

'The boys, of course. Look, enjoy being child-free. If you become more serious, and start having them around all the time, you'll miss it.' Briony narrowed her eyes. 'Or are you more serious already?'

Lu gave a nervous laugh. 'Don't be silly.'

'Why's that silly? What's wrong with the man? He seemed quite fanciable to me, and you obviously think he's great—you've been glowing like Christmas tree lights since you two got together.' They turned into Jolly's department store, Briony slowing down to examine the make-up counters.

'He's got children, and you know I've always said I don't want any.' Lu rubbed a pinkish tester lipstick on her wrist. Too blue; she wanted something with more red in it for the summer.

'If you don't want children, then mightn't it be a good idea to go out with a guy with kids of his own? How old are they?'

'Seven and ten. I know what I want, and it's not to be someone's wicked stepmother.' Lu picked up another lipstick to try.

'You could always be a loving, caring stepmother.'

Lu shuddered. 'I've illustrated enough fairy tales in my time to know that the stepmother is always wicked. Think of "Cinderella", or "Hansel and Gretel". Or "Snow White"—wicked, evil women, every one.'

'Life isn't like a fairy tale. Besides, mightn't that make him Mr Right? You don't want children, and a man who already has children won't want any more. You'd be let off the hook. And as for his little darlings, well, they'll be with the mother, you won't need to see them much.'

'No, they live with him half the time.' Lu dabbed grey eye shadow on the back of her hand. It shimmered prettily, the light catching little sparkles of anthracite and silver. She tried it on her eyes.

Briony sniffed a pot of eye liner gel, before replacing it. 'So that's not ideal. But you're never going to find the ideal. You have to compromise somewhere down the line.'

'Maybe you're right. Maybe I should think about it more positively.' Lu studied her face in the mirror, not sure if sparkly grey eye shadow worked with brown eyes, then suddenly thought of Snow White's wicked stepmother. 'At least his children are boys. There wouldn't be all that competition.'

'See? You're already starting to think of the benefits.' Briony gave a little shrug. 'Listen, nobody's perfect, same as you're not perfect. Mr Right doesn't exist. There's only guys with flaws that you're prepared to compromise over, and guys with flaws you're not going to compromise over.'

Lu left the make-up counter. 'Briony, Nick has children, and that alone makes him Mr Wrong.'

'Mr Wrongs are always much more fun than Mr Rights. Look at Jerry!' Briony gave a hard little laugh.

'I thought he was your Mr Right.'

'Whatever gave you that idea? But we're not talking about me and Jerry; we're talking about you and Nick.'

Lu followed her through to the clothes section. 'Perhaps we should be talking about you and Jerry.'

Briony frowned and shook her head, peering at the back of a cream blazer to see the price. 'No point in talking. We're in a really funny place right now. Let's not talk about me. I don't know what I want.'

'I do,' Lu said seriously. 'And it doesn't involve children.'

'So what are you doing with Nick? Because if that's true, you're wasting each other's time and should split up.'

Lu's heart lurched. 'Don't say that. Just because you go out with someone, it doesn't mean you've got to marry them. It's the twenty-first century; you're allowed to have fun and for it not to be serious.'

'So this is a no-strings fling?' Briony snorted as she slipped the cream blazer off the hanger and tried it on. 'Yeah, right. You look remarkably like a woman in love to me.'

'Do I?' Lu could feel herself colour up, her heart beat faster. She considered the reflection of herself standing next to Briony in the cream blazer. Did she look like a woman in love? Her skin was pink, her hair was shiny, she was slimmer than she'd been for ages. She smiled at herself, thinking of Nick. 'Honestly, you do talk rubbish sometimes. No, when Mr Right comes along, I'll be off like a shot, you'll see. And until then, I'll have a great time with Nick. We're going away next week to northern France.' Lu caught sight of Briony's expression in the mirror. 'I know, it's not quite the Caribbean, but I'm sure it'll be really interesting. We're going to drive around the Somme looking at the places he's going to plant his poppies.'

'The Somme? Wasn't that nothing but mud and people getting killed?' Briony gave that supportive best friend look as she took off the blazer and put it back on the hanger. 'My, that's romantic.' She didn't sound convinced.

'At least it's France,' Lu said. 'Little bistros, lovely food, lots of wine . . .'

'And cemeteries! What more could a girl want? Still, you'll be with the man you don't love. It'll be great.'

*   *   *

France to Lu meant sitting outside restaurants in marketplaces shaded by plane trees, lingering over a glass of chilled white wine, perhaps lazily watching a game of petanque played by old men in dusty trousers and crisp white shirts. A dog trotted past, a cat arched its back, wood pigeons cooed in the trees above, and the old men made muted exclamations like *bof* and *alors*, and waved their

arms in expansive gestures . . . . one had
done a particularly good shot.

And after lunch, perhaps a str . . . . town,
gazing at crumbling eighteenth-c . . . . cades
punctuated by green-shuttered windo . . . . paint
faded and peeling in the strong sunlight . . . . ybe
down to the river, a wide expanse of wat . . . . ed
with weeping willows that made a lattice . . . . of
shadow patterns across the beaten-earth pat . . . .
air cooler against the skin in the shadow of
trees, the touch of leaves trailing against a han
the murmuring of the pigeons and the lovers
strolling along, their feet not making a sound.

Lu imagined strolling with Nick, the two of
them leaning in towards each other, their fingers
intertwined, in no hurry, taking the time to sit on a
curly-armed park bench, watching the river flow
by, her head on his shoulder, his arm around her
back, caressing her neck while they talked about
everything and nothing.

What she didn't imagine was an open landscape
with field after vast field of monochrome crops,
the harsh yellow of rape the only relief from the
shades of green that stretched across the wide
horizon. Not entirely flat, but this was land
ploughed and tilled and planted with the efficiency
of an agricultural factory, with no hedges or fences
to disturb the green flow.

'I thought there would be poppies everywhere,'
Lu said, looking around for splashes of red as they
drove through the fields.

Nick, at the wheel, shook his head. 'Too much
spraying with weedkiller and fertiliser. They only
grow on the verges now. It's going to be an uphill
struggle to get the farmers to change their ways.

ɔ many vested interests, and not
The nts to remember the war. This area
eve scarred; it's not just the land, but the
wa le feel. A lot of people would rather
w out it.'

f n see that. But it's not as if you want to
  poppies every year; it's just for the
énary.'

So far everybody keeps telling me there's no
ay the farmers will give up an inch of their
productive land to commemorate the war,
centenary or not, and that they're only interested
in profit. For example, the Somme area's main
gastronomic delicacy was eels,' Nick said. 'But
there's so much pollution in the river from the run-
off chemicals from the fields that there's been a
ban on catching them the last couple of years. It
hasn't stopped the farmers using chemicals. Still,
it's more fun if it's a challenge,' he added
cheerfully.

Lu, looking out on to the massive fields, thought
it was an impossible challenge. Nick sounded
positive, but then he always did. She supposed that
was an advantage when you were in charity
marketing and fund-raising. Darling Nick. He'd
picked her up after lunch, then driven all the way
from Bath, through the tunnel, a quick bite of
something to eat in Calais, then back on to the
autoroute for another hour or so, and now a long
A road towards Albert. He must be tired, but he
didn't show any sign of it, just said he liked driving.
Lu knew he hankered after a sports car but instead
drove a practical estate, good for shovelling in
boys and their kit. And rubbish—Lu picked up an
old chocolate bar wrapper from the floor and

tucked it into the pocket of the door. 'What's the plan for the weekend?'

'I want to drive around a bit, get a feel for the lie of the land. Then the main places to see are the museum at Péronne and the Newfoundland Memorial Park at Beaumont Hamel. I expect you want to go to Thiepval.'

'Please. I'd like to see Jack's name on the memorial.' She stared out of the window at the relentless fields lining the autoroute. Battlefield tourism; it seemed a contradiction in terms. Still, she was here with Nick. She patted his thigh, overcome with a rush of happiness. It didn't matter where she was, so long as she was with him.

Albert turned out to be a far cry from the sunlit honey-gold buildings of Lu's imagination, being fairly industrial in places, with streets of terraced brick houses, the doors opening directly on to the pavements. No plane trees or greenery of any sort to be seen. There were hardly any cars on the road, and the whole place felt deserted, which was odd, given that it was only nine o'clock in the evening, with dusk just falling.

The hotel wasn't much better. It felt sad and unloved, although the receptionist was pleasant enough as Lu filled in her registration card and showed her passport. Their room was up some winding stairs on the second floor, and looked out on to the street. Rough beige carpet, nubbly beige curtains, beige candlewick bedspread; not a chic, shades-of-neutral sort of beige, more an absence-of-colour sort of beige, like being drowned in oatmeal. Even the wardrobe had a beige laminate finish.

Nick dropped the bags and looked around.

'Sorry it's not more romantic,' he said.

'We'll have to make our own romance,' Lu said, going across to him and putting her arms around his neck. 'Or are you too tired?'

In answer Nick pushed her on to the bed, which may have been beige but, they discovered, also had a good mattress.

In the morning they got up late, too late for the breakfast provided by the hotel, so they ran across the road to a café, dodging the raindrops, and ate croissants and apricot jam and drank dark, strong coffee. Nick spoke good French, Lu discovered, and she relaxed into letting him take charge as she couldn't go much beyond the basics herself. 'But I do know what farmyard animals say in lots of languages,' she added. 'In France cockerels say *cocoricoo*, in Germany it's *kikierikkii*, in Turkey it's *Gaggala-gaggala-gu*.'

'You're so clever,' Nick said, squeezing her knee under the table.

It was still raining after their late breakfast, but the café proprietor assured them that it was due to clear in the afternoon, so they decided to go to the museum at Péronne first. They drove along an absolutely straight road for about twenty minutes before arriving in the town centre.

Péronne looked more like the France of Lu's daydreaming, having plane trees around a market square and an old moated château built of dark rust-red brick, which housed the museum, although the overall effect was somewhat spoiled by loud music blaring out of speakers on the buildings. It was so loud, it was a relief to enter the museum.

The room by the reception area was devoted to

an exhibition of modern illustrations from a graphic novel. The name Jacques Tardi meant nothing to Lu, but she knew that graphic novels were taken very seriously in France and had a long tradition there. The illustrations were of an ordinary soldier in the First World War (based on Tardi's grandfather, according to the audio guide). Lu could have stayed in the exhibition all day, finding the detail fascinating. Tardi was working in pen and ink, and something called *lavis*, which she guessed was French for watercolour. There were photographs of the illustrator's friends posing for sketches, holding guns or pretending to struggle through barbed wire.

'Is that how you work, from photographs?' Nick asked.

'I have done, but now I mainly use my imagination, or I sketch from life.' Talking vegetables were hard to come by, she thought of saying, but that sounded superficial when surrounded by images of war. Lu realised Nick was taking a polite interest in the illustrations, but she could see that for a non-professional they weren't quite as fascinating as she found them, so they went into the main body of the museum, which was a series of ultra-modern glass and concrete cubes within the ancient fortress walls. The first room was about the causes of the war, and Lu listened intently to the audio guide, trying to untangle the complicated manoeuvrings of the then superpowers, France, Germany, Britain, Russia and Austria-Hungary, as she followed the trail of maps set into the floor.

The next room was dedicated to the engravings of Otto Dix. 'We saw him at the Imperial War

Museum, remember?' Lu said to Nick. They were as she remembered, sharp and darkly powerful. Dix had been a young student when he'd been drafted into the German Army, and these were nightmares come to life. Life in the trenches, harsh and cruel. There seemed to be no light, just blackness and the scratching of a pen. Skeletons, a screaming horse, empty black eyes under the line of a helmet. This was where all the manoeuvrings led to. They went into the next room silently, even Nick seeming subdued. More maps, more explanations. Displays of uniform were set in the floor, almost like shallow graves. Lu turned from them and studied the cases round the sides, hoping that there would be relief from the more conventional displays. Propaganda and medals, newspapers, letters home.

There was an extract from Helen Thomas's book, about her husband's last night on leave before returning to the war, and to his death. It was written so simply, so openly: about how they'd spent the evening reading Shakespeare sonnets to each other, then talking of their love for each other and their children all through a cold winter's night with the frost on the windows. Lu found herself crying. The tears spilled down her face out of her control, almost as if they were happening to someone else. Nick put his arm about her shoulder and handed her a handkerchief. She blew her nose, and shook her head as if to shake the sadness away. There was no use for words. She walked round to study a cavalry officer's uniform, scarlet and gorgeously gilded with tassels. It had taken a few years for armies to realise that scarlet was a brilliant target and that shiny silver breastplates were no match for machine guns and shells. She moved on quickly into the next room.

More destruction, more death. Through a glass wall she could see the river flowing outside, much as she'd imagined in her French daydreams, with the sun sparkling on the wet willow leaves after the rain. She focused on the greenery, unwilling to turn and look at another display of the mechanisation of death. Nick slipped his hand into hers and squeezed it, and she was grateful for the warmth.

They went quickly through the next and final room and out to the river. Lu gulped down the fresh air, overwhelmed in a way she hadn't been at the Imperial War Museum. There was too much here that was real; she couldn't distance herself from it. It had become personal for the first time.

'Okay?' Nick's eyes were concerned. 'You look pale.'

'Okay,' she answered, and it occurred to her that they hadn't exchanged more than a dozen words in the entire time they'd been in the museum.

'Let's have some lunch.' They walked back under the shadow of the ancient walls. A blackbird had made its nest on a crumbling ledge. Lu could see the opening mouths of the chicks frantically cheeping as they waited for their mother to return. A poppy grew from a crevice, scarlet petals against the brickwork, the colour of dried blood.

They scouted round the town square looking for the ideal little bistro of Lu's imaginings, but most of the choices were bars or an Irish pub. In the end they settled on a place that looked as if it was part of a tourist chain, but the food was better than a tourist chain would have been in England, although as expensive.

Over lunch they talked about Nick's project, and how it was going. The line of poppies was only one strand in a wider scheme to promote awareness of the impact of war on returning soldiers and their families, but it was important.

'It'll be photogenic,' Nick said. 'The reality is, a colourful band of poppies will get more media coverage than a soldier struggling to talk about his experiences.'

Lu listened, caught up in his enthusiasm and commitment, and knew he would succeed, even though it was going to be difficult. Everything seemed possible with Nick. It was the way he dealt with things, from the determination in his face when he spoke of dismissive politicians to the gusto with which he tackled the food on his plate. She felt her heart swell as she touched his cheek.

'What?' he asked, his expression puzzled.

'Nothing,' she said, smiling and shaking her head, awash with warm and fuzzy feelings she couldn't put words to. 'Nothing.'

Nick took her hand and kissed it, his eyes closing for a moment as he pressed his lips against her skin. 'You're lovely,' he murmured.

They lingered over lunch for so long it was late afternoon by the time they emerged, blinking, into the clouded light. The jaunty music was still blaring from the loudspeakers as if it was a fete, although there were no signs of any festivities.

'Where now?'

Nick opened the map. 'We're here,' he said, pointing to Péronne. 'I thought we could drive across to Thiepval following the line of the

Front—it's called the Souvenir Route, so it should be marked. It takes in most of the major battlefields of the Somme offensive, like Longueville and Delville Wood, so it should give me an idea of what I'm taking on.' He suddenly grinned at her, his face lighting up. 'I bet you a tenner that in five years' time I never, ever want to speak to a farmer again.'

'Will I know you in five years' time?' Lu said without thinking, and then caught her breath, because he was pulling her to him, his expression serious, and she felt a deep thrill run through her as she realised that the answer might be yes, they would be together in five years' time; that their futures were joined.

Eventually they drew apart, and Nick gently swept the hair back from her face, his expression tender.

'Come on, you, or we'll never get there.' He opened the passenger door for her, and she got in, his hand lingering on her hair.

They followed the signposts along a straight road bisecting the massive fields, then turned off the main road on to smaller lanes. Lu watched the clouds in the big skies, the way the wind ruffled the wheat and made shimmering, elusive patterns. And dotted in between were the cemeteries.

She'd thought they would be vast expanses of graves, but from the road they weren't as she'd expected; instead they were more intimate, smaller enclosures containing lines of headstones. Every village had at least one, if not two or three, and along the road in between the villages were signs pointing to others up lanes and trackways. Nick explained that the British, unlike the French and

139

the Germans, had had a policy of burying soldiers near where they fell, rather than gathering them into one massive cemetery.

One commemorative cross stood on ground that had been left all lumpy and bumpy. The result of the constant shelling, Lu assumed, thinking back to the lunar landscape of the Otto Dix drawing in the Imperial War Museum. It made her realise how the current landscape had been flattened and smoothed by the constant ploughing and tilling so that something raw and visceral was transformed into bland uniformity.

She saw the Thiepval monument before she realised what it was. Large and square, set high on a ridge in this mainly low-lying landscape and surrounded by trees, it dominated the land. By now it was too late for the visitor centre to be open, and all the other visitors had gone, but the early-evening sun was still shining, so they parked in the empty car park and walked along a gravel path through woodland. Then the land opened up and to their right stood the monument.

There was no way you could call it pretty. It stood foursquare on the brow of the hill, a massive mix of terracotta brick and limestone, a least a hundred feet high and the same across, a great solid tripartite arch. Across the top was written: *The Missing of the Somme*. The lawn in front of it was roped off, so they walked around the side, and as they got nearer, Lu could read the names engraved on the sides. Thousands of them, arranged by battlefield, and then by rank. Seventy-two thousand in all, the soldiers who were known to have died on the Somme but whose final resting place was unknown. It made her feel better that the fallen did at least have somewhere that their name was listed, so they could be remembered. No one else was there but the birds sang, and the British and French flags set on top of the monument flapped loudly in the breeze.

On the far side of the monument was a cemetery, French soldiers to the left and British to the right. The British gravestones were identical, shining white headstones with whatever information could be gathered from the remains about the unknown man who was buried there: rank, regiment, whatever. The French ones were black concrete crosses with small plaques set into them: *Inconnu*. There was a dignity about them, but Lu couldn't help feeling that the practice of individualising the gravestone, wherever possible, was preferable.

Set in the base of the monument was an iron door. Inside was a file with information on who was commemorated on the monument. Lu looked up Jack's name and found his location: the second pillar to the right. She glanced briefly at the visitors' book. The crassness of some of the remarks stung: 'so unbelievably HUGE', 'cool', 'a VERY good monument', but she guessed from the writing that they were schoolchildren. A lot of people had written 'we will remember'. She found a pen in her bag and added her name. Under Comments she wrote: *Here to remember Jack Havergal.*

She went up the steps to where Nick was waiting for her. Beneath the great central arch she realised quite how large the monument was. The scale of it, the numbers of names written over every inch, made her feel faint for a second. Nick took her hand and they walked over to the second pillar on the right. She scanned the lists, searching for Jack's name. Ah, there he was, high up and a little to the left, sandwiched between T.M. Hastings and G.F. Johnson. She wanted to touch the lettering, but it was too high for her to reach. Delia's father. Known Unto God.

Nick put his arm around her. 'I don't know why I'm crying,' Lu said, sniffing furiously. 'He's only a name to me. I didn't know him. A few months ago I didn't even know he existed. In some bizarre way, I'm not even upset. I just can't stop crying.'

Nick held her tightly, and she felt safely encircled in his arms. 'My family were very lucky,' he said as Lu rested her cheek against him, feeling his voice resonate in

his chest. 'My grandfather was at a training camp in Chatham throughout the First World War; my father was too young for the Second. All the uncles survived, as far as I know. Seeing this . . . I realise how fortunate we've been. What about your father's family?'

'My father?' Lu pulled away from Nick, wiping her face with the handkerchief Nick had given her at the museum. 'I don't know anything about my father's family. For all I know, I have grandfathers and great-uncles here . . .'

'Why don't you know them?' Nick said gently. 'You never talk about him.'

'There's not much to say. He left us.' Lu pushed her hair off her face. 'When I was six he went off with another woman, and that was that, more or less. Pixie had to bring me up on her own.'

'That must have been hard for her.'

'I suppose. She did her best, but . . . well, you've

seen her. She's not exactly like most mothers.' They walked to the edge of the monument and Lu looked out over the Somme countryside, so peaceful and green. 'I don't talk about him because . . . it hurts. It hurts that he didn't want to be with us, he didn't want to be with me. He didn't even take me to the zoo, or any of the other things that divorced fathers are supposed to do.'

Nick held her hand. 'I can't understand not wanting to stay in touch with your child. Surely he must have visited.'

'Nope. Not once. It was as if we'd never existed.' Lu traced an arc with the toe of her shoe. 'Occasionally he writes, but it's too late. I don't want to have anything to do with him.'

'When Morwenna went,' Nick started to say, then stopped and cleared his throat. 'When Morwenna went, she assumed she would have full custody. It was hard to make sure I got more than just the usual one weekday night and the occasional weekend, especially when I was . . .' Lu squeezed his hand tightly, looking up into his face as he continued. 'I was pretty devastated when she went. I knew our marriage wasn't working, but I thought somehow we could keep it together. I wanted us to stay together.' He turned to Lu and smiled. 'Not that I want to be back with her now, don't worry about that. Morwenna is definitely in the past.'

'Good,' Lu whispered, as Nick hugged her to him.

The sun came out as they descended the steps, the evening rays hitting the building so the limestone glowed and the terracotta brickwork flared vivid orange. It almost hurt Lu's eyes to look at it. They walked along the grassy path through the trees, and suddenly the sky above their heads was full of darting swifts chasing midges, their bodies black against the blue, blue sky.

*   *   *

That night, back in the hotel room, Lu whispered to Nick, 'Make love to me.'

His touch was tender, there was no sense of haste; he held her close, kissing her face, their bodies working together, eyes locked as if they could read each other's soul. 'I love you,' he whispered, 'I love you.' And she wrapped her legs tightly around him, pulling him deeper into her, and told him she loved him too.

Chapter 7

Happiness must be catching, Lu thought, lying in bed and seeing the morning sun stream through the nubbly beige curtains. Nick was still asleep, so she nuzzled under his arm. 'Wake up,' she whispered, blowing air at his ear. 'Wake up and make love to me.'

'Mmm?' Nick rolled towards her, grabbing her to him with both sleepy arms so Lu was pressed against his chest.

'Wake up,' she insisted, prodding his stomach. 'No croissants for you today, Mr Jones.' In answer, Nick rolled right on top of her, crushing her chest. 'Get off me!' she squeaked breathlessly.

Nick's voice was in her ear. 'I thought you

wanted me. I thought you said you loved me.'

'I do, I do, I do, but you're going to squash me. Nick!' He seemed to get heavier for a second, then rolled back off her and looked at her with his beautiful blue eyes. She touched his face, as if she had never realised before quite how beautiful he was. 'I do love you.'

He smiled. 'I love you too.'

They missed breakfast at the hotel again.

*   *   *

Lu was resistant to the idea of the Newfoundland Memorial Park. Perhaps it was the word 'Park', which made her think of manicured lawns with notices to Keep Off the Grass and flower beds planted with scarlet salvias and gentian-blue lobelias, and stern-faced park keepers in peaked hats with officious attitudes. Logically, she knew that it was unlikely that a park created in the 1920s in northern France would have much relationship to a nineteenth-century English stereotype, but that was the problem with clichés: they didn't respond to logic. But Nick wanted to go, so go they would, though for herself she would have stayed in bed with him for ever and ever, just them together in a little beige room on the second floor. She sighed happily as they drove along. To be honest, she'd go anywhere he wanted to go.

'There are so many cemeteries,' she said, as they drove past yet another one.

'Do you want to stop?' Nick asked.

'Shall we?' She didn't care where she went or what she did, as long as it was with him. In answer, Nick pulled in at the next one they saw, marooned in the fields far away from any other habitation. Lu pushed open the gate and went through to a brick-built entranceway, like a loggia. She walked up the steps and under the roof. Beyond she could see the cemetery unfolding before her, line after line of identical white gravestones on either side of a wide grassy central path. It looked like a lecture theatre, with the gravestones replacing the rows of seats. Each line had a border in front, and as she walked, she recognised the flowers: London Pride, hardy geraniums, typical English plants from an English country garden. The grass was immaculately cut, not a weed sprouted. It looked as though the Queen was about to visit in the next five minutes, except there was no waiting welcome party; there was no one at all except herself and Nick and the gravestones.

She began to read the names on the stones along the line nearest to her, thinking she could at least say the names of the dead men so they were, in some way, recognised. A Soldier of the Great War. VIth London. Known Unto God. A Soldier of the Great War. VIth Battalion, Scottish Regiment. Known Unto God. A Soldier of the Great War. Ist Highlanders. Known Unto God.

She spun around, scanning the writing on the gravestones. There was a name dotted here and there, but most were simply soldiers of the Great War, Known Unto God. Unnamed graves. The Dix engravings at Péronne had shown bodies flung over the edges of trenches or tangled in barbed wire, a random hand reaching from out of the earth. That was what had happened to these men. Their poor bodies, or what remained of them, had been left to rot until the remnants could be gathered into the cemeteries, by which point there was nothing to identify them and no one to remember them. Her face was wet with tears again, and because there was no one else there apart from Nick, she didn't bother to hide them.

Nick was at the end of the cemetery, near the cross. Here five sycamores had been planted in a semicircle. The perfection of the path was broken by the scattered seeds, like helicopter blades. Birds sang in the trees, a tractor ploughed somewhere in the distance.

'There are so many of them, and no one knows their names,' Lu said, blowing her nose on Nick's handkerchief.

'I know,' he said. 'That's why we have to remember.'

Lu felt dragged down by sadness. There were so many—somebody's son, brother, father—lost without a name on their gravestone. Some didn't have a regiment listed; she saw one that was simply to an unknown lance corporal. She shivered as she imagined that perhaps all that had remained was an arm in a sleeve with the lance corporal's stripes on it.

'Promise me you won't ever do this,' she said fiercely. 'I couldn't bear it.'

'Do what?'

'Get involved with . . . something as senseless as a war.' She knew she sounded stupid even as she said it, and she hugged him, shutting her eyes tightly as if by sheer willpower alone she could protect him from harm.

Nick laughed softly. 'Oh love, don't upset yourself. I'm way too old. It's my boys we have to worry about.' His voice changed as he said it, and he kissed her hair.

They walked slowly back towards the car. Like at Thiepval, there was an iron door set into the wall of the loggia, and inside the cupboard was a file. Lu flipped through. There were plans showing the location of all the graves, notes about what had taken place nearby, the nationalities of the men who were buried here: mainly British, but also Canadians, Australians, New Zealanders, South Africans, Indians, French and even two Germans. Nothing could make the scale of destruction of human life better, but at least it was being remembered properly and with every respect.

Lu looked back across the cemetery, and beyond to the fields. There was a newly planted crop in the adjoining field. Fresh green shoots grew in regimented lines, stretching far away across to the horizon. She wanted to leave something in the cemetery, to give something back, anything that would show she cared. But there was nothing to give.

* * *

They drove on to the Memorial Park. Lu groaned inwardly at the sight of several coaches lined up in the car park. Notices on the front windows showed they were taking part in various battlefield tours. War tourism: it didn't seem right, although she knew it was exactly the same as what she and Nick were doing. She hoped the park wouldn't be too commercialised. But Nick was insistent that they came, and all the guidebooks said it was worth seeing, so . . .

They went first to the museum building, which

explained what had happened at Beaumont Hamel on 1 July 1916. Lu's preconceptions were confounded: there was no commercialism, no slickness, nothing but respect. Outside the building there weren't any flower beds, or any other attempt to prettify the site, just pine trees edging deeply undulating earth mounds, the remnants of trenches. Lu had always imagined them in straight lines, but they were much more random than that, cutting across each other in something closer to a herringbone pattern than a grid system. Beyond the trenches was no-man's-land, and some hundred feet from the last trench was a stumpy black tree, dead branches sawn off, more like a fingerless mitten than a hand reaching to the sky. This was the Danger Tree.

On 1 July 1916, some eight hundred Newfoundlanders had set off from the third trench; only a few made it as far as the Danger Tree. Those who reached it realised that it was impossible to continue with the attack, so retreated, only to be shot in the back. Lu turned and looked behind her. The trenches weren't far away; it would take less than a minute for her to run to safety, but only sixty-eight of those eight hundred Newfoundlanders had made it. And they had been the third wave; the soldiers of the first and second trenches had already set off and been lost, so the Newfoundlanders would have been running over the bodies of the dead and wounded from the first two trenches.

Jack had been somewhere near here. Perhaps he had stood shivering in one of these very trenches, waiting for the Big Push, before running forward and being shot down. Percy would have been with him, but he'd been luckier, merely losing his leg and not his life in the fields of the Somme.

Nick and Lu walked along the perimeter path, past two more cemeteries, the enemy trenches and another cemetery, ending up at a mound with an enormous bronze caribou on top, facing in the same direction the poor Newfoundlanders had taken on 1 July. There was a park guide there, a chatty young Canadian in a scarlet coat.

'They estimate that about one hundred and seventy bodies are still lying out there,' the guide told them, looking out towards the Danger Tree. 'Bits come up every now and then, and we're able to identify them.'

Nick asked some questions, but Lu couldn't pay attention, her brain unable to absorb any more information. From this point she could see the land ahead, the lines of the trenches, no-man's-land and the Danger Tree, then the enemy trenches. They were so near. The patch of land they were fighting over was so small. Perhaps Jack was somewhere out here, deep in the bumpy earth. It was a peaceful place to lie for eternity, she supposed, but the whole battle had been so short, brutal and ultimately meaningless. They had attacked to no purpose. Nothing was gained. Later, in November, there were more attacks, and finally the enemy trenches were captured. But then the Germans retreated to the Hindenburg line, so the whole thing had been pointless. All those lives, so little gain.

*　　　*　　　*

Lu had never needed a cup of tea more in her life,

so they drove to the nearest village and found a café draped with Union Jack bunting and memorabilia aiming squarely for the battlefield tourist.

The tea room was long and thin, with elaborately plastered ceilings. It looked as if it might once have been the foyer and waiting room of a railway station. The bar area had been made from sandbags neatly piled up and covered with varnish and the military theme continued with the decoration: rifles and bayonets, shell cases and other bits of Army paraphernalia, all heavily rusted.

'They look as if they've just been dug out of the ground,' Lu said, drinking her tea from a mug decorated with a cartoon image of a British Tommy who looked a bit like a Mabel Lucie Attwell toddler crossed with a leprechaun. It was the best cup of tea she'd had in France so far, as they seemed to have got the concept of putting the tea bag in the hot water immediately, rather than leaving it on the side to be dunked in lukewarm water.

'I expect they have—the farmers are constantly finding various bits. There's a special unit that deals with any ordnance discovered.' Nick drained his mug. 'Poor sods. Makes you realise the scale of the war.'

'Would you have done it?' she said to Nick, thinking of the thousands, millions of Jacks and Percys who had waited miserably in the trenches. They must have known their chances of survival were minimal and yet they'd still obediently gone over.

'What? Fought?' Nick shook his head. 'I don't

151

know. I think so. You can't let countries just march into other countries and say they belong to them. And if I'd been a Tommy in the trenches . . . yes, I'd have gone over the top, I think. I'd have been worried about letting everyone else down.'

'Even though you knew that you'd probably be dead in a few minutes?'

Nick pulled a face. 'Yes, I still think I'd go. Sounds weird, I know, but I think I'd feel we were all in it together, we'd all take our chances together and that would be that. It's what men do.'

'And I bet you wouldn't talk about it.'

'Probably not.' Nick laughed. 'No—we wouldn't talk about it, we'd just do it.'

'Men are different,' Lu said with feeling. 'I can't imagine a group of women behaving like that. We'd want to talk about it and decide if it was a good idea or not.'

'And nothing would get done.'

'Look around you,' Lu said. 'In the circumstances, I think that would have been an excellent thing.'

'Women should be running the world.' He kissed her. 'There's a museum here. Do you want to see it?'

Lu secretly felt she'd seen quite enough war museums for one weekend, let alone in one lifetime, but she followed Nick. She would have followed him anywhere, she thought, suddenly overwhelmed. She couldn't resist stroking his arm as he paid for their tickets, wanting to rub her cheek against him, wanting him. He turned and smiled at her. Oh, she loved him.

The museum turned out to be housed in the long back garden of the tea room, although it was unlike any suburban garden Lu had ever seen. Two trenches had been dug along the length, with the earth piled up between them to represent no-man's-land. Lu and Nick went left first, to the German side. It was all very makeshift, the sides of the trenches propped up with planks of wood, and mud everywhere, but in a strange way it seemed real. Certainly more real than the Trench Experience at the Imperial War Museum, which had presented a clean and orderly version of trench warfare. The mannequins in their trench coats looked cheerful, smiles painted on to every face. Perhaps they were smiling at the music, which Lu thought sounded like Irish rather than German songs. She wasn't certain if it was supposed to be part of the museum or whether it came from the garage next door over the wall made from spent shells. How many were in just this wall alone? Thousands. She shivered. No wonder the landscape had been blown to pieces.

The middle section between the two trenches was skewered with iron spikes designed like elongated pig's tails, each curl festooned with a strand of barbed wire. Lu remembered the Jacques Tardi drawing of the soldier crawling through the wires. You wouldn't get a clear run to the Danger Tree, of course; you'd have to negotiate the lines of barbed wire. Perhaps this was what had happened to poor Jack: he'd ended up caught on strands of wire and died hanging there, trapped and unable to move, prime target for a sniper's rifle. There was a mannequin of a sniper cheerfully pointing his rifle out of a porthole towards the British side, and there, up on the mound of no-man's-land, a hand reached out from the soil.

Lu felt sick as they walked back and round the top of the display to the British side—they knew it was British as the soundtrack changed immediately to Vera Lynn and 'Keep the Home Fires Burning'. Wrong war, surely, Lu thought as they walked the length of this trench. The British appeared much tidier, more organised and better equipped than the Germans, which Lu was pretty certain was not the case in reality. More body parts stuck out from the soil of no-man's-land, hands and feet, but also a couple of artfully placed skulls.

'I'm surprised they haven't draped a body or two over the barbed wire,' Lu said, pointing.

Nick smiled. 'This whole place is geared up for school parties, and I bet the kids love it. My boys would. They love gruesome things. They don't think it through.' Lu didn't know what to say. Yes, boys loved disgusting things, farts, bogies, blood and gore, but did that mean they had to be encouraged? Even Nick, who was as sensitive and caring as Lu could wish for, was less horrified, and more interested about the war. She secretly suspected that he'd have been first in line to join up, and probably got his stupid brave head blown off. Her thoughts were confirmed by his next comment. 'I was thinking of bringing the boys along at some point. Do you think it would be too much for them?'

'I don't know.' Lu shrugged. 'I don't know them.'

Nick frowned. 'I was thinking . . . it's about time you met them. What about next weekend?'

154

Chapter 8

Lu had given great thought as to what she should wear to meet the boys. She wasn't competing with Morwenna, of course not. She could never be the children's mother, and wasn't trying. Instead she wanted to look like perfect girlfriend material: jeans tucked into flattish purple suede boots, with a zebra-print belt slung around her hips. A plain white T-shirt. A short good-quality jacket in a soft green lovat tweed. They were going to take the boys to Longleat (hence the flattish boots). She hoped Longleat would occupy them enough so she and Nick would get some time together. Would the boys like her? Lu looked at herself in the mirror. Her shoulders were so hunched up they were practically rubbing her earlobes. Anyone would think she was about to go for a job interview, one on which the rest of her life depended, instead of meeting two primary school children. Would they like her? She wrenched her shoulders down, loosened the belt a notch and felt slightly less sick. Only slightly, though.

What is the matter with you? They're children. C-H-I-L-D-R-E-N. She pulled a face at herself in the mirror, then went to look for her usual silver bangles on her bedside cabinet. No sign. She raised her head for a second, thinking back. She'd done some work last night. She went to the living room and collected the silver bangles from beside her drawing board, along with her wristwatch. She hated wearing anything on her wrists when she worked, as if slipping off the jewellery was like shucking off the shackles that tied her to the ordinary world and released her into the imaginary kingdom where her creativity roamed. Would they like her? She slipped the bangles on to her wrist, and fastened the watchstrap. Twenty to. If she didn't get a move on she'd be late. I want to be late, something inside her squeaked. I don't want to go-o-o.

Be calm. Breathe. Close your eyes. Imagine your aura becoming a pale-blue cloud, a happy blue cloud, calm and serene, calm and serene. Would they like her? Would they like her? Would they like her? It was all very well saying 'calm and serene'; it was quite another matter feeling it. Pixie would probably have painted her with zigzag orange and red lines all round her. Lu gave up on her aura and let herself out of the flat and on to the street, car keys in her hand, bag swinging from one shoulder. Loud music might be the answer. Dandy Warhols on the stereo, she wove the car through the agonising, aggravating slow-moving Sunday traffic out of Bath towards Nick's cottage. She was going to be late.

She arrived, parked by the green, and sat in the car for a few minutes with the engine off. She was going to see him. Nick was waiting for her. She smiled, thinking of his face, of him stretched out naked on the bed last weekend in France, like a cat in a sunbeam, eyes half closed but watching her as she got up and moved about the room, getting ready to go out but very aware of his eyes on her body. Nick was better than any aura visualisation.

Calm and serene, she got out of the car. Of course they'd like her.

As Lu approached the house, she saw a flash of movement from the downstairs window. Someone had been watching and waiting for her. She paused at the front door, but no one came, so she knocked using the dolphin door knocker.

A few moments later and there was Nick, a broad smile on his face. 'Good to see you,' he said, kissing her formally, then holding the door wide open.

'And you,' Lu said, wanting nothing more than to snuggle under his arm and be held by him, but he was closing the front door and calling up the stairs.

'Come and meet Lu.' Nothing. Lu waited politely. Nick shook his head, slightly flustered. 'I'm sorry, I don't know where they've got to. They were here a minute earlier. Guys? Come and meet our guest.'

'Don't worry,' Lu said, grabbing his hand and stopping him from going up the stairs. 'They'll come in their own time.' She touched his chest lightly, raising her face to his. 'I've missed you.'

His face lit up, and he turned towards her, all attention focused on her. 'I've missed you too.'

'I wish we were still in France.'

'Me too.' Nick stroked her face. 'I forget how good-looking you are. Each time I see you . . .' His voice trailed away and they stared at each other. Lu could feel the electricity blazing between them. She'd never felt like this before, this feeling of being a newborn foal, all wobbly legs and uncertainty.

Nick pulled away, looking down. Following his

gaze with hazy, unfocused eyes, she saw a small boy. 'This is Tom.'

'Hello, Tom,' she said with a kindly smile, holding her hand out to him. 'I'm Lu.'

Tom put both hands behind him. 'Do you have a dog?'

'No,' Lu said, mentally flailing around for a more satisfactory answer. She straightened up, pulling her hand back. Stupid—boys didn't shake hands, that was what grown-ups did. 'My gran's got a Westie,' she offered. Not good enough. Tom peeled off like a fighter jet and whooshed back up the stairs.

'Tom, that's not how we speak to guests, come back here,' Nick called up the stairs into Tom's slipstream, before turning back to Lu. 'I'm sorry, I don't know what's got into him.'

'That's okay,' Lu said, blinking. This wasn't what she'd imagined.

'Come and have a drink,' Nick said awkwardly, as if alcohol was going to be the only thing that got him through the day. 'I don't know where Ben's got to—he was here a few minutes ago.'

'Never mind,' Lu said, tucking her arm into his, suddenly totally happy to have him on his own. Stuff meeting the kids. 'How's your week been? Did you manage to follow up the man on the council?'

'Yes, I've got a meeting booked for Tuesday, which is good,' Nick said as they went into the kitchen. 'What do you fancy? Tea? Coffee? Wine?'

'You,' Lu said, putting her arms around his neck and kissing him. 'I fancy you.' Oh, but he was a wonderful kisser, even though she could sense that he wasn't a hundred per cent lost in the moment along with her . . . She pressed herself against his body; she hadn't realised how starved of human contact she'd been, how hungry she was now, how intensely she felt, how—

Nick pulled away from her, furiously clearing his throat and pushing his hair back. Somehow he'd teleported right to the other side of the kitchen. 'This is Lu,' he said gruffly, sounding a bit like Father Bear.

Lu felt as caught out as Goldilocks as two pairs of blue eyes studied her. As far as looks could speak, she'd broken the chairs, eaten all the porridge and stolen the beds. 'Hi,' she said weakly, giving a feeble wave. Now she knew what Nick was going to look like if he was ever seriously pissed off with her, she thought, wilting under the unwavering gaze of both his sons. 'Let me guess— you must be Ben,' she said to the taller boy, tugging nervously on her jacket. Gosh, he looked like his father—Morwenna's genes had been swamped.

'Yes, this is Ben,' Nick said. His voice was too loud. 'Hey, Ben—Lu's an illustrator. Perhaps you could get her to help on that art project you need to do for school.'

'Yes, I'd love to help,' Lu chipped in with a whopping fib.

Ben's stare became even more withering. 'Mum and me did it last week. When you were away.'

Nick's face fell. He looked lost and confused, and Lu longed to cuddle him, stroke his brow and generally look after him. But she couldn't. Instead she said, 'Why don't we set off for Longleat now? It's a lovely day and I'm sure we can grab some lunch there—my treat. I expect the boys would like that.'

Nick recovered. 'That sounds a good idea. Right, guys, go and get your things. Departure time in ten minutes.'

The boys left, leaving Lu feeling she'd cracked it. Child-rearing? No problem. It was like lion-taming—not that she'd done much of that in her life, but she understood the principle. Never let them see you're afraid. Never let them take control. Be in charge. She smiled serenely at Nick. See? Easy-peasy.

*   *   *

At the big roundabout there was a notice pointing to Longleat. Nick turned the car into the entrance, and Lu expected to see the house, the safari park—everything—laid out before them. But there was only a long, long driveway, with grassy banks on either side, punctuated with a variety of trees, and beyond, more trees.

'I've never been to Longleat before,' Lu said, looking about her. 'Stupid really, when it's on my doorstep.'

Nick glanced over to her. 'Not if you don't have kids. We haven't been for ages, have we, guys?'

'We went with Mum,' Tom piped up from the back seat.

Lu saw a shadow flicker across Nick's face. Annoyance? Regret? He claimed he hardly ever thought about Morwenna, and Lu had accepted that. She suddenly realised that it had suited her to believe him when it had been just the two of them, but now, with the evidence of his past relationship clattering away on Game Boys in the seats behind

160

her, she found it hard to believe. He'd been married to Morwenna, for heaven's sake, had two children with her. There had to be some emotion left.

Lu glanced behind her at the boys. Both were engrossed in their game, their faces intense with concentration. She could see Nick in both, Ben especially, in the mops of thick, untidy hair, even though theirs were a sandy honey shade while Nick's was dark brown. He was there in the shape of their brows, the way their eyes were set, and something about the expressions that flickered over the boys' faces reminded her of him. She loved Nick; it would be easy to love these boys who looked so like him.

Filled with affection, Lu lightly touched Nick's thigh. He smiled in response as he slowed the car down before a ticket booth. The prices were written up, various options explained: house only, safari park, passport.

'Christ, it'd be cheaper going to the theatre,' Lu murmured in amazement. What seemed a bit pricey for one became astronomical when multiplied by four. No wonder people said it cost thousands bringing up kids. No wonder Nick was broke.

'A family passport, please,' Nick said, and handed the ticket man his credit card.

Lu felt a warm glow at being part of a family— Mum, Dad, two boys in the back—and smiled graciously at the ticket man, who was concentrating on the card machine. She'd be an incredibly young and glamorous mother, to have two boys like Ben and Tom. A yummy mummy. She leaned forward, but it was obvious the ticket man couldn't care less about her, yummy mummy status or otherwise, as he handed the tickets to Nick, who passed them on to Lu. 'You don't have to do everything in one visit,' Nick said, starting the car again.

Lu flicked through the tickets, reading all the information. There seemed to be so many things to do. Oh yes, she remembered watching a television programme about the murals in the house. They'd be worth seeing. And she quite fancied looking at the paintings; the collection sounded varied, even if there was probably a high proportion of seventeenth-century gods and goddesses cavorting on clouds, which left her cold.

'I'm looking forward to seeing the house,' she said to Nick. 'It's ages since I've been to a stately home.'

'Boring,' Ben said from behind her.

Oh yes, she'd forgotten to be the perfect girlfriend. 'If you don't want to, that's fine,' she said, smiling brightly. It was supposed to be their treat; she could always come another time.

'I'm afraid the boys tend to want to do all the running-about things,' Nick said.

'That's what we'll do then,' she said. The drive turned left, and suddenly they were on the edge of an escarpment, with the landscape dropping away dramatically into a valley. 'Wow.'

'This is called Heaven's Gate,' Nick said, slowing the car down.

'There's the safari park,' Ben said, pointing.

Lu was on the wrong side to see easily. She could make out fences, with what looked like camels behind them. 'Aren't there lions here?' The Lions of Longleat—didn't she remember that as their slogan? When she was a child she'd always wanted to come and see, but Pixie didn't believe in depriving animals of their freedom, so they'd never done anything like a safari park. She remembered the prices at the ticket booth and suddenly wondered if Pixie's high-minded stance might also have been dictated by the equally high entrance prices, and felt a stab of appreciation. Pixie might not have been the perfect mother by any means, but Lu had never felt poor growing up, just different.

They drove down past the house with its amazing turrets and towers all intricately carved in honey-coloured stone, then to the car park beyond, already covered with hundreds of cars. Nick found a place shaded by a large horse chestnut tree in full flower, like a lighted Christmas tree in the middle of May.

'Right,' Lu said, getting out of the car and inhaling the warm spring air, wonderful after a week in the city. Perfect girlfriend, here she was. 'What first?'

It turned out there was a family strategy already in place, starting with the safari boats, because apparently they developed queues as the day wore on. Some of the attractions were aimed at much younger children—my readership, thought Lu—and were dismissed out of hand by Tom, Ben and Nick.

Lu had had an image of Nick and her strolling hand in hand along shady paths while the boys frolicked ahead of them in an engaging but contained way. This was not how the boys, or indeed Nick, had thought of the day. Their version of Longleat was a relentless round of activity. If only they could have been plugged into the National Grid, no one would need to build more nuclear power stations. Even their pizzas were wolfed down faster than, well, wolves. Lu felt giddy with the non-stop action, like being stuck on a perpetual merry-go-round. After a while you just longed to get off. At least Nick was in tune with her thoughts, because he suggested that the next attraction should be the maze. The boys charged ahead and through the ticket barrier, but he turned away and sat down on a bench, then patted the seat next to him.

'It'll occupy them for about ten minutes, if they remember the secret,' he said. 'Hours otherwise.'

Lu snuggled next to him. 'I've never done this sort of thing before. We didn't do tourist stuff. Music festivals, yes, stately homes, no.' Would it have been different if her father had stayed? Would they have done things like this together, a little nuclear family? As far as she could tell, Longleat was stuffed with families.

'A deprived childhood,' Nick said, hugging her to him. 'Let me make it up to you.'

Lu luxuriated in being on her own with Nick, but it didn't last nearly long enough for her. Soon there was a shout of triumph, and they turned to see the boys waving from the central tower. Lu and Nick waved back, Nick with vigour, Lu half-heartedly, wishing the boys could have got lost in the maze for a couple of hours. The prickings of jealousy she'd felt earlier stirred inside. Not that she was jealous of a couple of little boys. Certainly not. Just . . . she wanted to be with Nick, have his undivided attention.

'Adventure playground next,' Nick said, getting

up.

At the adventure playground Lu bought ice creams, although she did wonder if that was wise, given that the boys were already running as they went in. Hands were stamped so they could go in and out as many times as they wanted. How many times could one child want to go into an adventure playground? wondered Lu. But as she entered the wooden stockade that encircled the playground, she realised that here was an energetic child's dream come true. Things to climb, to whizz round on, to hang upside down from, and in the centre a tall tower that the boys were heading for at speed. She noticed that in front of each activity there were cut-outs of elephants, tigers and monkeys.

'Yippee, I'm in,' Tom said, ducking through a cut-out of an elephant and haring up the slope after Ben towards the wooden tower.

'There are height restrictions,' Nick explained to Lu as they followed at a more sedate pace. 'They've got to be a certain height before they can go on some of the things, and the heights are shown by the various animals. This must be the first year Tom's been tall enough to go for the big one.'

Lu nodded knowledgeably, not having a clue what he was talking about and thinking she knew more about fantasy worlds for little girls than the real life of children.

The tower was set on a small grassy mound like a Norman motte and bailey, according to Nick. Lu could imagine Rapunzel leaning out of one of the openings at the top, her long blonde plait hanging down for the prince to climb. She knew without being told that Nick's boys would consider such a thing soppy. Would Nick?

'Do you remember Rapunzel?' she said. Nick was puffing slightly with the climb. She'd have to put him on a diet at this rate.

He gave her a look as if he could sense her good intentions for his future weight loss. 'Which one's Rapunzel?'

'The one with the hair,' Lu said. 'The witch cuts off her hair when the prince is climbing up her plait, and he's blinded by falling into thorns.'

'And then what happens?'

'I can't remember. They all live happily ever after, that goes without saying, but I'll have to check. I think it might be that she cries and her tears cure him.' She paused on the climb as some excited children raced past her. 'Must be the first time a relationship has been mended by a woman crying; most men run a mile.'

Nick laughed. 'That's certainly not a fairy tale,' he said. 'I had a girlfriend, oh, years ago, way before Morwenna, and whenever you did something wrong she cried. Her eyes would go all big, and then the tears would just fall out, great big blobs of water running down her cheeks.'

'What did you do?'

'Run!'

They entered the tower. Looking up, Lu could see a ledge and then, whoosh, a sheet of silvery metal unfurled, straight down at first, then gently curving away out of the foot of the tower in front of where they were standing. A cluster of children loitered around the top of the ledge. One of the children was Ben, but Tom was standing at the bottom with Lu and Nick.

'The death slide,' Nick said, peering up. 'I've

166

never understood the fascination for them.'

As he spoke, a small girl peeled off from the group nervously jiggling around at the top and dropped herself over the side. Lu saw how she slid down the steep drop, then, as the curve took over, the slide supported more of her weight. She came effortlessly to a halt at the bottom, before scrambling up and rushing off past Nick and Lu to a set of stairs at the side.

'It looks fun,' Lu said, as another child launched over the edge and seconds later shot past. She personally hated anything that involved her feet parting company with the ground, but if you liked that sort of thing, then the slide looked like just the sort of thing you liked.

Nick looked relieved. 'Tom's a bit nervous, so it would be great if an adult could go down at the same time. Hey, Tom. Lu loves the death slide! She'll go down with you, and I'll see you both when you come out here.'

'Don't you want to go with him?' Lu looked up at the glinting metal sheet.

'Heavens, no—I'm terrified,' Nick said cheerfully. 'You go up the stairs, then come down. That's all there is to it.'

So much for my knight in shining armour, thought Lu sourly as she crossed over to where Tom was clutching the barricade. His knuckles were white. 'Come on, Tom. Show me where we've got to go.'

They climbed up what seemed like suspiciously many steps. How high was this slide? It had only looked about thirty feet up from the bottom, but it felt as if they were climbing more like a hundred. Tom trudged up silently beside her, his face pinched.

Right. They were at the top. Now what? Lu looked over the edge, then recoiled. Oh God. What had looked like thirty feet from the bottom was now about three hundred. She couldn't do it. Tom looked sick. I know just how you feel, mate, she thought.

A fairly constant stream of children were scrambling up, sitting on the edge then launching forwards. Tom was clutching the guard rail; he was obviously terrified. Like father, like son. Like girlfriend. Lu was about to suggest going back down the stairs—there's no shame in knowing your limitations, she could imagine herself saying— when she saw Ben waiting his turn. 'Do you want to go down with Tom?' she asked him.

Ben shook his head. 'He's too scared,' he said matter-of-factly. 'He won't ever do it.' Then, whoosh, Ben was over the edge and sweeping down, all before Lu could offer him a tenner if he took his little brother down. She looked across to Tom and caught his expression, a sad mixture of embarrassment at being called scared by his brother, and fear.

'Looks like we're on our own,' Lu said to him. It couldn't be that difficult, could it? She slipped her feet out of her boots and nudged them to the side. 'Shall we go down together?' She held out her hand.

Tom's warm hand slipped into hers, and she felt a wave of triumph. 'Let's sit down.' They sat, feet dangling over the edge. From here the slide looked more menacing than before, the drop further. Could she really be about to do this? They wouldn't let you if it wasn't completely safe, she told herself. Just a moment in free fall, and that was it.

Going over the top. That was what the Tommies in the First World War called it. The moment when they scuttled out from the relative safety of the trenches into the fire of the war zone. You were shot for cowardice. But I'm a coward, thought Lu, as her heart was gripped by fear. Perfect girlfriend get stuffed; she wasn't going to do it. She was going to accept her fate. After all, Tom was Nick's child. He was nothing to do with her.

She turned to Tom to say that she'd changed her mind, but his face was looking up at hers, his eyes bright with anxiety, his grip tight. He trusted her.

'On the count of three?' Tom nodded, his mouth set.

Oh shit. 'One . . . two . . .' Was she really going to do it? She must be out of her tiny mind. Oh shit, oh shit . . . 'Three!' and then there it was, that sensation of falling, falling, her worst nightmare, Tom shooting ahead, a burning sensation on her elbow and then it was over and she was stumbling to her feet at the other end, heart pumping.

Tom's hand wrenched out of hers. 'Come on, let's do it again.'

'You go,' she managed, the air for words of more than one syllable having been knocked out of her. And he was gone, racing up like the other children, off for another try. She stood, checking that her body was in one piece. Being a perfect girlfriend was harder than she'd thought.

Chapter 9

Lu might have ended up with carpet burns on her lower back and elbows for all the wrong reasons, but it didn't do her relationship with the boys any harm over the next weeks. Tom in particular seemed to have accepted her as a fixture in his father's life, and although Ben was more reticent, he tolerated her. Toleration was okay, Lu thought. It was realistic. Just because their father loved her, it didn't mean that they had to love her too.

Before she'd met the boys, she'd complained to Briony about Nick having a double life, one with her and one with the boys. Now she'd become part of the fringe of the second life and she wasn't sure she liked it. When Nick was alone with her, he was lovely as usual, but when it was her and the boys, he was focused on them. Sometimes it took all her powers of seduction to get him to look in her direction. The summer half-term was particularly bad, as Nick had the boys all week. When she challenged him about it, he apologised and said he felt he had to compensate them for having to adapt to sharing him. 'What about me adapting to sharing you?' Lu said lightly, and Nick had laughed as if it were a joke. But it wasn't. She almost preferred the previous situation, when she hadn't known what it was like to share him with someone else.

At least then she'd got more work done. It was galling standing on the edge of a football pitch watching twenty-two little boys run around when she knew that back home she could be working on

170

a book, or going out to lunch, or doing some shopping before going to a party or private view in the evening. Instead she had to watch the match, then listen to Nick and Ben dissect it, then Nick and Tom, then Tom and Ben while Nick made supper for them all, then watch *Doctor Who* or *The X Factor*, then go back home because Nick didn't feel the boys were ready for her to stay over. And what was going to happen in the imminent school holidays when the boys would be around more? Was she going to have to keep going back and forwards like a shuttle bus, only allowed the honour of Nick's bed on the few occasions the boys wouldn't be around?

'It's early days,' he kept saying, as if they hadn't been seeing each other for nearly six months now. Six months might not be very much compared with twelve years with Morwenna, but it was a long time for Lu.

'When won't it be early days?' she asked, but Nick never knew the answer to that. She just had to be patient.

Briony wasn't the least bit sympathetic when they went out for a midweek drink after work. 'If it bothers you so much, then leave him. You've always said he's not Mr Right. So what are you hanging about for?'

'Because I love him,' Lu said, gritting her teeth as they took their drinks from the bar and went to sit outside to catch the evening sun, hopefully a harbinger of a scorching summer in July and August, as promised by the weathermen.

Briony gestured with her hand. 'Gotta be patient, then.'

'Like you are with Jerry?' Lu sniped back,

irritable and fed up. She regretted it immediately when she saw the expression on Briony's face. 'Sorry.'

'Not your fault. Actually . . .' Briony settled down at a table by a wall covered in jasmine, white flowers like a thousand little stars. 'I think Jerry might be on borrowed time.'

'Really?' Lu floundered internally as she sat opposite her. Briony and Jerry had been together for so long, Lu had assumed that their relationship behaved like a grumbling appendix, bickering on into the future but never actually rupturing. The idea that they might split up was impossible. She squinted at Briony, trying to make out her expression, wishing she'd brought sunglasses, terrified of what her friend was going to say next.

'I was at an artist's studio last week looking at his work, and he asked me out for a drink afterwards. I went, it was very nice, then he asked me to dinner, and that was very nice too, and then I went home. And Jerry was slumped on the sofa drinking beer and watching *Big Brother*, and I don't think he noticed that I'd been gone. And I thought . . . well, I thought, I don't know why I'm with you. And I've never thought that before.'

The scent of jasmine filled the air, sweet in the evening sunshine. Lu swallowed. 'Did you say anything?'

Briony shook her head. 'Nope. But I could have an affair. Not with the artist—I didn't fancy him enough, and besides, his work's really good; I'd rather represent him at the gallery. But I could do it.' She nodded, more to herself than to Lu. 'I really could.'

172

The conversation with Briony had unsettled Lu. Was this how Morwenna had felt about Nick? Not a sudden passionate meeting with her lover and caution being thrown to the winds, but a slow attrition of love and respect. It was easy to paint Morwenna as the wicked witch, but Briony was Lu's friend. Briony was good. And what of her own father, who had also left for another woman? Had he had a moment when he'd looked at Pixie and thought: I don't know why I'm with you?

She rang Nick when she got home, even though it was late and she knew he went to bed early on week nights. He answered, his voice heavy with sleep.

'Hi,' she whispered. 'It's me. Were you asleep?'

'Mmm.' She could imagine him rubbing his eyes. 'Is everything okay?'

'Fine. I just wanted to speak to you.'

'Okay.' He sighed, still half asleep.

She smiled, thinking of him. 'Go back to sleep.'

He made a little grunting noise, then, 'I love you.'

'I love you too. Go on, go to sleep.'

'Okay.' He put the phone down, and she wondered if he'd remember the phone call in the morning. It didn't matter. She knew why she was with him. She would be patient.

*   *   *

The next week Lu didn't hear from Briony, so she assumed—hoped—that her flirtation with temptation had been momentary, or that if it was going to develop, it wasn't happening fast. She was more concerned with avoiding Yolanda. The

173

second Sugarsnap book was nearing completion, and she would have to decide whether she was going to sign the next contract. Two more books, three months per book. That took her to Christmas. Most illustrators would have been pleased to know there was money coming in for six months.

But I'm not most illustrators, she thought, filling in yet more green paint and letting her answering machine pick up Yolanda's calls. I can't carry on doing this sort of work. She knew Yolanda would be wanting her to sign the contract, and that she ought to do it, but she couldn't make herself pick up the phone. Instead she let it ring.

It was ringing on Thursday, the day Lu was taking Delia to hospital for her operation, and without thinking she answered it.

'Aha—I've caught you at last.' Yolanda's voice was triumphant.

Bugger, Lu thought. I knew I shouldn't have picked up. She stood by her drawing desk, looking down at the work nearly done. At least she didn't have to feel guilty about that because for once she was on time. 'Hi, I was just going out. To take my gran into hospital,' she added, hoping to win the sympathy vote. 'I can't be long.'

'I'll be brief. What's happened about the second contract?'

Lu could imagine Yolanda as a gunslinger, lounging on the veranda decking outside the saloon, chewing a cheroot in the corner of her mouth.

'Oh, well, I . . .' Heck, she seemed to have turned into James Stewart.

'We need a decision.' Yolanda's voice was tough.

She'd stopped lounging and was now poised for the shoot-out, her hands resting on the edge of her gun belt.

'This is a really bad time,' Lu stalled, looking out on to the green from her sitting room window. A woman in a singlet and jogging shorts walked her dog on the pavement outside, openly peering into the ground-floor windows as she passed. Lu turned away, facing into the room. 'I've got to pick up my gran, she's going into hospital for an operation. I can't be late. Can I call you back?'

'But will you?' There was no mistaking the menace in Yolanda's voice, the dark glitter of her eyes from under her black Stetson. 'I've had the impression you've been screening my calls.'

'I've been away.' James Stewart was a good guy, and the good guys always won. Right? Lu took a deep breath. 'The thing is, Yolanda, I can't face doing another Sugarsnap book. I've thought about it, but I can't. I'm not a machine, I can't just churn it out. I have to feel inspired.'

Yolanda snapped back, 'Think of your gas bill. That works for most people.'

Lu transferred the phone to the other ear. 'It's not just about money. It's about what you believe in. The work has got to be worth doing. And the world really doesn't need another book about peas and other vegetables.' Lu looked across to the bookcase, stuffed with all the varied books she'd worked on in the past. Fairies, animals, castles, farmyards and forests, casts of thousands to the simplest line drawings. There was more to life than peas.

'Lu, the world always needs another book about peas and other vegetables. There's a whole allotment's worth of fruit and veg that's been untapped. This series could run and run.'

'Like runner beans?'

'Great idea for a series. You could have French beans, string beans, broad beans—with an underlying message about childhood obesity—'

'I was being ironic.' She could hear James Stewart: *it's your legumes or your life*. 'My life's too short for this.'

Rat-a-tat-tat, Yolanda shot back, 'Are you saying you're not going to do it?'

For a moment Lu teetered. She touched the edge of the painting on the drawing board. This was work, this was her job; if she said no, then what would she do? But if she said yes . . .

'I'm sorry, but no.'

The intake of breath at the other end was like the gun being pulled out of the holster. Lu squeezed her eyes shut, waiting for the blast. It came.

'What the hell am I going to say to the publisher? Don't think there's more work waiting for you, because there isn't. It's this contract or nothing.'

'That's blackmail.'

'No, it's the real world. It's about being professional. A job is a job.'

'No it isn't. It's about doing work you believe in, work you're proud of, work that matters. If it doesn't matter, then what's the point?'

'You eat. Last chance. Are you taking this job or not?'

It was like looking over the edge of the death slide. She glanced around the sitting room of her flat, the one she'd worked so hard to buy, the beautiful objects she'd filled it with over the years. 'Not.'

*   *   *

Her hands were still trembling when she picked Delia up.

'Where have you been? I was wondering if I ought to get a taxi.' Delia looked cross rather than relieved.

'Sorry, Gran.' Lu picked up Delia's case, thinking it was pathetically light.

'I've put all of Scottie's things in that bag. Can you manage?'

'Yes, of course.' She picked up Scottie's bag, which was much heavier than Delia's and clunked as she swung it into the car. Delia stood on the front doorstep, suddenly dwarfed by the house behind her. Lu came back.

'You'll be okay,' she said, giving Delia's thin shoulders a squeeze. 'It's a routine operation, isn't it?' She had meant it to be a rhetorical question, but she could hear the anxiety in her own voice, the child's need for reassurance.

'Oh, don't you worry about me,' Delia said. 'Now where's Scottie gone? Scottie! Scottie! Ah, there you are.' Scottie scampered around the corner of the house, trailing a tartan lead. Delia stooped and caressed the little dog's head. 'You'll be safe with Lu,' she said. 'She'll look after you.'

'Of course I will,' Lu said. The dog's eyes shone like blackcurrants through the rough white hair that fell over his face. If he had been a teenage girl he'd have spent all day flicking back that fringe, only to let it fall forward so he could peer though it

177

mysteriously. But he was only a dog, so he didn't do mysterious.

Delia put the lead into Lu's hand and gripped it between hers. 'Look after him,' she said, her face puckered with anxiety.

'Oh, Gran, of course I will. You'll be fine and back in no time.'

'He has half a tin, morning and evening, and I put a few treats out for the evening. Then there are doggy chocs—he can have five of those a day; he's not to have more or he'll put on weight. I've written it all out and it's in his bag.'

'I'll look after him,' Lu said solemnly. Delia had never fretted about her like this. Or perhaps she had, but Lu had never noticed. 'Come on, or we'll get caught up in the rush hour.'

She helped her grandmother into the car, thinking how frail her wrists were. Then, once Delia was ensconced, she opened the boot of the hatchback. 'Come on, Scottie, jump in!'

Scottie looked up at her as if the concept of jumping was not one he understood. Sighing, Lu bent and scooped him up and into the back, portable as a handbag. Perhaps this was what she was best suited for, dog-sitter, not illustrator. Or perhaps she should start doing dog portraits. She stared at Scottie, who stared back, then curled up in the corner of the hatchback. He'd already managed to leave a scattering of white hairs across the interior. I'm not a doggy person, she thought as she closed the door.

*　　　*　　　*

They drove to the hospital, Delia clutching her

178

handbag in front of her as if a passer-by might suddenly wrench open the passenger door and snatch it from her. Lu parked, despite Delia's insistence that she could manage on her own, and what about poor little Scottie, shut up in the car?

'I'll wind the windows down; it's not as if it's blazing sunshine.'

'Dogs get heat stroke, you know—Lu, you will be careful with him, won't you?'

'Of course I will,' Lu said, beginning to get a bit annoyed by the fussing over the dog. Her beloved gran was going to have an operation, and all she could think about was the dog. 'I'll look after him like he was my own baby,' she said.

Delia shot her a sideways look. 'I thought you always said you didn't want children.'

'That doesn't mean I wouldn't look after one if I had one,' Lu pointed out, taking Delia's bag away from her. 'It's because I'd look after my child too well that I don't want one; it'd worry me to death. I'd be forever tidying up after it, and feeding it on organic gourmet stuff and tying its nappies into origami parcels. If it survived the intensive cosseting and managed to get to eighteen without being suffocated or having serious mental health issues, I'd be so devastated when it left, I'd collapse into a little heap, never to recover again.' She slammed the car door shut with her bottom and clicked the central locking, then cocked an arm for Delia to take.

Delia tucked her arm into Lu's. 'And that's supposed to reassure me?'

'Yup. Mind out for the kerb.' They walked to the hospital entrance and the automatic doors swooshed open for them. Lu asked at reception where they should go, and they followed the directions up to the ward. Delia stepped forward and checked herself in. Lu trailed behind the nurse as she showed Delia where her bed was.

'Do I have to get undressed?' Delia said, touching the pale-blue cellular blanket. There was a hospital gown folded on top of it, creases so sharp they looked as if they might hurt when worn.

'Heavens, no, wait until this evening if you like,' the nurse said cheerily as she clacked busily down the ward.

Lu and Delia looked at each other. Lu wanted to do something, anything—plump pillows, arrange grapes—but there was nothing to be done.

'You'd best be getting back.' Delia looked very small against the hospital curtains.

'I can wait.' She didn't want to leave her grandmother alone in this place. She wanted to kidnap her, take her home where she could be her usual cosy self, not this shrunken little old lady.

'I don't think Scottie will like being cooped up in the car.'

'He'll be all right. I'll take him for a walk later, I promise.' Lu looked around. 'Can I get you anything?'

'I'll only be here for a couple of days; there's nothing to need. Go on, I'll be fine. You get back.'

Lu hesitated. It seemed callous to be leaving, and yet there wasn't anything she could do. 'Perhaps I could find you a cup of tea or something.'

'Lu, off you go. I'm not a child.'

'I know. Well, if you're sure . . .' She gave Delia a hug. 'Don't give the nurses too much trouble,' she said.

180

'I'll do my best,' Delia replied.

'What, to give trouble?' Lu tried to make it a joke, and Delia gave a faint smile. 'I'll see you tomorrow, after the op.'

'Don't bother, I'll probably be all woozy.'

'I want to bother.' Lu squeezed her tight. 'Take care,' she whispered.

*   *   *

I should have been a dog, Lu thought, watching Ben and Tom play with Scottie. She hoped she could at least bathe in the glow of having brought Scottie along, even if she wasn't his owner. Delia's operation had gone smoothly: the troublesome teeth had been successfully extracted, leaving Delia swollen like a chipmunk and drinking through a straw. The hospital felt that it would be best for her to stay on the ward where they could monitor her, so instead of coming home she would spend the weekend there. Lu reassured her that Scottie would be fine.

And of course, Scottie was more than fine; Scottie was the star attraction. The boys welcomed him like he was the answer to their dreams. She would have been thrilled to have received a quarter of the attention the boys gave the little dog, although she had to admit that Scottie was better value than she was, tirelessly interested in fetching, chasing and running about.

'Where do they get all this energy from?' she asked Nick.

'I don't know—I'll have to stop feeding them,' he said, putting his arm around her.

Lu leaned into him, feeling his warmth and

solidity. 'Don't stop feeding me,' she said. 'That roast was brilliant. You are clever.'

He kissed her hair. 'Am I? It seemed fairly ordinary to me.'

'No, you're brilliant and clever and extraordinary and wonderful and . . .' Lu buried her face in his chest.

'I'll have to make a roast more often. I had no idea it was so impressive.'

'I wish I could cook,' she said.

'But you can cook,' Nick answered quickly. 'You're a great cook.'

'That's nice of you to say so.' Lu turned her face towards him, expecting the kiss that came. It was lovely sitting here with Nick, so close to each other emotionally and physically. She offered a silent prayer of thanks to Scottie. Not only had she gone up in the boys' estimation, but he was occupying them so she got Nick to herself.

'I've got Tom's birthday party in a couple of weeks,' Nick said. 'That's going to test my cooking skills.'

'Will it? I'd have thought it'd be easy. Packets of crisps and whatnot.'

'But there's the cake to do. Thank heavens you can get decent birthday cakes from the supermarkets.'

'Seems a pity not to make a real one.' Not that Lu had ever made one herself, being a member of the 'if it fits in a toaster, I can cook it' school of thinking, but Delia always said they were easy; you just had to follow the recipe. Cakes had been one of the few things Pixie had made, her speciality being hash brownies.

'Maybe I'll stir myself and get inspired,' Nick

said. 'But there's quite enough to organise without having to worry about a cake. I'm going to take them swimming first, that should tire them out. Morwenna's going to take Tom up to London next weekend as a birthday treat. I'm not quite certain what they're doing, but I thought it was only fair that I should do the party with all the school friends.'

Lu felt herself drift away as Nick talked about Tom and parties. She wanted to be interested, but there was only so much boy talk she could take. 'Do you think I ought to call Yolanda up and grovel?' She bit the side of her thumbnail. She'd told Nick all about what had happened earlier, while he was making lunch and she did all the gofering, and he'd been nothing but supportive. She'd known he would be; that was the way he was.

Nick looked at her. 'Why should you? You don't want to do the job, so there's an end to it.'

'But if I don't work, I'll have no money coming in. Maybe there'd be something else I could do.' Even as she said it, she knew it was unlikely. Yolanda wouldn't find her more work until she felt she'd made her point. That might be months away. Lu gave the nail another go, feeling the edge ragged against her teeth. 'There's money due that I've invoiced for, and the last trickle of royalties from the picture books I did a million years ago, but that will dry up over the next six months and then there will be nothing. Nada. Zip. Zilch. I ought to grovel.'

'Be positive. Of course you'll get another job, and if not, cross that bridge when you come to it. You don't have to think about it now.'

She looked at him. 'That's easy for you to say:

you've got a salary, and sick pay and holiday pay and a pension.'

'And two boys who need looking after, and an ex-wife.'

'I know. Why does everything have to be about money in the end? Why can't it be about good work?' Lu tucked her thumb into her palm to stop herself biting the nail any more. 'I know I can do better work than I've been doing for the last five years, I know I can. I want to do a proper picture book.'

'So. What do you need to do to get a proper picture book?'

'Sleep with the right editors.' Nick raised his eyebrows at her. 'That probably wouldn't work either, actually. They're all female.'

Nick laughed. 'I was going to say don't be defeatist, but in the circumstances I won't. Go on, this is your world, not mine. What would you need to do to get a picture book deal?'

'Writing one would be a start.'

'And then?'

'Doing some roughs for the illustrations, then designing the whole book, then going to finished artwork on a couple of illustrations, then making a dummy.'

'What's that?'

'It's a mock-up of a finished book, but without doing all the work. You'd just do the cover properly, and a couple of illustrations so they could get an idea of how the whole book was going to look. You send it out to editors and hopefully they fall in love with the project and give you a mega advance.'

'What's stopping you?'

'Dunno.'

'Hey, Dad,' Ben called. 'Come and play with us.'

'In a minute,' Nick replied, before turning back to Lu. 'When we went to that museum at the Somme, you said you'd like to do something like that illustrator had done, the comic books. So why don't you?'

'They're graphic novels, not comics,' Lu corrected absently. 'But Jacques Tardi's already done that, and brilliantly. Besides, there isn't much of a market in the UK for graphic novels for adults, and I've always illustrated and written for children.'

'But you could do something new perhaps, a crossover book aimed at lads like Tom and Ben that could also appeal to adults. A sort of graphic-novel picture book.'

'There speaks the marketing man. People don't want new things, they want more of the same.' She kicked a bit of grass, thinking how such a book might look. 'I suppose there might be a market for it.'

'Da-a-ad.' Ben stood over the football, Tom and Scottie panting furiously beside him.

'Well, there you are then. Write your story, do the illustrations, send it out.' Nick got up. 'Coming.' He ran off and joined them.

Lu watched, silently seething. Did he really think it was that easy? She'd have liked to see how he felt if she suggested that raising a few million was just a matter of making a couple of phone calls. He was running now with the boys, tackling Ben, getting the ball, shooting for goal, but Scottie was heading him off, little legs flying as he raced after the ball, yapping all the way, Tom following

185

closely behind. The ball shot past the goal mouth by inches, and Nick groaned theatrically.

'Pathetic,' Ben shouted, rugby-tackling his father.

Nick spun him round, lifting him up by the waist so that Ben hung at right angles for a second before Nick dropped him to the ground. He looked up briefly at Lu. 'Come and join us.'

'In a minute.' Lu hunched into herself, cross and grumpy. It was all very well for Nick to say write a picture book, but it wasn't something you could just knock up in your lunch hour. You had to have a good idea for starters, something original, something they wouldn't have seen before. She went back to biting her thumbnail. It was quite a good idea of Nick's to do something like Jacques Tardi's work, but aimed at a much younger age group. She could see it working. She put her head in her hands. No, she could see everyone saying: it's a really interesting idea but there isn't a market for it. You can't make a picture book out of the First World War. Yolanda certainly wouldn't like it.

'Come on, Lu, you'll enjoy it,' Nick called out to her.

Yeah, right. She knew she was being ridiculously grumpy, but hey, she was a grown-up, she was allowed to be grumpy if she wanted to. Scottie yapped cheerfully, dropping to the ground to watch Tom line up a free kick. Traitor, she thought darkly. You're supposed to be on my side. Tom scored a goal, then ran around waving his arms in the air before inexplicably falling to the ground in a heap. Exhaustion? No, he was up again, belting down the length of the pitch in hot pursuit of Ben,

186

Nick and the ball.

It was obvious they weren't going to stop any time soon. She could either stand on the sidelines like a lemon—Sour Face Lu—or join in. Not that any of them were bothered whether she joined in really; the boys couldn't care less so long as they had Scottie.

Nick jogged up to her and bent over, his hands on his knees. 'Bloody hell, I'm unfit.'

'You ought to be on a diet. You'll probably have a heart attack.'

Nick roared with laughter. 'That's my girl. Always looking on the bright side.' He held out his hand to her. 'Come on then. Prove you're fitter.'

She stared balefully at him.

In response he suddenly grabbed her bag and ran off.

'Oi!' Lu stood up. 'Give that back.'

Nick swirled it round by the handle. 'Come and get it then.'

'Right. That does it.' Lu ran after him, and he scooted off across the pitch, zigzagging away. 'Give me my bag!'

'Nah-na-na-na-nah,' Nick sang, waggling the bag, but she was faster than he was and caught up with him.

'Gotcha,' she said, grabbing the bag, half laughing, half puffing. Nick got her in a bear hug, tugging at the bag. He was much stronger than her, but she hung on. 'Don't you dare!' she squeaked. 'No, Nick, stop it. Stop it!'

'Only if you'll play with us.' He was out of breath too.

'I will, I will.' Nick let her go then, and she twisted round to face him. 'That was blackmail,' she said, fondly stroking his cheek.

'My speciality,' Nick said, and kissed her quickly, before running towards the boys. 'Hey, guys, Lu's playing.'

'Me and Dad against you and her,' Ben called out to Tom, who pulled a face.

'I don't want to play with her, I want to be on Dad's team.'

Lu stopped running. 'Well, thanks. And the name's Lu, not her.'

'Guys, guys,' Nick said, putting up his hands. 'We're not playing teams, just having a knockabout.'

'But it's more fun with teams,' Ben moaned.

'We're having a fun game. No, Ben, enough.' Nick put up his hand as Ben whined and dragged his feet across the grass. 'Here—Lu,' and he kicked the ball across to her. Lu ran with it for a bit, then passed across to Tom, but Scottie intercepted it.

'I've got it,' Tom shouted, running after Scottie, and the game started up again.

Lu had to admit, it was fun running around with the boys and a football, much more fun than aerobics or running on a treadmill. Her shoes coped quite well on the slippery grass, and she was as fast as any of them, except perhaps Scottie, and he had four-wheel drive. 'Here, here!' she called, and Tom passed to her. Now she was dribbling the ball down the field—oh no, Nick had stolen it from her. Right, she'd get it back. Adrenalin pumping, she tried tackling Nick, laughing as she reached for the ball, enjoying his hands on her, getting the ball out and passing to Tom, a quick hug and a kiss before Nick was running backwards, calling out to

Tom to warn him that Ben was looming up to steal the ball. He'd got it now, no, he'd missed a kick, it was loose, she was going to be first to it. And then she'd got the ball, and the goal was in sight. She ran, kicking the ball in front of her, she was going to shoot—oh, how great if she got a goal, she could feel the triumph now – and there was nothing to stop her and she swung her leg back to kick and—

Ugh. She landed on the ground with a thump, her left knee taking her weight. Ben was grinning at her as he sped off with the ball. 'You tripped me,' she gasped, hardly able to speak. 'You little sod.'

'Lu!' Nick was looking shocked.

'He did it on purpose,' Lu spluttered, sitting on the ground and rubbing her sore knee. She couldn't believe it—why had he done that? Jesus, it hurt, the pain was excruciating. Involuntary tears flooded her eyes. 'I've buggered my knee.'

Ben stopped running, came towards her hesitantly.

'Christ, it hurts.' Lu rolled up her trouser leg. 'Look what he's done.' There was a long pause as they all looked. The evidence trickled down her calf, thick and scarlet, the skin on her knee blue-purple where the top layer had been scraped off. Seeing the damage made it sting even more. She hugged her leg to her.

Nick stretched out a hand. 'Let's get you up.' His voice sounded quite normal, as if nothing had happened.

Lu stayed put. 'I might never walk again.'

Nick laughed. He laughed! She was in agony and he was laughing at her. 'Girls!' he said to Tom and Ben, rolling his eyes. 'Useless.'

Lu stared at him, the pain in her leg a dull throb compared to the stabbing in her heart. He'd stopped being her lover; he was Ben and Tom's dad—no, worse, he was playing the bloke game, us men against you girls. And she couldn't win. If she complained that Ben had deliberately tripped her, he'd say it was just a game. If she demanded he tell Ben off, she'd look like a spoilsport. If she said she wasn't a useless girl, it'd be proof that women had no sense of humour.

She got up slowly, her leg feeling as if it was on fire. Nick put an arm around her but Lu shook her head. 'I'm okay—I'll just sit on the bench for a bit. You guys go on with the game.'

'Sure?' Nick sounded concerned but also relieved.

She nodded, and started to limp towards the bench. Her jeans had stuck to the blood; she could feel them tugging at her skin as she moved. Behind her, the game started again.

*   *   *

Lu did the washing-up while Nick put the boys to bed. What now? Perhaps I should just go, she thought, stacking a plate on the draining board. I knew the children were going to be an issue before I started. He's always been Mr Wrong. Perhaps I should just pack up and go.

'But why the bloody hell should I?' she asked Scottie, who was lying on the kitchen floor beside her. 'Ben tripped me up. He should have been told off.'

Scottie cocked his head to one side.

'I know, I know. He's a child. Nick's his dad.'

190

Oh, Nick. She screwed her eyes up. She loved him, that was the problem. And he loved his boys.

Scottie started snuffling round the skirting board, hoovering up crumbs. At least he'd been a hit with the boys. 'You're right,' Lu said, wiping her face with a soapy hand. 'I've just got to be grown up about it.'

Nick came into the kitchen and put his arms around her. She could feel his breath on her hair as she relaxed into his embrace, all anger dissolving. 'Hello, gorgeous,' he murmured. 'How's the leg?'

'I'll live,' Lu said, leaning back into him. 'Did you say anything to Ben?'

'Ben? No—why?'

She turned round to face him, washing-up brush still in her hand. 'Nick, he did it on purpose.'

Nick looked shifty. 'Oh, I don't think so. It was just part of the game. Glass of wine?' He went over to the fridge.

Lu started scrubbing at a saucepan, trying to remember. Had it been part of the game? She could remember the running about and, yes, Ben charging up to her, his leg going out . . . 'He did trip me,' she said, turning.

Nick sighed. 'It's called tackling. Maybe he was being a bit enthusiastic, maybe he got carried away. It's not an issue.'

Lu felt like pointing out that her knee was probably scarred for life, but resisted the impulse. 'It is for me.'

There was a short pause. The air was charged with icy-cold particles, everything was in sharp focus and Lu suddenly thought with shock: this might be it. Nick seemed a million miles away, even though he was just the other side of the kitchen. 'Then we'll have to agree to differ,' he said carefully, as if the wrong words might shatter things for ever.

'I don't want to have an argument with you.' Lu spoke equally carefully, feeling her way along the edge of the abyss.

'And I don't want one either.' Nick gestured to the fridge. 'Glass of white?'

'Please.' Lu managed a smile, despite being close to tears with relief. The danger was receding. 'Oh no, I shouldn't—I've got to drive back.'

Nick cleared his throat. 'Why don't you stay over?'

'What about the boys?'

'They asked if you'd stay.'

'Really?' A rush of delight thrilled through her and she grinned at Nick. The boys wanted her to stay. She caught an edge of something sheepish in his expression and narrowed her eyes. 'It isn't me they want, it's Scottie.'

Nick made a deprecating gesture. 'That may have had something to do with it.' He crossed the kitchen and held her face in his hands. 'But I want you to stay. I want you to stay very much. Will you?'

Lu nodded. She loved him. That was all there was to it.

Chapter 10

Lu collected Delia from hospital on the Tuesday after her op. She was still a bit swollen and bruised around the edges but otherwise as fit as she'd ever been, along with umpteen reassurances from the hospital staff that there was nothing to worry about. Delia was more worried about Scottie, and it was good to be able to tell her that he had spent the weekend playing football, being walked or generally being fussed over by two boys. It had been a great success.

Lu didn't tell Delia about her knee (which was scabbing up nicely) or the row. That was something she had to process for herself. Had she been right to be upset? Had Nick been right to play down the incident? They had come very close to the danger zone. Would Nick have taken her side if it had been some other boy who had tripped her? Was it a sign that when the chips were down, his loyalty would always be to his boys ahead of her? She tried not to think about it, but it popped up unexpectedly, making her head ache.

And then Briony split up from Jerry.

'To be honest, it's a relief more than anything else,' Briony said, apparently without a concern in the world, as they made their way through a group of French schoolchildren cluttering the pavement outside the Abbey. 'Jerry asked me if I was shagging Simon, and I said yes—was that a problem? And he just blinked and said he'd have to think about it.' She gave a belt of raucous laughter. 'I can't believe I was with him for all

193

those years. He's just pathetic.'

Lu couldn't take it in. The picture it conjured up was so unlike what she expected from Jerry, she almost felt sorry for him. They crossed the road at the Guildhall. 'Who's Simon?'

'That artist I told you about.' Briony turned into the Guildhall market with a little skip, as if full of the joys of spring. Briony didn't usually skip.

'I thought you said you didn't fancy him.'

'I'm allowed to change my mind.' Briony spun round to Lu, a big grin on her face. 'Of course I know Simon's just a transitional relationship, but I'm having fun—and I haven't had fun for such a long time. I don't know why I put up with Jerry for so long.'

Because you loved him, Lu thought but didn't say, as Briony placed her order at the deli. The blackboard behind the counter announced that today she was being served by James. You can put up with almost anything if you love someone, Lu thought, ignoring Briony flirting outrageously with James as she chose her samosas. Even coming second. And I do love Nick.

'Listen,' Briony was saying as they came out of the market on the other side and crossed the road to the Parade Gardens. 'The weekend after next, Simon's cousin has an exhibition opening in St Ives, and we're going down—his cousin has a flat over his studio that we can use. It's got two bedrooms, so why don't you and Nick come down too? There's a party on the Saturday night, then we're having lunch with a big group on Sunday before coming back. Apparently loads of art-world people from London will be there—Simon said his cousin knows Damien Hirst and people like that.

194

It'll be absolutely amazing—you've got to come.'

'I'd love to, but I can't,' Lu said as they went down the steps. She'd not been to St Ives before, but she knew of it: a little Cornish fishing town with an artists' community and an outpost of the Tate Gallery, and wonderful beaches and restaurants. It was somewhere she'd always wanted to visit, but she didn't even bother to try to work out a scenario where it might be possible. 'Nick will have the boys that weekend.'

'Can't he change weekends? Go on, ask him.'

'No, he won't. If he's made an arrangement with them, he keeps it. He says it's bad enough being divorced, he's never going to let the boys down again.' Even if it means letting me down, she thought wistfully. 'Besides, it's Tom's birthday party. And I'm making the cake.'

Briony raised her eyebrows. 'You? Making a cake?'

*   *   *

It really couldn't be that hard to make a special birthday cake, Lu thought. It just needed a bit of forward planning. She'd got a couple of books from the library on cake decoration, and back home, she flipped through the pages, looking at the pictures. The trouble was, they all seemed rather mundane, and Lu wanted Tom to have the cake to end all cakes. She'd offered to take the party catering off Nick's hands, and then had also said she'd arrange all the games too, after Nick had brought them back from swimming.

'In for a penny, in for a pound,' she'd said, laughing as if it was just some casual arrangement.

Secretly she planned to show them all that she could organise a party just as well as any mother.

She stopped at a picture of a treasure chest. It was half open and revealed chocolate money and jewels in the form of lots of sweets. The bright colours appealed, but it looked like an easy cake to make, to be honest. Perhaps she should go for something easy given that it was her first attempt, but then she discarded the thought. What made the cake look good was the decoration, and she was going to decorate Tom's cake to within an inch of its life. After all, she was an illustrator; if she couldn't decorate a simple birthday cake, who could? Morwenna, came back the answer. Morwenna, who was such a talented artist. Morwenna always made her own cakes for the boys.

Lu slammed the recipe book shut. She wouldn't make any old cake; she would do her own creation. She picked up her pencil and started to doodle. Tom's favourite things were football—yawn—and Harry Potter. Perhaps she could do the owl from the books. That would be quite easy, given that it was a snowy owl: you'd just need plain old icing sugar with a couple of orange fruit gums for eyes. She could cut down the sides of an ordinary circular sandwich cake, then plonk it upright on the base to make a rocket shape. Bit of icing smothered all over, using a fork to make a feathery pattern, and that would be that. She looked at her drawing. Yes, it would work, but it was far too simple.

What else could she do? The Sorting Hat? She sketched it out, giving a floppy tilt to the end of the hat, as if it was melting. Yes, she could imagine the shape—maybe she could make a cone by lining her metal sieve with paper. Then she could put chocolate buttercream all over it. Whoops! She scribbled over the drawing as she realised it would bear a startling similarity to one of Scottie's poos.

The flying car would have been a possibility, but how could she make it fly? It would have to sit mundanely on the cake base, and if it was going to do that, she might as well make a Ferrari or a Porsche and give up on the Harry Potter theme. She bit the end of her pencil. What else was there? Perhaps she should think again about football.

Pencil in hand, she began to sketch, boys playing football. 'And not tripping each other up,' she muttered to herself, drawing one boy's intent expression. He was going to get that ball in the goal if it killed him. The soldiers had played football at Christmas, she remembered Nick telling her, the German and British lads having a good game and forgetting the war for twenty minutes. She wondered who'd won as she drew the young men, the sky lowering overhead, the Danger Tree to one side, burnt branches ominously still next to the movement of the boys. All those men, some of them just boys . . .

She stopped and wiped her eyes, then studied her drawing. There was something about it that worked. It was rough, but there was an energy there. She flipped the page and sketched the Kitchener poster—Your Country Needs You—and a boy staring at it, his cap perched on the back of his head. She could see from the way he stood that he was eager to go, caught up with patriotic fervour. Innocent. Like Tom, but nearly grown up. He wanted to go to war. Quickly she wrote:

The boy who went to war.

She stared at the words. There was something hypnotic about them; they stood out on the page as if she was viewing the drawing through stereoscopic glasses.

The boy who went to war.

She took a sharp intake of breath, then settled down again, all thought of cakes forgotten. This was what she'd been waiting for.

*   *   *

The boy became an obsession. Page after page she filled with drawings of him, and when she wasn't drawing, she was reading soldiers' diaries and other accounts of the First World War. Gradually the boy—Arthur—came to life, and over two intense weeks a story started to form under her pencil.

Arthur tried to sign up, was turned away by the recruiting officer for being too young, went home, stole his father's bowler hat and returned. He was nothing if not determined. This time he was let in, although the recruiting officer recognised him. He thumped him on the back and said, 'Good show.'

Arthur liked the Army; it was better than working on the land and being a plough boy. He liked the drilling, the marching up and down, the boring repetition of mindless tasks, although he grumbled along with everyone else. The food was good, better and more plentiful than at home. He'd grown six inches by the time he went home on leave, and the girls at the station looked at him in his uniform with admiration, eyelashes fluttering at the sight of the handsome soldier. His sisters were thrilled with him, showed him off like a prize, and his mother cried when he gave her his Army pay. He'd only kept a bit back for baccy, which he'd got the hang of smoking because all the other chaps did, and he was a man now. Arthur liked being a man.

She drew like a woman possessed, filling sketchbook after sketchbook. Nick was a tremendous support, never complaining when they met and all she could talk about was Arthur. He helped, too. Some of it was practical—his office had several shelves full of First World War books and photographs—but mostly he acted as cheerleader for the project. She would show him her latest drawings and watch his face intently, seeing his expression change from surprise to delight, sometimes puzzlement if the drawing didn't quite work and he couldn't make out what she was doing. And as Arthur got more involved in the war, Nick's reactions became more serious, and he would put his arm round her as he studied her work, as if he needed the physical contact to remind himself that it was all long ago in the past.

'How's it going to end?' he asked after silently looking through that day's work. Shelling had made Arthur's landscape into a moonscape. Barbed wire twisted across craters. A hand reached out from the earth.

'It's fiction; he's going to live to tell his tale to his grandchildren.' Lu shook her head. 'In real life . . .' She thought of all those graves across the Somme. 'Only one in eight died. Perhaps he was lucky.'

Nick cuddled her in close. 'I hope so.'

The day before the party, she came back to the present and darted round the supermarket collecting family-sized packs of crisps, finger rolls, cocktail sausages, pizzas, juice, cola, bumper packs of sweets, anything that looked heavy with either carbs or sugar or both. She reckoned the boys would be starving after swimming and would wolf food down pretty much regardless of what it was. It was what boys did. She made the cake the night before, and thought it was pretty cool. She managed to smuggle it in without any of them seeing.

Tom tried to persuade her to reveal what sort of cake it was, but she shook her head as he went through the list. Football, car, a rocket? No, no, no.

'It's not going to be fairies, is it?' he said, looking worried.

'No, not fairies,' she said, laughing at the expression on his face at the thought. 'Don't worry, you'll love it.'

The other guests turned up, dropped off by estate cars or MPVs that whisked away at speed. Lu was disappointed; she'd imagined herself handing out glasses of chilled white wine and being a serene yummy mummy, but obviously the real yummy mummies had other things to do with their Saturday afternoons.

'So what is the cake going to be?' Nick said as the boys clambered into the minibus he'd hired to take them swimming. 'Fancy giving me a clue?'

'Not a chance. You'll have to wait and see along with Tom.' Lu kissed him. 'Have fun.'

Nick climbed into the driver's seat, checked that everyone had their seat belt done up, and they set off. Lu stood on the doorstep, waving as they disappeared round the corner at the end of the road, then went back into the house.

For a moment she wondered if she was perhaps being a bit too ambitious, but then shook her head. Nothing ventured, nothing gained. She planned to do the tea when they got back, then some games— pass the parcel, pin the tail on the donkey, musical bumps, sleeping lions, all the things she imagined a traditional party consisted of. Her own birthday parties had been haphazard affairs, and she'd longed for something with balloons and streamers, perhaps even a magician to saw the birthday girl in half. No such luck, although Pixie did her best. It depended on who she was seeing: the reggae band had been a good year, followed less successfully by a small man with a Zapata-style moustache who played the bongoes while Lu's friends hung around giggling, but the best had been the rave music and dancing until they dropped. Of course everyone had wanted to come to her parties, once word had got round about how weird they were, and as a result Lu had been invited to many of the sort she longed to have herself.

But she'd never had a traditional birthday party like that, until now. She'd got about ninety minutes to transform the cottage. Out came the bags of crisps, to tumble into bowls; the sausages went into the oven; she cut squares of cheese and speared them with cocktail sticks, put out hula hoops and party rings, boiled eggs and made vast quantities of sandwiches. She'd had lots of clever ideas about streamers and sparklers, all of which evaporated as she worked. Who'd have thought it would take so long just to put out a few biscuits and make some sandwiches, especially when you'd forgotten to leave the butter out to soften first? Parties were harder work than she'd thought. I'll have to tell Pixie that, she thought, because even if my parties were weird, they were good. It must have taken a lot of effort. And money. She winced as she remembered the supermarket bill. She couldn't ask Nick for all the money back; she was going to have to lose the receipt somewhere at the bottom of her handbag.

Never mind. It would be worth it. Lu looked at the kitchen. It looked like an illustration of the perfect party from a picture book, she thought. She'd have been proud to have painted it. She turned, hearing the rumble of the diesel engine outside, and for some reason the sound triggered the thought: Oh heck, I've forgotten to put the pizzas in.

The boys piled back into the house, hair drying in spikes, talking, shouting, jostling. She ushered them in and felt a glow of satisfaction at their delighted expressions, all the while trying to remove the wrapping from the pizzas and get them in the oven before Nick could see.

'It looks amazing,' Nick said, coming into the kitchen and giving her shoulders a squeeze. He looked exhausted, and damp round the edges.

'It was nothing,' she said airily, wiping a dab of egg mayonnaise off her face. 'Nothing at all. I don't know why people make so much fuss about parties.'

Nick raised his eyebrows, but anything he might have said was drowned by the noise of the boys.

They demolished everything. Nick and Lu were kept busy replenishing glasses, passing food, removing anything that looked as if it was about to be used as a missile.

'Tom's mum,' a boy called, catching Lu's attention. 'Please, Tom's mum, can I have some more juice?'

'Don't be stupid, that's not my mum,' Tom said, his mouth full of half-baked pizza.

'Who is she then?' the boy asked.

Tom shrugged dismissively. 'Just somebody.'

'My name's Lu,' she said, surprised to be fighting tears as she poured out the juice. Just somebody. She'd worked this hard, and was that all she was. Just somebody. Don't be silly, she told herself. Tom didn't mean to hurt you; he was probably embarrassed. And after all, what was he supposed to say? That's my dad's girlfriend? Too much to ask of an eight year old. But it still hurt.

'Everything okay?' Nick said, passing her with an empty carton of juice.

'Yes, of course.' Lu looked around. 'Is it time for the cake?'

She brought the cake in—Hedwig, with fruit gum eyes and surrounded by a ring of candles—to satisfactory oohs and aahs. The singing of 'Happy Birthday' was followed by unsuccessful candle-blowing, as she hadn't thought through the problems involved in having a large owl in the centre of a lit circle. Nor had she thought how they were going to slice the cake once it had been admired and Tom had been promised his wish, even though it had taken several puffs to blow out the candles behind Hedwig. It was trickier dealing with children than she'd imagined without their teachers to keep them in order.

She checked her watch. The schedule was now way out. 'We probably ought to move them to the front room in a second for the games.'

'Pee break first', Nick said.

'Mmm,' Lu said. 'I reckon that's your department.'

Nick laughed and clapped his hands. 'Right, guys, Lu has organised a whole lot of games and stuff, but first, upstairs and wash your hands.'

Chairs scraped back, feet pounded as they hurtled through the hall and up the stairs like wildebeest on migration across the Masai Mara. Strange how ten boys could make so much noise, Lu thought weakly, longing for a cup of tea. But no time for that as they thundered back down the stairs and into the front room.

She'd imagined them all sitting nicely playing pass the parcel. She hadn't reckoned on the difficulty of a) getting them to sit, nicely or otherwise; b) getting the music to rise above what seemed like a hundred competitive voices; and c) the attractions of chuck the parcel. Nick policed the circle as Lu raised her voice. She was used to giving school demonstrations; this should have been a doddle. With relief, the final layer was unwrapped, the toy discovered, grabbed by the winner's neighbour, slung around the room, discarded.

'Pin the tail on the donkey next.' Lu stood up, wondering if giving a group of boys a violent weapon, even something as small as a drawing pin, was a wise idea. The boys jostled, nudged, swore and bumped each other as the blindfold was put on and they lunged at the donkey. They're supposed to have a good time, and they are, she thought, as her beautiful donkey got stabbed in the eye.

'What did you have planned next?'

'Sleeping lions,' Lu said forlornly, looking at her list and thinking the chances of getting this lot to lie down quietly were minimal.

Nick obviously thought the same. 'Right, guys, let's go outside and play football,' he said, and off they went, leaving Lu feeling like the cowboy trapped in the stampede, without even a horse to use as a barrier, while the herd charged over and around her. She went to clear up in the kitchen. Out in the garden, Nick had got them playing football, running off all that sugar. The doorbell rang, and she went to answer it.

'Sorry, I'm early, I hope that's okay,' an anxious-faced woman said.

'The boys are playing football in the garden. Come in and have a glass of wine. Or a cup of tea,' Lu added, seeing the surprise on the woman's face. She showed her into the kitchen and filled the kettle, but there was another ring at the door. More parents—a couple this time. They knew the first mother and greeted her with kisses and exclamations of delight. Lu made tea, feeling left out of this love fest. No one seemed to feel any need to include her in the conversation. Not that she wanted to discuss holidays in the most wonderful villa on Corfu, but it would have been nice to be asked. She poured the tea into a selection of mugs, then handed them round.

'What an amazing-looking cake,' the father said, taking a mug. 'What was it—a bomb site in the snow?'

'My interpretation of Hedwig,' Lu said stiffly, as the doorbell rang again. How dare he be rude? She smiled sweetly. 'Help yourself to a piece.'

More sets of parents crowded in, others drifted out into the garden, and she served tea and cake, smiling and nodding, uncertain if these were friends of Nick and Morwenna or just acquaintances. They all looked about ten years older than herself at least, and not a yummy mummy among them, unless it was the sort of mummy who saw pies and said yummy. She went out to give Nick a cup of tea. He was still involved in the football game, along with a couple of other fathers and the boys. It looked ultra-competitive, she thought, steering away from a bit of tackling that looked as if it was about to cross the divide between physicality and violence.

'Who was that girl?' she overheard one woman say just as she came back up the garden towards the kitchen. 'The one who was helping.'

Lu stopped, then edged towards the window, expecting praise. It had been a pretty amazing party, if she said so herself.

'The nanny, I suppose,' came the reply. Huh, Lu thought. Did she look like a nanny? What did one of those look like anyway?

'No, it's the girlfriend,' another voice said knowingly.

'Girlfriend? Since when did he and Morwenna split up?'

'Heavens, ages ago. Didn't you know?'

'Poor Morwenna.' There was a satisfied clucking of tongues.

'It's not poor Morwenna at all, at least not from what I heard. She moved in with that man—oh, what's his name? You know, the one who runs the garden centre.'

'Really? No! So she left him.'

'Oh yes. Mind you, there's no smoke without fire, they say. Nick seems to have got himself sorted out with this one rather quickly.' Lu could just imagine this unknown woman's face, bulging with implications. She knew she should stop eavesdropping—didn't Delia always say that eavesdroppers never heard any good about themselves—but she felt a horrid compulsion to stay and listen, however painful it was.

'So you think it was going on all along?'

'I've no idea.' The woman sounded saintly, as if she was the last person in the world to gossip. You bitch, thought Lu. You're making it sound like I'm the one at fault, and I'm not. Nick's marriage break-up was nothing to do with me. It's not my fault. 'But look at how she's dressed,' the woman carried on.

Lu looked down at herself. How was she dressed? Normally, was the answer. Jeans and T-shirt. Okay, the jeans were pretty tight, but they were only jeans, and the T-shirt was from Gap, for heaven's sake. It showed her midriff, but it was hardly siren kit, and her shoes weren't that high, but from the reactions of the other women she might as well have been wearing a black rubber corset and suspenders. She put her hand over her mouth to stifle any sound, hating herself for being upset by a bunch of stupid gossiping women. It didn't matter what they thought, what they said, she told herself. Except it did, it did.

She was about to leap into the kitchen and defend herself when she caught sight of Nick, pushing his hair back from his face, his arm around Tom's shoulder. He caught her gaze and made a thumbs-up sign at her. Lu pulled herself together and did a thumbs-up back as he came towards her. She wanted to tell him about the women, but knew she couldn't. He'd be devastated that they were talking about his marriage like that; he'd always made such a point of stressing that he and Morwenna didn't bitch about each other.

'Looks as if people are making tracks,' he said. Hooray, thought Lu. I want them to go and leave me alone. He gave her a quick kiss. 'You've done everything brilliantly, thanks so much.'

A boy came up and shook Nick's hand formally. 'Thank you for having me,' he said.

'You're welcome,' Nick said, ruffling the boy's hair with a smile.

And me, Lu thought. I'm here too. But she might as well not have been for all the notice he took of her. The boy loitered.

Suddenly Nick turned to her. 'Shit—party bags! I completely forgot. Did you do any?' he hissed.

'Party bags?' She stared at him wide-eyed. 'Party bags!'

'You didn't . . .' He put his hand to his forehead as if desperately thinking up Plan B.

'No, I didn't think . . . Sorry.' There it was. At the final hurdle she'd failed.

'Doesn't matter. My fault, I should have remembered,' he said. 'I'll just quickly wrap up some cake or something. These kids have quite enough stuff as it is.'

They went through to the kitchen, and Lu could see the heads turn and the sharp eyes, despite the smiles. Not everyone, of course, but enough to make her conscious of her tight jeans and smooth stomach, the unfriendliness of some of the women in their loose-fitting polo shirts. She felt young and urban and out of place. A tarty bimbo who couldn't even come up with a few party bags.

In a moment of clarity she suddenly realised that if she were to become the boys' stepmother, this would happen again and again. The explanation of who she was, the raised eyebrows, the calculations of those who knew Morwenna and were measuring Lu against some invisible standard, which she would fail to measure up to. Because there wasn't any way she could win at their game. She'd always be an interloper, always the suspicious girlfriend, the wicked stepmother—unless she turned into one of the bitchy women herself and ganged up against anyone else who was different.

I can't win, she thought. I can't win. Whatever I do will be wrong. But then later, after they'd all gone, and Tom had reluctantly gone to bed, Nick slipped his arm around her waist and kissed her neck, and she remembered why she loved him once again.

*　　　*　　　*

'You know what they say?' Lu said, leaning against the bedroom door.

'No, what do they say?' Nick said absent-mindedly. He pulled his sweater over his head. 'God, I'm knackered. I'd forgotten how bloody exhausting birthday parties were.' His head came out the other end dishevelled, and he ran his hand over it in a vain attempt to make it smoother.

209

'It's about what men want . . .' She pulled her T-shirt over her head, sucking her tummy in as she went. 'A cook in the kitchen, and a whore in the bedroom.' She undid her belt, then slowly unbuttoned her jeans, her eyes fixed on his. As she slithered the jeans down her legs, she made sure that she was facing him square on, breasts pushed together by her arms. She'd bought a set of expensive lingerie that she couldn't afford, just for him, his very own birthday present. Nick stopped what he was doing and Lu smiled inwardly, knowing she had his full attention. She stepped out of her jeans.

'You certainly showed today that you were a cook in the kitchen.' Nick leaned back on the bed. The echo of 'whore in the bedroom' was almost audible.

Lu slid one bra strap down her arm, watching Nick's eyes follow it. She swung herself up on to the bed, then straddled him.

'And the whore in the bedroom?' She spoke lightly, pressing down against him.

'Perhaps I'll decide that later.' His eyes were half closed.

Lu leaned forward to kiss him, their mouths exploring. She could feel Nick's hands on her hips. And in the background, vaguely, a noise.

Nick heard it too. He stopped kissing her and turned his head towards the door.

'It's nothing,' Lu said, kissing round his neck and shoulders, trailing her hair so that it tickled him. 'Nothing.'

Nick reached up and held her head to his, his arms strong and powerful, his mouth hungry for her.

A creak outside the door. Then . . .

'Dad . . .'

In one swift move, Nick pushed Lu off him so she sprawled on the far side of the bed, then swung the duvet over both their bodies as the door opened.

'What is it?'

'I don't feel well.' Tom looked small by the door, his hair tousled and his toes peeping out from his pyjama trousers.

Nick rolled on to his elbow away from Lu. 'What's the matter?'

'I feel sick.'

Nick reached over Lu and groped around on the floor for his trousers. 'Hang on.' He slipped them on under the duvet while Lu lay, covers up to her chin, expensive lingerie hidden. 'Let's get you back to bed,' he said to Tom, and ushered the boy from the room.

Lu wondered what she should do, but couldn't think of anything. Tom wanted his father, not her. She remembered the way people had looked at her, either as the hired help, or assuming she was some home-wrecker. It simply wasn't fair.

Nick came back after a few minutes. 'Sorry about that. He's just a bit overexcited,' he said, undressing and getting into bed again. He slid his hand across her belly. 'Now, where were we?'

Lu rolled towards him. 'We were discussing whether I was a whore or a cook.'

'Or both,' Nick said. His hand traced the line of her bra, then slipped inside. 'This is very fetching underwear you nearly have on. I think I need to examine it more closely.' She hooked her leg over his hip, drawing his body close to her as he bent his

211

head to her breast, his tongue encircling her nipple. She rolled her head backwards, feeling the waves of pleasure fluttering at her insides, like being tickled internally by feathers. His hand moved further downwards. Oh but she loved him, she loved what he was doing to her, do that again, oh, yes please, she loved—

'Dad,' wailed a small voice. 'Daddy.'

Nick stopped. 'Shit.'

Their eyes met. No, Lu's said.

The voice wailed again. 'Daddy, I need you.'

Nick made a 'what can I do?' gesture with his shoulders. 'Sorry.'

Lu slumped back, her eyes shut. 'It's not your fault,' she said.

'I'll be back in a minute.' Lu felt him get out of bed and pad across the room, the door opening and closing. Jeez, but she'd been on the brink. Bugger bugger bugger. She rolled up into the duvet, trying to stay mentally in the right place so they could pick up where they'd left off when Nick came back.

Nick didn't come back.

Eventually she got up, pulled his sweater over her head and stomped downstairs to the landing. The light was on in the bathroom. She pushed the door open to see Nick on his hands and knees cleaning up vomit. Hedwig, by the look of it. It had got everywhere. Sheets and a Batman duvet cover were bundled up in the bath.

'Is he okay?'

Nick nodded. 'He seems to have dropped off to sleep. Probably better out than in.'

Lu looked around. It was certainly out. 'Have you got another cloth?'

Silently Nick handed her a cloth and she started scrubbing the wall, thinking it was a pity someone had decided to only tile halfway up it. If only they'd had the foresight to anticipate projectile vomiting by an excitable eight year old. It didn't half stain the plaster. Hopefully it was just the excitement and not food poisoning. The last thing she needed was to be sued. The only plus was the thought of projectile vomiting going on in all those other houses, especially those of the smug women.

Nick looked up and winked at her. 'And who says true romance is dead?'

Lu smiled back at him, because she knew he was trying, but she couldn't say a thing.

Chapter 11

Everybody was fretful the day after the birthday party. Tom seemed to have recovered from his vomiting, but was bug-eyed from lack of sleep. Ben arrived back from his sleepover, which seemed to have featured a lot of computer games and not much sleep. Nick made lunch, but because he'd been running late, Tom and Ben had snacked on party leftovers and didn't want to eat anything, which made Nick first short-tempered and then guilty, so that after lunch, instead of helping Lu with the clearing up, he went to help Tom build a model while Ben did some homework in the sitting room.

Lu found herself with her hands in the sink, wishing that Nick had a dishwasher. They were waterlogged by the time she'd finished, Nick not having anything as sensible as washing-up gloves. She flicked through the Sunday papers. The main article was about yummy mummies. She slapped the paper down. What a waste of time, given that to be one it helped if you'd started off looking like Elle Macpherson or Claudia Schiffer. I could be partying with Damien Hirst, she thought. I could be having lunch in St Ives. She could just picture them all sitting in the sunshine outside some colourful fishermen's pub, the sea breeze ruffling their hair, eating delicious but simple food and drinking chilled white wine. They were out having fun, while she was stuck inside reading about people having fun.

I'm bored, she thought, looking round for something to do. There was a great mound of clean clothing waiting to be ironed. She picked up a pair of small underpants, then dropped them back. I must be mad to even be thinking of it, she thought. It was bad enough having to wash up non-stop, let alone start on the ironing. Restless, she went upstairs to see what Nick was doing. She stopped outside Tom's door, listening to them talking. They were obviously having a good time, father and son bonding over model-building. She felt like an interloper.

She traipsed downstairs again and went back to the Sunday papers. She could of course go home, but she didn't want to go home, she wanted to have a nice time with Nick. Our time. I want some quality time too, she thought, putting the kettle on for a cup of tea. While waiting for the kettle to boil, she picked at Hedwig's buttercream icing until she felt sick like Tom.

Finally, finally Nick and Tom emerged and they

all went out for a walk, despite Ben's complaints. Tom ran ahead and Ben trailed behind, and for a few moments Lu was alone with Nick.

'Do you think I look tarty?' she asked.

'You? Of course not. You look great,' he said, slipping his hand around her waist. 'Why?'

'I just wondered,' she said, kicking at a bit of branch on the path in front of them. 'I didn't feel I fitted in terribly well yesterday with those people.'

'I hardly know them myself,' Nick said. 'They're just Tom's friends' parents, that's all.'

'Oh. I thought they were friends of yours and Morwenna's.'

'Not particularly. I know who they are and we've been round to supper with a couple in the past, but . . .' Nick shrugged as if that was all that needed to be said. Perhaps it was. He began to talk about some work problem, and Lu listened with half an ear, fed up with office politics. She didn't know how Nick managed to keep his enthusiasm going, she thought darkly. Except that he was always enthusiastic. She had to admit that sometimes that could get annoying.

*   *   *

When they got back to the house, Tom revealed that he hadn't begun his homework and that if he didn't finish a project he hadn't actually got round to starting he would be in serious trouble.

'Morwenna could have said something,' Lu said, tight-lipped.

'Perhaps she didn't know. You wouldn't be a love and make supper, would you?'

'I was thinking of going back home.'

215

Nick looked stricken. 'It's not that late, is it?'

'No, but . . . I'll go after supper. You help Tom.'

He quickly explained what he'd been planning to cook, kissed her forehead and went, leaving her yet again in the kitchen.

She tipped the sausages into the pan and they started sizzling nicely. Broccoli and mashed potato, Nick had said. She could do that. She started peeling the potatoes, and it occurred to her that she should have started with them, because they took ages to cook. She put the sausages on to a lower heat; they would have plenty of time to cook through. Where was Nick? She craned her neck in case she could hear him somewhere, but there was nothing except the sound of Armageddon coming loudly from the sitting room.

She walked through to find Ben perched on the edge of the sofa, furiously zapping something on the Xbox.

'Ben, you couldn't come and help with supper, please?' Lu said in a pleasant voice. Ben gave no sign of having heard her, so she repeated the question. 'Would you like to help with supper, please?'

'Can't—I've just got to the ninth level,' Ben mumbled, still intent on the screen. Thud thud thud went the missiles.

'Sorry?' Her own heart was going thud thud thud too, she realised. What if he refused again?

Ben glanced at her, a look of extraordinary annoyance, then hunched over the console with even more intense concentration. 'I'm busy,' he hissed. 'Go away.'

Lu's jaw dropped. What now? She'd asked nicely; he ought to come and help. Otherwise she was going to have to be the little woman slaving alone in the kitchen so the men could eat. But she didn't know what to do in the face of his intransigence. She thought of snatching the console from him. She thought of turning the power off. She thought of whacking him over the head with a saucepan. They all seemed good ideas—if she wanted World War III to materialise in Nick's sitting room as well as on the Xbox.

'Right,' Lu said. 'I'm going to tell your father.' It sounded pathetic even to her, like sneaking at school. She despised sneaks. She bit her lip. She wasn't Ben's mother. She didn't want to be his mother. She just wanted him to help out. That wasn't an unreasonable thing to ask. She stared at the back of his head, but he'd got some invisible force field that stopped him registering her presence. It was all very well taming lions by showing no fear, but it wasn't quite as easy-peasy as she'd thought to control a ten-year-old boy intent on a computer game.

'I'm telling your father,' Lu repeated, and flounced into the hall, aware that it had to be the weakest exit line in history. One unexpected bonus of Malcolm's disappearance was that at least Pixie could never say it. She paused at the foot of the stairs. Had she been as difficult as Ben? As intransigent?

She went upstairs, muttering to herself that she wasn't Ben's mother and that Nick should sort him out. It was outrageous that he was getting away with not helping—and he was being rude to her. She flung open Tom's door, but neither Nick nor Tom were anywhere to be seen.

Perhaps they'd gone out to the car. Lu stomped

217

back downstairs and hovered in the hall, torn about what to do. Physically hoicking Ben out of the sitting room like a snail from its shell seemed a definite step too far. She'd just have to manage on her own. She went back to the kitchen, where the large saucepan full of water was boiling furiously, steaming up the windows.

How many potatoes did one need anyway? Didn't boys eat continuously? She'd better do lots. Nick's potato peeler dug into her hand. It was old, and she longed for her economically designed one that peeled smoothly. Still, you couldn't have everything.

There, that had to be enough potatoes. She tipped the peelings into the garbage, then checked the saucepan. The water was bubbling away nicely, just like her temper. She flung in handfuls of the peeled potatoes, squeaking as the hot water splashed. Then she put another saucepan of water on for the broccoli and started on the table. The stripped pine top looked as homely as a Boden ad. She put out cutlery for the four of them, just like any other nuclear family, all the while simmering with resentment. Ben ought to be doing this. It wasn't much to ask, a pretty small contribution. She jerked open the drawer that had the candles in it and shoved them into the candlesticks. Okay, so she'd rather it was a candle lit supper for just her and Nick, but there was no reason to lower her standards just because there were children present. Not her children either.

Candles lit, she went back to the stove, where the potatoes had come back to the boil. She gave them a prod. Rock solid. She tried to remember when she'd put them in—was it five or ten minutes ago?

Eventually Nick came through. 'I think I've managed to find the answers,' he said, swiping a handful of olives. 'Tom will live.'

'My hero,' Lu said, giving him a kiss. He really was very handsome, she thought, running her hands over his back. 'Where have you been? I wanted you to . . .' She couldn't think of a way to explain without sounding like a whingeing sneak.

'You wanted me to what?' Nick murmured.

Lu pushed him away and went back to the stove. 'Nothing.'

'How's it coming along?' He peered into the frying pan with the sausages. 'Shouldn't these be on a higher heat?'

'What?' The sausages did look very white and flabby, not brown and crispy. 'I suppose so—I'm not used to your cooker,' Lu said, turning up the heat so that the fat started to spit and the sausages hiss.

'Potatoes look done,' Nick continued. She could have murdered him.

Bits of potato were bobbing on the surface of the water. 'Right.' She grabbed the pan, and carted it to the sink. 'Do you have a colander?'

'Errr—in here.' Nick pulled out a colander from a corner cupboard. Lu poured out the potatoes, watching them disintegrate into a sodden mass. No need to wonder if they were ready or not.

'Dad,' came a wail. 'Dad—can you come and help?'

Nick looked at Lu. 'Can you manage?'

'Of course,' she said through gritted teeth. 'It'll be ready in five minutes.'

'Dad,' came the wail, even higher-pitched than

219

before. 'Come here!'

'Duty calls.' Nick grinned apologetically, then loped out of the kitchen.

Damn, she'd forgotten to put on the broccoli. Leaving the potatoes in a soggy white mush in the kitchen sink, she chucked the broccoli into the pan. There was no time to wash it, and besides, logically, boiling water would kill off any lingering germs. The sausages still looked pink and flabby, despite the fat in the pan resembling treacle. The heat was on max. Why weren't they going brown? She dug the packaging out of the bin and looked at it, but there were no clues to be found there beyond the promise that they only needed fifteen minutes in a pan, being turned once. She turned them over, but the undersides were resolutely pale as sunbathers on the first day of the holidays. Perhaps they'd brown up while she made the mash.

She tipped the potatoes back into the pan, where they splatted against the sides, and searched the drawers for a masher, not that it looked as if they needed such a thing. Oh well, she'd have to make do with a fork. She started mashing the potatoes up, the fork scraping the sides of the pan like nails on a blackboard. She dropped in a knob of butter, then a dash of milk. At least that was what she intended, but as she poured, the milk gave a sudden lurch and spurted out. She stirred it in. The mash was resembling a thick soup. She'd just have to call it creamed potatoes and leave it at that. Now for the broccoli.

Da-dah! Out of the saucepan and into the colander, perfectamundo, so long as you ignored the little green florets left on the sides that showed she'd overcooked the broccoli too. Why was it

220

always so difficult in someone else's kitchen? You'd have thought putting stuff in a pot of boiling water would be the same everywhere in the world. She tipped the broccoli into a bowl, then half spooned, half poured the mash into another. The sausages were still not done. How long could sausages possibly take? She could heat the plates while she was waiting, she supposed. She found four dinner plates and ran hot water into the sink, then let it out again as the surface had little white and green specks on it. A quick swish round the bowl, then more hot water. She dropped the plates into the sink, and put the vegetable dishes out on the table. 'Supper!' she called up the stairs. 'Come and get it.'

Footsteps upstairs demonstrated that she'd been heard. She went back into the kitchen and pulled the now warm plates out of the sink, rubbing them quickly with a tea towel. The sausages were a pale biscuit shade. It would have to do; they'd been cooking for twice their allocated time at least.

Nick and Tom turned up, Tom heading straight for his place. 'Why have we got candles?' he said.

'Because it's nice,' Lu said, her smile straight out of the 1950s.

'Does Ben know it's supper?' Nick asked.

'I don't know,' Lu said, bright as polished steel. 'Why don't you call him?'

'Ben!' Nick bellowed towards the sitting room. 'Supper!'

Lu slapped the sausages on to the plates, then distributed them to the four places. 'Help yourself to veg,' she said. Tom looked suspiciously at the pale sausages but didn't say anything. Lu sat down. She wasn't going to say anything either. Nick also seemed to have gone quiet as he spooned mash on to his and Tom's plates.

Ben came in and slumped into his seat. 'Have some veg,' Nick said, dishing out broccoli for everyone. It slopped suspiciously on to the plates. The silence was equally suspicious. So? Lu thought. I can't cook. I do restaurants, not family dinners. It's food. What's your problem? But as Ben, Tom and Nick weren't saying anything, neither did she.

Ben broke the silence. 'Where's the gravy?'

'There isn't any,' Nick said. 'Eat up, Ben, or it'll get cold.'

Ben sat back. 'You can't have sausages without gravy.'

Lu looked across at Nick for support, but he didn't say anything. 'Not everyone has gravy with their sausages.'

'We do,' Ben said, looking towards his father.

'Well I don't,' Lu snapped.

Ben gave a disgruntled noise. 'And they're not cooked,' he said, prodding one of his sausages.

'Fine,' Lu said, getting up and whisking Ben's plate from under his nose. 'You don't need to have them.' She marched to the dustbin, flipped the lid up, and swept the sausages into the bin. Then she came back and slapped the empty plate under Ben's nose.

'Lu . . .' Nick said.

Ben looked round, aghast. 'What's she done that for?'

'I'm sorry if my cooking doesn't make the grade,' Lu said, her voice tight with control. 'You should have come to help instead of expecting to be waited on hand and foot.'

'What about my supper?' Ben looked horrified at the thought of no food.

'Here, have mine.' Nick passed his plate over to Ben, taking the empty one away. 'I'll make some gravy.'

Lu stared at him as he got up and started rummaging in the cupboards. Was he deliberately undermining her? He made the gravy from powder as Ben and Tom sat in silence, the food congealing on their plates. Lu decided she would demonstrate that yes, sausages could be eaten without gravy. Her knife and fork scraped unnaturally loudly on her plate.

Nick came back with a jug and smothered the boys' sausages with a brown blanket. It did look more appealing. Lu declined his offer, but she nudged one of her sausages over to his plate.

Nick shook his head. 'I'm not hungry,' he said tersely.

Lu stared at her plate, not hungry either. She'd never seen him angry before. He was always so outward-going, but now he was contained and quiet, the air vibrating with controlled anger. He wouldn't meet her eyes. I'm the one who should be angry, she thought to herself, not you. It's not me who's at fault. But his inward control scared her. The boys picked up on it, eating quickly though without apparent pleasure. When they'd finished, Nick cleared their plates and gave them a KitKat each, although Lu knew he'd planned an apple pie he'd bought from the village WI and ice cream. The boys scarpered, chairs scraping back, a harsh, grating sound.

Lu waited for the storm to break.

Nick leaned back on his chair, his hands on the

223

table. His eyes were hard. 'Was that really necessary?'

His voice was icy cold, and Lu's anger surged up to meet it. 'Why is it my fault? Excuse me, he's not the one who's cooked for you all single-handedly, without an ounce of help from anyone else, and I did all the party food and was treated like a bimbo or the hired help, or ignored, with no thanks from anyone, and then . . . and then I've had to put up with rudeness. And you, you didn't back me up.'

'You're behaving like a spoilt brat—you threw the child's food away.'

'I don't think I'm the spoilt brat around here.'

Nick took a sharp intake of breath. 'What did you say?'

'You wait on them hand and foot, you run around after them, you spend all your time and energy on them . . .'

Nick stood up. 'They're my children,' he shouted at her across the table.

'They're not mine,' Lu shouted back.

The words reverberated round the kitchen. Suddenly she could smell the scent of defeat in the air.

Nick rubbed his forehead. 'I'm sorry if you thought Ben was rude to you, but he wasn't really. He was just being a normal ten year old.'

Lu shivered. 'I want you to put me first.'

Nick let his arm drop as if defeated and turned away from her.

'I want to be first with you,' she repeated. Her hands hung limply by her sides.

'They're my children,' he said, without looking at her.

'So they've got to come first, without question.

Is that it?' She felt sick.

'Don't ask me to choose,' Nick said, shaking his head. 'I love you. Don't ask me to choose.'

And the heat had gone from them, and nothing was left except sadness and loss.

'I love you too,' Lu said. Tears were making salty tracks down her face. 'But I want to come first.'

Nick ran his hands through his hair. 'If you had children . . .'

'Don't tell me—I'd understand,' and the bitterness of the words stung her tongue.

'They're my children,' Nick said again, not meeting her eyes.

'And I come second.' She'd known that from the start. She sat down with a thump, suddenly thinking she might be sick. No, the pain inside wasn't nausea, it was like having her guts skewered by ravenous seagulls. She tipped forward, holding on to her knees. 'I can't leave you,' she said.

Nick knelt by her, his arms around her. 'You don't have to,' he said, tears in his voice.

'You're a good father and you love them, and that's how it should be. But I'll always be second, and I want to be first with someone. I want to be first with you, but I know I can't ask that from you, it wouldn't be right: they're your children and you love them, but I love you so much and I want to be loved by you in the same way, but you can't, you can't,' she sobbed.

'No, no, don't say that,' he murmured into her hair. 'I do love you.'

'But you love them more.'

'As well, not more. As well,' he said, his grip tightening around her. 'Don't leave me. I love you.'

'Hold me,' she whispered, thinking that this was the last time, the last time she would ever see him, touch him, that this was the end. She had to remember everything about him, to keep in her heart. The feel of his hands on her back, the feel of his sweater rough against her cheek as she pressed her face into his shoulder, the way she fitted perfectly into his arms. She wanted to stay there for ever, safe within his loving arms. But the pain was too strong, a buzzing in her head, driving her forward. He loved her, but he couldn't put her first. And she couldn't ask him to, because if he did, it would destroy the man he was, the man she loved, loyal and true, a good father. The best father. She squeezed her eyes tight shut, wanting the future to vanish, wanting only to stay like this with Nick for ever, the rest of the world shut out and excluded, no future, only them together in their own world. If only they could have stayed in France, the world of falling in love, the two of them discovering, exploring, delighting in each other. Nick was the man she loved because of his children; they had shaped him as much as he had shaped her. 'I love you,' she mouthed silently into his shoulder. 'I love you, I love you, I love you. I'll always love you.'

*   *   *

She collected her things together quietly and put them in her overnight bag. There wasn't much to collect as it turned out. She had made hardly any impression on his life, she thought. There wouldn't be much of a Lu-shaped hole to fill. She was quiet,

226

feeling that all the life had been sucked out of her. Perhaps there came a point where there were no emotions left. Or perhaps she was holding herself in because she knew that the only emotion left to her was pain. I can't believe I'm going, she thought, picking her case up and taking it down the stairs.

Nick was waiting in the hall. 'Don't go,' he said.

She shook her head. 'I have to.'

His face contracted in a twinge of pain. 'I love you.'

'But not enough. No,' she added quickly, putting a finger to his mouth. 'It's my fault, not yours. I want all of you, and I know I can't have that. It's best like this.'

'Best?' Nick turned his head away from her and stared at the ceiling, the skin around his eyes red.

'Don't cry,' Lu said, trying to smile, but her mouth went down instead of up. 'It *is* best. Otherwise we're going to have this argument again and again until we exhaust all the love we have.' She gave him a hug, allowing herself one last delicious moment against his body before pulling away. 'Look after yourself.'

'And you.' He touched her cheek, and she pressed her hand to his for another stolen moment before turning and going quickly through the front door. Her feet carried her down the path, not looking back; she didn't think she could carry on, but she got to her car, and there were her car keys in her hand. She hesitated for a second, but then unlocked the door and got in. Engine on, slip into gear, disengage the handbrake, one last look at him standing by the cottage, beloved Nick, her life, her everything, and then her foot pressed the

227

accelerator and the car moved ahead and on to the road, and he was left behind.

Chapter 12

You can get over this, Lu told herself. It hurts, of course it hurts, because you are only human, but it was the right thing to do. You always knew it would end, because he was never Mr Right. You knew that from the start. And breaking up hurts. But it had to be done at some point. Better now than a few years down the line. Better now.

'No no no,' she howled, hugging her knees into her chest and rocking backwards and forwards. 'Not now. Not never. I want him. I want him.' And the tears would start again until she was exhausted.

The weight dropped off. Another morning, another couple of pounds. But all she felt was a mild curiosity at her body's reactions; she couldn't get excited about it. She thought she'd never get excited about anything ever again. The shell of Lu went through the motions of being a living person, but inside she was hollow and dry.

One day this too will pass.

She liked to say the phrase when things were bad. One day this too will pass. But oh, she'd never felt half this much pain over previous break-ups, especially given that she was the one who had left Nick. The summer decided to chime in with her mood by raining every day. Outside, it was bleak and grey. Inside . . .

Yes, it would pass, one day. And the answer, as it always had been, was work. Lu had meant to develop her own website some day, instead of relying on Yolanda. It seemed that 'some day' was today. She bought a domain name, found a hosting site, began designing her pages, uploading images of work she'd done. It was absorbing and took time, both of which were desirable in her current state.

She also began work on a range of greetings cards inspired by Scottie. This meant comforting afternoons at Delia's sketching Scottie in a variety of positions. There was Noble Scottie (watching television), Alert Scottie (Delia waving a biscuit behind Lu's head), Cute Scottie (Delia rattling the biscuit tin in the kitchen), Athlete Scottie (neighbour's cat in garden), Scruffy Scottie (scratching his ear with his hind leg, something he needed no prompting to do), and Sleeping Scottie (default position).

After the sketching sessions, all three of them would settle down to tea and biscuits, and then Delia would have her computer lesson. Lu had decided that her grandmother would enjoy becoming a Silver Surfer, despite her arthritic hands, if they just took it really slowly. They were already inching towards Internet competence. There had been a small setback because none of Delia's homework was ever saved, even though she swore she'd done it. Lu privately suspected a cyber version of 'Scottie ate my homework', but the problem was solved when she discovered that Delia hadn't grasped how to turn off the computer, and, in the absence of a button marked 'off', had been gaily pulling the plug out from the wall. She also signed Delia up for a course on Computing for the Terrified: Complete Beginners at the local university. She had a feeling that it was going to be the instructor who would be terrified, because Delia was doubtful of the merits of taking the course, but there it was. Her grandmother would join the twenty-first century even if Lu had to drive her there every week.

Lu also persuaded Delia to tell Pixie about the adoption. Pixie reacted with a mixture of astonishment and chagrin that Lu hadn't seen before. Lu felt horribly guilty about having known before Pixie, until she realised that some of Pixie's reactions were less about being excluded and more about the fact that her predictions regarding Delia's personality, based on her birth chart, were now shown to be founded on what Pixie called misleading information (always said with narrowed eyes), as if Delia had been deliberately trying to catch astrology out.

And then there was Arthur. Lu's drawings now took on a harder, sharper tone. Arthur's face had the same innocent freshness it had always had, but the lines she drew were harsher, the blacks blacker. She didn't know who she was drawing for, only that there was a story emerging from under her pen. The story helped her to stop thinking about Nick.

It was the right thing to do. He had children.

She had to say it aloud ten times, twenty times, a thousand times a day like a mantra. Come on, Lu, she told herself. You've made tough decisions before, and it's always been for the best. You should have stuck to the list. That was your problem. Were children ever on the list? No. No. A million times no.

Stick to the list.

230

Lu paused. Was she really being successful by sticking to the list? Here she was, her heart breaking yet again. Perhaps she should be rethinking her approach. She thought back to all the men she'd discarded for what had seemed like such good reasons at the time. Had they really been that bad?

Not really. Sometimes the reasons why she'd split up with them seemed trivial and superficial, almost as if she were looking for a problem. She shook her head. That way madness lay. It wasn't her fault that they were useless. It was like looking at houses. You only wanted to live in one, so it was right to carry on looking until you found the perfect one. No one thought it was odd when people moved house, trading up. Where was the difference with men?

She took a deep breath. If Nick wasn't Mr Right, there were plenty of others out there. She didn't need to lower her standards, go out with someone who had obvious flaws—like children—because the right man was waiting for her.

It was strange how the pep talk didn't work as well this time. She had to admit to herself that Nick had got under her skin more than she'd bargained for. She couldn't think why—he'd got hardly any of the qualities on the list. And he had children.

Lu got up from her drawing desk and searched in her bag for her sketchpad. She flipped through it, hunting for something she could remember drawing. It was Tom. In the drawing his cheeks were round, his hair sticking up on end, the line of his skull beautifully shaped. He was a lovely child, she thought, remembering how scared he'd been on the death slide. How scared she'd been, for that matter. But they'd done it. They'd conquered their fears and gone over the top. She rubbed her elbow. It had hurt, but she'd done it. And Tom had then done it again and again. At least she'd made some contribution. She wondered if, in time, when the family went back to Longleat, or some other adventure playground, Tom would remember Lu, who had helped him get over his fear. Probably not. She would become some girl whose life had briefly touched theirs, and who had then gone again, not leaving a mark.

She started to cry, sliding down the wall until she was crouched in a foetal position, overcome with the pain of leaving, playing out that last dreadful day, wishing she could go back and change it somewhere, she didn't know where, so that she was with Nick and they could be happy again. She felt she would never be happy again, ever.

*   *   *

The crying stopped, because it always did. Lu gradually came back to herself, emotionally wrung out, washed clean as an empty jam jar. She stood and stretched, even though she felt a thousand years old, her body sore and tired. Her elbows felt sharp in her palms as she clasped her arms around her body, finding some comfort from her own touch. One day this too will pass. Well, it was taking a bloody long time to do it, frankly.

It would be great if you could just fast-forward some bits of your life. She was sure that in six months' time she would be with someone new and looking back on this time of grieving over Nick as if it had happened to someone else. Three months even. Leaving always hurt, but she'd got over it in the past, and she'd get over it again. She frowned, remembering that it didn't usually hurt quite this badly.

Perhaps I'm just getting old, she thought. Maybe heartbreak is like hangovers, getting worse as you get older. Or maybe Nick had mattered more than she cared to admit. But I knew he was wrong from the start, she told herself. She needed a new list, a What Is Wrong With Nick list. She took out a clean sheet of paper from the drawer under her desk, chose her favourite black gel pen and began.

He's untidy.

He's a bit scruffy.

He's always cheerful—which is unbelievably irritating sometimes. She smiled inwardly, thinking that if Nick were reading this he'd be protesting that she could have been describing Scottie. And he's funny, she added. And charming. And he licks his fingers in the kitchen when he thinks I'm not looking. And looks guilty when I catch him out. And when he smiles his eyes light up and he gets a little crease down the side of his cheek that isn't there otherwise, and . . . Lu touched her own cheek, remembering, then shook herself. This wasn't what she was supposed to be doing.

What Is Wrong With Nick.

He's broke.

He has an ex-wife.

He has children.

He has children.

He has children.

That was what she needed to remember, not all

the other stuff. He has children, and that's not what I want. Even though the boys were all right most of the time. Actually, looking back, she'd enjoyed being with them; even playing football with them had been fun until Ben had tripped her. She looked at the drawing of Tom. Perhaps she had over-reacted a bit. And about the cooking. So silly, to break up over sausages and gravy. She could feel the sadness starting to seep into her mind, like smoke insinuating itself under a door.

But Ben will get worse, she rallied, chasing the sadness away. Ben will become a teenager and so will Tom and they will be ghastly, grunting, reeking beasts, and you really really don't want to be dealing with that.

There. She inhaled deeply. The depression had gone. Nick looked far less attractive now, sandwiched by two leering behemoths of Satan. It was the right thing to do.

*   *   *

'I am never going out with a man with children EVER again,' Lu said to Briony as they stood in the queue for the Banksy exhibition. She had heard that the exhibition at Bristol City Art Gallery was popular and that the queues had been lengthening over the summer, but she hadn't expected it to take quite so long. They'd already been waiting for half an hour, and it looked as if it might take another half-hour to get to the entrance.

Briony raised her eyebrows. 'That's a bit extreme,' she said.

'No.' Lu shook her head. 'No, no, no, no, no. I

mustn't do it. It's a bad idea. I should have just said no.'

'But I thought you liked Nick,' Briony said.

'I did.' Lu felt her face crumple. Oh Nick. Why hadn't she met him earlier, before he'd had children? But she couldn't cry here, not in the queue. She pulled herself together. 'I always knew he wasn't Mr Right, so I should never have started it.'

Briony put her arm around Lu's shoulder. 'You always said that, but I thought you two were getting along so well it didn't matter.'

'We were getting along well. He's lovely. But his children are always going to come first.'

Briony gave a snort. 'What do you expect? He wouldn't be much of a dad if they didn't.'

'I know.' Lu stuck her hand out, wondering if it was going to rain on them. Moisture was definitely in the air. 'But they're not my children, are they, and they won't ever be. And I want to be first for my partner. I don't want to be shunted off into the sidelines as if I'm disposable, someone who doesn't matter.' The knot in her stomach tightened. She had wanted to matter to Nick so much. And he had mattered to her. 'I really tried,' she said. 'I went to Longleat with them, I made cakes, I played football. I wanted them to like me.'

'But they did, didn't they?' Briony looked up at the sky. 'I bet it starts raining before we get in.'

Lu didn't care about the rain. If anything, it suited her mood. 'I think they did like me. I liked them. It's funny, but I miss them a bit. Their energy and optimism and innocence. But . . .' She stopped, wondering how she could explain it to

235

Briony, especially when she hadn't worked out how she could explain it to herself. 'I felt like I was never part of their unit. Nick had a side to him that I could never be part of, and when he was with them, I was always excluded.'

'What else did you expect? To become the boys' mother?' Briony rummaged in her bag. 'Drat, it is going to rain, and I've forgotten my umbrella. Have you got one?'

Lu shook her head. 'No, I didn't think to bring one.' A big blot of rain dropped on Lu's face, then another. 'I knew I wasn't their mother, and I wouldn't have wanted to be.'

'So what are you complaining about?'

'I'm not complaining . . . okay, I am complaining. I suppose I felt I couldn't ever be part of their unit, and I knew that Nick would always put that first. However much he loved me, when the chips were down, he would love them more.'

'But it's a different sort of love, surely.' Briony turned up her coat collar. 'Was Nick upset too?'

'Yes, of course. It was ghastly. And it hurts.' The rain came down, the sort of fine rain that makes you think it isn't really raining until you realise that you're sopping wet. 'God, Briony, it hurts so bad. I feel as if I've sawn off my legs, my arms with a rusty hacksaw.'

'Perhaps you can get back together . . .'

Lu shook her head. 'It was the right thing to do.' She didn't want to even think about getting back together. It was such an attractive idea, she'd had to take Nick's number off her mobile to help her resist the temptation to ring him. 'I've been telling myself that so often, I think I should just write it down on a piece of paper and hand it out on the street. It was the right thing to do.'

Wet through, they finally got into the exhibition. Banksy had taken over the museum, so there were two rooms dedicated to his work, and then throughout the rest of the building he had added to or altered one or two exhibits in every room. The gypsy caravan was plastered with parking tickets and eviction notices. A stuffed lamb in the taxidermy section had a little mask over its face, like the one worn by Hannibal Lecter in *The Silence of the Lambs*, while a few cases along, a beaver displayed a shiny gold cup for salmon fishing. Lu and Briony had serious conversations about whether the exhibition was art or merely a series of clever and amusing jokes; about the merits of conceptual art and what was the point of art anyway, but as they went round, Lu found herself drawn more to watching the children than the art. They ran around the museum excitedly, finding the Banksy exhibits in each room as if it were part of some huge treasure hunt or spot the difference competition. Tom and Ben would have loved it, she thought, appreciating the look on the faces of a group of boys as they spotted the phallus lurking among a group of authentic stalagmites. Perhaps she should email Nick and tell him about it, suggest it might be worth braving the queues sometime in the summer holidays. She shoved her hands deep in her damp pockets. No. Not to be thought of. It was over. It was for the best. It was the right thing to do.

*   *   *

An enquiry came via the website. An American publisher was looking for an illustrator. They'd seen some of her previous work, had tracked down her website. It was a good job they were offering, a picture book. Lu wondered where she stood regarding Yolanda, but she hadn't heard from Yolanda since turning down the second Sugarsnap contract. Perhaps she should have grovelled, but on the other hand, perhaps not. There were two sorts of break-up, she thought wryly. Those that ended with a bang and those that ended with a whimper. It looked as if the ending with Yolanda had happened, and she hadn't even noticed. She emailed the American publisher saying yes, she was free, and could they send the brief over. It would keep her in work for the next few months. There were also the Scottie cards to try to sell, and then there was Arthur.

Lu flicked through the pages. It was nearly done now. One of the questions she was sometimes asked at school demonstrations was how did she know a book was finished? Sometimes you thought it needed more work and went on, and then it was spoiled. Other times you thought it was finished, but then later—perhaps even after it had been published—you realised that it had needed more work. Lu knew that the more time she had with a project, the better she could judge if it was finished or not, and as she gained more experience she made fewer errors of judgement. Still, it was a tough call.

Especially when you didn't want to send it out. It was a strange thing. As long as the book was at home, on her drawing board, she felt it was safe. And of course it was, tucked away from any rejection and dismissal, removed from critical voices. She stroked the painting in front of her. Let's face it: it was done. There was nothing more to do beyond scan it and make up a dummy.

Scanning the pictures in always took more time than she expected, and so did dropping the text into the spaces she'd deliberately left in the artwork. Printing out the pages was the easy bit. She laid them out in order along the floor. Now to make them up into a book. Using rectangles of cardboard cut from a plain white shoebox, she made the front and back covers, binding the rough edges with masking tape, plus a long thin rectangle that was to be the spine, then taped them together to make one piece. She glued the cover pictures into position, tucking the edges over and hiding them with more paper, then sat back and admired her work. She now had a cover.

On to the insides. She compiled the book, putting the pages in order and back to back. The full illustrations were at the beginning, two paintings across each spread so that when the book was opened they made one long image. It was years since she'd made up a dummy, but the skills came back as the afternoon passed.

By the evening she had something that resembled a book, with illustrated covers and the first three spreads also fully worked, and the remainder in rough form. It was enough to give an art director a feel for how she saw the finished product.

Here were the boys setting off for war, their heads held high, joking, laughing. Then reality started to bite: the trenches, the misery of the weather, the mud. One of the older men she'd drawn had been based on the footage she'd seen at the Imperial War Museum, but she realised now she'd drawn him as Jack, the tilt of the head she'd seen in the photograph repeated here. He was cheerful, encouraging to young Arthur, and as she looked, she realised that in Arthur she had drawn Tom as he might become: the same line of the skull, the same rounded cheek, although that became more hollow as the book went on. The lines of gravestones rose unbidden in her head. So many of them had been Known Unto God. Those boys, those lovely boys with all their potential, lying apart from their families, lost to the world. She wiped a tear away, careful not to let it fall on the page and spoil the illustration.

It was all futile. Her efforts were utterly ridiculous. It was a stupid idea. Who on earth would want to read about the First World War in picture book format? It wasn't going to be for little children, and adults could read proper books about the war, books written by experts, not someone who hadn't even got history GCSE. Lu went to the kitchen and filled the kettle, the water spurting angrily out of the tap and splashing back at her. She'd wasted her time, she'd wasted the whole of the summer; in fact the whole year had been a complete waste of time. She hadn't even been able to track down Anne for Delia.

And she'd wasted time on a man she'd known was wrong for her right from the start. Nick was off with his boys and she deserved someone who put her first. It was what she wanted: someone without children, someone who didn't want children. Nick was lovely, but Nick was the past; he was as dead to her as Jack was. She gripped the worktop, knuckles aching with the effort. I will not get upset over Nick, I will not, I will not. Not ever again. It was the right thing to do. He is wrong for me, he was wrong from the start, he doesn't offer what I want.

She straightened up. I will not waste any more of the year crying over Nick. I will not. She resolutely shoved Nick into the furthest corner of her brain, the equivalent of a disused croft on an Outer Hebridean island. The kettle had boiled, so she made herself a cup of tea and went back into the sitting room. The dummy of the book lay open. She looked at it with a distant eye. What a silly thing to have wasted her time on. Well, she had, and that was all there was to it. She might as well send it out and then she could forget about it, concentrate on building her career up again.

It was the beginning of September, autumn was starting; she could smell it in the air, clean and fresh with a hint of woodsmoke. September meant the harvest was gathered in; it was a time for new beginnings: schoolchildren in uniform too big for them playing conkers, if boys played conkers still. Ben and Tom would have known. Ben . . . He was going to start his new school this term, moving up from being a big fish in the small village primary school to being an insignificant minnow in the scarily big secondary school on the edge of Bath. She shut her eyes for a second, sending a silent wish into the ether that he would be safe and happy.

New beginnings. She settled back at the computer and began to write.

241

Dear X,

I am writing in the hope that you would be interested in publishing my book *The Boy Who Went to War*. It is an illustrated picture book aimed at the 7+ market and is about the young boys who enlisted in the First World War . . .

As she typed, she shook her head. Who on earth would be interested in this? It was the wrong market, the wrong age, the wrong everything. No, the sooner she got rid of this stupid idea and went back to her usual work, the better.

She dug out her index box and flicked through the cards of all her professional contacts. Editors, editors, editors . . . Who to send it to? Who on earth might be so foolish as to give this a second glance? She shook her head. She'd been in the business for more than ten years; she really should know better. Her finger stopped at Veronica Meadows, one of the best-known children's book editors, who published all the big names. Lu had met her a couple of times at professional gatherings, but had never had the nerve to send her anything. Far too grand for the likes of me, she thought, although she could hear Nick in her head urging her on, saying aim high, don't be defeatist. But Nick had gone. He'd been a dead end, and she'd known that from the start. Her finger moved on. She found several names and drew up a list. Who to try first? Ronnie Widnes had been the editor on a project she'd done ages ago. She'd start with her. She went back to her letter and filled in Ronnie's name, then added a quick paragraph about how they'd worked together on a nursery rhyme treasury some years back.

Lu stretched, and printed out the letter. It wasn't brilliant, but it would do. The whole project was a waste of her time, and the sooner she gave it up the better. Still, it was worth a couple of rounds of postage, since she'd spent the time making the dummy. She'd put it in the post tomorrow. And then she'd start something completely new.

Chapter 13

Two months later, as Lu drove along the A36, she gave Delia the occasional nervous glance. It had seemed a good idea at the time, going to the small town where Jack had come from, but now she wasn't so sure. Perhaps it would be too much for her grandmother. It was now nearly five months since Delia had had her wisdom teeth out, and although she appeared to have made a full recovery from the operation, Lu had noticed that the house wasn't quite as immaculate as before. Over the summer she'd hoped it was because Delia was outside gardening rather than doing housework, but it was now November and there were cobwebs in the corner of the sitting room.

Lu didn't deceive herself that Delia was online surfing; she kept saying she didn't see the point of it. She agreed that it was very convenient for looking up train times, but pointed out that as she hardly ever went anywhere by train, the additional convenience was limited. She'd then added that she hardly went anywhere at all nowadays, her shoulders hunched into that shrunken look Lu hated to see. So Lu had suggested this trip. She'd thought it would be a nice afternoon excursion for them both, not too far a drive, a little bit of a wander round the town—there was bound to be somewhere they could get a cup of tea—and then back home. She had just sent off the finished artwork to the American publishers and there were no new jobs on the horizon, so she was free, and it was a clear, bright day, chilly but sunny. So long as Delia kept wrapped up, she'd not get cold.

'Okay, Gran?' Lu asked as they waited at a set of traffic lights.

Delia smoothed her skirt with gnarled fingers. 'Do stop asking me that. I'm as fine as I was five minutes ago, when you last asked me.'

Lu drummed her fingers on the steering wheel, wishing that the lights would hurry up and change. If she turned left here, she'd end up in Nick's village. He wouldn't be there, of course, it was a working day for him. Besides, driving past an ex's house was the sort of stupid, obsessive thing that ditched girlfriends did, not women who were in control of their lives, who knew where they were going.

The lights changed, and Lu suddenly swung left, earning a toot from the car behind her. 'Scenic route,' she said breathlessly to Delia.

It was scenic. The road twisted up and down valleys, the hedgerows bright with scarlet berries. The trees had still got their leaves, a spectrum of red, gold and yellow spiked with the dark greens of the conifers. The fields were either green or freshly ploughed, catching the sun like rippled chocolate. They dropped down one steeper valley and across a ford at the bottom, scattering ducks

244

and a fat white goose, water droplets sparkling. Lu's heart lifted as she drove into Nick's village.

Never had it looked so picture-postcard perfect, hamstone glowing, gardens bursting with the last purple Michaelmas daisies and pink nerines, white daisies like stars across the grass verges. She pulled up on the far side of the green and looked across to Nick's cottage. The terrace glowed in the sunshine like jewels. No sign of his car—she hadn't expected that—but . . . Her heart stopped as she thought she saw movement in the dormer window. No, it had been left open, and the curtains were moving in the breeze.

'Are we there? I thought it was going to be a bigger place.' Delia was looking around and fumbling at her seat belt.

'No. I just thought it was pretty and decided to stop.' Lu's voice was hoarse and came out wrong. She didn't sound like herself. She put the car into first gear and drove on.

Jack's town, when they got there, was a pretty hamstone place with plenty of brightly coloured hanging baskets strung along the fronts of the buildings. Lu imagined that in summer they were strewn with pink and scarlet petunias clashing with blue and white lobelia, but now they boasted variegated trailing ivies. There was a farmers' market here once a month; Nick sometimes used it. Lu pushed him out of her mind, instead clocking a hotel in the centre with a noticeboard outside announcing afternoon cream teas. Sounded right up Delia's street, she thought, parking a little further on, near the church.

They walked the short distance to the church slowly, Lu matching her steps to Delia's pace,

245

Scottie trotting happily beside them. As they got nearer, Lu realised that there was a large war memorial to the front of the churchyard. 'To Our Glorious Dead 1914–1918' was written on the front, with the dates for the Second World War a later addition underneath. It had been Remembrance Sunday a few days before, and wreaths covered the bottom of the memorial, scarlet poppies blaring against the stone plinth.

Lu glanced at Delia. 'Do you want me to look?'

'It's what we're here for,' Delia said stoutly.

Lu found Jack halfway down on the side nearest the church. She called Delia to her and put her arm round her as her grandmother studied Jack's name, her wrinkled face inscrutable. 'Fancy that,' Delia said eventually. 'All this time, and he's been sat here, just down the road.'

Lu refrained from saying that Jack was actually in some forgotten field on the Somme. Apart from anything else, she herself felt more connection with the name on the memorial than she had done at Thiepval. Delia's shoulders felt fragile under her arm. 'Do you want to sit down, Gran? There's a bench in the churchyard.'

The wrought-iron gate creaked as they went through into the churchyard, Delia's arm tucked into Lu's. Lu settled her on the bench against the church wall, Scottie at her feet.

Delia turned her face towards the sunshine. 'It's a strange thing,' she said. 'I know he was my father, but he's just a name when all's said and done. Percy was my real dad. Still, I'm glad I know what happened to Jack, and where he came from.'

'I wish I could find your mother.'

Delia closed her eyes. 'Oh, you've done wonders

246

already. And it's only curiosity. I've made it this far without knowing.'

'But I want to find her for you.'

'I reckon I'm lucky to know who Jack was.' She squinted at Lu. 'Go on now. You see if I've got any relatives buried here.'

There were plenty of gravestones to look at. Lu thought it was a pity churches didn't usually have a map of the graves, in the way that the war cemeteries in France had. An image of Nick studying one of the information sheets at Longueville flashed past her. Drat. She shouldn't have given in to the temptation of going to his village and seeing his house; it had stirred up all the emotions she was trying so hard to control. However hard she tried, she couldn't push him completely from her mind. It's early days, she told herself. A few more months and you'll be going Nick Who?

But as she walked the lines of the graveyard, so haphazard, so unlike the regimented rows of the war cemeteries, his memory walked beside her. Her mind was so full of him that she almost missed the first Havergal gravestone and she had to go back and check. Jeremiah Havergal 1795–1848. Beloved husband of Elizabeth Havergal, 1799–1853, daughter of Thomas Foster of the county of Berkshire.

'Look, Gran—I've got one!' Lu waved at Delia, who was sitting in the sun showing no signs of springing into action at the news. 'And there's another over here.'

It was a bit like a treasure hunt, Lu thought. She should have brought Ben and Tom and set them the task of finding all the Havergal gravestones. It would have been as good as the Banksy exhibition. In the end she found eleven stones with the name Havergal on them. She noted down all the names and dates and any other information, thinking that tracing them on the birth, marriages and deaths website would be something for Delia to do online. Then they could work out how they were related to all these people.

The air was full of the scent of bonfires and freshly mown grass. Lu inhaled deeply, looking round and feeling a profound connection with this place. It had always been just her, Delia and Pixie. Now she had relatives.

She said as much to Delia as they walked back through the town towards the hotel Lu had spotted earlier.

'What about your father's family?' Delia said. 'He wasn't an only child; he had brothers and sisters. Quite a lot turned up for the wedding. I thought they were going to drink the place dry.'

Pixie had occasionally made references to the wedding—the flowers she'd worn in her hair, the dress she'd picked up from Camden Market—but she'd never mentioned Malcolm's family being there. 'Are you sure?' Lu asked as they paused to allow Scottie to lift his leg against a bollard. 'I thought it was just a load of their friends.'

'Them certainly. Bunch of hippies talking nonsense. But Malcolm's lot were also there. His dad was a builder, I think, from the south coast. Drove a brand-new Rover, as far as I remember— your grandad was that impressed.' Delia smiled at the memory. 'And there were a couple of bridesmaids, his sister's children I believe, but my memory may be playing tricks there. Can't remember her name; she had a big floppy hat on.'

'You mean I've got two cousins.' Lu swallowed. She had cousins.

'More than that, I'll be bound. Lots of children there were, talked all the way through the ceremony.' Delia sniffed, and gave Scottie a tug on his lead. 'Mind you, they might have belonged to them hippies.'

'Why didn't you tell me I had relatives?'

'I assumed you knew and didn't want anything to do with them. You don't talk about your dad. S'pity, he was a nice man. You should have given him a chance.'

'He didn't give us a chance.' Lu scuffed the gravel edge by the bollard with her shoe.

Delia pursed her lips. 'Now that's your mother talking. You want to take what she says with a pinch of salt, you know that. Auras indeed! No, your dad was all right, he was. Underneath all that hair.'

'I don't really remember him,' Lu said. 'At least . . .' She'd been younger than Tom when Malcolm had left. She could remember the bedtime stories, being swung around and around until she laughed herself sick, being shown how to plant seeds. She rubbed her fingertips together, feeling the soil under her fingers, moist and gritty.

'You were a real daddy's girl,' Delia said.

Lu frowned. 'I don't remember that.'

'Oh yes. That's why you took it so hard, I think. He wanted custody, you know. He fought real hard for you, but people didn't like the fathers taking the kids, not then. Children should be with their mothers, that's what we all thought, unless they were unfit. I don't know. Your mother wanted you, so she got you, but then she didn't want anything to do with him. All or nothing, that's your mum, and you're just the same.' Delia started to walk on. 'Come along now, Scottie. I need a nice cup of tea.'

*   *   *

Lu sat in the back of Simon's car, staring out of the window. Not that she could see much, as it was pitch black and had been for hours already, although it was only eight. She decided she hated winter. Everything cold, everything dying, everything damp. Simon's car was at least warmer than her flat, which was one benefit of going out. Briony had insisted, saying that Lu was becoming a hermit. It was ironic, in a way, that she had left Nick partly because she wanted the sort of cool lifestyle that didn't go with parenting two boys, and then when she'd got it, the cool parties had fallen flat. Right now, hand on heart, she'd rather be at home watching *The X Factor* in Nick's cottage with the boys than sitting in Simon's car on the way to a smart party, listening to him and Briony wittering on with inconsequential lovers' chat as if they'd forgotten she was in the back. What were they on about now? Christmas presents. Oh dear, now Briony was giggling coyly. Briony never giggled. She was never coy. Was this really the Briony who'd said she didn't fancy Simon? Proof at last of alien abduction? Lu gave a little clearing-her-throat sort of cough, to remind them she was there. It was a shame it wasn't a fancy dress party they were going to, because then she could have gone as a gooseberry.

250

She went back to staring out of the window, thinking about her outing with Delia. Delia had said her father had fought for her, that she'd been a daddy's girl. It was so hard to remember back in time, to get things clear in her head. He'd left them in the lurch, had left and set up with a new wife, a new family. He had never wanted to be with them, had never cared for them. That was what she'd always believed. The few memories she had of her father had always been warm and caring, but she'd always dismissed them; she remembered them because they were rare moments and that made them special. But to be honest, that didn't fit. Lu could remember mundane things, like being in a crowded street, all lit up for Christmas, holding her daddy's hand tightly. There was hot chocolate in her memory; she could taste it in her mouth now, but it was hardly of earth-shattering significance. The only negative memory she had of that time was nightmares about 'them' coming to take her away. She didn't know who 'they' were, but she was frightened of them. Despite the super-efficient heating system of Simon's Audi, Lu shivered.

The car turned into a driveway marked with big stone pillars with eagles perched on top, and back in the present, Lu shivered again. This looked like it was going to be a posher evening than she was expecting. The car turned a corner and there was the house, windows blazing light into the cold November sky. She could make out ivy-covered walls, and—yikes—battlements. It wasn't a house, it was practically a castle.

Briony looked round at her in the back and gave an excited grimace as Simon parked in between

251

another Audi and a Porsche. Lu knew that since meeting Simon, Briony was moving in more elevated circles than she'd ever done with Jerry and was loving it. Lu wasn't so sure. It was all very well thinking you could run with the hounds if you were of greyhound material, but Lu had a nasty feeling that she was more of Scottie's persuasion, albeit without the short, bandy, hairy legs. Oh well, she thought as she got out of the car. At least the food was likely to be good, and plentiful, and she was a starving illustrator who needed feeding.

Drinks were in the main entrance hall. In Lu's flat that would have meant squeezing as tight as sardines to get ten in, plus a couple more in the broom cupboard under the stairs (if it was good enough for Harry Potter . . .). Here the hall was larger than Lu's flat in its entirety, with a marble chequerboard floor pockmarked here and there with the effects of stilettos. Or so Lu assumed; somewhere so grand, so out of her normal life, it could have been the aftermath of some lord or other getting frisky with his shotgun before an afternoon's hunting, what? A double staircase rose majestically from the hall, and Lu had a brief fantasy moment about marrying the house's owner (*Jane Eyre* had always been a favourite novel of hers) and ending up swanning down the staircase in a crinoline (she'd also been fond of *Gone with the Wind*). Brief, because when Simon introduced her to the owner, he was everything she expected a Rupert to look like: floppy blond hair over a ruddy face that clashed with pink corduroy trousers declaring the ultra-confidence of masculinity and a self-worth probably borne of generations of shooting tigers and keeping natives in their place.

But he was kind and made her feel an honoured guest rather than the poor relation, so she only felt a few rebellious urges to register his name in her little book for when the revolution came.

The same couldn't be said of all of the guests, some of whom she felt she could have cheerfully lined up against the venerable ivy-covered walls and shot there and then. Melissas and Felicias, Olivers and Oscars, standing around in exclusive little groups discussing clubs and property, the impossibility of buying anything in London for under a million. Hadn't these people heard of the credit crunch?

The food was good, though. Lu tucked in, thinking that she might as well make the most of her brief visit to the high life. One Oliver, his good looks marred by enormous bags under his eyes, tried chatting her up by saying how much he liked girls with long brown hair, to which Lu promptly replied that at thirty-two, she considered herself to be a woman. She knew she was being snippy, and that her snippiness was quite possibly fuelled by inverted snobbery, but she didn't feel at home with these people. She couldn't find connections. Even the ones who talked about art—and there were a few—talked about it in terms of investment and status, the value of the art being determined by the price rather than the quality. She wondered how Pixie would have painted the conglomerated aura of the guests: a deep self-satisfied pink, she thought, in rich glutinous paint. Lu frowned as she loaded her plate for the second time. She would have to go to see Pixie to ask about her father.

'Hello,' said a vaguely familiar voice. 'We meet again.'

She looked up, forkful of smoked salmon in her hand. It was Marcus.

Chapter 14

Her memories of Marcus had blurred into an impossibly wonderful mix of George Clooney and the man from the Dolce and Gabbana ad. In reality he wasn't exactly the hybrid that she'd imagined, but he wasn't bad. Not bad at all. His hair was thick and springy, his eyes were a warm dark brown and his skin was lightly tanned. Obviously Minneapolis was sunnier than she'd thought.

'What are you doing here?'

'Why? Do I look like a gate crasher?' Marcus raised an eyebrow. 'I was invited by Rupert.'

'No, no, I'm sorry. I meant, I thought you'd gone to Minneapolis for ever. Are you over here on holiday?'

'Not exactly. Minneapolis didn't work out. What with the downturn, the business was vulnerable to failing completely. We ended up closing down the unprofitable bits and selling off the rest.' Marcus frowned. 'It's really hard making those sort of decisions with a workforce, but what can you do? Sometimes you have to cut out the dead wood or the whole ship will go down. I seem to have mixed up my metaphors,' he added, smiling at her. 'Never mind. The upshot is that I got back about a week ago. I was going to give you a ring, see if you were about, see if you remembered me.'

Lu wondered if that was true, then decided to

assume it was, given that it was so much more flattering. 'Of course I remember you,' she said. 'How could I forget?' She spoke lightly, because she had forgotten him, blotted out by Nick, but now it was all rushing back. He'd been Mr Perfect. 'Do you know that feeling when you haven't seen someone for a long time, and then you meet up with them and they don't fit your memories, and for that split second they look like complete strangers. And then they become themselves, and that's the image you carry around with you. Sometimes it's because they have changed— they've got older or fatter or something. Or maybe it's because you've changed.'

'I see,' Marcus said, frowning slightly.

'Not that I'm implying that you're older. Or fatter, or anything.' She gave a nervous giggle. This wasn't going well. For a second she remembered how easy it had always been to talk to Nick. There had never been any awkward moments, when things had become difficult, except for the break-up. And even then she'd been able to talk to him. 'Anyway, did you have a good time? What was it like working in the USA?'

If Marcus recognised her ploy to change direction he didn't say, because he started talking about the differences between the two countries. Lu hadn't been to the States, even on holiday, so she didn't have much to contribute, beyond laughing at his language misunderstandings. 'Two countries separated by a common tongue,' Marcus pronounced, as if it was his original idea. Lu smiled politely, and as if sensing her lack of interest, it was his turn to change the subject. 'Tell me what you've been up to in the last six months.

How's your work going?'

'While you've been away I've changed direction.'

'You're no longer illustrating?'

So he remembered what she did. That was a point in his favour. 'I'm still illustrating, I'm just no longer employed.'

He tilted his head. 'Freelance?'

'Well, I always was a freelance, but I used to do flat-fee work via my agent. Now I've ditched my agent and I'm working on my own projects.' It sounded grander than it was in reality: the mounds of sketchbooks filled with Arthur.

'That sounds like a dramatic step. A lot seems to have happened in your life while I've been away.'

Nick, for starters. Her insides contracted at the thought of him. Their relationship had been so intense, it was hard to believe it could have been contained within the time limits of just a few months. She hadn't known she'd been living in black and white, but when Nick had blown in, Nick with his loud voice and endless enthusiasm, suddenly life had become a rainbow of colours. Back in her childhood, she could remember having colouring books with black and white line drawings. The paper was harsh and shiny, but when you dipped your brush in clean water and trailed it over the illustrations, colours appeared like magic and the paper buckled under the soppy wetness of the brush. That was what Nick had been: the magic brush that had changed her life into Technicolor. And now he had gone.

Lu mentally shook herself. She'd decided she wasn't going to think about Nick any more. She'd known he was wrong for her right from the start, in the same way she'd known Marcus was right for her from the beginning, at the tenth anniversary exhibition at Briony's gallery. She smiled at him. 'Yes, the last few months have been quite dramatic, one way and another.'

They talked some more, had another glass of champagne, moved to a quieter room with lots of deep comfortable sofas, then another glass of champagne, and then Marcus was telling her about his last relationship, which had broken up because she had wanted children and he hadn't.

'I don't want children,' Lu said. 'It's funny, but I've always known that. I keep waiting for my biological clock to start ticking, but it doesn't and I don't think it's going to.' Then she paused. It seemed such a strange thing to be talking about on a first meeting. Although it wasn't really their first meeting; they'd already had a first date. In a way, Marcus was doing what she'd said she intended to do—checking that the first big deal-breaker on his relationship list wasn't there. Doesn't want children. Well, she ticked that one fair and square.

An image of Tom's face looking up at her as they went down the death slide came into her head, the warmth of his hand in hers. It hadn't been so bad, being with the boys. They were probably getting overexcited about Christmas right now. Perhaps Tom was a shepherd in the nativity play, complete with a tea towel on his head, and Ben would be finishing his first term at the big school. I hope it's gone well, she thought wistfully.

Marcus leaned forward. 'It's strange, when you say you don't want children, people think you're selfish. That's what my last girlfriend said to me:

you're selfish. But I don't see why. I said, why do you want them? and she said, I just do. Well, if that isn't selfish, I don't know what is. I want it, therefore I must have it. And what she saw as her future was a neat little bundle, or a mini-me who she could dress up and play dolls with. Nothing about changing nappies.'

'Or cleaning up projectile vomiting,' Lu said, thinking of Tom again. A much less appealing image than nativity shepherds. She could picture them cleaning the bathroom together, and then putting Tom's bedclothes in the washing machine. Poor little chap. My night of passion, she thought to herself, smiling wryly at the memory.

Marcus smiled at her. They were leaning very closely together, his shoulder near hers, their knees almost touching. He was wearing a crisp cotton shirt, and for a second Lu wanted to bury her nose in the fabric, so clean were the folds, so sharp the creases around the cuffs. He could have been modelling it for a clothes catalogue; in fact, looking around the room at the other guests, they could all have been some advertiser's dream, selling an aspirational upmarket product such as cognac or after-dinner mints. It was all so perfect, so exactly where she had wanted to be, and yet all she could think of was Nick's crooked smile as he mopped up after Tom, and him saying that true romance wasn't dead.

'Penny for them?' Marcus was saying, his smile stretching over perfect, even teeth, and for a second she hated him, just because he wasn't Nick. But Nick was the past.

Rupert plonked himself down on the end of the sofa. 'Now, you two lovebirds, enough of this cosy chit-chat. I'm rounding up volunteers for skiing in the Alps over New Year.' Lu could sense from the way Marcus shifted in his seat that he was as annoyed as she was at being called a lovebird, but Rupert appeared oblivious. 'Interested?'

'Where are you going?'

'Meribel. Muffin's cousin has bought a big pile with his redundancy money and is going to run it as a chalet hotel. It needs a complete refurb, but before he shuts it down, he's going to have a big bash for New Year. Might be a bit primitivo, mattresses on the floor and bring your own bedding, but I reckon it'll be a hoot to rough it for a change. Like being a student again.' Lu couldn't imagine that Rupert had ever really roughed it, as a student or otherwise. 'It's in a great location, right on the slopes, and the company will be good.'

'I might be interested,' Marcus said. He turned to Lu. 'What about you? Do you ski?'

Lu shook her head. 'I've never tried it.'

'Do come,' Rupert said, looking at her with intensity, as if he would be devastated by her absence even though he'd only exchanged half a dozen sentences with her before. 'There's lots of skiing, plenty of black runs for the butch and hairy, like Marcus, and easy bits for the beginner. It's the best place to learn. Briony, come over here and tell your friend she ought to come with us.' He waved, and Lu saw Briony swaying across the room towards them, Simon tagging along in her wake.

'Hey, Lu. You've got to go skiing!'

'Are you going to go?' As far as Lu knew, Briony's previous comments about skiing had indicated that only idiots wanted to waste money on sliding down mountains on planks, getting freezing cold and wet at the same time.

'Of course, darling,' Briony said with a nonchalant wave. 'It'll be fab.'

Lu giggled. 'Well, darling, I simply can't.' Marcus gave a snort of laughter. He was all right really, she thought.

'Why not? It'll be great,' Rupert said, patting her knee. 'You'll love it, I promise.'

Lu moved her knee. 'If I break my arm, I don't earn. Sadly I don't have some cushy job where I can get sick pay.' Her painting arm was the most wonderful excuse for why she couldn't go. Nothing to do with having no money at all.

'That's a pity, it sounds like it's going to be fun,' Marcus said. 'I bet you'd like skiing, and let's face it, it's going to be worth it just for the whole experience. Meribel's got a lot going on even if you don't want to ski. There's loads of other stuff to do.'

'Besides,' Briony said, waggling her finger at Lu, 'I know you've got insurance. If you break your arm, it pays for you.'

'I'm sure it won't pay out if I break it skiing,' Lu said, feeling under fire.

'I'm sure it will, and you're not doing much right now, are you?' Briony swigged some wine. 'Come on, this would be the ideal time to come with us and try out skiing. And just think, if you did break your arm, the insurance would kick in and then you'd be paid for lolling around doing nothing.'

Lu shook her head, hoping that if she didn't respond, they'd give up and change the subject. She certainly didn't want Briony to enlarge on the subject of Lu not doing much right now.

'I love the idea of your arm being insured,'

Marcus said. 'I'm not sure what I'd choose if I had to insure a bit of myself. My hands, maybe.'

'I'd insure my eyes,' Briony said, trying to perch on the sofa arm but sliding off so she ended up squeezing next to Rupert. Lu shifted a bit sideways to make more room, conscious that she was shifting closer to Marcus. She could feel his thigh running along next to her own.

'Because they're beautiful?' Simon asked. Lu was glad he didn't sound slurred, as he was driving them both home later.

'Ahhh,' said Briony, looking up soppily at him. 'Actually, I was thinking more about looking at artworks, but I'll go for beautiful. What about you?'

'It'd have to be my legs,' Simon said. 'Better than Betty Grable's, so I've been told.'

'By whom?' Briony's tone was dismayed as they all looked at Simon's legs, but it was impossible to check out the similarity given the fact that he was wearing trousers.

'By you, of course,' Simon said, smirking, and Briony went all giggly again.

'Oh, you,' she said, saucer-eyed.

The aliens had taken her. This might be a transitional relationship, but Briony was making the most of it.

Marcus touched Lu's arm, and she turned with relief to him, feeling more warmth than she'd felt before. 'Are you sure you won't come skiing with us?' he said, his voice low.

'It's not just my arm,' Lu admitted. 'It's lots of other stuff—everyone will be miles better than me, for starters, and it'll be boring being the one left behind all the time.'

261

'You'd go to ski school. You'd soon pick it up.'

'Do you know, the words ski school depress me almost as much as the word semolina. It just seems ridiculous, an adult going to ski school.'

'Lots of people do it; how else would you learn?'

'I don't want to learn, that's the thing.' But she did, in a way. She wanted to swish down mountains looking cool and elegant like a girl in a James Bond film from the sixties, gliding to a halt in an arc of snow. Trouble was, the reality was a seriously unflattering Day-Glo romper suit and bruises from perpetually falling down.

'You could come out and decide if you liked it, and if you didn't, there are other things to do. It's not just about skiing.' He looked at her as if considering. 'I bet you'd like cross-country skiing. There'd be no risk of breaking your arm, and you'd be out in the mountains with the wonderful scenery.'

'You obviously go every year.'

'If I can,' Marcus said. 'It's a great holiday. All you have to do is have a good time and enjoy yourself.'

'Put it like that, and I'm not surprised you go every year.' Lu didn't like to say that her budget didn't run to skiing holidays every year. Besides, where would she sleep? If she signed up now, she wouldn't want to commit to sharing a room with Marcus, but in a couple of months' time, that might be all she wanted to do. She glanced up and caught his eye, then swiftly looked down in case he could read her thoughts.

'C'mon, Bri, time to go home,' Simon said, putting his hands out and heaving Briony up from the sofa.

Briony surged up and into his arms. 'You're lovely, you are.'

'And so are you, my darling, but I think I ought to get you back. Coming, Lu?'

She nodded and stood up. 'That's my lift. It was nice meeting you again.'

Marcus stood too. 'I'll come with you to the car.'

Lu said goodbye and thank you to Rupert, then followed Simon and Briony out to the car, very conscious of Marcus beside her, his hand occasionally in the small of her back, steering her through the other guests. Simon poured Briony into the front seat and then went round to the driver's side.

'Why don't you think about it?' Marcus said softly. 'Maybe this is the year you try skiing.'

She found herself smiling back and saying yes, maybe it was.

'I'm glad I came tonight.'

'Me too.' She felt suddenly shy. 'It was good to see you again.'

He started to move towards her—oh, she hadn't been kissed by anyone since Nick, she wasn't sure she wanted, oh . . .

It felt strange having another man's mouth on hers, strange and somehow wrong, as if she was being unfaithful. That was ridiculous.

But he wasn't Nick.

No, he wasn't Nick, he was better than Nick. Her heart contracted. No, not better, different. And she had to stop thinking about Nick because it was impossible. In response to the thought, she kissed Marcus back with a passion she wasn't sure she meant.

Simon tooted the horn and they pulled apart,

263

Lu feeling horribly embarrassed.

'Dinner?' Marcus said, and she nodded. 'I'll call you.'

She got in the car and Simon drove off, impatient to get home. Not that it looked as if he was going to see much action tonight, as Briony was already snoring. Lu stared out of the window at the blackness, her hand to her lips, thinking about Marcus.

*   *   *

'And?' Briony said.

'And what?' Lu replied, then relented. 'Yes, he called, and yes, we're going out to dinner, and then . . . we'll see.'

'You fancy him, though, don't you.' It was a statement, not a question.

Lu thought about it as Briony placed her order with the waitress. The café had gone to town on the Christmas theme; red and green tinsel was draped everywhere. There was so much of it on the edge of the counter there was hardly enough room for the plates of brownies and cookies. 'Well, he is lovely to look at, and he's everything I could want from a man: he's considerate, amusing, good company, intelligent, good job . . .' And at least speculating about Marcus had stopped her thinking about Nick.

'But?'

'But,' Lu agreed. 'I don't know, I'm in a funny place right now. I want to fancy Marcus. I want to want to rip his clothes off. And there *is* something there.' She placed her order too, but no carrot cake for her today; she was on a diet.

'So there is some chemistry.'

'Oh yes, I wouldn't be seeing him again if there wasn't.' Instead of flowers, the café had stuck a couple of striped candy sticks into the little vases on the tables. Lu pulled one out and twiddled it in her fingers. 'It's like the whole thing with Nick has blown all my circuits and there's not much power going through the system.'

'You know what you should do? You should shag Marcus. Get your mojo back, get over the hump with a hump. Lay the ghost.'

'Like you with Simon?' Lu stroked the satin ribbon around the candy stick. Transitional relationships. They sounded so . . . neat. An organised way of getting over heartbreak. Not messy, sprawling, emotional tangles.

'Spot on. Look at me—I'm having a whale of a time. It couldn't be better.'

'Not sure about the friends, though.' Lu pulled a face, thinking of Rupert and co. 'What's all this about going skiing—oh, and thanks for letting everyone know I haven't got much work on at the moment. I really needed that.'

Briony groaned. 'Oh God, I'm sorry. I was a bit pissed.'

'And the rest.' Lu popped the candy stick back in the vase as their orders came.

'But listen, the skiing will be fabulous, I know it will. And if we both go, we know there's going to be at least one other person who's going to be dreadful.'

'I may have hidden talents,' Lu said, starting her unseasonal Caesar salad.

'Mmm.' It didn't sound as if Briony thought that likely. 'Simon says that there's lots to do in

Meribel even if we don't want to ski, and it does sound fun, a big group of us in a chalet with log fires and fondues and mulled wine and the snow sparkling and—'

'Sleigh bells ringing? I thought this chalet needs a complete refurb.'

'I don't think it's too bad right now, just he wants to make it six stars, super-luxurious. There's room for loads of people—it's got seven floors apparently.'

'Doesn't sound like the sort of shack Heidi lived in.'

'That was in Austria or Germany or somewhere. This is in France. Think of all that lovely food and wine, yum yum yum.' Briony took a forkful of quiche.

'I don't know. If I say yes—and I can't believe I'm even thinking of it; I'm so broke I can't run the heating as much as I'd like and my car needs work doing to it—but if I do . . .' Lu chased a crouton round her plate. 'It puts me in a tricky position re Marcus. If I go, it's sort of like saying I'm going to sleep with him.'

'Don't be daft. I suggested you came, it was nothing to do with Marcus. It's such a big place you'll be able to have a room to yourself, I'm sure. Besides, don't you want to sleep with Marcus?'

'Hey, come on, we've only just met.'

Briony waved an unrepentant hand at her. 'Actually you met eleven months ago, when you were convinced he was Mr Right, but okay, in theory, is it possible? Is there enough chemistry?'

'In theory?' Lu prodded a bit of chicken with her fork, buying time. Was there enough chemistry there? There had been when they'd first met; then

266

she'd fancied the socks off him, but now was different. 'I don't know. It's too early to say.'

Briony snorted. 'We both know your problem: you're still hankering after Nick.'

'I'm not hankering. Really I'm not.' Briony looked at her. 'Okay, maybe just a bit. But it was good with him.' Lu's voice trailed off. It had been good. Better than good, in fact.

'Tell me again. Why aren't you with him?'

'Because I finished it. Because he's not the man for me. We'd have broken up sooner or later. It just happens to have been sooner.' Lu stared at a line of dancing Father Christmas cut-outs on the wall ahead of her as if they had all the answers tucked away in their sacks. Nick would have made a good Father Christmas; he had the right energy for it, full of goodwill to all mankind. 'Perhaps it's for the best anyway. I know what he's like, he's so generous and kind, and I'm so broke at the moment he'd be wanting to bail me out all the time, and he can't afford to carry anyone apart from the boys. I'd be dragging him down if we'd stayed together. At least if we're apart I've only got myself to worry about.'

'But that's only about money, that's not about your relationship and how you felt about each other. You'd find a way to cope.'

'You know what they say, when poverty comes through the door, love goes out the window.' Lu pushed her plate away, unable to eat any more.

Briony tilted her head to one side. 'Are things that bad? I mean, financially?'

'I'm pushing it. I've just finished a job for the US, so I've got that money coming in, but there's nothing else, and I don't suppose anything will turn up this side of Christmas. I've done a picture book and been sending it out to editors, but it comes back so fast it's got scorch marks down the side of the envelope. They all say more or less the same thing—they love it but it's too adult, too young, too difficult to market, too different, too controversial, too demanding, too depressing, too dramatic. I've practically exhausted every contact I've got. I'm mad to be even considering going skiing in the circumstances.'

'Would you be interested in any other sort of work? I mean, non-illustration work. Because I could do with someone to help out from time to time.'

'Really?'

'On a casual basis, of course. I always need help with exhibitions and to cover for me at the weekends, or if I want to go shopping or something. And then you could afford to sponsor me—I've signed up to do a spinathon next month to raise money for the new baby unit at the hospital.'

Lu blinked. 'That sounds energetic—and very unlike you.'

'I thought I'd better get fit, what with going skiing, and I might at least raise some money for a good cause at the same time.'

Lu agreed to sponsor Briony, and she rummaged in her bag for the form.

'Workwise, you could start with helping me with the next exhibition private view—that's Tuesday week. I'm going to need help hanging the work and then doling out the wine and doing the selling bit—I'd give you commission. You'd be great, much better than the students I usually rope in.'

'That'd be wonderful. I mean, I hope to get some illustration work soon, but I could do with some cash now. You're a lifesaver.' Lu gave Briony a big smile as she filled in the sponsorship form. 'I am so fed up with being broke all the time and worrying about money.'

'So go out with Marcus. He's got stacks of dosh.'

Lu thought back to the break-up with Nick, how much love there had been between them. He'd looked so upset when she'd left, but he hadn't stopped her. He'd let her go. And every day her heart hurt just that little bit less. Every day the gaps between thinking about Nick became longer and longer. He was slowly receding from her life, and perhaps it would be Marcus who replaced him. Perhaps Briony was right, and she should shag Marcus and get Nick out of her heart and her head once and for all.

'I am going out with Marcus—for dinner. And then . . . we'll see.'

*　　　*　　　*

The next day Lu knocked on her mother's door— no point in trying the door bell; that hadn't worked ever since Pixie had had a bout of paranoia and decided that 'they' were bugging her house using electricity wires and disconnected it. She waited, noticing that a couple more plaster fairies seemed to have taken up residence in the garden. Their smirking faces were faintly sinister, but she imagined that they were meant to be benevolent spirits. A cat circled itself around her legs and she bent down to touch the warm fur, a reassuringly normal cat, white with splodges of marmalade, solidly built. Given that her mother had once aspired to being a white witch, it was a relief that it wasn't a lean black one. She was about to knock again when from inside she heard a faint tinkle of bells. The door creaked open an inch, then widened.

'Long time no see,' said Pixie, as she stepped back to let Lu in.

'Hi, Mum,' Lu said, giving her a kiss and getting a familiar whiff of patchouli oil. Pixie's hair was more auburn than pink today. She must have been at the henna again.

'I wish you wouldn't call me that,' Pixie said, a look of horror on her face, as if Lu had just announced she had decided to stand as a Conservative MP.

'But you are my mother,' Lu said, pushing past the hanging curtain of beads and bells that separated the little entrance porch from the main living room. 'What else am I to call you?'

'My name's Pixie. I am not a mum.'

No, Lu thought. You're certainly not that. When Lu had been younger, how she'd longed for a cuddly mum like the other kids had, someone who made cakes and wore aprons and had tea ready on the table when you got home. She'd been to her friends' houses; she knew that was what their mums were like. It was what she'd played at being when she'd made Tom's cake and done his party.

In some ways Pixie had been more successful at playing mother than Lu had been. Lu had felt cold-shouldered by the other, legitimate mothers, but when she was growing up her friends had actively wanted invites to her home, their eyes wide as they looked around the house, looked anywhere in fact, drinking it all in: the patchwork quilts draped across the sofa, the walls obscured by hangings depicting Ganesh or Ishtar or whichever god was being worshipped that week.

At least shifting to aura painting meant the decor had improved, although Lu wondered how her mother could live there without developing a headache, as the walls throbbed with psychedelic portraits.

'Gran thinks you're Susan.'

'Susan! How could anyone think I was a Susan?'

Indeed, looking at Pixie, she was as far away from Susan-ness as a person could be, short of a sex change. Her hair was short, spiked up every which way and the colour of tomato soup. Lu had forgotten what colour her mother's hair was naturally; she wondered if even she could remember. The colour made her skin look pale and tired, or maybe that was an effect of the heavily kohled eyes. Pixie's look today was perhaps best described as Pirate meets *I Love Lucy*. She was wearing a dress, a pretty green floral dress that a Susan might have worn in the fifties, but underneath it were skinny jeans, and she'd hoicked it up round her hips with a large buckled belt that a buccaneer might have been proud to wear sailing the high seas.

She shook her head so the hoop earrings jangled. 'Susan is such a boring name, sweetie. So conventional.'

'That's me all over,' Lu said, tilting her head with a smile. 'Boring and conventional. What about a cup of tea?'

In answer, Pixie led the way into the kitchen. It was a small room, with roughly plastered walls and

271

a hotchpotch of kitchen units. A large saucepan bubbled on the stove, steam escaping through the lid. Pixie was erratic in the kitchen. Sometimes there would be nothing to eat in the house beyond a couple of misshapen carrots that you would think twice about giving to a starving rabbit; other times lavish banquets would appear, quasi-medieval feasts with unusual flavours, studded with pine nuts, or else the favourite would be Indian, with chapattis draped around the room like circular flannels drying out. Lu lifted the lid of the saucepan to reveal a pale greeny-yellow liquid. 'Stock?' she said doubtfully.

Pixie picked up a spoon and gave the saucepan a poke. 'I'm dyeing a shirt using onion skins.' She lifted the contents up. It looked like the colour of baby diarrhoea. 'Mmm, I'm not sure I've got the proportions right. Camomile?'

'Camomile would be lovely.'

Lu looked out of the window while Pixie made the tea. The cottage was lower than the garden, so the plants were at eye level. Close to the house were herbs and other flowers that Pixie used to make concoctions of various sorts, such as feverfew for migraine. Another cat, this time a densely furred grey, sprawled over a lavender bush. Further down the garden Lu knew there were vegetables and a beehive, and apple trees. A man was working at the far end, digging, judging by the angle of his back and his jerky movements as he pushed down into the soil.

'Give him a yell for tea,' Pixie said over her shoulder to Lu.

'I wanted to have a chat with you,' Lu said, emphasising the you. She didn't want her mother's partner loitering around. He was a good fifteen years younger than Pixie, nearer in age to Lu herself, in fact. Lu had been appalled by it to begin with; he'd been twenty and Pixie had been thirty-five. It was bad enough having everything decided by the Tarot, without her mum having a toyboy. Teenage Lu had been so disgusted she'd gone to live with Delia for two terms before she'd relented and come back home. But Neil had survived the course, and twenty years on was still there, albeit renamed as Raven.

Pixie pushed open the window. 'Tea,' she yelled. 'Raven! Tea!' Raven turned, gave her a wave and a thumbs-up, then went back to his digging.

Pixie waved vigorously back, then closed the window. 'I think he's going to come in when he's finished,' she said, smiling with a little wrinkle of her nose. Lu stared at the ceiling. She had learned to tolerate Raven, but honestly, it was ridiculous, her mother, at her age, behaving like a teenager.

Pixie picked up a tray with the tea things on it and led the way back into the dimly lit living room. The windows were small at best, but a tangle of creeper filtered the light even more. It gave a subterranean feel to the room, heightened by every surface apart from the ceiling being covered with rugs, tapestries or paintings.

'I was expecting you,' Pixie intoned as she laid down the tray.

'Yes—I rang and told you,' Lu countered. 'You know I don't believe in the cards.'

'No, before you rang. The cards told me your thoughts were turning to home.'

Lu turned it over in her mind. She often thought of home; in fact, almost every time she walked into her flat she thought, thank God it's not like home. Did that count? And if it did, how could the cards know, let alone communicate the fact to Pixie who, for all her vaunted claims of sensitivity, often seemed to have the perception of a blind rhinoceros. Let it pass; it was enough that she was here. What did it matter if the cards had predicted it? She had other things to deal with.

'I was with Gran the other day,' she began, thinking this was a good place to start raising the subject of Malcolm.

'You're always with her,' Pixie said. 'Rummaging around with the family history and what have you. I don't know why she doesn't ask me.'

Lu knew full well why Delia didn't ask Pixie. Pixie's methods were as magical as the Internet searches had appeared to Lu, but were based less in tangibles such as computers and software, and more on intuition and feelings and the burning of incense. She was about to utter some platitude about living nearer to Delia, which made it easier, when she registered the tinge of jealousy in Pixie's voice. Lu and Delia had always been close; had Pixie felt excluded?

Lu had always seen her mother as someone who was so extreme she couldn't possibly care about other people's opinion of her. Pixie had always taken her own course through life, trampling on the feelings of others. Lu had responded by not caring about Pixie's feelings. Pixie was a cartoon character, someone to be amused and embarrassed by in equal measure. But seeing her fiddling with her belt buckle, her cheeks pink, Lu felt an unexpected pang of guilt. I don't have anything to feel guilty about, she told herself. I was a child and Pixie was . . . Pixie was doing her best, she had to admit. As she herself had tried to do her best with Tom and Ben.

'Delia would love to have your help,' Lu lied. Pixie looked up, eyes wide. 'Really, she would. She just didn't like to ask you.' How she was going to square this with Delia, Lu didn't know, but she'd do it somehow.

'Tell me how far you've got,' Pixie said eagerly. 'What are you looking up?'

Lu told her as much as she could. She explained that they'd managed to find out quite a lot about Jack, but that Anne was being more elusive.

'You should have come to me before,' Pixie said, looking smug. 'I'll find her. I have ways.'

It was on the tip of Lu's tongue to say yeah, right, and would those ways involve higher planes and spirit worlds, but she stopped herself. What did it matter to her if Pixie tried in her own way? And besides, for all she knew Pixie might be intending to use the same routes Lu had, and might spot something Lu had overlooked. She'd wait and see what her mother came up with, and if her methods worked, that would be fine, they'd have found Anne, and if they didn't, then they were in exactly the same position they were now.

But her voice was softer than perhaps it would have been earlier when she asked about Malcolm. 'We were looking at the war memorial when Delia mentioned your wedding. I didn't know I had cousins.'

Pixie looked vague. 'Oh yes, I think your father's sisters had children.'

'Why didn't I meet them when I was growing up?'

Pixie looked at Lu as if she were a halfwit. 'I wasn't speaking to your father, so it wasn't likely I'd have been speaking to his stupid sisters.'

'I'd have liked to know my cousins.'

'No you wouldn't, they were very dull. Just like your father. Dullest man on the planet. I don't know why you want to talk about this now.' She started to get up. 'It's very dull.'

'Then I'm as bad as my father,' Lu said, grabbing her hand and pulling her back down on to the sofa. 'Please. It's important to me. We never talk about him.'

'You never talk about him,' Pixie corrected her. 'If I say he's tried to get in touch, you bite my head off. You're a very black-and-white sort of person, you know. It's all got to be perfect, and if it isn't, then you don't want to know. You wouldn't do finger painting when you were little because you didn't like getting your hands dirty.' She shook her head in sorrow. 'It's all or nothing with you. I don't know where you get it from.'

'You, maybe?'

'Me? I'm the most open person I know. I've always been interested in new experiences, and moving forwards. There's nothing closed about me.' Pixie straightened up and inhaled deeply before breathing out. 'My spirit flows forwards and upwards,' she said, her hands following the direction of her spirit. 'I am open as the lotus, as free as—'

'Okay, Mum, you're open, and I'm closed and dull. What I want to know is, why did you marry him? If he was so dull and boring . . .' She waited for Pixie's answer.

Pixie's mouth twitched. 'Your grandmother

wanted me to,' she said eventually. 'I didn't—I didn't see the need. Anyone would think it was the Middle Ages. And she wanted me to wear white, which would have been a bit rich in the circumstances. I was seven months' pregnant with you, sweet pea,' she said, beaming. 'Not that I showed much. You were a teeny baby and a very neat bump. Of course, I was incredibly young, in my teens.'

Lu let that pass. There were much more interesting questions to ask. 'Didn't you love Dad?'

Pixie stroked the back of her neck. 'To be honest, sweet pea, I can hardly remember your father. He was really fun at the beginning, but then he changed, became all conventional. I didn't want to be a wifey. I've never wanted to do that—if I'd wanted to be like that I'd have stayed a Susan. And then your father got heavy . . .' Pixie made a face, as if she'd eaten something as disgusting as the contents of the saucepan in the kitchen. 'Those were dark, dark days. And I am a creature of the light,' she said, raising her eyes upward.

Lu looked at her hands, remembering what Delia had said. 'Did Dad really leave us?'

'Lunabella! How can you even ask me that, when you know what I went through, what our life was like. I had to struggle On My Own to bring you up.'

'Did he try to keep in touch?'

'Ha—he thought he could steal you away from me, as if marriage gave him the right to you.'

'It did.' She remembered Nick saying how he'd fought for an equal share of the boys.

'I didn't want to get married in the first place,'

277

Pixie said indignantly. 'I'd have managed from the start. He was just sperm. Anyway, you didn't want to know him. I said, do you want to see your dad ever again, and you said no. You were quite clear.'

Lu's chest was painfully tight. 'I was six.'

'You had an opinion, and I respected it.' Pixie got up. 'He went off with another woman and left us, and that's an end to it.'

Lu grabbed her hand again, forcing Pixie to stay. 'No it isn't. I won't let you walk away from talking about it. I don't think you're telling me the truth— Delia said he fought for me, so he didn't just walk out on us.' Her heart was thumping, it hurt to breathe. 'Did you stop him from seeing me?'

'No—you didn't want to see him. You screamed yourself sick when he came round, you said he was a bad man, you didn't want him, you only wanted me.'

'Why would I say that? I was only six.' She remembered Nick talking about his divorce, how Morwenna and he had tried really hard to make it easy for the boys, had controlled their own feelings, had tried not to say what they really felt, and especially not in front of the boys. She looked at Pixie, not famous for emotional restraint. 'You made me say those things.'

'It was what you wanted,' Pixie flung back at her, face flushed, eyes wide like a frightened pony. 'I only did as you wanted. You wanted to stay with me.'

'I loved my daddy,' Lu cried out as Pixie's face crumpled. 'I wanted to be with him. Why did you do it? Why?'

'It was for the best,' Pixie said, mascara everywhere. She took Lu's hands and held them in hers. 'Lu, darling, it was for the best. We wanted to be together, just you and me.'

Lu snatched her hands away. 'I don't believe you. Why would you do something so—'

'She was frightened.' Lu spun round to see Raven standing in the doorway. Pixie gave a juddering sigh and ran to him, sobbing into his chest. 'She thought he'd say she was an unfit mother and take you away. She was frightened she was going to lose you.'

Lu stared at him, open-mouthed. Raven nodded, his arm around Pixie. 'She told me about it, years ago, when you were being a pain about me coming over. You meant everything to her. We almost broke up because you didn't approve of me. Selfish, I thought you were, looking down your nose at your mum, always off round your gran's house, then complaining the first time she had a proper relationship.'

'She had loads of boyfriends,' Lu flung back. 'All the time.'

'Not staying over, not when you were little,' Pixie said, her eyes pleading. 'I tried my best, but Malcolm was right. I am an unfit mother.'

Lu stood up, despite her legs shaking. 'I can't think straight.'

Pixie embraced her. 'Say it's all right, sweet pea. I was trying my best. Say it's all right.'

Lu disentangled herself. 'I have to think.'

'You think, then,' Raven said. 'But remember, your ma's not an unfit mother and you know it, but he would have said she was. He had money to buy lawyers and she had nothing, except you. You were everything to her. She was frightened of losing you.'

Chapter 15

She was frightened of losing you. The words echoed in Lu's head as she reeled home, buzzing with adrenalin as the memories started to fall into place. Her father had wanted her, and was prepared—had possibly threatened—to say that Pixie was unfit as a mother to get her. Pixie's only chance was to get Lu to want to stay with her. That explained what she could remember of the time, all the fighting and raised voices, and being frightened that 'they' were going to take her away.

Pixie had planted the idea of 'them', or maybe she'd simply taken advantage of an existing fear. Either way, the upshot was that her father had been thwarted. He couldn't claim that Pixie was an unfit mother when Lu herself had apparently turned against him. And when Lu had turned from him, he had given up and left her. It explained the lack of contact over the years. Of course he could have tried harder to get in touch when she was older—Lu was certain that Pixie had passed on every attempt of his to contact her—but as he was rebuffed every time, perhaps it was understandable.

Lu frowned. She couldn't imagine Nick giving up on his boys, not ever, whatever they did, however much they pushed him away. He'd be there for them when they were ready to come back. It was something she admired in him, even though it had meant they'd broken up. But now . . . perhaps she understood a bit better how special that was.

And Nick would never have done something as underhand as threaten poor Pixie with being called an unfit mother. That was unfair, when Pixie was struggling to do her best. Lu shook her head. Her upbringing hadn't exactly been conventional, but she'd always had a roof over her head, food to eat, clothes on her back and, most importantly, creative freedom to let her imagination roam. Without Pixie, Lu wouldn't be the person she was.

Of course, Delia had helped. Lu winced inwardly, remembering what Raven had said. She'd been selfish—she was a teenager; what teenager wasn't selfish? But looking down her nose at Pixie . . . running off to Delia's . . . Hadn't she herself realised that afternoon how much Pixie had felt excluded? She hated to admit it, but Raven was right.

Lu put her head in her hands. What to do what to do what to do? She wanted to hate Pixie for what she'd done, to hate Malcolm for what he'd done, but then she'd have to hate herself for her part in it. Okay, not when she was a child, but growing up she could have investigated her parents' divorce more thoroughly. It wasn't Pixie who'd refused contact with her father when she was in her teens; it had been Lu herself. And sensible, organised Delia and Lu had ganged up on Pixie and her whacky ideas, excluding her from their orderly little world. Unfit? But then, Lu thought, aren't most of us? There wasn't such a thing as a perfect mother or a perfect father. And what about a perfect man?

*　　*　　*

281

Dinner with Marcus was just the antidote to her churning emotions about Pixie and Malcolm. However, while it was very pleasant being with Marcus, there was something lacking. It was hard to put her finger on what it was, given he was charming, considerate, confident. Perhaps that was the problem. He always said the right thing, always did the right thing. He was so perfect it was hard to get a sense of who he was. Conversation was easy but it never challenged her. Not until she casually mentioned that Briony was taking part in a spinathon, pedalling away to raise money for the premature baby unit at the local hospital. 'I expect she's already been after you for sponsorship?' Lu said, thinking of the tenner she'd donated that she couldn't really afford. But then if she could afford fancy lamb chops at a posh restaurant, she could afford to sponsor Briony.

Marcus nodded, cutting a bit of steak. 'Asked, and been refused.'

He sounded very definite, which took Lu aback. 'You don't believe in sponsorship?'

Marcus took a deep breath. 'It's not that I don't believe in it, but I do think it's a dubious way to raise money—after all, in what way could riding a stationary bike for eight hours possibly contribute to the world? Or sitting in a bath of baked beans.'

'It's just for fun,' Lu said, wondering if it was socially acceptable to gnaw her lamb chops rather than try to cut off the fiddly bits of meat with her knife. 'And if it raises money for a good cause, what does it matter what they do?'

'But is it a good cause?' Marcus said.

'It's for premature babies,' Lu said, bewildered. 'Of course it's a good cause.'

'Why of course?'

'Well . . .' Lu floundered, thinking this was like those stupid exercises she could remember from school: describe the inside of a ping-pong ball to a Martian. 'It's saving babies' lives, isn't it. Of course that's good.'

'Given that the world is likely to collapse from overpopulation, I think that's a dodgy argument.' Marcus mopped up gravy with a scrap of bread roll.

Lu put her knife and fork down and leaned forward. 'I know you don't want babies, I don't either, but you can't hate them that much, not so you don't want them to live.'

'You're making me sound like Herod, going out and slaughtering babies of a Saturday morning instead of sensibly trotting round the golf course like everyone else in middle management.' Marcus also put down his knife and fork. 'I don't hate them, I just don't see the point of keeping them alive when they've been born prematurely. It's a sentimentalisation of childhood and children that seems unnecessary.'

'But they're just little babies.'

'Who nature is discarding.' Marcus cocked his head on one side and looked at her, his eyes very direct. 'There must be something wrong with them, or else they would have gone to full term. Nature is merely acting in everyone's best interests, and I don't think it's wise to interfere.'

'So you don't take aspirin when you have a headache?'

'I take paracetamol, usually, but that's not the point. If I have a headache, it's a temporary affliction.'

'Not if you get migraines,' Lu said. She looked at Marcus, uncertain if she wanted to carry on with this conversation. She could feel the grains of interest running away, and she wanted to hang on to whatever she could. Men like him were hard to find. Her rational mind added that maybe there was a reason why he was single: repulsive views. Oh no, perhaps he was going to be a secret admirer of Hitler. Perhaps he believed in eugenics.

'I think it's unusual for migraines to last as long as a lifetime,' Marcus said.

'I don't understand what you're really saying here,' Lu said, thinking that she did, but she so didn't want to. Redeem yourself, Marcus, she pleaded internally.

'Think of it this way,' Marcus said. 'A premature baby is, by definition, one that hasn't reached full term. It's missed out on, what, sixteen, seventeen weeks of development. All the studies show that the vast majority of premature babies have physical or mental impairment—sometimes both. This affects their lives, if they survive, for ever. And the chances are we're talking serious handicaps, not just being slow to learn to read. Many of them will have to have operations to keep them going, painful, extremely arduous operations. Would you seriously wish that on a baby? Isn't that cruel?'

'You could say that of any operation,' Lu said, reeling against the onslaught.

'No, that's not true. You're not thinking for yourself, you're just going along with the sloppy line of thought that says, it's babies therefore it must be good. We want to save voles, but we put down rat poison. Why—are voles better animals than rats? They look more cute, but is that a reason to save their lives? Save the pretty ones, kill the ugly. That's close to eugenics. You'll be telling me you're a fan of Hitler next.'

Lu stared at him open-mouthed. How had he managed to work it so *she* was in support of eugenics? 'I never said anything about voles,' she said weakly, looking around the restaurant for support. Their Christmas decorations were far more restrained; just little silver stars scattered here and there.

'But I bet you support them. Furry foxes, cuddly seal pups, friendly dolphins—who by the way aren't that friendly.'

'We were talking about premature babies,' Lu said, trying to steer the conversation back to the subject.

'Who—and I do hope you agree with me on this one—it is cruel to torture.'

'Yes, but—'

'In addition, having a premature baby puts a huge strain on the parents and any existing children. A higher proportion of marriages where there is a handicapped child end in divorce.'

'But not all premature babies are handicapped.'

'A high enough proportion for me to oppose devoting funds—funds that could go to far more worthy causes, what's more—to striving to keep them alive.'

'I see.' Lu stopped. Well, that was that. She knew how she felt now about him. Not Mr Right, obviously. What could she have been thinking of? 'What you choose to give to charity, or don't choose, is none of my business.'

Marcus stared at his plate, then looked up. 'I've

upset you. I apologise.'

'No, I realise now what an excellent engineer you must be. Determined and logical.' Bullying, she added mentally, feeling cold.

The silence between them grew. She wondered if she should just get up and leave. If she went now, she'd catch the end of *Desperate Housewives*. She smoothed her napkin over her knees, thinking about Nick and how easy their conversations had always been. There had never been any sense of strain with him, until the end. And even then there had always been love and respect between them.

Marcus cleared his throat. 'My sister was premature,' he said very quietly.

Lu glanced up, but he wasn't looking at her.

'My mother was twenty-five weeks pregnant when she went into labour. They fought as hard as they could for the baby, endless operations. She was so small. Later I dissected frogs in biology in school, and that's what she looked like. A frog, splayed out in a plastic cot, tubes everywhere.' He fiddled with the gold signet ring on his little finger. 'She nearly died so many times, but she survived.'

'How old were you?' Lu said, her voice husky.

'When she was born? About four. We went from being a very ordinary, happy family to . . .' Marcus looked away from her as if to hide the vulnerability and pain he knew he'd exposed.

Lu didn't know what to say. 'I'm sorry,' she whispered. It was all she could think of.

'My father couldn't cope with it. She came home, and needed everything doing for her. And I mean everything. For years I thought that everyone's house was stuffed full of nappies. It was all right when she was small, because everyone knew that was what babies did, but later . . . You'd be amazed at how much room adult incontinence pads take up,' Marcus said, smiling at her as if trying to make a joke of it, but she could see the truth in his eyes, and caught her breath that he was trusting her with his story.

'Anyway, Dad bailed out quite early on, leaving me and Mum with Hannah,' he continued. 'Mum had to do everything for her. And she wasn't just physically handicapped, it was mental too. She couldn't control her emotions. She was like a baby; if something disturbed her, or discomforted her, she screamed and had tantrums.' His expression revealed how difficult it had been.

'Everyone said my mother was a saint, as if that let them off the hook from actually helping her, or doing anything. Mum tried her best, but she believed that Hannah should be accepted by society. She insisted on bringing her to playgroup, or on school outings or to parties. In the end she was told Hannah wasn't welcome, that she upset the other children. And she did: she'd scream or lash out. In that case, my mum said, none of us will go. So we stayed at home and no one visited us.'

'It must have been awful for you,' Lu said, nearly in tears, reaching across and squeezing his hand.

He squeezed it back. 'It wasn't ideal, to say the least. But in some ways I should be grateful. I stayed away as much as I could—the library was usually open for a couple of hours after school. I must have been the only child in the history of the universe who actually wanted more homework, so I'd have an excuse to stay. I couldn't work at home—even Mum could see that with Hannah

287

shouting and screaming I couldn't get anything done.' He sighed. 'My poor mum. Dad left, I left as soon as I could, and she was alone with Hannah, who didn't even know who she was.'

'Surely she must have been aware . . .' Lu couldn't imagine what that must be like, to be left caring for a helpless child who couldn't respond, who couldn't love you. Tom, with all the vibrancy and energy sucked out of him, no more hugs and those rare sloppy kisses.

'I'm afraid not,' Marcus said, his voice hard. 'She couldn't make connections with anyone. Mum was any old carer, assuming Hannah even understood the concept of being cared for.'

'What happened? Is she still alive?'

'Thank God, no. She died suddenly when she was twenty-two.'

'How desperately sad.' Lu shook her head in sympathy. 'It must have been so hard for your mother.'

'Yes. It was as if she'd been in prison for twenty-two years, a prison that condemned her to never sleeping more than three hours at a time, to constantly dealing with shit and vomit, to being shunned by society.'

Lu felt that deep sense of shame again, the same as when she'd looked at the gravestones on the Somme. The feeling of wasted lives, and how her own life was so superficial in comparison. 'I feel guilty,' she said. 'I've never really thought about what it must be like.'

Marcus patted her hand. 'I didn't mean to depress you,' he said. 'My family were unlucky; many premature babies aren't as badly handicapped as Hannah was. Some aren't handicapped at all. But I'm sure you understand now why I don't support premature baby units. I think nature should be allowed to take its course.'

'I can see that.' How little she knew of people. She'd assumed Marcus was strong and confident; she'd been fooled by his glossy, hard exterior. Let's face it, she'd been attracted to him because of the way he appeared on the surface. But underneath was someone different, someone vulnerable. She smiled at him, and squeezed his hand again. 'And you didn't depress me. I'm glad you shared that with me.'

Marcus cleared his throat. 'Not many people know about Hannah,' he said. 'It's not a secret, but—'

'I won't tell anyone,' Lu said quickly. 'I wouldn't dream of betraying your confidence like that.'

'Thank you.' Marcus looked directly at her, and Lu felt something flutter inside.

The rest of the meal passed pleasantly. How strange that she'd thought of leaving, Lu thought at one point, finishing off her apple crumble. Marcus was telling her about a conference he'd been speaking at and making her laugh at the absurdities of the regulations.

'Do you speak at a lot of conferences?' Lu asked.

'Enough,' Marcus said. 'It's expected by the company, to a certain extent. I've got one next week, in fact, up in Oxford. I'm speaking on the last day, telling a whole bunch of professors and dons about science applications in business.'

'How impressive,' Lu said, thinking of all the episodes of *Inspector Morse* she'd watched and how intimidating the dons and professors invariably were. 'I'd be terrified.'

'It's no big deal,' Marcus said. 'They're people, just the same as you and me.'

'Yeah, but a bit more intelligent,' Lu said, thinking this wasn't the moment to reveal her meagre collection of exams passed.

'It's a particular type of intelligence,' Marcus said with a shrug. 'It doesn't mean they're any good at being creative,' and he bowed slightly in Lu's direction, 'or making money. Which is why,' he added, taking the bill from the waiter, 'I am paying for dinner.'

'No, at least we should go halves,' Lu said, reaching for her bag, determined to pay.

But Marcus was too quick. He handed his card to the waiter. 'It's mine, because I first upset you and then bored you about the premature babies.'

'I wasn't bored,' Lu protested.

'Never mind,' Marcus said. 'My treat.'

Lu hesitated for a moment. She wanted to pay her own way, but on the other hand, she was broke and he certainly appeared to have all the trappings of wealth. 'Just this once,' she said. 'But next time it's on me.'

She let him help her on with her coat, his hands sure on her body. He was so well mannered. If he asks me to come home with him I'll go, she decided as they left the restaurant. They hovered outside. 'I go this way,' she said, indicating right.

'And I'm this way.' He pointed up left.

'Thank you for a lovely evening,' she said, beaming invisible waves at him: *Kiss me*.

'The pleasure was mine,' he said. He touched her hair, then bent his head and kissed her. Gently at first, then something hungrier, as if let off the

290

lead. His mouth ate hers, lips tingling, teeth occasionally touching, passionate, exciting. One of his hands slipped around her waist, pulling her body towards his. So much for gentlemanly restraint, thought Lu, coming up for air.

'Come back to my place for coffee? It's just round the corner.'

Just a few minutes earlier she had told herself she was going to say yes, but still she hesitated.

'Sorry, I didn't mean to be pushy.' Marcus moved back. 'Perhaps another time.'

Backing off did the trick. 'No, it's fine,' she found herself saying.

*   *   *

Marcus had been telling the truth: his flat was literally just round the corner, a ground-floor and basement conversion of a Georgian house. In theory it wasn't that different from Lu's flat, because most of the Georgian houses followed the same pattern: two rooms on each floor. It was simply the scale that was different, Marcus's main room being big enough to run a five-a-side football tournament in. It was minimally furnished with low-slung chocolate leather sofas, and above the fireplace hung one of Jerry's nudes. It looked good, Lu had to admit, a dramatic splash of colour in the otherwise neutral room. She could live with it, she thought.

'Nice place,' she said.

'Thanks.' He moved through double doors, across a dining area (Lu clocked the Arne Jacobsen table and chairs) and into the kitchen, where he took out a bottle of wine from a special wine refrigerator, the sort Lu had only previously seen in restaurants. 'In a way, the recession has worked in my favour. I was going to sell up when I went to Minneapolis, but because the market is so depressed at the moment I decided to let the flat instead. So it was waiting for me when I came back.' He handed her a glass.

'I thought we were supposed to be having coffee,' Lu said.

Marcus's smile broadened. 'My mistake. Whatever you'd like.' He moved towards an espresso machine.

'Wine's fine,' Lu said, smiling at him with her eyes over the brim of her glass.

They went back to the sitting room and Marcus put on some music, Van Morrison, late-night, mellow music. Seducer's music. And how did she feel about being seduced? Not bad, she thought, the memory of that passionate kiss in her head.

That memory was soon added to with another, and another. It felt like years since she'd smooched with someone on a sofa, although the leather squeaking and creaking made her want to giggle.

'I thought, just my luck to meet someone like you before I was going to Minneapolis. And then coming back and finding you were still free . . .' Marcus nuzzled her shoulder. 'The men around here must be stupid,' he murmured, his breath hot against her neck.

Nick wasn't stupid, Lu wanted to say. Nick was . . . not to be thought of, she decided, and kissed Marcus again. He was a passionate kisser; she'd have stubble rash the next day for sure. His hand slipped inside her shirt, warm against her skin.

Then under her bra. She suddenly remembered him talking, way back on their first date, about the precision technical equipment his company manufactured. His technique was certainly precise. Her equipment fitted neatly into the palm of his hand. His hand moved further down, and that was far enough.

Lu sat up, pushing him away slightly. 'It's late,' she said. 'I've got to get home.'

If he was disappointed he didn't show it. Instead, he walked her all the way back to her flat, even though Lu protested he didn't need to. Still, it was nice that he did.

'This is me,' she said, conscious that her flat was in a far less grand house in a far less salubrious part of Bath. Not that Marcus seemed to notice.

'Listen.' He held her chin so she was looking directly at him. 'I want to see more of you, now I'm back. A lot more of you.'

'Sounds good,' Lu said.

'This conference in Oxford. It finishes Friday afternoon and I was planning to come back, but I was thinking—perhaps you'd like to come up and join me for dinner on Friday evening, and stay over? I'm staying in a very good, very romantic hotel.' He kissed her neck.

Oh, Lu thought. That was like asking her outright if she'd sleep with him. But they were adults, they liked each other. Wasn't that—bed—where this was heading, and why not at a romantic hotel in Oxford?

'Are you asking me to . . . ?'

'To accompany me. To get to know each other better. No strings, but'—he pulled her towards him—'perhaps a few hopes?'

293

Lu grinned back. 'Perhaps.'
'So you'll come?'
She nodded. 'I'd love to.'

*   *   *

What had she got herself into? It was mad—in effect she'd agreed to sleep with a man before the relationship had got that far. Normally sex was something that happened, or didn't, as the case might be. You might hope, you might expect, but it wasn't organised beforehand. Lu told herself to stop fretting; she'd got nearly a week to change her mind, if she wanted to.

She spent Sunday with Briony taking down paintings from the old exhibition and wrapping them in bubble wrap ready for collection by either the customer—hooray!—or the artist—boo-hoo. About a third had sold but Briony was disappointed by the result. The work for the new exhibition was already waiting to be unwrapped and then hung on Monday and Tuesday. Lu helped with that too, and filled Briony in on dinner with Marcus, and the fact that they were having dinner next Friday, but somehow not that the dinner was going to take place in Oxford and be followed by a stay in a romantic hotel. She wasn't quite sure why she didn't tell her that. Perhaps because Briony was so busy telling Lu about how wonderful Simon was, and what a great time they had together; it rather put Lu off from sharing. This year their roles seemed to have reversed, Briony having gone from being in a serious relationship to playing the field, and Lu moving from playing the field to being . . . She pulled

294

herself up. She wasn't in a serious relationship, what was she thinking about? Right now, she didn't have a relationship with Marcus, and as for Nick, that had been . . . well, she'd always known that wasn't going to last, so it couldn't have been serious.

'Cheer up,' Briony said, giving her a push. 'We've just got a few more to do, and then we can relax for a bit before getting everything ready for this evening.'

'Sorry? Oh yes, the paintings.' Lu looked around at the sea of bubble wrap, and the walls covered with lots of small jewel-like pictures that Briony hoped would sell well just before Christmas, small meaning reasonable prices, in her opinion.

Briony gave her a quick appraising glance, but didn't follow up until they were both sitting down with a cup of tea, having five minutes' rest before starting to put out the glasses. 'What's the matter?' she said, perched on the edge of the table with a packet of digestives and sounding more like the usual Briony. 'And don't say nothing. I can tell when you're brooding.'

Lu gazed at her tea cup. Despite the opening, she didn't want to tell Briony about Marcus and his invitation, and the slightly uncomfortable feeling it gave her. She could predict Briony's response: you're not a nun, go out and have a good time. Instead, Lu told her about Pixie and Malcolm and what Raven had said. 'And now I don't know what to do. I feel angry with her for manipulating me, but I also feel sorry for her, and guilty for being horrible to her as a teenager, and on top of it all, I'm confused about my dad. It just seems an awful mess, and I don't know how to sort it out.'

'Wow.' Briony blew out her cheeks. 'That's a lot to deal with all in one go. Why didn't you say anything earlier?'

Lu shrugged non-committally. 'I've been so confused by the whole thing, I haven't been able to talk about it. Besides, I felt I'd rather had my quota of sympathetic shoulder from you.'

'Don't be silly, that's what friends are for.' Briony dunked a digestive into her tea, nodding ruminatively. 'You're right, it's a mess. One question . . .' She popped the digestive into her mouth and chewed while Lu waited. 'The big question: do you love your mum?'

'Of course,' Lu said immediately.

'Of course,' Briony echoed. She picked a bit of digestive from her front teeth. 'You didn't even have to think about that, did you?' Lu shook her head. Briony looked smug as she continued. 'Your mum has probably spent the whole weekend crying her eyes out because she thinks she's lost you again. Her aura has probably washed away.' She smiled at Lu, inviting her to be complicit in the joke, but Lu didn't respond. She wasn't going to make jokes about Pixie's auras again, however daft they were, and besides, Pixie probably *had* spent the weekend crying her eyes out. Poor frightened Pixie.

'I'll go and see her tomorrow,' Lu said.

Briony slid off the table. 'Good. And now that's sorted, it's back to work. You fetch the glasses and the crisps, and I'll get the wine. Party time!'

*　　　*　　　*

Helping Briony out in the gallery was better than nothing, Lu thought as she manoeuvred through the crowd. And in terms of private views, it might even be preferable to be a helper, as you didn't get caught up in boring conversations with Briony's neighbours, but instead could slide gracefully away, waving a bottle of wine to indicate that you were on duty and therefore, sadly, couldn't have another conversation about the progress (or otherwise) of Clive's novel.

Lu topped up glasses and chatted about the art on the walls. She made several definite sales, and a few maybes that she thought might translate to a red dot by the end of the evening. Briony would be pleased with her, she thought, weaving her way round an intense conversation about post-modernism and coming face to face with Nick.

It was so unexpected, she felt poleaxed, as if she'd just run into a door. Oh no, she was going to be sick, she was going to cry, she was going to faint. Everything in her head buzzed and danced, her body was shaking. It was Nick.

'Hello.'

He looked the same as usual, but she could see the lines of tiredness around his eyes. He was wearing a sweater she'd bought him in France, one that had fitted perfectly then but was loose now. Blindly she put out a hand to steady herself and he caught it. His hand, his fingers. She grasped it for a second, before coming back to herself and dropping it.

'Hello,' she said, wondering what to do now. She couldn't look at him.

He leaned forward and they kissed, politely, like

old friends. 'How are you?'

'I'm fine.' It was a lie. Her heart was beating as if she'd drunk six espressos in a row. 'How are you?'

'I'm fine.' He paused, looked at his hands as if he didn't know where to put them.

Hot tears pricked her eyes. 'I'm sorry, I'm being stupid, I just didn't expect to see you here . . .' Oh God. She opened her eyes wide and fixed them on a small painting of a scarlet elephant with an orange howdah, willing herself not to cry.

'It's okay. Let's go outside.' Nick's arm was round her as they went out to the pavement, along with the smokers.

'This is so stupid,' Lu said, trying to smile. Three breaths . . . one . . . two . . . three. Her emotional flood receded. 'Sorry about that. Let's start again. How are you?'

'Still fine.' They looked at each other, eyes searching, trying to find the words to bridge the gulf between them. She wondered if the smokers could sense the tension between them, the sadness and sense of loss. They had always been such friends.

'How are the boys?' she asked. 'How's Ben settling into the new school? And Tom?'

Nick gave a rueful laugh. 'Tom's been in trouble for dropping a water bomb off the balcony into the school hall, and Ben has broken his wrist trying to do wheelies on his bike.'

'Is he okay?' A broken wrist sounded serious.

'He's fine, torn between being thrilled because he can't use his hand for writing essays, and disgusted because he's missed out on football this term.' He shrugged. 'Typical boys. And what about

298

you? How's the book?'

'Oh, the book.' She didn't like to say it was currently lying on her desk, having been rejected by nearly everyone in publishing. 'I've sort of lost impetus with it.'

Nick shook his head. 'Lu, no. It was wonderful.'

'It's nice of you to say that, but . . .'

'It was.' He touched her arm, his hand gentle yet she felt it through to her soul. 'It was the best thing you've done.'

'Oh I don't know,' she said, scrunching her hair in her hands because she was confused being next to him, not being allowed to touch when she was so used to being physically close.

'*I* know,' Nick said. 'And I know it was the best thing you've done.'

'And you're an expert?' Lu said, trying to keep it light, trying to look as if none of it mattered.

'No, but I know when something's real.' He checked himself before carrying on. 'And it is good. You know it is. There's real power there.'

'Yes, of course, it's an emotive subject, but where's the market?'

'Why worry about the market? Isn't that what being an artist is about? Expressing yourself, and hoping other people will buy your vision, but holding on to your dream even if they don't.' Nick's voice became softer. 'You have huge talent. You should use it.'

Lu wanted to believe him. She wanted to believe him so badly, but in the end it was only words. Anyone could say them, anyone at all. She shook her head, unable to speak.

'I miss you,' he said, but she put up her hand to stop him.

'Don't say it. Don't say it or I'll cry again.'

'Lu . . .'

'I'm sorry, I can't have this conversation any more,' she said, pushing past him and going back into the gallery, straight through the guests and up the stairs to the toilet, shutting herself inside. She sat on the seat, head in her hands. Oh God. Oh God oh God oh God.

It was the shock of seeing him, that was what it was. If only she'd known he was going to be there, she could have been prepared. Briony should have said something. Lu frowned, working out that Briony probably hadn't known. Nick was on her mailing list and therefore he was sent notification of all the exhibitions. She checked her mascara, dabbing away at her eyes, trying not to smudge it. Calm down, she told her reflection. You left him because it wasn't going to work out. Her reflection didn't look that impressed.

Think about Marcus, think about Marcus. Lu tried to bring Marcus up in the permanent home cinema that lodged in her brain, Marcus smiling and being charming, the feel of his hand in the small of her back as he considerately walked her home, the clean coolness of his mouth against hers.

Her heartbeat slowed and she was able to breathe more easily. Marcus, that was where her future lay. She would find the money to go skiing. She would have a lovely time with her friends. She would wear salopettes and a bobble hat and only fall over in a cute way that never hurt or looked ridiculous. She would go, even though her credit card would buckle and groan under the strain, and Nick would cease to matter to her.

Already didn't matter to her, she corrected herself. It was only the shock of seeing him again. Plus she was probably feeling a bit emotional, having had the conversation with Briony earlier about Pixie. She breathed deeply again, her emotional guard fully charged and in place. Be serene and calm. Then she opened the door and went back down to the gallery. But though she looked for him everywhere, Nick had gone.

* * *

Lu stood on the pavement with the exhibition artist, Simon and a big group of friends as Briony locked up. It was raining, and there were lots of umbrellas open and cries of hurry up! Lu slung her bag over her shoulder, and as she did so her phone beeped. She'd got a text.

'I'll follow you to the restaurant,' she called out, huddling into the doorway of the gallery as the others moved off, laughing and talking very loudly.

R u ok? N. He'd sent it an hour ago.

Yes. Sorry about that, she texted back.

The reply came back almost immediately. *Can we meet?*

Lu leaned back against the gallery door, her eyes shut. What was the point of meeting? To start up again? She'd already had enough pain this year. And she was with Marcus now. Quickly she texted back: *I can't. I can't.*

* * *

Lu didn't go on to the restaurant. Instead she trudged back home in the rain, half hoping that

301

Nick would call or text her. No, more than half, even though she knew she shouldn't. Seeing him had opened up the wound that had started to heal over, and however much she told herself not to get upset, it was impossible not to. Nick had meant more to her than she had realised, but Marcus was where her future lay.

She slept badly that night, her dreams confused fragments of reality and fantasy. Someone kept stealing her handbag whenever she put it down; it wasn't there when she looked for it again. Scenes shifted from the gallery to her flat to a house that she'd never been to before and yet she knew it was home. Once she thought she was beside the sea, but as she woke she realised it was the sound of the wind and the rain rattling the Georgian sash window of her bedroom.

The morning was dark and stormy, and Lu pottered around her flat before getting dressed, feeling as if she'd got the hangover from hell, although she'd hardly drunk a thing the night before. The dummy of *The Boy Who Went to War* was on her desk, still in its envelope. She ran her fingers over the cover. Nick had said it was the best thing she'd ever done. He said she was talented, an artist. That there was power there.

She turned the computer on, found her format letter. Dear X . . . she hesitated, then—what the hell. She typed in Veronica Meadows instead of X and printed it out. Quickly she popped the letter and the dummy in a new envelope, addressed it, then sealed it tightly before she could change her mind. There.

Her gaze caught the photograph of Jack. She'd got used to having him there while she'd worked on the Arthur book, hoping he'd approve of what she was doing, but now she ought to return him to Delia. Unless . . .

*   *   *

Pixie's expression went from pinched to uncertain to beaten when she answered the door and saw Lu there. She wasn't wearing her usual war paint and her skin looked fragile and taut over her cheekbones.

'Mum,' was all Lu said, but Pixie's face crumpled even further.

'I'm so sorry,' she wailed. 'I'm a bad mother.'

'Don't be silly,' Lu said, hugging her tightly. On the drive over she'd mentally prepared a long speech about how she was feeling, how confused the previous visit had left her, but that all dissolved in Pixie's sobbing. There wasn't really any need to say anything, just to hold her mother and be held by her. Pixie's hair smelled musty and familiar, the scent of home.

Eventually they pulled apart. 'Are you going to invite me in?' Lu said, wiping her face.

In answer, Pixie tugged her into the cottage, mopping at her face and sniffing. She looked at Lu. 'Camomile?'

Lu nodded. 'Please. Is Raven here?' she asked, following Pixie through to the kitchen. It wasn't that she didn't want to see him, just that their last encounter had been strained to say the least, so she was relieved when Pixie said he was at work. He worked for the council, an office job entailing a suit and his hair in a neat plait. Lu had often wondered if they called him Raven or Neil at work, but had never got round to asking. She'd never asked much about him, she realised. She wasn't even sure quite what he did at the council.

Pixie bustled about making camomile tea and chatting cheerfully about the misery she'd endured over the past week, the misery she'd endured in the past full stop.

'But you're here now,' she said, patting Lu's hand.

'I've got an ulterior motive,' Lu said, reaching into her bag and pulling out, with difficulty, the photograph of Jack in its heavy frame. 'This is Jack. I've got as far as I can. I thought you might like to try.' She told Pixie where she'd got to with Jack's story, and how she was also looking for Anne Morgan.

Pixie took the photograph. 'I'll get back to you in a couple of days,' she pronounced, propping Jack up against a pile of butternut squash. 'It shouldn't take long.'

Lu gave her a sideways look. What was she planning to do? 'It is the original,' she said carefully.

Pixie flapped a hand. 'Don't fuss, I'm not going to damage it. I'll give it back to you on Friday.'

'I'm going away for the weekend. To Oxford.'

'After the weekend, then.' Pixie narrowed her eyes slightly. 'Oxford sounds nice.'

'I'm meeting a friend.' Lu stared out of the kitchen window, thinking of Marcus. It seemed a long time since she'd last seen him, and suddenly the idea of meeting him in Oxford seemed sheer madness. But it was what she wanted; she wanted to be wined and dined and bedded by Marcus, who was Mr Perfect, the man who ticked every box on the list. Abruptly she turned back to Pixie. 'Would you read the cards for me?'

Judging by the splutter of camomile tea, Pixie certainly hadn't anticipated that. When she'd stopped choking—'Hayfever, sweet pea,' despite it being December—they went through to the sitting room, where she pulled a long coffee table round to the front of the sofa and covered it with a purple silky cloth that Lu remembered once using to make a princess's cloak. She'd been told off thoroughly, although with hindsight Lu wondered if it was the aspirations to royalty that offended, rather than the insult to the cards.

Pixie produced a cedarwood box and reverentially opened the lid. 'The usual?'

Lu nodded. Pixie used several Tarot packs, but Lu's favourite showed the characters on the cards as romantic knights and fair maidens. As a child she'd secretly hoped she looked like the maiden on the star card, and had squirted lemon juice on her brown hair to make it blonder, though it had resolutely refused to curl at the tips no matter how many times she twirled it around her pencils.

'Shuffle,' Pixie said, handing the pack to Lu.

Lu carefully took the cards and started to shuffle. It wasn't easy, as they were larger than the usual pack of playing cards. It was a long time since she'd done this, but as she shuffled, familiar patterns came into her mind and she let them circle round. As a child she had believed utterly in the Tarot; as a teenager she'd rejected it along with everything else her mother stood for; and as an adult . . . she liked to think she was open-minded.

Tell me what to do, she asked the cards as she

selected seven of them at random and silently passed them to her mother, who carefully laid them out on the table.

'Oooh, look, cups!'

Lu looked. Cups were the modern-day hearts, and represented romance.

Lu hardly ever had cups; it was one of the things that made her both doubt and trust the cards. She had had romance in her life, so the cups should have been there, but it had never turned out that the romance was with The One, so the cards were right to deny her and stick resolutely to pentacles, swords and wands—or diamonds, spades and clubs. Now cups had pitched up, and in force: six of the seven cards were cups. Maybe this was it, maybe Marcus was The One.

'That's the past, that's where you are now, and that's the future. That's you.' Pixie pointed to a flaxen-haired maiden, then tapped one of the cards, the knight of cups, on his white horse. 'Who's he?' she said, a knowing smile on her face.

'No idea,' Lu said. It was strange, but she thought the knight looked a bit like Nick. Weird, when it was obvious that Marcus was the knight in shining armour, sitting proudly on his white charger.

'Is it that nice man I met at your flat ages ago?' Pixie made an interrogative hmm noise. 'The one with the lovely aura?'

'I don't see him any more,' Lu said, because one strange meeting at Briony's gallery didn't count as a meeting, and Pixie was obviously fishing for information so that she could mysteriously see the future in Lu's cards. 'I'm not going to tell you anything about my love life, so you might as well forget it. Tell me about work.'

Pixie handed her the pack, and Lu selected another card and slid it across to her mother.

'That's a nice one. There are going to be trials and troubles, but you'll be triumphant in the end. Look, there you are, waving your flag of victory.'

Lu peered. The card showed a knight in a verdant landscape, his horse wheeling underneath him, a long scarlet pennant fluttering overhead. She couldn't help but find it comforting. So that was work. She pursed her lips, thinking about romance.

'There's a man,' she started to say before being interrupted by Pixie's squeal. 'I won't tell you if you make a fuss.' Pixie looked innocent. 'There's a man. I'm thinking of . . .' Lu couldn't say 'sleeping with him', not to her mother, not even to a mother like Pixie. 'Of taking things further. Is it what I should be doing?'

Pixie silently handed her the pack. Lu shuffled, focusing all her concentration on Marcus and trying not to let any Nick thoughts slip in. She selected a card and passed it across to Pixie. Her hand shook slightly and she realised her heart was beating faster.

Pixie turned the card over. The wizard. 'Is this man a teacher?' Lu couldn't really say yes, although she'd already learned more about semi conductors than she'd known there was to know. Pixie looked nervous, then shook her head. 'I can't answer your question.'

'Can't, or won't?'

Pixie shook her head. 'The cards are always right, but it's a question of interpretation. The wizard might represent a person, an older man you

307

look up to, or he might have something to tell you. There are many interpretations I could make, but it's not clear to me.'

Not blooming clear to me either, Lu thought, that's why I asked. There wasn't any point in getting cross. It was all nonsense anyway. She picked up the wizard. He wasn't young, like the knight of cups, but an older man with a long beard, Merlin-like. What was he trying to tell her?

Pixie gently took the card from her. 'Listen to your heart, sweet pea,' she said. 'If you listen, it'll tell you what to do.'

* * *

It was a beautiful dress, sleek and sophisticated, cut so cleverly it appeared to be one fluid, flowing piece of fabric, but actually made of clever sections so it hung around Lu's body perfectly—the sort of dress an upmarket interiors magazine editor ought to wear. She had bought it some years ago in celebration of a nice royalty cheque (those were the days . . .) but had never quite found the right occasion to wear it. Her need to look sleek and sophisticated, or even like an upmarket interiors magazine editor, was limited. But dinner with Marcus—why, the dress had been made for such an event. She would look sexy, but not so sexy that she couldn't back out later. Not that she was going to back out, of course. Listen to your heart—that was what she was going to do, even though it was such an obvious platitude. Listen to your heart—that could mean almost anything.

She hummed a little tune to herself, imagining Marcus unzipping the dress at the hotel and then

. . . and then her imagination stopped. She couldn't get past the clothed bit into the naked bit, but no matter. It would happen, and they'd all live happily ever after, tra la la. She folded the dress carefully and put it in her overnight bag along with a selection of bras and knickers, and socks and jeans and skirts and shoes. It was so hard to know what to choose, and she wanted to look perfect for tramping round muddy fields or dawdling through a museum. Either seemed equally plausible occupations for a weekend in Oxford, and required equally different clothing.

Everything was going to be perfect, Lu thought. Marcus said that his conference finished at four, and they'd arranged to meet for tea at five. The hotel wasn't far from the station, so she was going to take the train. She hoicked the bag off the bed and practically extended her arm by four inches as it plummeted to the ground. A little bit of editing was going to be required. She would decide what to travel in first, and then take it from there.

She hauled the bag into the bathroom and tried her jeans and jacket on. That was a trusted formula for travelling, and she could change into the dress when she got to the hotel. One decision made. She could wear the jeans if they went on a muddy walk. She took them off and put them to one side. Now, what else could she wear with the jacket? She turned to examine the contents of the bag, but stopped as she caught sight of her lower half in the mirror.

What had happened? She knew what had happened: in an effort to cut costs, she'd cancelled her regular waxing appointment at the beauty salon and this was the result, closer to a badger on

Regaine than smooth perfection. She couldn't go away for a romantic weekend and be hairy.

Rummaging in her cupboard, she found an old tube of hair remover. She examined the label, looking for a sell-by date. It surely didn't go off; it must be so full of chemicals it was indestructible. She squeezed a dollop out and sniffed, but as it always smelt foul, it was hardly a help. She weighed the tube in her hand. Dilemma. Risk the chemicals, or go hairy? Decision made, she stood in the bathroom, spatula at the ready. Here goes.

The phone call came just as she had smeared hair remover over her bikini line. Perhaps it was Marcus, checking she was still coming. Peering out of the bathroom, she realised that the curtains in the front room were wide open, so she dropped to her knees, keeping her naked lower half out of view of any passers-by in the street outside. The phone was insistent.

'Coming, coming,' she muttered, shuffling along on her knees, legs wide to avoid too much stickiness spreading. I must look like a surrealist dwarf from *Snow White*, she thought, with my long white beard in the wrong place. Or a miniature Scotsman without a kilt but with a bushy sporran. She could feel the squelching in the creases of her thighs as she reached up for the phone. If only Marcus could see me now, she thought, picking it up and smiling in anticipation of his voice.

But it wasn't Marcus. It was Delia's neighbour, Mrs McAllister, telling her that Delia had been taken in to hospital.

Chapter 16

'You idiot,' Lu said, plonking herself down on the bed. 'What on earth possessed you?'

'It needed doing,' Delia said, as if that was all the explanation needed. She was looking wan and every day of her ninety-two years, a pale-blue cellular blanket draped around her shoulders. Underneath it, several wires ran to a machine by her side.

'You're nearly ninety-three. You don't go round climbing ladders to clear the moss from the gutters; you phone me up and I do it, or I arrange for someone to come.'

'Tsk,' Delia said. 'I know you're busy.'

Lu shuffled round on the bed. Somehow a whole week had gone past since she'd last visited, and she couldn't use work as an excuse because there wasn't any.

'I'm never too busy to come and help. Besides, it's a complete waste of all our time if I have to come and visit you here.' She could feel her inner thighs twitching. Damn, she probably hadn't washed all the chemicals off her skin. Tonight I will make love to Marcus, she thought, and the skin on her thighs flared all over, though whether it was anticipation or allergy she couldn't say. A faint smell of ammonia wafted upwards, and she hoped that was hospital rather than hair remover. 'So what's happening? Do you want me to give you a lift home?'

Delia shook her head. 'They want me to stay in.'

Lu felt a cold chill as she looked at Delia's

beloved face, already imagining the worst. 'Why?'

'Nothing serious.' Delia was matter-of-fact, slightly annoyed if anything. 'They want to do some tests. They think I might have had a heart attack or something.'

'Gran! Mrs McAllister said you'd fallen off the ladder.'

'Oh don't fuss, it's nothing. They just want to check me out, that's all. Which is why I'm so pleased to see you.' She looked up at Lu expectantly. 'I'm worried about Scottie. Mrs McAllister says she'll keep an eye on him, but it's not the same. Could you have him for the weekend? It'd be a great relief to me.'

Lu looked at the bedspread. 'I was going away this weekend,' she mumbled, not meeting Delia's eyes. Having been uncertain about the hotel, she now wanted nothing but to stay in a room with linen sheets and a luxury bathroom. And then there was Marcus. Something told her that he wasn't a doggy person.

Delia's face crumpled. She seemed to have shrunk in the bed. 'Scottie will be fine with Mrs McAllister,' she said, her wrinkled fingers pulling at the sheets.

It was one of those horrible moments when you know what the right thing to do is, but you so don't want to do it. Lu's brain wanted her to rationalise, to come up with some compelling argument that would let her off the hook. On the one hand there was the prospect of passionate first-time sex with an exciting new man. On the other, a small hairy dog and her grandmother's anxiety. I'm not a saint, she told herself. I've got other plans.

'Of course I'll take care of Scottie,' she said, as

312

the prospect of passion dwindled. 'Don't worry, just concentrate on getting better.'

'There you are!' It was Pixie, resplendent in a swirling cape designed for swishing about romantically on deserted moorlands. 'What did you think you were doing? You should have asked me!'

Delia explained that she wasn't decrepit yet and could clear her own gutters very nicely thank you, and Lu told Pixie about the suspected heart attack.

'They might fit a pacemaker,' Delia added. 'But I don't like the idea of it.'

'Now, Ma,' Pixie said. 'Don't be difficult. If that's what they say you need, then that's what you should have.' She sat on the edge of the bed on the other side to Lu. 'Look what I've brought with me.'

She took out the photograph of Jack and started to tell Delia all about Jack's childhood. It was a very colourful account, with lots of details about getting into trouble for scrumping apples, but not much that one could call hard evidence. Pixie was in her element, though, and Delia looked happy, saying well I never at appropriate intervals. Lu decided against pointing out the inconsistencies.

A doctor came round and explained the medical situation to them. Delia had had a mild heart attack, and yes, they wanted to fit a pacemaker. But she also had a raised temperature, possibly caused by an infection from the bump on the head she'd got when she fell off the ladder. Pixie and Lu both looked at Delia, who looked sheepishly back. Until the infection cleared and she'd had forty-eight hours without a temperature, they couldn't fit the pacemaker.

'So when will that be?' Pixie asked.

313

'Probably at least a week, but it may be more. And she'll have to stay here so we can monitor her.'

'But Scottie—' Delia started to say. Lu quickly reassured her.

'Don't worry, I'll make sure Scottie is fine,' she said, before turning back to the doctor. 'Will she be home in time for Christmas?'

'Once she's had the pacemaker fitted, she can go home the next day, but I understand you live alone?' Delia nodded. 'You'll have to be with someone. Could it be one of you?'

'You'll come and stay with me and Raven,' Pixie said firmly, her hand on Delia's. 'We'll have Christmas at my house. You too, Lunabella.'

Lu nodded meekly, happy to let Pixie be in charge, and the doctor continued on his rounds. And Pixie was definitely being in charge. She bustled around Delia's bed, tucking in everything she could see until Delia was pinned flat to the bed, gave the curtains a good shake, and sent Lu off to find fresh water. When Lu came back with a refilled jug, Pixie was studying Delia's medical notes in a way Lu guessed she'd picked up from watching *ER*. She'd slipped off her cloak and donned orange diamanté reading glasses, which gave her the appearance of a librarian re-imagined by Andy Warhol in blocks of bright and unlikely colours.

'I thought you were going away for the weekend to see your friend in Oxford,' Pixie said, as Delia took advantage of being out of Pixie's sight line to surreptitiously tug at her blankets to loosen them.

'I was, but I've got to look after Scottie.' Lu brightened, thinking that if Pixie was in such a

314

managing mood, there might be one more thing she'd like to manage. 'Mum, could you look after him, just for the weekend?'

'Oh no, the cats wouldn't like it at all. Grimalkin went off in a huff the last time he visited and we couldn't get her down from the roof for ages.' Pixie deftly tucked Delia back in.

Lu looked around. There wasn't anything for her to do here. She gave Pixie a goodbye hug. 'I'll be off to collect Scottie then. Bye, Gran.' She pressed her face against Delia's soft cheek. Don't die, she told her silently.

'Goodbye, my darling.' Delia touched Lu's face. 'You're a good girl.'

'Thanks, Gran.' Lu shifted from one foot to the other, not wanting to go but knowing there was nothing she could do. Delia was in safe hands, and of course she had the added advantage of her daughter looking after her. 'Is there anything at all I can do before I go?'

Pixie smiled and shook her head, but Delia tried to twist round in the bed. She failed due to being anchored so snugly. Instead she beckoned to Lu. 'The photograph. I don't want it here. Can you leave it at home when you pick up Scottie?'

'Of course,' said Lu, picking up Jack's photograph. She couldn't resist kissing Delia again. 'Love you,' she whispered.

*   *   *

Now what? As soon as she left the hospital building she turned her mobile back on and rang Marcus. No answer—his mobile was obviously turned off, as he himself was going to be at the

315

prospect of sharing his weekend with an animated hearthrug. Oh well, there would be other occasions, she rationalised, but disappointment hung in the air like a mist; she could feel it emanating off her. Or maybe that was just the hair remover, which was beginning to burn.

Delia's house seemed very empty without her. Scottie was so delighted to see Lu he farted. I guess this is the epitome of welcome, she thought, locating his lead and basket, food and bowls. She went to tell Mrs McAllister next door that she'd taken him. Mrs McAllister made a good show of looking sad.

'I'll miss the wee fellow,' she said, wee being the appropriate word as Scottie lifted a stumpy leg over her wallflowers.

Yeah, right, Lu thought as she drove back home. My weekend of passion, me and Scottie together. Pixie would say it was the fates combining against her and Marcus. Lu was about to text him the bad news when suddenly she rallied. Stuff the fates. It wasn't ideal, but she wasn't going to give up without a fight.

She rang the hotel: yes, they accepted dogs. And they could offer parking.

'Scottie,' she said. 'You shall go to the ball!'

*   *   *

In retrospect, Lu thought Marcus reacted really rather well. He was expecting a glamorous weekend in a posh hotel with a new girlfriend, a situation that would, hopefully, involve a lot of good wine, delicious food and excellent sex. A few quirks were to be expected—an allergy rash on the inner thigh caused by out-of-date depilator, maybe—but in general the weekend was planned and plotted. When he saw Lu his smile broadened and he embraced her, getting tangled in a short tartan lead at the end of which loitered the whiskery face, complete with lolling tongue, of Scottie. It was eternally to his credit that his smile only faltered slightly as she explained the situation.

'My grandmother's ill—I had to bring him. The hotel said it was fine.' She looked up at him nervously. 'I hope you like dogs.'

'To be honest, I've not had much to do with them.' Marcus looked down at where Scottie was cheerfully engaged in spreading white hairs over his dark navy suit trousers, creating dense cross-hatching against the pinstripes. 'Are you sure the hotel is happy?' His voice sounded hopeful of refusal.

'Yes, I rang up, and they've confirmed it again at reception now. Dogs are allowed here.'

Marcus clasped his hands together. 'Excellent. In that case—welcome . . . what's his name?'

'Scottie,' Lu said. 'I know, unbelievably unimaginative.'

'Better than something like Pushkin for a cat.' He leaned down and tentatively patted Scottie on the head. 'Hello, Scottie. Beam me up!'

'Thank you so much for being understanding. I really didn't know what else to do,' Lu said as Marcus stood up, wiping his hands.

He arranged for Lu's bag and Scottie's bed to be taken up to their bedroom, with an ease that impressed Lu. 'Shall we go up and have a drink?'

'That'd be lovely.' Lu followed Marcus, Scottie trotting happily beside them. The hotel had been created from a former prison, now all in luxurious plum and midnight blues. They went up to the bar in the lift, padded like a madman's cell, emerging into a tall room that you could imagine being an exercise room, or perhaps a judgement hall. The windows were so high up only a man on stilts could see out. Everything was midnight blue—the walls, the upholstery on the chairs and sofas—although the carpet was Black Watch tartan. It was very sophisticated and oozed sexiness, but the atmosphere had the opposite effect on Lu. Or maybe it was harder to feel sexy when you were towing along a small scruffy terrier.

'How was your conference?' she asked, as they settled down on a cosy velvet sofa made just for two. 'Did your speech go well?'

'I think so,' Marcus said. In between ordering champagne he told her about the conference, the excellent and varied points he had made, the applause at the end, the intelligent questions. 'I'm not going to plead false modesty,' he said, 'but I rather think I was one of the conference highlights, hence . . .' He indicated the champagne.

Lu raised her glass. 'To your speech.'

Marcus inclined his head. 'It was good,' he admitted. 'I think there'll be quite a few people talking about it this evening and over the weekend.'

'What was it about?' Lu asked, and while Scottie lay at her feet, snoring gently, Marcus told her. And told her. The trouble was, while Lu understood individual words, they made no sense when put together into sentences. It was a bit like reading Stephen Hawking's book on particle physics: you felt you understood it the moment you read it, but when you stopped to think about it, you realised you were still none the wiser.

Invest in a dictionary of business jargon, that was the answer. Then she could get to grips with what a PE ratio was—nothing to do with gyms, she gathered. It was unfair on Marcus to expect him to explain every little term. When he said things like 'getting my ducks in a row', she imagined a line of fluffy ducklings bustling up to stand behind their proud mother. He'd already explained the difference between a bull and a bear market, but she still wasn't quite sure which was the desirable one. It was one of those things—like being asked to spell 'necessary' aloud, or define the word 'crepuscular', or explain French phrases used in novels without a translation—that seemed designed to confuse and unsettle you, even if you thought you knew what the answer was before the question had been asked.

She was never more aware of her lack of formal education than when she was with Marcus. If she was to be his Miss Right, she was going to have to do some research. She stared into his chocolate-brown eyes, thinking it might be fun to learn about a different world. Everyone she knew was involved in the creative sector. Marcus opened up new horizons, a new way of life.

Drinks finished, Marcus suggested going to their room to freshen up and change before dinner. Lu nodded. They were the only people in the lift, and as the doors closed, he took her in his arms and drew her to him in what should have been a glorious snog, except that Scottie jumped up at them, lead rattling like the ghosts of ancient prisoners past.

'I hope he's not going to do that every time I want to kiss you,' Marcus said as the lift door opened on their floor.

'I'm sure he won't,' Lu said, despite not knowing. She didn't suppose that Delia went in for wild embracing at home, so she could hardly think it was what Scottie was used to. 'Oh my,' she said, stepping out of the lift and looking around her.

The hotel bedrooms were in what had been a wing of the original prison, with an open central light well, and tiers of cast-iron walkways and staircases running between them. Every eight feet or so was a heavy cell door. Marcus went across one of the walkways, over the open space to the other side. Lu followed, thinking it was a good thing she didn't suffer from vertigo. He opened one of the cell doors, and it slowly swung back to reveal not a tiny chamber but a large double bedroom, following a similarly dark colour scheme as the bar area, but this time in plum and chocolate, like being inside a gigantic marron glacé. Looking up at the vaulted ceiling, she realised that the room had been formed from two of the original cells.

'How many prison jokes can you think of?' Lu said, hiding her nervousness with a smile. Suddenly being here in this room made what was to come seem all too real. It was one thing to agree to come away on a weekend with Marcus after a passionate kiss at the end of an evening; quite another when she was alone with him in a room dominated by an enormous double bed. The door clanged shut behind her.

'Look, Scottie, some nice person's brought your bed up. And there's your bowl. What were the

320

names of the people in *Porridge*? Fletcher, wasn't it?' Lu bent to unclip Scottie's lead. 'And the other one . . . what was he called?'

Marcus shook his head as he tugged his tie undone. 'Search me.'

Oh no, he was getting undressed. 'He was Kate Beckinsale's father in real life, I think. Something Beckinsale, I suppose.' What was she doing jabbering on about *Porridge*? Anyone would think she was nervous. Which she wasn't. Or maybe just a little. She sat on the bed, then decided against it and circled round to examine the small windows, which still had bars across them. 'It's a bit creepy,' she said.

Marcus came over and held her, and this time Scottie did no more than bark a couple of times as he kissed her thoroughly. Lu wanted him to reassure her that it would be okay, but instead he pulled away. 'I'm going to grab a quick shower and change before we go down to dinner,' he said. 'Okay?'

'Of course.' He went into the bathroom— another cell—and shut the door. Lu sat on the bed feeling uncertain. It wasn't that she didn't want him; it just seemed strange, as if she'd made an agreement and now he felt there was no need for her to be wooed. And she wanted to be wooed. Seduce me, she thought as she looked at the bathroom door. Make me feel desire. Make me want you.

She looked round the room, thinking it was literally a luxurious prison. Sighing, she located her bag and opened it up, pulling out her dress. She didn't need a shower, having spent hours earlier showering off the hair remover. She dressed quickly, hurrying so as not to be discovered by Marcus in any stage of nakedness. Once in her beautiful dress, she began to feel better, more as if she belonged here. She looked around the bedroom, examining the various things that had been left on display. There was a typed history that she started to read. Heavens, the original castle on the site was old, Norman Conquest era. She got to the bit about torture at the prison, then shoved the history in a drawer. This weekend was supposed to be romantic, not tortuous.

The bathroom door opened, and Marcus came out, humming gently, a towel round his waist. She realised she was sitting like the Queen, knees together, hands neatly in her lap, and jumped up. 'Everything okay?' he said absent-mindedly, as he looked in the wardrobe for a shirt. He'd been here for a few days, judging by the number of shirts hanging there.

'Yes, fine,' Lu said. 'The story of the prison is a bit gruesome.'

'Really?' Marcus slipped his shirt on. Lu bent down to examine the strap of her shoe, not wanting to see him without the towel, not at this stage. It felt wrong, as if she were coming to it cold. The champagne didn't seem to have affected her at all. She longed for another drink as fervently as an alcoholic.

Marcus went back and forward between the bathroom and the bedroom, apparently oblivious to what Lu thought was an awkward situation. Although perhaps that was the solution. Pretend this was everyday, pretend they were already lovers and were simply getting ready to go out. Otherwise it was too embarrassing. Finally he was ready, and with one last goodbye stroke to Scottie, they went downstairs.

The dining room was in the basement. The torture chamber, Lu thought, looking around her nervously, although to be honest it could be any smart basement restaurant with low lighting and lots of small tables.

Lu chose from the menu while Marcus read the wine list. 'What would you like?'

'White wine, please. Something light.' And lots of it, she felt like adding. The waiter came, and they placed their orders.

'Have you thought any more about going skiing?' Marcus said, leaning back.

'I'd like to go, but I don't think it's practical, to be honest,' Lu said.

'You don't want to be practical,' Marcus said. 'Think of the adventure, the challenge . . .'

The cost, Lu thought, as Marcus continued to extol the virtues of skiing. He did seem keen, as his pitch lasted long enough for the wine to come: white for her, red for him. 'Sorry.' He grinned sheepishly. 'I've been boring on about skiing.'

'It was interesting,' Lu said, not entirely truthfully, as the waiter poured their wine.

'I got you the Pinot Grigio in the end,' Marcus said. 'I toyed with the white Rioja, but decided against it; I thought you'd find it a bit too heavy if you like light whites. Too much alcohol.'

'I'm sure this will be delicious,' Lu said, taking a good sip. 'I didn't know you could have too much alcohol in wine,' she added. 'It sounds like a good idea to me.'

'If your purpose is to get drunk.'

323

'Perish the thought,' Lu said, not wanting to sound like a complete alcoholic.

'It's not good to have too much alcohol. There's the practical problem that it prevents people from calculating exactly how much they've had to drink, but there's also the issue of the character of the wine itself. This red, for example,' and Marcus swirled the wine around the glass. 'It needs a certain amount of alcohol to give it body, but too much and the wine is off balance.' He took a sip. 'This is about right.'

'Heavens, and there was I thinking all you needed to know was your credit card number for the next bottle.' Lu took a sip. 'You know a lot about wine; is it one of your hobbies?'

'I wouldn't say that,' Marcus said. 'Just knowledge I've acquired.'

There was a slight pause. He's probably nervous too, Lu thought, and that's making him pompous. She knew she was being more giggly than she was normally. Not that she was nervous exactly. If anything, she felt unmoved, but that was probably a sign of defensiveness. You'd have to expect the first time with someone to feel a bit strange, she thought, especially when you'd broken up with someone else. The memory of leaving Nick hit her, that dreadful moment when she walked out of his house, and she dropped her head for a second, overwhelmed by loss. But she wasn't going to allow herself to be self-indulgent, she thought. She was here with Marcus, and he was an altogether different prospect. This was a new beginning for her. This was the future.

Dinner was delicious, but Lu got more and more clumsy as the meal went on. She kept dropping the cutlery, and knocked over her wine glass. Cue mad mopping with her table napkin. She didn't seem to be able to do anything right. And the food didn't help. She'd ordered fish, and the mechanics of de-boning a Dover sole appeared to have escaped her. All adeptness had gone from her fingers and she ended up with something that resembled mashed potato rather than delicate fish fillets on her plate. It wasn't the alcohol; it was the thought of what was to come. Her stomach had gone beyond the pleasurable flutter of anticipation to a full-blown nervous storm.

'Shall I take you to bed?' Marcus finally said, an amused smile on his face.

Lu drained her glass. 'Yes please.'

They kissed in the lift going up, Marcus with his hand on her left buttock, as if it were a peach he had to test for firmness. Lu closed her eyes tightly and willed herself to feel something. They went along the walkway, Marcus gently jiggling the room keys. He was so self-assured. She'd been attracted by that assurance at the beginning, so it was perverse that she found it extremely annoying now. It's the weirdness, she told herself. Normally sex just happens. It isn't planned and arranged. It's about being caught up in the moment. She tried to remember how she'd felt when they'd last seen each other, that moment of passion.

Scottie was thrilled to see them, scampering round and yapping. 'I hope he's not going to do that all night,' Marcus said, yawning and pulling his sweater over his head.

Shit. 'I've got to take him out for a wee,' Lu said.

Marcus looked up disbelievingly.

'Sorry,' Lu said, swiftly clipping Scottie's lead on and ushering him outside. Back down in the lift, and out to the front of the hotel. There Scottie meandered round sniffing the shrubs in planters while Lu shivered, her breath freezing in the cold night air. We could do a runner, she thought. My car's here; I'd just have to ask reception for the keys. She looked through the doors into the hotel. Reception was all lit up and twinkling like a mirage.

What was she thinking of? Anyone would think she'd never had sex before, or that Marcus was repulsive. And he wasn't, he was gorgeous. Everyone said so. Scottie lifted his leg and a pungent stream ensued. Decision time. Except it wasn't a decision. She was here and she was going to have a great time. There was just this literal hump to be got over. First time is always tricky, she thought. The moment of truth.

Lu and Scottie trailed past reception, but no one looked up. Up in the lift—again. She was getting used to its vagaries, the way its doors shushed open. Then along the walkway, feet silent on the carpet, and into the room.

Marcus lay in the bed, his arms akimbo, hands cradling his head. His top half was naked, and she could see dark chest hair against tanned skin. Attractive, except she felt like a prostitute called from room service. She unclipped Scottie's lead and told him to go to his bed. The dog obediently hopped into his basket, circled round and lay down, nose pointing over the edge. Lu went to the bathroom, trying not to look at Marcus naked in the bed, and brushed her teeth. Her reflection looked perfectly normal, as far as she could see from the seductive low lighting.

As she went back into the bedroom, she hesitated. What she really wanted was for Marcus to take the lead and then she could follow, but he was lying back on the bed waiting for her. Surely he couldn't expect her to undress in front of him like a stripper? Why, he was virtually a stranger to her. Don't be silly, Lu thought. You're behaving like a virgin, and that's the last thing you are. Come on, take charge. You lead, if he's not going to. Not that she was going to strip in front of him. She wasn't that drunk; in fact, she felt nearly sober, apart from an other-worldly sensation that she was watching herself.

She sat on the edge of the bed and kicked her shoes off. Back towards him, she lifted her hair up to expose the back of her neck. 'You couldn't undo my necklace, could you? The catch is tricky.'

Marcus edged nearer. She could feel his warm breath on her shoulders, his hands touching her skin, caressing her neck. That was better, Lu thought, leaning back into him. She felt his hands on the catch, then the necklace coming loose. He reached past her and put it on the bedside locker. She stayed still, waiting. He unzipped the back of her dress, then slipped it off her shoulders, kissing her neck, her shoulder, the top of her arms as the fabric fell to her waist, leaving her naked. Yes, that was better. She twisted round to him, warm skin against skin, his hands on her body, her pulling him towards her. And then she was on her back, wriggling out of her dress, lifting her hips so the material dropped to the floor, Marcus looming over her, kissing her, touching her.

'Hang on,' she whispered, and deftly tucked

herself under the duvet. Now they were face to face, naked under the covers, not that she'd got as far as exploring his body; her hands were firmly above the duvet, which was acting as an imaginary Plimsoll line. He stroked the hair off her face, his eyes half closed. He looked . . . a bit dopey, to be honest. Don't think like that, she commanded, plunging towards him and kissing him with all the passion she could muster, eyes tightly shut. This was Marcus, aka Mr Gorgeous, the Perfect One, Mr Right. Marcus who ticked all the boxes. His hands were exploring the lower decks, and she wanted it to work. But—and she had to admit it to herself—not much was happening. There wasn't enough sexual thrill to moisten a postage stamp.

Scottie in his basket gave a low growl, and the noise reminded her of Nick snoring gently on the sofa, then waking up and seeing her, his smile so genuine, so delighted that she felt warm all over just from the memory.

Marcus was still rummaging around, but Lu felt so detached, he could have been searching for a lucky ticket in the bran tub. What was it about her that meant she was unable to respond? Perhaps anxiety over Delia, or the prospect of performing in front of an audience, albeit a gently snoring canine one?

Something of her response must have got through to Marcus, because all of a sudden he stopped, and she opened her eyes to find him looking at her. His expression was wary.

'What's wrong?' he said.

Lu licked her lips nervously. What she should have said was something like, it's fine. Perhaps with a dollop of groaning on the side. 'I don't know,' she whispered instead.

Marcus withdrew his hand.

'I'm sorry,' Lu said. 'I wanted this to work, I don't know why it's—'

'Are you frigid or what?' His voice was harsh with disappointment.

'No, and I'm not a lesbian either,' Lu said. 'I've just . . . changed my mind, that's all.'

'Changed your mind?' Marcus sounded incredulous. 'Changed your mind?' His voice rose. 'What do you mean, you've changed your mind?'

'I'm allowed to,' Lu squeaked.

'Jeez.' Marcus flopped back against the bed.

'I'm so sorry, it's just I don't fancy you.'

'Great. Is that supposed to make me feel better?' He sat up and swung his legs out of bed as if about to leap out. 'What the fuck are you doing here then?'

'I thought I did, I thought you were Mr Perfect.' Marcus gave a disgusted snort. 'No, I did,' Lu persisted. 'You're everything I want in a man. It's just I don't—'

'Fancy me,' Marcus said. 'Yeah, I've got that message.' He suddenly turned round, his face dark. 'What's going on here? What are you doing? Are you stupid, or what?'

Lu suddenly realised she was in a vulnerable position. She had voluntarily got into bed naked with this man, and all the staff would testify to their candlelit dinner. Even if she screamed the place down, no one would hear through these thick walls. What had she been thinking? 'Yes, I'm stupid,' she said, hugging a pillow to her. 'Stupid enough to think you were the man for me.' So stupid, she thought, staring at Marcus. 'You're not

Mr Right,' she said indignantly.

'I never said I was,' he replied, equally indignant. 'What the hell's your problem?' There was a low growl and suddenly Marcus yelled, 'Fuck!' He shot out of the bed, batting at his lower legs. 'Call your bloody dog off! The bastard's bitten me.'

Lu scooted over to Marcus's side of the bed. Marcus, hands cupped in an effort to protect the crown jewels from Scottie's sharp little teeth, was hopping around trying to kick the dog off his right leg, and Scottie—judging by the determination that shone out of his eyes—was not letting go. 'God, I'm sorry—Scottie, stop it, let go.'

'It hurts,' Marcus said, giving such a kick that Scottie was spun off his feet.

'Just sit down for a sec,' Lu said. 'Stop fighting him.'

'I'm not fighting him,' Marcus moaned, hopping about and jiggling. It was not a good look. 'He attacked me.'

'He was only trying to defend me,' Lu said, trying not to laugh at the sight. Oh dear, it really wasn't funny. 'Scottie, drop! Drop it!'

Scottie dropped.

'Look what he's done,' Marcus wailed, collapsing back on the bed. 'I'm bleeding.'

And he was. Lu rushed into the bathroom and grabbed handfuls of cotton wool and loo paper. When she came back she handed them to Marcus, then, realising she was still naked, found her knickers plus the T-shirt she'd planned to wear the next day and slipped them on.

Marcus had wrapped himself in the duvet and was examining his leg, dabbing at it with a cotton

330

wool ball. The wound didn't look as bad as she'd first thought, although it was dreadful that he'd been bitten at all.

'Are you okay?' she said, not sure of what the best approach was.

'I'm probably going to die of tetanus.' Marcus was hunched over his leg.

'It doesn't look that bad . . .'

'Or blood poisoning.'

'Isn't tetanus blood poisoning? I thought it was the same thing.'

'No, it's quite different. Tetanus is lockjaw.'

Lu realised that she was lacking in the Florence Nightingale stakes. 'How's your jaw feeling?'

Marcus threw her a filthy look.

'Sorry.'

She sat on the bed, wondering what to do next. Scottie came over to her, and she gently stroked his head. Really, it was quite impressive, little Scottie tackling a great big man like Marcus, just to try and rescue her. 'Good boy,' she murmured. 'Good dog.'

'Good dog?' Marcus was outraged. 'He's taken a whopping great chunk out of my leg. He ought to be destroyed.'

'No! You couldn't put Scottie down. He was trying to protect me; he didn't understand what was happening.'

'*He* didn't understand? *I* didn't understand.' Marcus gave a deep sigh, and moved round to look at Lu. 'I don't understand,' he said, his tone softer.

'I don't understand either,' Lu said. 'I like you a lot and you're really good-looking and interesting and everything I've ever thought I wanted.'

'But?'

331

'But . . .' Lu stroked Scottie's head. 'Something is stopping me. I don't know what it is, but it's there, and there's nothing I can do about it.'

'Bit late in the day to find out.'

'I know, and I'm so sorry. You see, I really wanted this to work. I really, really did.'

There was a long silence. Lu looked around the room, thinking of the previous occupants, from romantic trysts to banged-up prisoners, a whole spectrum of delight and disaster.

Marcus broke the silence. 'I'm tired. I'm going to sleep and we can sort this out in the morning.'

Lu considered. Should she go? Her car was in the car park, but she'd had enough to drink to be well over the limit, although she felt stone-cold sober.

'What about me?'

'Oh, just go to sleep. I promise I won't pounce on you in the night. Frankly, it's the last thing I'm interested in right now.' Marcus yawned, rolled over in the bed and turned out his bedside light. 'Just keep the bloody mutt away from me.'

Lu led Scottie round to his basket and settled him down with a dog biscuit. She knew she shouldn't reward him for biting Marcus, but he had been brave. Her knight in scruffy hair. He was softly crunching the biscuit as she slipped into bed. Marcus was hunched over on his side, his back unforgiving.

'Sleep well,' she said automatically as she turned out her bedside light. Then, because she meant it, 'I really am sorry.'

'Never mind,' Marcus mumbled. 'Let's face it, you're either frigid, a lesbian or still in love with your ex-boyfriend. Take your pick, I'm past caring.

G'night.'

She wasn't a lesbian.

She wasn't frigid.

Lu stared into the darkness, wondering about the third option.

Chapter 17

Lu got up early after a restless night and took a sleepy Scottie for a walk around Oxford. She wished she knew the city better, because she ended up trailing down a row of high-street shops that could have been anywhere in the country, instead of wandering romantically through dew-spattered meadows twinkling in the misty sunshine. Not that they would have been dew-spattered even if she could have found them, given that it was a wet mid-December morning and not May. Still, at least Scottie enjoyed the walk, sniffing enthusiastically at every corner and doorway and leaving his own trail where, Lu guessed, quite a few lads had been the previous night.

Breakfast was a stilted affair, Marcus businesslike as if he'd already decided to cut Lu out of his life. She was sad, in a way, because it was always sad when a door closed. But regrets? She looked at his handsome face and knew she had none. He wasn't Mr Right, after all.

They packed, and Marcus checked out. Lu offered to pay her share of the bill, but Marcus pursed his lips. 'It's on expenses.'

Lu adjusted Scottie's basket under her arm. 'I must at least pay for Scottie.' But Marcus put his hand up in a way that made it obvious he would rather just forget about the whole incident. They went out to the front, where their cars were parked.

'Goodbye.' Lu held out her hand. For a second she wondered if he was going to take it, but eventually he did. 'Sorry about the leg.'

'If it festers, I'll sue.' He didn't smile as he got in his shiny car, so she wasn't sure if he was joking or not. Suddenly she realised he was a major-league bore, so there were no second thoughts as he drove off and she loaded Scottie and his bed into her rust-bucket of a car, beyond hoping that Scottie's teeth weren't too infested with bacteria.

The drive home was easy, which was good, given the thoughts that pounded against Lu's brain. She didn't want to listen to them, she rejected them, she pushed them away, but still they kept surging back, persistent and insinuating. What about Nick? How do you feel about Nick? You still love him, don't you? Don't you?

'I don't know,' Lu cried aloud, hands gripping the steering wheel as she turned off at Junction 18 towards Bath. 'I don't know.'

*   *   *

Lu was home by eleven, her weekend stretching emptily in front of her. She imagined that Nick would be with the boys. School had finished for the term by now, she guessed, so they were probably doing something together. Football or swimming, maybe. Tom liked making models for some war game and could spend hours in the games shop having battles with his army of space dragons. She wondered if the boys still believed in Father Christmas. Tom probably did, but secretly, to avoid derision from his older brother. They could even be in Bath right now doing their Christmas shopping.

Which was something Lu really ought to be doing herself, not that she had many people to buy for. Scottie scampered around the flat as if it was the first time he'd been there. She hoped his foray into the defence industry hadn't given him an appetite for biting suitors. He'd never bitten Nick. Nick had said he'd missed her when she saw him at the gallery, and it had sounded like an invitation to open up the chance of getting back together. But she had run away from him as if she'd been frightened. She sat down, then stood up again, unable to settle, restless as Scottie, feeling trapped by the four walls of her flat. Finally she grabbed a Christmas card. 'To Nick, Ben and Tom,' she scrawled. 'Happy Christmas.' She hesitated, then wrote 'Love Lu' and quickly sealed it into an envelope before she could change her mind.

She rang the hospital. Delia was fine, and her temperature was dropping. Visiting hours were two to five. 'Shame I can't bring you,' Lu said to Scottie, who cocked his head at the sound of her voice. 'Delia would like to see you far more than me.'

The doorbell rang for one of the flats upstairs; only a dull burr in Lu's flat, but despite that, Scottie barked like mad, rushing around. He bashed into the table and the photograph of Jack tottered, then, before Lu could catch it, fell and smashed.

Lu knelt. For some reason this was the last

straw, the trigger, and she started to cry. She wasn't sure what she was crying for: something lost? Her head ached from the drama of the night before and she felt she had already had a full day. Leaving Nick was the right thing to do, she told herself. The frustration as Nick put the boys first, his puzzled face saying, 'They're my children.' 'But not mine,' she'd replied. And yet, and yet . . .

No, Lu thought, wiping her face. He was wrong for her, he came with too much baggage, he pushed her, challenged her, he was too different. She tried to ignore the niggling voice that told her she was frightened because he challenged her beliefs about herself: Lu Edwards was an independent young woman, without baggage dragging her down.

She picked up the pieces, avoiding the shards of glass. The frame was broken too; it collapsed in her hands, held together only by the black paper backing and glue. It could always be reframed, she supposed, although it was nicer—more authentic —in the original frame. As she pulled out the photograph of Jack, thankfully untorn, she realised there was something underneath it, a piece of paper that had been sandwiched between the photograph and the backing. It was small; even when she unfolded it, no bigger than a card. The soft edge on one side indicated that it had been torn from a notebook. The writing was copperplate, the pencil marks faded and hard to distinguish.

Lu stood and took the letter over to the window to see better.

336

25 June 1916
My darling Annie,
I miss you so much. I think about your dear sweet face all the time but we're being kept busy here and I don't have much time for writing. I told Mother we were engaged and she's very happy. She gave me her ring to give to you, with her blessing, when we next meet. I hope it's soon!!! Mother wants us to be married at home, but I don't know what you'd like.

It's grand weather here, I hope you are enjoying it yourself. My arm is better. I find holding the gun for a long time is tiring and makes it ache but mustn't grumble, there are chaps in a worse state. We've been hanging around here for three weeks, the chaps are getting bored, we play tricks on each other but it's only fun and they're good lads really, the grandest set of chaps I know.

If anything happens to me, my darling, Percy will do what he can, and I have promised I will do the same for Maud. He's a good chap, I know I can trust him to do his best.

Anyway, that's all from me right now. Write as soon as you can. Look after yourself.

Your loving friend,
Jack

There was another piece of paper folded in with the letter, a newspaper clipping from the births, deaths and marriages columns of *The Times* dated 27 July 1920. In journalese it told of the untimely deaths from the flu epidemic of the wife and two of the children of the Royal Academician Wilfred Morgan of Kensington, London. The younger daughter, Anne, had recently been a land girl in Somerset.

The last item was a birthday card, a basket of kittens. Lu peered at it more closely and realised it was hand-made. Whoever had drawn it had had real ability. She opened it up.

My darling Delia,
 A little bundle of kittens for a little bundle of joy. I hope you like them. Kiss Auntie Maud and Uncle Percy for me, but save the biggest birthday kiss for your mama who loves you and is looking forward to having you home with her as soon as she can.
 Your loving Mama

The card was in an envelope, and Lu checked the postal date, peering at the faded printing. It was unclear, but she was pretty certain that it was December 1919. She examined the photo frame to see if there were any other letters, gently prising the backing away. It was so fragile it left black flecks on her hand, but there was something else there, a wodge of paper. With the handle of a watercolour brush, she edged it out far enough to take it by the tips of her fingers and pull it out. As she pulled, she saw that it wasn't a letter, but the wrapping round something. Carefully she opened it up, catching her breath when she realised what was there.

*   *   *

For a moment Lu was sure that her grandmother was dead, and her heart constricted. Delia's face was white, her jaw hanging slack, her eyes closed. An eyelid fluttered. No, she was just sleeping upright in the chair, her hospital gown skew-whiff about her neck. She looked vulnerable and defenceless, not the feisty gran that Lu knew. Instinct said you shouldn't wake someone who was asleep, but Lu reached out for one of Delia's hands, lying palm up on the rug that covered her knees.

'Gran,' she called softly. 'Are you awake?' Delia's face gave a flicker and she moistened her lips. Not dead then. Lu's heartbeat returned to normal. 'It's me, Gran.'

'Lu?' Delia's voice wavered and Lu held her breath. She'd heard from other friends about aged relatives not remembering who they were, and dreaded the day when Delia would not know her. Delia made a little noise, like a kitten's mew, as she opened her eyes, watery and unfocused, blinking in the light.

'How are you feeling, Gran? They said on the phone your temperature was down.'

Delia blinked. 'Mustn't grumble. They say at this rate I'll have the op in a few days. The things they do nowadays. Don't know why it's supposed to be a good thing, having wires in your chest. Sounds a terrible idea to me—and what if the batteries run out, that's what I want to know. I might just stop.'

'I think it just helps your heart to keep going, like a back-up. It sounds a good idea to me. You're precious.' Lu squeezed Delia's hand.

'Is that so?' Delia smiled faintly.

The lady with the tea trolley came round, and Delia had tea and biscuits. She looked better now, more herself than when Lu had first come in. Lu told her that Scottie was doing well and was settling in at her flat, deciding that now wasn't the time to reveal his unexpected protective qualities.

'I've got some things to show you,' she said when Delia had drunk half her tea. She spread them out on the bed. 'I found these behind the photograph. The first one's from Jack to Anne.' Lu read the letter out, looking up from time to time to see how Delia was taking it. Delia's face was attentive.

'So he was going to marry her,' she said when Lu finished.

'It looks that way. And look what else I found.' She brought out the wodge of paper and unfolded it so Delia could see. It was a ring, a fine pale-gold band with a tiny ruby set into it. 'I think this is the ring he mentions in his letter.'

Delia picked it up, her lips pursed. She placed the ring in the palm of her hand, the rubbed gold gleaming softly against the creases, and gave a deep sigh.

'Okay?' Lu asked gently. Delia nodded, but didn't say anything.

Lu put the letter down and picked up the envelope with the birthday card. 'Then there's this.' She held it out to Delia.

Delia shook her head. 'You read it.' Her voice was husky.

Lu read it out loud, then the newspaper cutting. She cleared her throat. 'There aren't many records of the Women's Land Army, but I've managed to

340

do a bit of tracking online. Anne was born in London in 1896, so she was twenty when she had you. What I think happened is that she was working as a land girl on the same estate as Percy, and through him and Maud, Jack met her and fell in love. When Jack was sent home in the spring of 1916, they were able to be together briefly, and at that point decided to get married. But Jack was sent back to the Front before they could. He died not knowing that Anne was expecting a baby. He and Percy had had a pact that if either of them died, the other would do their best to look after their loved ones, so maybe when Percy was invalided back home he got in touch with Anne, or maybe Maud knew about the pregnancy anyway. Anyway, I think that between them they decided that Maud and Percy would look after the baby until Anne could do so herself. Anne's father was an artist, but that doesn't mean he would have accepted an illegitimate baby. Then, after the end of the war, Anne died in the flu epidemic, along with her mother and a younger brother. So Maud and Percy formally adopted the baby; in those days you could do it privately, you didn't have to go through the procedures you do nowadays. As Percy had lost his leg in the war, he couldn't carry on being a gamekeeper, so they moved into Bath and started a new life with you. Maud had always looked after you, so perhaps it was easier to let people assume that you were their natural child. I think it was Maud who sealed the letters and the ring, and the cutting behind the photograph, to keep them safe for you.'

Delia was very white under the bright hospital lights. A tear slid down her cheek as she gripped the ring in her hand. 'But he was going to marry her.'

'Yes, Gran,' Lu said. 'He loved her, and she loved you. She didn't give you up casually. She died, poor thing, before she could make a home for the two of you together.'

Delia wiped her eyes. 'It must have been hard for her, being unmarried, and her lover dead in the war. There must have been a lot of them, when you think about it.' She held out her hand for the card. Lu passed it to her and Delia examined the little watercolour, a small smile playing on her face. She looked up suddenly. 'Now we know where it comes from.'

'What?'

'Your talent, and Susan's painting too. We never had any artists in the family before you two, but her dad was an artist, you say.' Delia traced a wrinkled finger over one of the kitten's little faces. 'She painted kittens like you do.'

Lu looked at the painting. 'I don't know if it's like my style, but I'd be pleased to have painted this. She had real ability. And he was a Royal Academician, no less. I haven't had time to trace his work, but he should be easy to find out about. Something we can do together, now you're so good at the Internet.'

'So you come by it honestly.' A shadow passed over Delia's face and she closed her eyes. Lu carefully took the cup away from her.

'I'll come and visit you tomorrow, Gran,' she said softly. 'Sleep now.'

Delia opened her eyes. 'It may have got a bit delayed, but I think that's the best birthday card I've ever received.' She squeezed Lu's hand.

'Thank you for finding this and showing me. It's the best Christmas present too.'

'You're not too upset? I mean, about being . . . you know.' She didn't like to say illegitimate.

Delia looked surprised. 'Of course not. I'm an old lady; if I haven't got over that by now, I never will. I wanted to know for interest, of course I did, and it's nice they wanted to get married, and that my real mother didn't give me up casually, but it's not important. Not now—it's too long ago. My husband was important, bless him, when he was alive, and now it's all about Susan, and you. I'm not a better person, or a worse person, because of what my parents did or didn't do. We can't do more than be ourselves, wherever we come from, and we must be content with what we've got.' She squeezed Lu's hand. 'If I die when they stick their wires in, you promise me you won't be sad. It makes me sad when I see you all unhappy, like you have been these past months. Now. You go home, and promise me you'll be happy.'

'I'll try, Gran. But it's hard sometimes.'

'You young people, you want it to be easy all the way. Life's hard, and there's not much you can do about it. Just make the best of what you get.'

*   *   *

Briony roared with laughter when Lu popped into the gallery to tell her about Marcus and Scottie. 'So that's a no,' she said.

Lu shrugged. ''Fraid so. But it means I definitely won't be going skiing. Mind you, when Gran comes out of hospital she's going to stay with my mother, so I'd have been looking after Scottie anyway and not been able to go. Mum is not a doggy person. Hell's bells, neither am I, come to think of it. I just seem to have been landed with him.'

'The killer hound.' Briony giggled, and pulled a stack of catalogues off a chair so Lu could sit down.

'I'll have to watch out or he'll scare away all my future boyfriends. I've spent my whole life without baggage, and now I've got a dog to tie me down.'

'What do you mean, you haven't got baggage? You've got loads,' Briony said, sticking an address label on to an envelope.

'I haven't,' Lu said, feeling affronted. 'No kids, no animals, no dependants of any sort.' She took a stack of envelopes from Briony and started to stick address labels on them too.

'What about your mum? And that's not even starting on all the stuff about your dad. Heavens, Lu, you're dragging a pantechnicon's worth of baggage around with you.'

'I'm not,' Lu said, more doubtfully this time, smoothing down the corner of a label with her finger.

'You pretend you can't see it, that's all. But you're just the same as everyone else.' Briony flattened a pile of addressed envelopes with her palm, ready to be franked. 'I'm not getting at you, love. Everybody's got baggage and you're no different. I mean, let's face it. Your dad's the reason you're commitment-phobic.'

'No he isn't, and I'm not commitment-phobic.' Lu looked around the gallery as if for support, but there were only the little Christmas paintings on the walls, and they were silent, although most of them had a little red dot next to them.

'Lu, you're a textbook case. You're looking for Mr Perfect because you're playing out all your issues with your dad leaving you.' Briony put out her hand.

'You've been reading too many self-help books,' Lu said, handing over her meagre pile of addressed envelopes. 'It's addled your brain.'

'I was with Jerry for seven years; there's nothing about commitment-phobia I don't know. Being with Simon, I see what a relationship could be like that has a future. I know it's just fun at the moment, but he doesn't go into hyperspace if I talk about what we might do for our holidays in six months' time. I couldn't get Jerry to make plans for next week. Yes, I've read all the books, and he's a classic. Do you know, he's actually quite keen on me again now I've gone.' Briony gave a contemptuous snort, shaking her head as if shaking Jerry out of her hair. 'But I think you're a different sort of commitment-phobic. Think about it—you fall for them at the beginning and they can do nothing wrong. Then it starts to get real, and because they're real human beings, they're not perfect. The faults show, at which point you leave them. Take Nick,' she said slowly, as if she was stepping carefully. 'You knew he had children right from the start, but you still went out with him. So when you broke up, it wasn't because he had changed, it was you. You were frightened because it was getting serious.'

'That doesn't make me commitment-phobic. I just haven't met the right person . . .' Lu trailed off. It sounded weak.

'I think we meet possible right people all the

time,' Briony said. 'It's just a question of recognising them, and knowing which bits we're prepared to compromise on.'

'Do you think I ought to call Nick up?' Lu said in a small voice.

Briony made a tsk noise. 'It's not a question of what I think, it's what you think. Nick's a great guy, but he's got kids and that's a lot to take on. It might be something you don't want to compromise on. That's your choice. But I'll tell you something, great guys are few and far between.'

*   *   *

As she got home, the phone was ringing. Lu ran to answer it, Scottie barking at her feet. For some strange reason she thought it might be Nick on the line, but when she picked up, a woman's voice asked if she was Lu Edwards.

Lu answered in the affirmative, thinking, Buggeration, I've now got to speak to someone about double glazing.

'I'm Veronica Meadows. You sent me your book.'

Lu lost all sensation in her legs as her brain gurgled to a halt. Was this really Veronica Meadows? Surely it couldn't be. Not *the* Veronica Meadows, the scariest woman in publishing, sounding quite pleasant and normal, a human being rather than a monster. Lu's brain restarted. Veronica Meadows was saying nice things. Very nice things, words like innovative, moving, touching. Important. Lu gulped. She understood the words individually, but the sentences they were forming didn't seem to work. Unless, unless . . .

346

but it couldn't be. Surely it couldn't be true after all the rejections from lesser publishers that the great, the important, the wonderful Veronica Meadows liked her book, liked it so much that she was inviting Lu to come up to London so they could discuss it further.

'Great,' Lu blurted, aware that she didn't sound like someone who could tie her shoelaces let alone write a book. 'That sounds great.'

Veronica Meadows paused before smoothly suggesting a time and place.

'Great,' Lu said, blinking furiously.

'I look forward to meeting you,' Veronica Meadows said before hanging up.

'Great,' Lu said into the receiver.

She put the phone down slowly and stared at it. Had that just happened?

Quick, quick, write down the time and place: 6 January, 12.30 at the publisher's office, then they'd go to lunch afterwards. She stared at what she'd written, then, like steam coming out of a kettle, she exploded into a high-pitched squeal and ran around the room. Veronica Meadows likes my book, she thought incredulously. Who to tell first? Briony? Pixie? Delia? But there was only one person she wanted to share the news with, and he wasn't there.

*　　　*　　　*

They collected Delia from hospital in Lu's car, Pixie's having broken down yet again. Despite that, she was in high spirits. 'It's the solstice tonight, Ma, so Raven and I have prepared a special dinner. I hope you'll like it.'

'I thought the solstice was in the summer,' Delia muttered as they helped her from the car.

'There are two, the summer one on the longest day, and the winter one on the longest night. The turning of the year. From now on the days get longer.'

'I could do with that.'

Lu checked that Delia's scarf was snug around her collar and that her hat was firmly on. Her coat looked baggy, as if it didn't fit properly. 'You've lost weight, Gran,' she said, tucking Delia's wispy hair under her hat.

'Hospital cooking. I hope yours is better, Susan.' Delia put her arm into Lu's and they began walking up the path. Lu could feel her grandmother leaning in to her and moderated her pace.

'Pixie, Ma, please. I can't bear to be called Susan. It's just not who I am.'

'Hoity-toity,' Delia muttered, though in a fairly benign way, but Pixie didn't hear because she had rushed ahead to open the front door. 'Is Scottie here?'

'He's at home, safe and sound,' Lu said. 'I thought it best because of getting you settled in and the cats, but I'll bring him over to visit tomorrow.'

Delia sighed, but she seemed to accept it. Once in the cottage, they settled her down in the front room. Raven hovered in the doorway.

'Hey, Mrs Forester. How are you doing?'

'Just getting my breath back,' Delia puffed.

'Cool.'

'No, I'm quite warm, thank you.'

Lu's eyes met Pixie's and they both smiled.

348

'Raven, fix us a cup of tea. Normal, please.' Pixie turned to Delia. 'I got in some ordinary tea bags, just for you.'

They had tea, and talked for a while, until Delia's eyelids started to close and her head began to nod. Again Lu and Pixie's eyes met. Silently they cleared the tea things and went into the tiny kitchen.

'Do you think she's all right?' Lu watched Pixie's face as she put the tea things in the sink.

'Just tired from everything, that's all,' Pixie said. 'Her aura's quite happy.' And for once Lu didn't want to dismiss her mother's auras.

Pixie stroked Lu's hair. 'But your aura isn't happy, Lunabella. Do you want to tell your old mother about it?'

'My aura's fine,' Lu said quickly. 'A publisher's interested in my new book.'

Pixie narrowed her eyes and stared at a point about two inches above the top of Lu's head. 'Mmm, I can see that, but there's something else. You're sad.'

'No I'm not,' Lu said, opening the lid of one of Pixie's herb jars and sniffing.

Pixie looked at her for one long, steady moment. Lu replaced the jar.

'All right, I am sad. There's a man I like, but I've blown it with him.'

'The nice man I met? The one with the lovely aura?' Lu nodded. 'Shall I read the cards and see if he's going to come back?'

'Thanks, but no. I don't need the cards to tell me my future.' Lu stretched her arms out in front of her, feeling the tight muscles across her back pull and then ease as she relaxed. 'I shall

349

concentrate on my career, as that seems to be going well for once.'

'That's nice.' Pixie hesitated. 'I hardly like to say it, but your father has sent you a Christmas card.'

It was on the tip of Lu's tongue to refuse to even look at it, as usual, but instead she thought of Nick saying that you couldn't give up as a parent, that you were always there. 'Okay,' she said, as casually as she could. 'No harm in looking.'

Pixie certainly hadn't seen that one coming, judging by the way her mouth dropped open. Then she bustled out, returning a few seconds later with a card in her hand.

Lu took it, feeling the heavyweight paper. Not a cheap card, then. To Miss Lunabella Edwards c/o Pixie Edwards, Columbine Cottage. Funny to be called Miss Lunabella: more like a character from *Gone with the Wind* than a contemporary illustrator. Turning her back on Pixie, she slid her finger under the envelope flap and opened it.

The picture was of a dove with a little banner that said Peace. It could have been an ordinary Christmas card, or it could have been a message, Lu thought. He wanted peace, after all these years. She opened the card, not sure of what she would find.

Dearest Lunabella

I hope this reaches you, and that one day you'll feel able to contact me. I would love to see you or even hear you on the phone. I love you very much, even though I haven't seen you for so many years. You are the most special person to me. Happy Christmas and best wishes for the New Year.

Your loving father,
Malcolm

'He always did write a nice letter,' Pixie said, reading over Lu's shoulder. Lu whisked the card away. 'I'm sorry. You needed your father. I probably should have let you go with him, but I couldn't. You were all I had.'

Lu held the card in her hand. Her loving father. She looked up at Pixie with troubled eyes. Pixie who loved Lu and had been frightened of losing her. But could you ever lose someone you loved? Didn't they remain with you, were part of who you were, even if you didn't see them? She read the card again, wondering about her father. He said he loved her.

'It's okay, Mum,' Lu said, putting the card in her pocket and giving Pixie a hug. 'The past is the past. As you're always telling me, I should look to the future.'

Pixie pulled open a drawer and took out a pair of oven gloves shaped like lobsters. 'I've done a special stew just for the solstice. I expect it'll be ready by now.' She put the lobsters on her hands and waved them in the air.

The edge of the card was sharp in Lu's pocket as she ran her finger along it. He loved her, though she'd refused to even look at the letters he'd sent her for years. She was the most special person to him.

She tilted her head to one side. It was easy to write that. It didn't make it true. But then she remembered Nick with his boys. They were most special to him; there was a bond there that carried on regardless. True love that never gave up,

351

whatever the circumstances, that could reach out over time and space like Anne's card to Delia. Could you ever lose someone you really, truly loved?

Chapter 18

After supper Delia went to bed, claiming she was worn out with all this palaver, although it wasn't clear which palaver she was talking about: hospital, the solstice, or the mishap over the food, Pixie having forgotten to put the oven on so they ended up cobbling a meal together. Pixie went up with Delia, leaving Raven and Lu to clear up and make camomile tea. Raven hummed bits from 'The Holly and the Ivy' as he stacked the plates.

'You're good for my mum,' Lu said suddenly. 'Thanks for being here.'

Raven blinked in surprise, then smiled shyly. 'Cool.'

Lu didn't know what to say to that, so she just smiled back, and they carried on clearing up, both of them humming along.

Pixie came down just in time to miss the washing-up.

'I'll be off now,' Lu said, handing her a tea towel.

'Won't you stay for some camomile tea?'

Lu shook her head. 'It's late, and I'm tired. I've got stuff I want to think about.'

'Oh.' Pixie looked as if she'd just been caught nicking stuff from the sweet shop. 'Is it about me? Your aura's all fuzzy.'

'I'm not surprised,' Lu said. 'And no, it isn't about you.'

'Good.' Lu didn't need to read auras to see Pixie's relax. 'Delia wanted to speak to you.'

Instinctively Lu looked up, as if Delia could see through floors. 'I'll go up now.'

Delia was looking very small in the spare bed, under a poster of William Blake's *The Ancient of Days*. 'Are you all right?'

Lu sat on the edge of the bed. 'Don't worry about me, it's my job to worry about you.'

'You always worry about your children, even when they're grown up.' Delia sighed. 'I worry about Susan.'

'Don't. I think Mum is one of life's survivors.' Lu smoothed the velvet patchwork bedspread with her hands. 'And she's got Raven to look after her.'

Delia nodded. 'I wanted you to have something.' She held out her hand. It was the ring.

'But you can't give me this,' Lu said.

'It won't fit my old fingers,' Delia said, as if that explained everything. 'Now don't argue, just put it on and keep it safe.'

Lu tried it on a couple of her fingers, finally settling on the fourth finger of her right hand. She looked up and realised that Delia was thinking what Lu was thinking: she and her great-grandmother had the same size hands. 'Thank you.'

'Now you look after that and mind you don't lose it, or I'll be most cross.'

Lu kissed her cheek. 'And you look after yourself and get some rest, or *I'll* be most cross.'

'You're a good girl,' Delia said sleepily, her eyes

closing. 'Remember to bring Scottie to see me tomorrow.'

* * *

Lu put the key in the lock, and immediately heard Scottie whimpering and scrabbling at the door, interspersed with little yelps. She let herself in and he flung himself at her, bright eyes shining, stumpy tail wagging so hard his bottom half wriggled as well. She reached down and scooped him up.

'That's what I call a welcome,' she told his happy panting face, then put him down quickly. 'Yeugh, dog breath.' She wasn't a real doggy person, she thought, but it was nice to be popular, even if it was only with an animated hearthrug. We want to make connections, to reach out to others, to feel our lives are intertwined with another's. Lover, parent, child. Scottie yapped.

'Yes, and dog.' Lu went into the flat and put out Scottie's food which he wolfed down in three seconds flat. 'No time limit, Scottie. You take as long as you like.'

Lu stopped, hand to her chest. This was it. She'd started talking to the dog. She was officially alone, a sad and mad old spinster. Ah well, there it was, she thought cheerfully, dumping her bag down on the worktop. 'Come on, Scottie, let's go out for a wee.' She unlocked the back door and went out into the courtyard garden, Scottie trotting after her.

He sniffed around the plant pots, snuffling like a detective on a mission, although exactly who else had been weeing against the plant pots, Lu didn't know. Cats, perhaps, the fiendish felines. 'Come on, Scottie. Do your stuff.' But Scottie was far too busy investigating the lower corner of a large terracotta pot.

Lu wrapped her arms around herself against the cold—surely the temperature had dropped dramatically this evening—and looked up.

The night sky was vast, pierced by thousands of pinpricks of light, and in the middle hung a beautiful round moon, like a silver disc. She could make out the craters and moon mountains, and from this distance they didn't look wasted and barren but shining and inviting. She joined the shadows to make up the face of the Man in the Moon. Not a happy man, judging by the dark eyes and the yearning mouth.

She felt the edge of the envelope in her pocket and took the card out again. The dove of peace had been outlined with glitter that twinkled in the moonlight. The writing inside the card was harder to make out, but she didn't really need to read the words; she already knew them by heart. A pang of guilt twitched at her heart. He'd written to her before, reaching out, trying to make the connection, but she'd always rebuffed him. She knew she should be angry with Pixie for misleading her, but then Pixie was Pixie. To be angry with her was like being angry with a child.

Lu stared at the ground, ashamed of her own behaviour. She said it was the boys who'd made her split up from Nick, but the truth was, she'd been jealous of them, of Nick's unfaltering love for them. Their connection with their father had been assured, whereas hers had felt tenuous and vulnerable. But who had made it so? Not Nick. His behaviour had been steady and consistent. All those men in the past, the Mr Rights and Mr Perfects who had turned out to be Mr Not Quite Right and Mr Far From Perfect, they'd never set themselves up to be that; it had all been in her head.

The moon hung in the night sky, round and perfect. It looked so close, as if she could reach out and touch it, and yet she knew she could never stretch across the gap and grasp its shimmering perfection. Lunabella, beautiful moon. It was the solstice, the longest night, the turning of the year.

*   *   *

So here she was again, outside Nick's house. She steadied herself, trying to stop that sick feeling of anticipation. There was a large wreath on the door, red holly berries everywhere, red as poppies. She took a deep breath before knocking.

Nick opened the door. Did she see his face lift for one second at the sight of her, or was it her imagination? She couldn't say. It had become very neutral now. 'Hello,' he said, pausing as if deciding whether to give her a kiss in greeting or not. Obviously not.

'Hello,' Lu replied, standing awkwardly and thinking this was a bad idea.

He cleared his throat. 'I wasn't expecting to see you.' He wasn't wearing shoes and his toes in socks twitched as if embarrassed.

'I'm sorry. Is it inconvenient? I was going to phone, but then I thought I'd come by.' Lu didn't care if he realised it was just an excuse; she was beyond that. There were some things that couldn't be said over the phone. 'I've got some news—a publisher is interested in Arthur.'

'That's good news. Congratulations.' Nick gave a taut smile. 'I always said you were talented.'

'Lu!' A shape rushed in from the hall and buried itself in her waist.

Lu stroked Tom's head, the strange sweet scent of boy. 'Hi, Tom.'

Just as suddenly he released her. 'Is Scottie with you?'

'He's in the car.'

'Can we take him for a walk?'

Lu looked up at Nick. 'I only popped by. I'm on my way to take him to see my grandmother.' Which ignored the fact that Nick's house was miles out of her way, as Nick knew just as well as she did.

Tom's face fell, then lifted again. 'Come and see my new model,' he said, tugging at her hand.

'Tom, Lu's on her way to see her grandmother, she's probably in a hurry,' Nick said. 'She doesn't want to see your model.'

'Yes she does,' Tom said impatiently. 'Don't you?'

'Of course. If that's okay with your father,' she added, thinking that Nick might not welcome her coming in. 'He might have other plans.'

'No he doesn't,' Tom said blithely. 'He was going to watch the news on telly, that's all. Come on.'

Lu glanced up at Nick, who was rubbing the bridge of his nose as she allowed Tom to drag her through the hall and into the sitting room. A Christmas tree filled up one corner of the room, decorated thoroughly in every colour imaginable, with no attempt at being tasteful. A golden star lurched drunkenly at the top, nearly touching the

357

low ceiling of the cottage. Underneath, Tom's Warhammer models were scattered all over the floor, dragon armies massing, the leaders out front mounted on eagles, dragons and prancing stallions.

Nick, in the doorway, cleared his throat. 'Would you like some mulled wine?'

Lu glanced up at him. 'That'd be lovely, if it's not a problem.'

'I told you, he's not doing anything.' Tom rolled his eyes. 'Look at this—I painted it all by myself.'

Nick clicked his tongue as if to say 'Kids!' but he left the room as Tom showed Lu the finer points of his model.

'This is my dragon master.' He held up a brightly painted monster with a tiny figure clutching its neck. The character—presumably female, given the preposterously exaggerated breasts, minute waist and skimpy outfit—waved a sword with vigour. At least if she had to conform to physical stereotypes she was a fearsome warrior. Tom had lovingly painted it all, hardly any overlaps between sections.

'This is good, Tom,' Lu said. 'I like the way you've done the scales.'

Tom cradled the dragon in his hands. 'It took for ever!' he said proudly. 'Dad wanted to help, but he's no good.'

'I'm getting so old I can hardly see what it is, let alone paint each individual scale,' Nick said, bringing in two glasses of deep purple wine, gently steaming. Lu took one, inhaling cinnamon and spices. Nick had arranged a mass of Christmas cards on the mantelpiece, and she couldn't help scanning them to see if hers was there, but she couldn't see it.

Ben stuck his head round the door and was about to depart when Nick saw him. 'Come and say hello to Lu.'

Ben sidled in, looking wary. 'Hi.'

'Hi, Ben,' she said, getting up from where she'd been sitting by Tom. 'I'm sorry about last time I was here. I shouldn't have thrown your supper away.'

Ben shuffled on to one foot. 'I was rude, Dad told me.'

'But I'm the adult.' Lu hesitated, not sure of what to do.

'I drive Dad mad as well.' Ben suddenly grinned. 'He says he's going to beat me so hard my eyes pop out and hit the back wall.'

Lu looked at Nick, amused at his embarrassment. 'Does he?'

Ben flicked a mischievous glance at his father. 'All the time.'

'Yeah,' chipped in Tom. 'And he says he's going to put us out on the streets to starve,'

'Come on, guys, give me a break,' Nick said, hunching his shoulders. If he'd been Tom's age he would have been squirming. 'It's Christmas.'

'It'll cost . . .' Ben put out his hand.

'In your dreams.' Nick turned to Lu. 'Tell me about your publisher.'

'Possible publisher. Nothing's been agreed formally, but they're interested. I'm going to meet the editor after Christmas.'

'That's great news. I'm really pleased for you.'

Lu looked at her glass. 'I wanted to tell you because it was really thanks to you. Without your encouragement, I wouldn't have carried on.'

'I don't think I had much to do with it, to be honest.'

'You did.' Lu suddenly felt like crying. There was so much she wanted to say to him, and yet it was impossible. She wanted to take him in her arms and tell him how much she missed him, how much she regretted leaving him, how she wanted to try again, but instead she was stuck in polite, minimalist sentences. 'I wanted to say thank you.'

Tom tugged her arm. 'Can Scottie come out and play, even if we can't take him for a walk?'

Lu glanced at Nick. 'It's up to your father.'

'Don't you want to go?' Nick looked uncertain. Did that mean he wanted her to go? Or hoped she would stay?

Lu shook her head. 'I'm not in a hurry.'

Nick rubbed the back of his neck. 'Perhaps we could go for a short walk.'

'Yey!' Tom exploded from the floor like a jet-propelled rocket.

It took a few minutes to get them all kitted up in boots, scarves and coats. Lu let Scottie out of the car and he greeted Tom and Ben like long-lost friends, bouncing up and down at their knees. She clipped his lead on and gave it to Ben, who scarpered down the pavement, Tom in indignant pursuit shouting, 'It was my idea, that's not fair.'

Nick just smiled. 'They'll sort it out between them.' He suggested a circular route round the village, going via the recreation ground. 'No football games, though,' he added, looking sideways at Lu.

They walked on for a little way in silence. Colour had drained from the village; the Michaelmas daisies and nerines were long gone, replaced at some houses by planters of pansies. No gaudy flashing Christmas lights either—it was far too smart a village to allow anything like that—although here and there people had threaded starry white lights through the trees. The main colours were the deep green of box and yew hedges, and the red holly berries, echoed in the wreaths tied with red ribbons that adorned most of the doors.

Nick strode on, hands deep in the pockets of a grey herringbone tweed coat that had seen better days, a navy scarf around his neck. Lu wanted to ask what he was thinking, whether he knew why she was here and how he felt about that, or if he genuinely thought she'd simply popped by. Just because it seemed so important to her didn't mean it was important to him. They reached the recreation ground.

'Can I let Scottie off the lead?' called Tom.

Lu nodded. It was good to see the two boys and the dog running around, the boys' cheeks scarlet with exertion in the cold air, their endless energy as they ran around with an imaginary ball, shooting at an imaginary goal, then the celebrations when they scored. 'You'll have to get a dog,' she said, turning to Nick.

He shook his head. 'It's bad enough being responsible for two boys.'

'You're a good father,' Lu said.

'Thanks.' He looked at the ground, embarrassed. 'I try to be. But it's hard when you're not with them all the time.'

'You're a good father,' she said again, touching his arm.

He looked at her, his expression unreadable.

361

Was he remembering the sausages? Or the night at the hotel when he'd first told her he loved her?

'I discovered a letter from Jack to Anne,' she said quickly, looking away from him. She told him what she'd found, what she'd managed to discover about Anne's background, and what she thought had happened. 'Delia's given me the ring.' She took off her glove and showed it to him.

He took her hand and bent his head as if to examine the ring more closely, and for one wild second she thought he was going to kiss her hand. But then he straightened and let it fall.

'How did your grandmother take it?'

'Better than I thought she would. It's ironic: she always kept on going on at me when I was younger about how boys were only after one thing—'

'But we are, we are,' Nick said, laughing, and for a second it was as if they hadn't broken up, and he was going to kiss her, but then the reality hit both of them and they stepped away from each other, back to no-man's-land.

'There's lots more to discover about Anne's background and her history, but I don't think Delia minds so much about being illegitimate now she knows that they intended to get married, and that Anne didn't abandon her, but died before she could bring her back home.'

'I think we underestimate the different values of different generations,' Nick said. 'I'm sure there are things I value that my boys won't bother with, and other things they'll be horrified about.'

'Like drink-driving,' Lu said, putting her glove back on.

'Or damaging the environment. I don't think I'd heard about global warming when I was their age, but both of them are expert on it.'

'That's school.' She watched Tom and Ben running around with Scottie. They were having such fun together, their breath coming out in short bursts of mist in the cold air. Dusk was arriving; lights were coming on in the houses that edged the recreation ground, making little patches of golden glow.

'And books about vegetables.' He smiled at her. 'So have you given those up for good?'

'I think so. Whatever happens, I mustn't let myself get caught up in doing work just because of money. It has to have some artistic merit.' She looked up at him, thinking how he'd made the same decision when he'd moved into the charity sector. 'It probably means I'll be broke for the rest of my life, but there are some things that are more important than money.'

If Nick saw the parallel with himself he didn't say anything. 'Will you do something on the war again?'

Lu shook her head. 'It depends on the publisher—if the book's a success, they'll want a follow-up. Arthur was special to me. I don't know if I could do something as good ever again.'

'Of course you could,' Nick said. 'You can do anything.'

Lu looked at her hands in their pale-grey gloves. 'I wish that were true.'

'You can.' For the briefest second he touched her arm. 'Shall we walk on? You must be getting cold standing here.'

She wanted to say that she'd stand there with him for ever, if that was what he wanted, but he was already calling to Ben and Tom and pointing

363

to the far side of the recreation ground. They began to walk across after the boys and Scottie, now back on his lead.

'I've brought back your First World War books; they're in the car,' Lu said.

'You could have kept them. There wasn't any hurry.'

'I thought it was best,' she said, as they threaded their way through a kissing gate and on to a footpath running between two rows of houses. She wanted to explain how it was impossible to move on when there were so many reminders of Nick around. He haunted her. And if he rejected her now, she was going to have to come to terms with it. She shivered, not wanting to raise the subject and risk that rejection, but it was what she was here for. 'It's been hard, moving on.'

He understood immediately. 'But it had to be done. I have the boys, and I can't change that, and it's not what you want. I can see that.'

'I don't know what I want,' Lu said slowly. 'I thought I knew exactly what I was looking for, but when I got it, I didn't want it.'

'What are you saying?' Nick's gaze was direct.

She remembered going over the death slide, the leap into the unknown. 'That I've made a mistake. That I'd like to try again.'

'But I'm all wrong for you,' Nick said. 'I'm a single parent with two boys, for starters. I'm broke. I'm knackered most of the time. I don't drive a sports car, or wear a suit. I don't do lists. If we got back together, wouldn't all the same stuff come up again?' He fingered the sleeve of his coat. 'I can't be what I'm not. I'm not some business tycoon, just a very ordinary bloke muddling through life. I don't have a five-year plan or a daily to-do list—heck, I don't even have a shopping list.'

Lu grabbed his arm and stopped him in his tracks. 'Do you think that's what really matters to me?' she said, looking into his eyes. 'Do you think I'm really that shallow?'

'Of course not. You're hugely talented and creative; look at the book you've just written. It's brilliant. You're on an upward swing, and I don't want to be the guy pulling you down.' He started to walk down the footpath after the boys.

'But I wouldn't have written it without you.' Lu trailed her hand along a garden wall. 'I wouldn't have had the courage to leave my agent, to move on, without your support. You made me believe in myself, that I had something to offer. Can't we try again?'

'I don't know.' Now it was Nick's turn to stop. He looked down, as if the truth could be discovered written in the tarmac of the path. 'I'd worry you'd regret it.'

'Isn't that my decision to take? You can't take responsibility for me, and I can't take responsibility for you. You told me to be brave and take chances. So here I am, taking the biggest chance of my life.' She put her hand on her chest, feeling her heart beating wildly. 'I behaved badly, and I know that now. I behaved like a child, not an adult. I accept that the boys come first—'

'Not first,' Nick cut in, looking up. 'It's different. I'm their father—oh, I can't explain.'

'Because I don't have children.' Lu nodded. 'I can see that. But I love lots of other people too—my grandmother, Pixie, Briony—all of them in different ways. I could love the boys.' Nick smiled

365

at that. 'I want to come back,' she said softly. 'I miss you.'

'I miss you too,' Nick said, and Lu's heart leaped up, only to be cast down again. 'I just don't think it's as easy as saying, let's get back together, and then it's as it was. Life doesn't work like that.'

'But nothing worth having is easy,' Lu said. 'It's all a risk, that's what living's about. I thought I knew what I wanted, but it was all about external things. It's not about ticking boxes, it's about how you feel when you're with someone. And I've never been happier than when I've been with you.'

Nick leaned back against a wall. 'I don't know. I want to say yes, but—what if you leave me again? I couldn't go through all that a second time. It's too painful.'

Lu shrugged. 'I want to be with you, but yes, it might happen. It's a risk, but what's the alternative? Living without love? We just have to keep trying.' She thought of her father, writing to her year after year, with no response. Writing into the darkness with only the memory to keep him going. She looked around her. 'I have a card to post. Is there a letter box near here?'

Nick looked surprised at the change in direction. 'Er, yes, just a bit further along.' They walked to the letter box, their steps matching. Lu wondered what Nick was going to decide. He'd said he wanted to say yes, but he was afraid. She looked up into the sky, where the first evening star was coming out. He wanted to say yes. He'd loved her once; he could love her again. All they had to do was stop being afraid.

Lu took the card out, and for a second held it on the lip of the opening. Her handwriting looked very firm and solid. Malcolm Edwards. She hesitated. If she posted the card, she was starting something when she didn't know how it would end. Was this what she wanted to do?

And then she let the card go.

'It's a bit late for a Christmas card—it'll never get there in time,' Nick said.

'I hope it's not too late.' Lu touched the letter box, then smiled. 'No, I don't think it's too late. I've decided that if you love someone, you can't ever lose them. They stay on in your heart, whatever happens in the future.' She looked at Nick, saving the details of him, the tousled dark hair, the troubled blue eyes, even the way his nose was slightly pink with the cold. Perhaps this was the last time she'd see him.

'I was thinking about what you said,' Nick said, shifting from foot to foot. 'About taking risks. You know I've got more baggage than Terminal Five, and there's nothing I can do to change that.'

'But I don't want you to change that. Oh yes, I always said it wasn't going to last because you had children, but that was because I didn't know, I didn't understand. You are the man you are because of the boys, not despite them.' She glanced up at him. 'You're like a package deal at the supermarket—three for the price of one.'

'That's one way of looking at us.' Nick sighed, his breath a frosty white cloud in the evening air. 'It's cold. Let's walk on.'

They started walking, then Nick put his arm around Lu's shoulder. She leaned into him as her arm went round his waist. 'It's not just you who has baggage,' she said, as they turned the corner into a lane dotted with thatched cottages behind picket fences and yew hedges. The frosty road shimmered in the moonlight and through the darkness she could just make out the boys some way ahead, their voices ringing clear as bells in the still night air, interspersed with Scottie's yaps as they ran back towards the green, towards home. 'I've hardly begun to sort out how I feel about my father,' Lu continued happily, feeling the warmth of Nick's arm around her. 'Then there's my crazy mother, and my grandmother who's not well. I'm probably going to end up looking after Scottie full time, you know.'

Nick squeezed her shoulder. 'The promise of Scottie is the only thing that makes the risk worth taking.' He turned to face her, his eyes meeting hers.

Lu put her arms around his neck, smoothed his hair back from his forehead. 'A risk like this?' she asked lightly, although her heart told her she wasn't taking a risk.

Nick grinned. 'The boys would never forgive me if I missed out on the chance of Scottie,' he said, then kissed her. And even if he was Mr Wrong, she knew that this time it would be all right.